Paths of the Dead

Lin Anderson has published several novels and one novella featuring forensic expert Dr Rhona MacLeod, which have been widely translated. Her short story *Dead Close* was chosen for the Best of British Crime 2011 and is currently in development as a feature film. Also a screenwriter, her film *River Child* won a student BAFTA and the Celtic Film Festival best fiction award. Currently Chair of the Society of Authors in Scotland, she is also co-founder of Bloody Scotland, Scotland's International Crime Writing Festival.

By Lin Anderson

Driftnet
Torch
Deadly Code
Dark Flight
Easy Kill
Final Cut
The Reborn
Picture Her Dead
Paths of the Dead

NOVELLA

Blood Red Roses

Paths
of the
Dead

LIN ANDERSON

PAN BOOKS

First published 2014 by Pan Books
an imprint of Pan Macmillan, a division of Macmillan Publishers Limited
Pan Macmillan, 20 New Wharf Road, London N1 9RR
Basingstoke and Oxford
Associated companies throughout the world
www.panmacmillan.com

ISBN 978-1-4472-4566-7

1 3 5 7 9 8 6 4 2

A CIP catalogue record for this book is available from the British Library.

Typeset by Palimpsest Book Production Limited, Falkirk, Stirlingshire
Printed and bound by CPI Group (UK) Ltd, Croydon, CR0 4YY

For Andy Rolph

1

The final hymn drew to a close and Amy took her seat. Around her, the bustle of a hundred people ceased and a silence of expectation fell.

She pondered again why she'd agreed to accompany her friend to a spiritualist church on a Sunday morning. She hadn't been inside a church in years. Any church. She still prayed, that habit had endured. Usually last thing at night, before she dozed off, she said the Lord's Prayer, more from habit than religion.

The minister had moved to one side and a young man took his place on stage. With his shiny cheeks and open-necked shirt, he reminded Amy of a rather earnest salesman, who'd recently tried to persuade Alan to buy a car he couldn't afford. She recalled how kind Alan had been to the man, and felt a sudden surge of love for her big student son. Second year at university studying engineering and doing well, even if he was always short of money. He'd turned out all right, despite not having a dad around. She smiled, thinking of Alan's amused expression when he'd heard where she was going that morning. 'Don't ask Aunt Bella to get in touch from beyond the grave. She terrified me when she was alive,' he'd said.

The medium moved nearer the front and gave them a tentative smile. *He looks so young*, Amy thought, *and gullible*.

He introduced himself as Patrick Menzies and wished them 'God Bless'. Then he explained that mediums like himself were able to communicate with those who had passed over. However, he couldn't summon the departed.

'They come to me,' he said, 'but only when they are ready, willing and able to do so.'

At this, the medium inclined his head as though listening to a silent voice just behind his left shoulder.

A ripple of excitement swept the room.

'This is it,' Doreen whispered beside her.

He spoke so quietly that Amy strained to hear. 'Yes. Welcome. I can hear you. God Bless.' He nodded a few times. 'Who do you want to speak to?' Pause. 'Yes. I understand.'

A small sob caused Amy to glance along the row to where a young woman was silently mouthing 'Please'.

The medium gathered himself and, opening his eyes, focussed on the audience. The tension in the room was palpable. It wasn't only the young woman who was desperate to be singled out.

Amy sat back in her seat. Alan was right. This was all nonsense. Yet she seemed to be the only person in the room who thought so. She checked on Doreen, who appeared as intent as the rest. Who did Doreen think might get in touch? Her mother, dead these past ten years? Amy heard an intake of breath from the young woman on her right as the medium began to speak.

'Is there anyone here called Amy?' His eyes swept the audience.

'I'm Amy.' Her young neighbour shot to her feet.

The medium looked puzzled, then turned and listened again. 'God Bless. Yes, I understand.'

The young woman interrupted this exchange in excited anticipation. 'It's my Gary, isn't it? Gary, can you hear me?'

Amy found her own heart pounding as all eyes turned from the other Amy to the medium.

'I'm sorry, I don't believe this is Gary coming through.'

'You asked for Amy. I'm Amy.'

The medium seemed perplexed by this and resumed his conversation with his silent visitor. Eventually, he said, 'I'm sorry, but this definitely isn't your Gary.'

The young woman gave a moan and slumped to her seat in despair. Amy felt a rush of sympathy, mixed with anger. How cruel to come here hoping desperately to talk with a loved one and for this to happen.

Meanwhile, the medium was cradling his head as though in pain. The minister hurried to his side and whispered something.

'No. No. I'm fine,' the medium insisted, straightening up again.

Amy was shocked at how white his face had become.

He looked upwards for a moment as though in prayer, then inclined his head to the left and listened.

'Oh no. That's terrible.'

The disquiet that resonated at his words silenced the murmurs surrounding the stricken younger Amy.

'I must ask the audience again. Is there an Amy in the hall?'

When Doreen touched her arm, Amy shook her head. 'It's nothing to do with me,' she said under her breath.

'It might be,' whispered Doreen, excited by the prospect.

Amy had no intention of raising her hand. She didn't want to hear some message from Aunt Bella, or anyone else for that matter.

'Please,' the medium pleaded, 'the Amy I seek is in the audience. Will she please reveal herself.'

Amy gripped her hands together and tried to ignore Doreen's whispered encouragement.

'Okay, I'll tell her. God Bless.' The medium turned to the audience once more. 'The spirit has asked me to say that it isn't Aunt Bella.'

Amy's heart stopped, and fear in all its forms swept over her. She opened her mouth to speak but no words came. Then she heard Doreen's voice.

'My friend's called Amy.'

The medium swung round and locked eyes with her. 'Are you Amy?'

'It can't be me you're looking for. I don't know anyone who passed on recently.'

The medium regarded her with concern. 'You know an Aunt Bella?'

'She died two years ago. My son Alan said I wasn't to speak to her,' she added, not knowing why.

'Your son's called Alan?'

'Yes. When I told him I was coming here this morning, he made a joke about his Aunt Bella. He said he hoped she didn't try to contact us. He was terrified of her when she was alive.' Amy's attempt at laughter died in the heavy silence.

The medium looked taken aback. 'You last spoke to Alan when?'

'An hour ago, just before I came here. He always comes over on a Sunday for . . .' Amy tailed off as she registered the medium's face. *He looks like a ghost*, she thought.

The medium, obviously distressed, was speaking to one side again.

4

'God Bless. Are you sure?' He turned his attention back to Amy. 'I am so sorry, Amy, but this *is* Alan I'm talking to.'

His announcement was followed by uproar in the hall. Amy shouted through it, 'That's nonsense. I spoke to him before I left.'

The noise abated as the audience strove to hear the medium's reply.

'Alan has asked me to give you a message.'

Amy rose to her feet, a rushing sound in her ears. She wanted the stupid man to shut up. She wanted him to disappear with his shiny cheeks and his ugly words. She shouted 'Stop it!' at the top of her voice, then turned on her heel and made for the door.

2

She was sitting in the minister's office, a cup of cold tea on the desk in front of her. Beside it lay her mobile. Amy had already left three messages for Alan, none of which he'd responded to. She'd tried the house phone as well, which wasn't answered either.

Alan has simply gone out, Amy told herself. It was Sunday after all. He often took the dog for a walk, or cut the grass for her. If the mower was running he wouldn't hear the phone. Maybe he was at the pub. He sometimes went for a pint on a Sunday, met up with some of his old mates, before the two of them had dinner together. The thought briefly consoled her. She glanced at the door, willing Doreen to appear and tell her she'd brought the car round and was ready to take her home.

But it was the medium who opened the door instead.

His shiny cheeks had reddened. *He looks like a clown*, Amy thought cruelly.

'Mrs MacKenzie. May I speak to you?'

'I think you've said enough.'

He seemed to shrivel under her glare. Amy wasn't naturally unkind and immediately felt a little sorry for him. He obviously believed in the rubbish he peddled, as did most of his audience. Since she had been part of that audience, he would assume she did too.

'I don't believe in this stuff,' she said. 'I just came along with a friend.'

He'd picked up on the conciliatory tone and as a result felt able to enter the room properly and shut the door.

'It would help *me* if we talked.' His request sounded completely sincere.

Amy contemplated the idea that he might be suffering from a mental illness. If that was the case then she shouldn't be mean to him.

'You'll have to be quick. Doreen's just gone to get the car.'

He glanced at the mobile on the desk. 'Have you called your son?'

'He's out at the moment.' Amy said this as though she knew it for definite. 'What do you want to talk about?'

'This is very difficult. I don't want to alarm you, but Alan gave me clear instructions.'

'Stop this!' Amy shouted angrily and rose to her feet. 'There is nothing wrong with Alan. He was in perfect health when I left him—'

The medium interrupted her before she could reinforce this further.

'I'm so sorry, Mrs MacKenzie. Alan told me to tell you to go to the police. I think your son may have had a violent death.'

Amy felt the hysteria rise and there was nothing she could do to stop it. 'You're mad, or ill. I don't know which. I'll go to the police all right, but it will be to make a complaint about you – and this place.' As the final words emerged, the door swung open and Doreen appeared.

'Take me home,' Amy cried as she pushed past her

friend, desperate to get away from the shiny red cheeks and the soft mouth that had uttered those terrible words.

Doreen made one attempt to speak on the way home, but Amy swiftly cut her off. She had no intention of repeating what the medium had said in that office. Her anger at the man was growing swiftly into fury. How dare he tell her those things. How dare he tell anyone that he could speak to the dead. It was appalling that a church allowed him to appear like that, frightening people. All the time she raged internally, a small but insistent voice reminded her that the medium had known about Bella. How could he have known about her sister? How could he have known about her conversation with Alan about Bella? The thought brought a chill to her heart and a desperate need to get home. To open the front door and call Alan's name. To see him emerge from his old room and ask her why the hell she was looking so worried.

When the car drew up outside the house, Doreen quickly offered to come in with her, but Amy wouldn't hear of it.

'I'll give you a call tomorrow. Let you know what time I'm coming round on Friday,' she said.

Doreen nodded, playing along with Amy's attempts at normality.

She waited on the front step until Doreen drove away, before slipping her key in the lock.

'Alan, I'm back,' she shouted. When the dog didn't come running and Alan didn't answer her call, she said out loud, 'He's out with the dog,' as though that settled everything. When she found a note on the table in the kitchen telling her he'd gone out with Barney and would be back around five, she said *I told you so* to herself. After she put the kettle on, she tried Alan's mobile again. When she heard its ring tone coming from the sitting room, she felt absurdly pleased. Alan had a forgetful nature and had left his mobile here more than once before. Beginning to feel less concerned, Amy spooned two large scoops of tea into the teapot and added hot water. This cup of tea she would definitely drink.

She was fine until four thirty. She'd busied herself until then doing tasks she would normally have left until Monday. When Alan visited, they usually spent time in the garden. Him cutting the grass and her pottering. Occasionally they went for a pub lunch. In fact, had she not agreed to go with Doreen to that silly church, they might well have been walking back from the Cumberland Arms at this very moment. Amy *tsked* in annoyance.

By five thirty she had started to pace the house, pretending to do things that didn't need doing. The chicken she had stuffed and roasted had been lifted out and was now rapidly cooling. The roast potatoes Alan loved had been cooked to a crisp, the broccoli turned to mush. By six o'clock Amy had taken to standing at the front window, looking out periodically, trying to conjure up Alan's tall figure, Barney at his side, coming along the road. She would give him a good telling-off when he did arrive, she decided. Especially if he'd stopped off for a pint and not called to warn her he would be late. *But he doesn't have his mobile*, she remembered.

She hadn't been able to eat her own meal, the gnawing sensation in her stomach having nothing to do with hunger. By seven she was frantic and could no longer pretend normality. Using Alan's mobile, she called everyone in his contacts list, asking if they had seen him. Most of them sounded bemused to have been phoned by Alan's mother. None professed to having seen him that day, except a girl called Jolene who admitted she'd been with him that morning. She sounded mildly embarrassed at revealing this and Doreen wondered if she was a girlfriend, but was too worried to ask.

'If he gets in touch, tell him to call me,' she said.

'I thought he was coming to see you today,' the girl said, sounding wary.

'He did. He took the dog for a walk and isn't back yet,' Doreen told her. She knew she sounded like a fussing mother, so left it at that and hung up.

Doreen called her at seven thirty.

When Amy heard her voice she almost put the phone down. Rightly or wrongly, she found herself blaming Doreen for what had happened in the church. And for what was happening now.

When Doreen asked outright if Alan was okay, Amy told her he had gone for a walk with the dog.

'He was in when you got back?'

'He left a note.'

'But that was hours ago. Have you called him?'

'He left his mobile behind,' Amy told her.

There was a short silence while Doreen decided what to say. 'Maybe you should call the police. Just in case.'

Amy didn't answer, although inside her head she was screaming.

'Do you want me to come round?' Doreen asked.

'No,' Amy said sharply. She could not bear to look at Doreen, to remember her eager face as she'd urged her to respond to the medium's call. Amy put the phone down.

She stood for a moment, her instinct yelling at her that

something was wrong. Terribly wrong. A suffocating pain clutched her chest, her head swam, no air filled her lungs. She sat down heavily on the chair beside the phone table. *Please. Please.* She felt the pain and despair that had swamped the other Amy when it hadn't been her Gary, and knew then that neither of their prayers had been answered.

She stuck it for another hour before she made up her mind to go out and look for him. Anything was better than sitting around here worrying. Being midsummer, it was still light. Amy put on her coat even though the evening was warm and lifted her handbag. She was at the gate when she realized if Alan came back he would wonder where she was. So she went back inside and wrote him a note, telling him she had his mobile and to please call it when he got home.

Outside she hesitated again, with no idea which direction to take. She tried to think where Alan would go with the dog, then a thought struck. If something had happened to Alan, surely Barney would have come home alone? The idea seemed a distinct possibility which relit her hope.

Now where would he head? Probably the country park. Even as she acknowledged this, Amy knew what she was doing was pointless. The park was huge. There was no way she could find him there, yet she kept on walking in that direction.

She was nearly at the entrance when the mobile rang. She grabbed for it, her heart leaping.

'Alan? Where the hell are you?' It was the young woman Jolene from earlier.

Before Amy could interrupt, the girl went on. 'I've had your bloody mother on the phone. And you were supposed to meet me at the flat half an hour ago.'

'It's not Alan,' Amy finally managed to say.

There was a strangled sound of embarrassment then Jolene said, 'He's not shown up yet?'

'No. I've gone out looking for him.'

'Could he have gone for a drink with one of his old mates?'

'I don't think so. We always eat at the same time when he visits and he wouldn't be late without calling.'

'He is usually good about that,' Jolene conceded. 'What do you think we should do?' Her tone was verging on fearful, which Amy immediately registered.

'You think something's happened to him?' Amy said.

'There's bound to be a simple explanation, and if he doesn't have his mobile, he hasn't been able to contact you.'

It was the same excuse Amy had been using to quell her own fears. 'You don't understand. That man at the spiritualist church told me Alan was dead,' she blurted out. 'And he knew about Bella. How could he know about Bella?' She was babbling now, but couldn't stop herself.

'I don't understand.' Jolene sounded shocked.

Amy had reached the park entrance. The summer evening had brought local residents out to enjoy the late sunshine. The scene looked so normal. If anything had happened to Alan in the park, surely someone would have helped him? A collie was running and fetching a ball. Just as Barney would have done. Amy felt a catch in her throat. 'I'm going home to wait for him,' she said and rang off.

When she got back, the house was in darkness. Once inside, she picked up the house phone and began by calling all the hospitals with Accident and Emergency departments. When she had no luck there, she called the police.

3

According to the GPS reading, the geocache was definitely somewhere near this tree. Steve checked the massive trunk, running his hands over its surface, looking for a crack or fissure he might have missed.

Then a thought struck him. What if the cache was buried? He hadn't noticed any disturbed earth, but maybe someone had hidden it by covering it with leaves?

He set about clearing the ground in a two-foot circle round the trunk. On the opposite side from where he'd been sitting, the soil *was* disturbed. Excited now, Steve took his trowel from the backpack and began digging.

By the time the trowel had revealed the presence of something long and canvas-like, he was already unsure. Most caches were reasonably easy to find once you reached the GPS reading. It only needed enough space for an interesting object and a logbook for you to sign. It looked as though he was unearthing a holdall.

Slightly worried, Steve stopped to glance about him. The wood was deserted. Few people came this high, preferring to stick to the lower woodland paths and open spaces. He hadn't seen anyone from the moment he started his climb.

The holdall was clear of soil now. It looked too big for a geocache, but then again, he'd found one buried in a small suitcase before. He located the zip and cautiously pulled it open.

Inside were clear plastic bundles, bound up with rubber bands.

Steve immediately shut the zip and began throwing earth back over it. *Jesus, Mary and Joseph. What a fucking fool!* He should have realized as soon as he saw it that it was a hold-all. *Jesus, they would have scouts out checking on it. They might even have someone coming to pick it up at this very moment.*

When he'd scrabbled enough soil back in, he covered it with a thick layer of leaves, shoved the trowel in the backpack and stood like a rabbit caught in headlights, his heart crashing in his chest.

What the hell should he do now? Forget it ever happened? Or call the police and tell them what he'd found? *For fuck's sake, there must have been twenty packets in there. How much was it worth?* He buried that idea as quickly as it came to mind. You didn't steal from drug dealers, not if you wanted to stay alive.

He took another look about. He could make out a few strollers below, some with dogs, but up here among the trees there was no one but himself. He checked his GPS, registering where he had found the cache.

He would have to call the police. Tell them about the drugs. But he didn't fancy using his mobile. And he didn't fancy doing it from here. He should find a payphone and call them anonymously. Where the hell would he find a payphone? They didn't even have them in the pubs now. Everybody had a mobile.

He could go to a police station and report it. He contemplated that for a moment. Then again, if it went to court, he might have to appear as a witness. Not a happy thought.

And he knew what happened to folk who grassed up drug gangs. Somebody would find him out. Then he'd pay.

Steve moved away from the cache, his heart still racing, his mouth dry. He wanted to tell the police about his find, but he was sufficiently scared of the consequences to be unsure. What if they thought he had something to do with the drugs, or had seen someone plant them there? It would be easier to just walk away and forget it. He wasn't responsible for doing the police's job for them. Then another and more horrific idea struck him. What if the police were watching the stash and had seen him dig it up? Maybe even caught him on camera? They would think he was the guilty one.

He had to get the hell away from there. And fast. Steve took off, heading directly downhill. That's when he found the dog, or more correctly, tripped over its body in the long grass. It was a black cross-breed and it was dead, blood staining the ground around its opened neck.

It wasn't the first time he'd seen a dead animal on the hill, although they tended to be cats, often stoned to death. The creeps that came up here to drink and get high thought killing a cat was fun. Creeps like the ones who'd buried the drugs.

All the more reason to get out of there. The path he was following split, one side heading towards a small hill surrounded by a ditch. He'd been here before in his rambles. It was a popular spot to use for a geocache. There were five upright stones on the hill's summit, all around waist height, like a miniature stone circle. He skirted the hill. Normally he would go to the top for a last view before leaving the park, but he had no wish to do that today.

That's when he saw a hand on top of one of the stones.

At first he did not – dared not – register the fact that it was not connected to an arm. His immediate thought was that it couldn't be real. But why would a fake hand be sitting on top of one of the standing stones?

Rather than climb the hill to check, he moved up the outer bank for a better look. From here the second hand was visible on the opposite stone. Between, lay a male figure, face down. Steve immediately linked this image to what he had discovered under the tree and had two thoughts. Maybe the man had interfered with the drugs stash and this was his punishment. And what if whoever did that was still here and watching him?

He took off then, fear and adrenaline coursing through his veins, galloping down the hill, dodging the trees and springing like a frightened deer, as though death bit at his heels.

4

Rhona stopped in her uphill climb and turned to look back. At 600 feet above sea level, Cathkin Braes Park was renowned for its panoramic views over the city of Glasgow, even as far as the craggy summit of Ben Lomond, clearly visible today under an azure sky.

She took a deep breath of fresh upland air, rich with the scent of the ancient woodland she had climbed through. A good day to be up on the Braes, even if the reason for being here was much darker.

She had been having a late Sunday lunch at Brel in Ashton Lane when the call came through. McNab had sounded bad-tempered. Not unusual for him, but Rhona guessed a weekend hangover was as much to blame as a call-out. Saturday night they had been celebrating his promotion to detective inspector, something McNab and many others had never thought possible. He'd confided to her in a drunken moment that, having reached this rank, he didn't really want it.

'You deserve it,' she'd countered. 'You're one of the best cops they have. Awkward, opinionated, self-centred, rude . . . but good.'

He'd tried to process the mixed message in his drink-fuddled brain, his face eventually brightening to a winning grin as he decided she had given him a compliment. Rhona remembered thinking she had missed out arrogant and over-confident from the list.

She looked up, catching the drone of a police helicopter, hovering like a monstrous bluebottle above a corpse. The crime-scene manager had already raised a tent on the summit and a cordon had been erected on the outer side of the surrounding ditch. Chrissy, her forensic assistant, had opted to arrive by helicopter rather than walk from the lower car park. Rhona watched as the helicopter touched down and Chrissy jumped out, ducked the blades and gave the pilot the thumbs-up, before making her way towards the cordon.

McNab disengaged himself from a huddle of boiler-suits near the incident tent on Rhona's approach and came striding towards her. Despite last night's celebrations, he looked his usual self, with his distinctive dark auburn hair and stubbled chin, although at closer quarters the vivid blue eyes were shadowed from lack of sleep.

'Dr MacLeod. Glad you could drag yourself away from your lunch.'

'At least I wasn't still in bed.'

He gave her a sympathetic look. 'I take it you didn't pull then?'

'Unlike you, you mean?'

McNab couldn't resist a self-satisfied smile. 'Making DI has its compensations.'

She'd seen the young woman watching McNab in the pub. It was shortly after Rhona had rejected McNab's romantic overtures. Unabashed, he'd made directly for his more ardent fan. Rhona had watched as the young woman gazed up at that distinctively roguish face, a fact not missed by the object of her admiration.

McNab caught her thoughtful look and added accusingly, 'You turned me down, remember?'

She hadn't always turned McNab down. At his best,
the former DS was a very pleasant way to spend an
evening. Although anything more permanent was definitely out of the question. She was spared thinking of a
suitable retort to express this sentiment by Chrissy's arrival.
Her forensic assistant, already suitably kitted up, looked
from Rhona to McNab and back, instantly assessing the
situation.

'You two on speaking terms?'

'As always,' McNab assured her with his signature grin.

By her expression, Chrissy didn't buy that, but decided
not to pursue the matter any further, which was unusual
for her. Instead she turned her attention to Rhona.

'Okay, boss, wait till you see what's in that tent,' she
said excitedly.

Dressed now in the regulation boiler suit, Rhona pulled back
the flap and stepped inside. The scent of death was immediately familiar, the death scene not so common, for the
tent enclosed what resembled a miniature stone circle,
consisting of five upright stones, half human height. Rhona
stood for a moment absorbing the scene and registering its
smells. She'd asked Chrissy to wait outside, much to her
assistant's chagrin. She wanted to form her own impressions,
register her own questions about what had happened here,
without Chrissy's excited commentary.

The victim was male. He lay on his front, his arms
outstretched in what seemed to Rhona an unnatural
manner. His face was turned to the right, his eyes closed.
He looked to be in his late teens or early twenties. There

were no obvious wounds on the body apart from the wrists, from which the hands had been severed.

The right hand lay atop the eastern stone, the left hand on the western one. Rhona circled the stones, using the metal treads laid down on the grass, observing the body from all directions, before stopping to look more closely at the hands. Just as the arms had appeared to be placed in position, the hands too had been 'shaped'. The index finger on each was extended, the other digits curled into the palm. The index finger on the right hand was pointing, she estimated, south-east, the left north-west, but they would know better once R2S, the Return to Scene specialists, had captured everything on video and stills and entered it in the crime-scene software.

She approached the right hand for a closer look.

The weapon of choice among Glasgow gangs was a blade, which could range in size from a flick knife, via a machete, to a samurai sword. The one thing they all had in common was how sharp they were. The hand had been severed cleanly and, judging by the wound and blood loss, it had been removed post-mortem. She checked the left hand and found the same, suggesting both hands had been amputated after death, when the heart had stopped pumping.

Rhona stepped inside the stone circle and got down on her haunches next to the body. At close quarters, she could see no obvious signs of struggle, nor the means by which he had died, although the natural process of decomposition had already begun. The arms, exposed below the T-shirt, and the legs below the shorts, showed signs of lividity as gravity pulled the blood downwards, producing a dark pink discoloration, similar in appearance to bruising. The areas under pressure, including that part of the face pressing on the ground, were free of hypostasis, suggesting the body had lain here since death occurred. The eyelids were also free of petechiae, tiny haemorrhages under the surface of the skin, characteristic of strangulation or crushing which sometimes gave the appearance of hypostasis.

Rhona took a series of photographs for her own use. The official stills together with a 360-degree video would be made available on the crime-scene software, but she liked to study her own shots at leisure. Concentrating on the face, she registered that the mouth, partially open, had something wedged inside. Investigating further, she extracted a small flat stone, on one side of which was scratched what looked like the number five.

Chrissy had decided she'd waited long enough.

'Can I come in now?'

Rhona nodded at the eager face in the doorway and Chrissy was in like a shot.

'What have you got there?'

Rhona handed her the pebble. 'It was in his mouth.'

Chrissy examined the stone closely. 'That looks like a five.' She glanced about her. 'And there are five stones in this circle.'

Rhona gave her a warning look, designed to suggest she should refrain from jumping to conclusions.

'I know it's unscientific,' Chrissy said, registering the look, 'but you have to admit it's weird.'

Rhona, not to be drawn, reclaimed the stone and put it in an evidence bag while Chrissy examined the nearest hand, which happened to be the right one. 'You don't suppose there's anything in the hands too?'

It was a possibility that had already occurred to Rhona. And it might explain why the hands had been made into a fist. Extracting the stone from the mouth had been relatively easy despite the onset of rigor mortis. Forcing open the hands was a different matter and best left until the post-mortem. Rhona said as much.

Chrissy looked disappointed, her mind already set on further 'weird' discoveries. 'So, what do you want me to do?'

Rhona set Chrissy to work on the immediate surroundings, while she began the detailed process of taking samples from the body. McNab had indicated that the duty pathologist had already visited by helicopter and established a suspicious death. It was her role now to collect as much evidence surrounding the death as she could, before the body was removed to the mortuary.

At such a remote location it would be easy to keep the public and media at bay, but its remoteness generated other problems associated with the length of time necessary to process the scene of crime – such as eating, and going to the toilet. She could only hope the crime-scene officer was on the ball on that score.

Dead bodies, in whatever state of decay, had little effect on Chrissy's appetite. In fact, the 'weirder' the circumstances, the hungrier she became. In a previous case, where a murder victim's head had exploded inside a metal skip as the result of a fire, it had been Chrissy who had scraped the residue from the walls. Despite this, she had sent a nauseated constable for a double smoked sausage supper halfway through the proceedings. Chrissy had her weaknesses, but a queasy stomach wasn't one of them.

Two hours later, it was McNab's face at the opening. Rhona gestured that she would join him outside. It was warm in the tent, the run of June sunshine continuing

unabated, which was both good and bad. In this temperature the body would decompose more rapidly. But from
the point of view of crime-scene personnel, it was easier
to be up here on the Braes in midsummer, rather than
midwinter in a freezing gale.

Rhona stepped outside, pulled down her mask and took
a lungful of fresh air.

'What?' she said in answer to McNab's look.

'Come see what we've found.' He gestured her to follow
him across the ditch onto the hillside, where a couple of
SOCOs were standing.

'Looks like we have more than one victim.'

The dog's body was hidden by the long grass, coated
by flies that rose in a buzzing frenzy at their approach.
The throat had been cleanly severed, the earth sticky
beneath. It was a cross-breed, well cared for, black with
a Labrador-type face. Around the neck was a red collar
without a name tag.

'Whoever killed our victim got rid of his dog too?'
McNab tried.

The state of the dog's body suggested a similar time
frame. Rhona said as much.

'Have we any idea who the victim is?' she asked. There
had been nothing in the pockets to identify him, mobile
or wallet.

McNab said no.

'How was he found?'

'A guy called the station today, early afternoon. Sounded
drunk or terrified or both. Said he saw what looked like
a human hand on a standing stone on top of Cathkin
Braes. The duty sergeant thought it was a hoax, but sent
someone up to check anyway.'

'Did you trace the call?'

'It came from a public phone box south of the park.' McNab turned his gaze directly on her. 'Want to know what I think?'

He wasn't really asking, so Rhona didn't bother with a response.

'I think the victim pissed off some Castlemilk drug baron and had his hands chopped off to teach him a lesson.'

It was a good enough theory. Except for the fact that she believed his hands had been chopped off after death. Rhona told McNab so.

That surprised him. 'So how *did* he die?'

'I don't know yet, but he wasn't stabbed.' The usual method of dispatch in gangland.

McNab read her puzzlement. 'What is it?'

'There was a stone in his mouth with the number five scratched on it. And I think the body was placed in a particular position after death. The hands too.'

McNab thought for a minute. 'Gangs have signature patterns and habits.'

'I haven't seen this one before,' Rhona said.

Neither had McNab by his expression, then he rallied. 'High on drugs, they're capable of anything.'

That was true too. Rhona changed the subject. 'Chrissy's going to moan about eating soon.'

'There's a food van down in the car park. When can we remove the body?' McNab tried his luck.

'When I've finished with it,' Rhona told him firmly.

Rhona sat on a camp stool next to the body and wrote up her notes by the added light of an arc lamp. Alone, Chrissy having departed for home, Rhona relished the quiet she shared with the dead. It was her habit always to write her notes this way. For practical reasons as much as anything. No one wanted to be in here, making it the quietest part of any crime scene. And communing with the dead brought a measure of peace, if not for them, then for her. Her purpose as a forensic expert was to ask questions and to collect evidence, to remain detached and analytical, but it was also in her remit to show respect for the victim, regardless of the circumstances of their death. These quiet moments allowed her to do that.

Studying the body in detail had produced a picture of a young healthy male, well nourished with no apparent signs of drug abuse. There had been no obvious evidence of recent sexual activity from the swabs she'd been able to take. She hadn't removed his clothing, deciding to leave that to the post-mortem, lest she disturb the wrist wounds more than necessary. A study of the hands had convinced her that their shape was intended, but why a perpetrator would choose to point the fingers or for that matter place the hands so precisely on the stones left her at a loss. The awkward shape of the body also perplexed her. There was a ritualistic feel to the scene. McNab was right, gangs had their structure and their modes of punishment, often as ritualistic as they were cruel. Burning, maiming, stabbing. Power and control were everything and the greater the fear, the more the control. But what was the reason for the stone in his mouth? And why the number five?

When she finally emerged from the incident tent, the sun was heading for the horizon. Being close to midsummer, it would not be gone for long. The mortuary team were on standby awaiting her departure. She watched them load the body onto the helicopter but refused their offer of a lift, choosing instead to make her way down the hill to the car park by means of a torch and the last rays of the setting sun.

Below her twinkled the lights of Castlemilk. From a distance Glasgow appeared peaceful, a slumbering giant of a city, spreading west and north, straddling the wide expanse of the Clyde from which its industrial might had been born. Yet a few miles to the north, you encountered Ben Lomond standing sentinel over the highlands.

The night air was soft and still; no breeze rustled the surrounding trees. She stood for a moment beside her car, revelling in the quiet, with the sudden thought that she was in the calm centre of a maelstrom yet to come.

5

McNab savoured his first whisky of the day. It hit the back of his throat then his chest with the intensity of a shot in the arm. He savoured the moment and its effect, already sorry that it didn't last long enough.

The bar was full despite it being a Sunday night, or maybe because of it. McNab wondered what the comparison figures were between pub-goers and church-goers. He'd read somewhere that twice as many people went to church than to football matches. It was a startling statistic that he wasn't sure he believed.

'To Detective Inspector Michael Joseph McNab,' he said under his breath as he took another swig. *But for how long?* was his silent retort. When he'd challenged Rhona about his promotion she had been characteristically adamant that he deserved it. A catchphrase attributed to a former Old Firm manager immediately sprung to mind: 'Maybe's aye. Maybe's no.'

He waved at the barman for a refill as his mobile vibrated. The screen presented him with the name Iona. He contemplated it for a moment then slipped the phone back in his pocket. Iona, a holy isle where St Columba first landed, bringing Christianity to Scotland. Iona, a nineteen-year-old, posing as older, eager and willing to bed a recently promoted DI. He'd been eager too, once

27

Rhona had turned him down. He wasn't so keen now.

He cursed himself for having given out his number. Never a wise move whatever the circumstances. Always sound willing as you mentally switch a few digits round. Then they think you meant it but were just that wee bit drunk and misquoted the number. Or tell them you can't give out your number, police policy to keep you safe, then take theirs and promptly delete it.

He'd been high on success the night of his party, not a little drunk and stupid into the bargain. Stupid enough to take her home with him. He pondered whether to ignore the call or send her a sorry message, maybe even claim to be married. Be cruel to be kind.

The second whisky had less effect. No searing heat and rush of energy, this one brought instead a mellow warmth. While experiencing it he felt a rush of . . . what? Affection? Desire again for the young body he'd played with the previous night? Whatever it was made him question whether he should ditch her quite so swiftly. Maybe he could string her along, call her when he felt like it. After all, that's how Dr Rhona MacLeod dealt with him.

A sexual hunger he'd thought he'd assuaged reared its head again. Iona had, despite last night, only exacerbated that hunger. He purposefully put Rhona MacLeod from his mind and decided to do nothing. Iona, like the island, wasn't going anywhere. And he had the perfect excuse for keeping her waiting. A murder.

First a strategy meeting for all involved. Rhona would say her bit along with the pathologist. For the first time it wouldn't be his previous boss, DI Bill Wilson, who would lead the side. He took another swallow, relishing both the whisky and the thought of his new role. No longer snapping at heels, but leading a pack. The thought excited him. The chance to deal with the murder did too. Even if it was just another gangland killing.

His mobile buzzed once more. He ignored it, telling himself he was off duty, but he couldn't resist a look. Iona's name flashed up again. God, she was keen, desperate even. Had he been that good? He allowed himself a moment's satisfaction. Now if it had been Rhona's name that had appeared, he might just have been tempted.

McNab ordered one more for the road, grateful that he was a short walk from his flat, where at least a half-bottle awaited him.

Heading for home, he was seized again by the familiar fear that had courted him since Kalinin's trial. His appearance in London as a witness for the prosecution had sealed the Russian oligarch's fate. It had also sealed his own. To be forever looking over his shoulder. Forever awaiting the reprisal. But then, didn't that go with the territory anyway? He was as likely to be a target for some Scottish psycho he'd locked up as for a Russian one.

The night streets were quiet and for the most part deserted. By the time he reached his flat, he would have welcomed the prospect of meeting another human being, just to be sure he wasn't invisible. He'd spent so long trying to stay unseen while awaiting the trial, he'd become paranoid whenever anyone looked at him. Now he wanted to be noticed, because it proved he was alive.

As he turned the key in the lock, his mobile rumbled again. He waited until he was inside then answered without looking at the screen. For a moment he wished for Rhona's voice, but got Iona's instead. In the shadowy emptiness of the flat, the smell of the previous evening still ripe in his nostrils, he didn't hang up. Hearing him answer, her own voice became tentative. She suggested a drink somewhere. He suggested here and now. She could get a taxi, come round. He repeated the address just in case she'd forgotten. It was hardly romantic, but she accepted. When he rang off, he cursed himself for a stupid bastard. *Last time*, he thought. *From tomorrow it will be work twenty-four seven. I'll tell her that.*

He looked about, trying to imagine what her eyes would see in the cluttered mess of his life. Then reminded himself she'd been here last night and was willing to come back. His one concession was to jump in the shower. As he re-emerged from the bathroom, he heard the taxi purr to a halt outside. McNab, naked and ready, went to open the door.

She undressed quickly while he watched, focussing not on her face but on her breasts, then her thighs and the hairless mound between. He'd registered the piercing there the first time, and the one on her left nipple. Neither had excited him, but touching them had excited her. He thought it a pity that she should puncture her beauty in this way, but said nothing.

She in turn had been fascinated by the scar where the bullet had pierced his back. She'd touched it as she'd approached climax, panting her excitement. He wondered what she was thinking in those moments. Was she visualizing the bullet penetrating his skin, the pain and the blood? Or was she celebrating his survival?

She came to him now, pressing her body against his erection, exploring his mouth with her ringed tongue. He lifted her and entered the moistness with one hard thrust. She arched her neck and moaned, anchoring her ankles in the small of his back, pressing him deeper, whispering in his ear what she wanted.

McNab turned and threw her onto the bed. Now it was his turn to arch his neck, his arm muscles taking his weight. Her tongue darted in and out between her pink lips, mimicking his thrusts, urging him on, the silver ring glinting.

Immediately it was over, he rolled off and onto his side. He knew if he gave the slightest indication he wanted more, she would be eager and willing, so he shut his eyes. Moments later, he felt the studded tongue circle his scar, once, twice, three times.

'No!' he rasped.

She gave a small sound of disappointment then conceded and curled alongside him. Eventually McNab heard the soft sounds of her sleep. This, he decided, would be the last time.

By the open window, her laptop on the table in front of her, Rhona ran a slideshow of her photographs of the crime scene. It didn't provide the quality of the 360-degree set of images R2S would provide, but each photograph highlighted something that had caught her eye or raised a question in her mind. As she watched, she was back there, the smell strong in her nostrils, the sound of the world outside the death bubble in the background. Even Chrissy's 'weird' conjectures replayed in her head. McNab's suggestion of a gangland killing had some validity, but somehow she didn't see them taking their victim to the top of Cathkin Braes to carry out the deed. And displaying the body in such a way didn't match either. As for the stone in his mouth? An image of it came up on the screen and she paused and enlarged it. The stone looked like red sandstone, common in Glasgow tenement building, but not naturally found on Cathkin Braes. The scratch on the surface definitely looked like a five.

She turned her attention to the manner of death. She had examined and sampled the body in as much detail as possible before its removal to the mortuary. Apart from the hands, she had found no other wounds. No blunt force trauma to the head, no stab wounds, no obvious needle marks. No evidence of strangulation or suffocation.

All the evidence she had was related to what had happened after death.

She checked over her notes once again, then closed the laptop. The air in the room was balmy, more like the Mediterranean than Glasgow. According to the weather forecast, the warm spell was set to continue. June in Scotland was traditionally drier than July or August, but this year had been exceptional.

She headed for the kitchen, poured a glass of chilled white wine and took it to the window. From here she had a fine view of the ordered garden of the adjacent convent. Bordered by scented flower beds, the centrepiece of the lawn was a statue of the Virgin Mary bathed in a rosy light. Whatever happened in her life, that peaceful view never changed. If it ever did, she would have to move house, she decided for the umpteenth time. Despite the late hour, she wasn't ready yet for bed. The long hours of northern daylight had disrupted her internal clock. That, and a brain not yet willing to give up processing what she had seen today on Cathkin Braes.

Rhona settled herself on the window seat to await the dawn.

6

McNab was startled into wakefulness by the drill of his mobile alarm. Glancing at the screen, he realized he'd set it to snooze at least thirty minutes ago. As he rose from the bed, a sudden memory of the night before came flooding back. *Fuck*. He'd done it again. He glanced at the body curled behind him, her face hidden by a curtain of hair.

This had to stop, he told himself as he headed for the shower. Both the whisky and the sex. The water beating the top of his head did little to relieve the pain that throbbed inside his skull. He consoled himself with the thought that true alcoholics never experienced a hangover, because they were never sober.

Once dressed, he shook Iona awake. She looked up at him sleepily, her mascara smudged, her lipstick faded. Without the carefully applied make-up she looked far too young to be in his bed.

'What age are you, really?'

'Old enough,' she said with a knowing smile.

'But too young for me.'

'You didn't think so last night, or the night before.' The pout only accentuated her youthfulness.

'I have to work round the clock now on a murder enquiry so this can't happen again.'

'But I thought . . .' she began.

'I warned you I was in a relationship,' he reminded her.

She sat up abruptly, exposing her breasts. McNab kept his eyes firmly on her face.

'With that woman at the party?' she said dismissively. 'I saw her turn you down.'

McNab headed for the door. 'Feel free to use the shower before you leave.'

Once outside he took out his mobile. He deleted Iona's number and blocked her calls, aware all the time that he knew the number by heart, anyway.

At McNab's entrance, the desk sergeant looked pointedly at the clock. '*Detective Inspector.*'

McNab wasn't sure from the sergeant's expression whether the marked rendition of his new title was a jibe or a compliment.

'I was just about to call your mobile.'

McNab waited to hear the reason why.

'A Mrs MacKenzie has identified the Cathkin Braes body as her son. She's waiting to speak to you. Has been for the last hour.'

McNab swore under his breath. The band of steel encircling his forehead tightened. The throb behind his eyeballs upped speed. He'd planned coffee and maybe a couple of paracetamol from DS Clark before facing the day. He hadn't anticipated the bereft mother of a mutilated corpse. Chances were she'd only viewed her son's face for identity purposes and he'd have to tell her about the hands.

DS Janice Clark threw him a sympathetic look when he entered the incident room.

'Where is she?'

Janice gestured to his new office. 'She's pretty upset. Do you want me in with you?'

It would have been sensible, but McNab rejected the offer. If he messed this one up, he'd rather no one was around to see, especially DS Clark.

The woman was seated with her back to him. She was so still she might have been fashioned from stone. Dealing with a crime scene, no matter how gory, was nothing compared to dealing with those whose lives had been shattered by the crime itself. McNab took a moment to compose himself before entering, wishing he hadn't drunk so much whisky the night before, or that he could have one now before facing her.

DI Wilson had been good at this aspect of the job. Compassionate and caring, with a determined manner that suggested it was only a matter of time before he caught the bastard that had done this to their loved one. It generally was.

On his entry, the woman turned and rose stiffly to her feet. McNab held out his hand, taking refuge in the formalities of introduction. Once completed, he suggested tea, although a full mug sat in front of her, its surface cold and scummy.

She shook her head. 'No, thank you.'

McNab took his place on the other side of the desk.

'I'm sorry for your loss, Mrs MacKenzie.'

She looked stunned, as though his words had suddenly reminded her of why she was here. McNab hurried on in case she should break down in front of him.

'I understand you reported your son missing yesterday evening.'

She nodded briskly, smothering a wave of emotion with practicality.

'Alan always comes round on a Sunday. He's a student, you see—' She halted, unnerved by her use of the present tense. She gathered herself and continued. 'I went to . . . church. When I got back he was out with the dog.' She stared into nothingness. 'He didn't come back.'

Her pain swept towards McNab like a wave. He felt it break over him and retreat to swamp her again. She sagged and caught the edge of the desk with her hand to steady herself.

'We'll find whoever did this to your son, but I'll need your help, Mrs MacKenzie.'

She looked up, searching his face for the truth in what he'd said.

'Will you help me?' McNab said gently.

She steeled herself. 'Can I have a fresh mug of tea? And I'd like to visit the Ladies.'

Ten minutes later, sipping tea, she told McNab the story of a good son who worked hard at university, came home to visit her regularly and who possibly had a girlfriend. None of which outwardly matched McNab's notion of a gangland member who'd broken the rules.

'You haven't met Jolene?' he asked.

She shook her head. 'I spoke to her on the phone when I was looking for Alan.' She opened her bag and extracted a mobile. 'This is Alan's phone. He forgot it when he went out with the dog.'

'That's very helpful, Mrs MacKenzie. Thank you.' He'd been about to ask about Alan's circle of friends, and anyone who might have wished him ill. The mobile was manna from heaven. 'One more thing, Mrs MacKenzie,' he said. 'How was Alan financing his degree?'

'He had a part-time job in a bar,' she said defensively. 'And . . . because of our financial circumstances, he was eligible for a maintenance grant.'

'Can you give me the name of the bar he worked in?'

'The Thistle – it's near the university.'

'Thank you.'

McNab rose, signalling the end of the interview, but Mrs MacKenzie seemed to be toying with the idea of saying something else.

'What is it, Mrs MacKenzie?'

She hesitated, then shook her head. 'Nothing. It's nothing.'

'Why not let me be the judge of that?' McNab said encouragingly.

'There was a man who told me Alan was dead,' she rushed on. 'I didn't believe him. But it was true.'

'What man?'

'It was on Sunday at the spiritualist church on Sauchiehall Street.' It all came tumbling out, like a desperate confession. 'I didn't want to go but my friend Doreen persuaded me. The medium called out my name. He said he had a message from Alan. He said Alan was dead and that I was to go to the police.' Her eyes were filled with horror and bewilderment.

McNab was equally astonished. 'What time was this?'

'Sunday morning about eleven. Alan was in the house when I left. Then this man said he was dead.' She stared at McNab. 'How could he possibly have known that Alan was dead?'

McNab wanted to know the exact same thing.

'Who is this man?'

'His name is Patrick Menzies.'

7

McNab regarded the sea of eager faces. He had been one of those faces, listening to the boss at the start of every murder enquiry. Sitting out there, you knew you counted, but you weren't responsible. You were led in the right direction. You weren't required to set that direction. DI Wilson used to tell him to think with his guts as much as his head. His head and his guts had told him this death was gang related. Most murders in Glasgow occurred within a domestic setting, usually through drink, or were the result of turf wars involving drugs, prostitution or gambling.

Most, but not all.

He raised a hand for silence and the chatter faded. He stood aside as an image of the crime scene appeared on the screen. McNab let those who had not yet seen this take time to absorb it before continuing.

'The victim, identified as nineteen-year-old Alan MacKenzie, was last seen by his mother around ten o'clock on Sunday morning. As far as we know, Alan took the dog, also found dead at the scene, for a walk on Cathkin Braes, while his mother was at church. In the early afternoon, an anonymous caller reported seeing a human hand near the summit, on a standing stone. When he investigated, he found Alan's body. The caller was agitated and refused to give his name. He also indicated he'd found a buried stash of cocaine uphill from the body. When we checked, the stash had been retrieved although the evidence was that it had been at the GPS reading he gave. He said he'd been geocaching and that's why he'd dug at that spot.' McNab looked around the room. 'Anyone here into geocaching?'

The heads swivelled round looking for someone brave enough to admit to this. Eventually someone did. DC Stevens, a young woman with a defiant look, put up her hand, to a titter of laughter.

'Right, Stevens, it's your job to find out the identity of our caller, via your geocaching contacts.'

The detective constable gave the surrounding and surprised team a triumphant look.

McNab continued. 'The victim's hands were removed after death and displayed on the stones. We don't know yet exactly how he died, although Dr MacLeod believes the hands were removed after death. Post-mortem is later today.' McNab paused. 'One more thing. The victim had a stone in his mouth with the number five scratched on it.'

He allowed for a few minutes' discussion as the troops absorbed the details, before calling them to order.

'Does anyone know anything about the spiritualist church on Sauchiehall Street, and a medium called Patrick Menzies?'

If he'd got down on his knees and asked someone in the team to marry him, he couldn't have had a more amazed reaction. A babble erupted.

McNab let them talk for a minute then posed the question again. It was his turn to be surprised when DS Clark raised her hand.

'I do, sir.'

'Then I'd like to speak to you in my office, Sergeant.'

She nodded, surprise evident on her face. McNab chose not to enlighten her. 'We have the victim's mobile, which he left behind at his mother's house. The Tech boys are downloading his contacts, texts, emails and web history. I want every lead there followed up. If Alan MacKenzie has any connection with the missing cocaine, I want to know about it.'

McNab dismissed them and, nodding to DS Clark to follow, headed for his office. Shutting the door firmly behind them, he indicated that she should take a seat.

He and Janice Clark went back a long way, her career path not that far behind his own. She was, in effect, his replacement as DS. Janice had always been immune to his charms, despite McNab's best efforts. After a third rejection, his ego bruised, he'd wondered out loud whether DC Janice Clark might be the other way inclined. The boss had given him a roasting for that, which he'd deserved. Janice's relief and joy when he'd survived the shoot-out at The Poker Club had made McNab feel even more of a heel.

'Well, Sergeant?'

'My mother goes to the church, sir. I've gone with her on occasion.'

McNab had expected some official connection, like dealing with a complaint from an angry member of the public about charlatans.

'Why would you go there?'

Janice seemed unfazed by his tone. 'My father gets in touch sometimes.'

Another surprise.

'Your father's dead, I take it?'

'He died of cancer two years ago.'

'And he talks to your mother through Patrick Menzies?'

'Yes, sir.'

'And you believe that, Sergeant?' His tone had moved from sarcasm to total disbelief, causing her to hesitate.

Then she came out fighting. 'At first I didn't, but after going there a few times . . .' She stopped and met his eye. 'I believe the only thing we know is that we don't know, sir.'

McNab sat back in his chair. 'That's a good line, Sergeant.'

'Yes, sir.'

His intimidating style didn't seem to be troubling DS Clark. McNab considered again how much they had in common. A fleeting thought also crossed his mind that Janice would make a good DI one day. Probably a better one than him.

'Anything else you wish to tell me, Sergeant?'

'I'm a member of the Scottish Society for Psychical Research, sir. Patrick Menzies has spoken at a number of our events.'

Having DS Clark admitting to him that she was gay would have troubled McNab far less than these continuing revelations. He struggled for a reply that didn't involve swearing.

'And what exactly is the Society for Psychical Research?' he finally managed.

'It investigates the paranormal, sir,' she said, then added, 'in a scientific manner.'

'Ghostbusters?'

She ignored the mocking question and posed one of her own. 'Why did you want to know about Patrick, sir?'

McNab decided it was his turn for a revelation. 'Alan MacKenzie's mother was at the spiritualist church on

Sunday morning. Patrick Menzies said he had a message for her. From Alan.'

Janice's hand rose to her mouth in dismay. 'The poor woman.'

'Menzies also told her to get in touch with the police, because her son had met a violent end.'

Janice didn't seem surprised. 'He's very good, sir.'

'In my experience, Sergeant, the first person to know someone has been murdered is usually the person who did it,' McNab said drily.

Janice looked horrified. 'But not in this case, sir.'

Being called 'sir' in a variety of tones was disconcerting. McNab remembered how often he'd used this method of challenging his superiors when a DS himself.

'I want to speak to Patrick Menzies.'

'Here or at the church, sir?'

'At the church. As soon as possible.' He wanted to see this place that purported to have a channel to the afterlife.

'I'll set that up, sir.' Janice rose to go.

McNab was used to vying for the last word. He and Chrissy McInsh were both experts at that. Unfortunately, when you were the boss, you didn't have to fight for the privilege. It took the shine off it, somehow. McNab contented himself with silence, which, he realized, was a first.

Alone in his office, he pondered his elevation to DI and the power it afforded him. Was it any better than throwing his weight around as a DS? At least then he'd been a free spirit. McNab understood with a sudden clarity that the further up the chain you went, the less free you became.

With this realization came an even more uncomfortable thought.

DI Wilson's door had always been open to his sergeant.

McNab had never had to fear baring his soul to the old man. DI Wilson wouldn't have spoken sarcastically to DS Clark. Just welcomed the fact that his sergeant had some insight on the case.

McNab pushed back the chair and stood up, irritated with himself, his thoughts and his actions. When he opened the office door, the hum of conversation in the incident room ceased, suggesting that he'd been the subject of it.

McNab approached Janice's desk, conscious that all eyes followed him there.

Janice looked up. 'Mr Menzies is at the church now, sir.'

'Then let's go, Sergeant.'

The babble erupted again as the door closed behind them. McNab realized the next issue with being the boss was that you were excluded from the general gossip and had to rely on your sergeant to keep you up to date.

He would have to bear that in mind.

The journey took a little over ten minutes. Finding a place to leave the car took almost twice as long. By the time they'd finally abandoned it, McNab's ill humour, edged by the remains of a hangover, had come back to bite him.

Janice, seemingly unmarked by his bad mood, led him towards a light-coloured elegant building with a pillared front entrance. McNab paused at the foot of the steps. In his youth, churches and chapels had looked the part. This building could have housed anything from a bank to a beauty parlour. He had long forsaken Catholicism, but he found himself annoyed by this.

The calm, ordered interior only served to irritate McNab further, as did Patrick Menzies when they were shown into his room. McNab's immediate impression was of an overgrown schoolboy with red cheeks and doe eyes.

Menzies came towards him, hand outstretched. He took it, knowing what it would feel like before he did so. Soft, warm and damp. McNab broke off contact as soon as possible.

'Can I get you some tea or coffee, Inspector?'

The voice was soft and cloying, or it was to McNab's ear. Janice, on the other hand, looked quite at home.

'Thank you, no.'

Menzies turned with a smile to DS Clark. 'What about you, Janice?'

McNab butted in before she could answer. 'DS Clark and I are in a hurry.'

The rosy cheeks flushed a little redder. 'Of course, Inspector.' The medium indicated a ring of seven seats in the centre of the room. *No doubt set out for a seance*, McNab thought. They all sat down, an empty seat between each of them.

'Tell me what happened at the service on Sunday morning,' McNab said.

'You mean with respect to that poor woman Amy MacKenzie?'

McNab nodded.

'Well, we finished singing the final hymn, then I got up on stage. I explained that I couldn't summon loved ones who had crossed to the other side. But only that they might choose to speak through me.' He looked to McNab, who nodded at him to continue.

'Then a voice came through. It was male and asked for Amy. I put this to the assembled congregation and a young woman said she was called Amy. She was looking for someone called Gary. My spirit connection indicated his name was Alan and he wanted to speak to his mother, Amy.' Menzies paused, looking stricken by the memory.

'When she didn't believe me, Alan told me to tell her it wasn't Aunt Bella. Whatever that meant, it frightened her and she left the room.' He paused a moment to collect himself. 'I sought her out afterwards to tell her the final part of his message.' He halted, looking stricken.

'Which was?'

'Alan was very distressed. He indicated he had died violently and urged his mother to go to the police.'

'This message from Alan. What form did it take?' McNab asked.

'A voice.'

'So you hear voices?'

Menzies examined McNab's critical expression. 'This is not an illness, Inspector. It is a gift.'

'Have you ever met Alan?'

'Not in physical form, no.'

'Have you ever heard his voice when alive, say on the telephone?'

Menzies shook his head. 'I had not met or spoken to Amy or Alan before yesterday's service.'

McNab's exasperation was growing by the second. 'Has Alan spoken to you since then?'

Menzies shook his head. 'No, he has been silent.' He looked down at his small, damp hands. 'But he is an unhappy spirit.'

McNab's suppressed *tut* turned out to be audible, causing Janice to flinch. He stood up, suddenly eager to be away from Menzies and his holier-than-thou attitude. As a boy, he'd met too many priests like Patrick Menzies. Men who thought they could talk to God. Who believed they knew what would happen to you after death.

'Thank you, Mr Menzies. We'll be in touch.' McNab

headed for the door. Glancing back, he saw Janice shake Menzies' hand and speak quietly to him. No doubt apologizing for her inspector's behaviour.

Once outside, McNab walked swiftly on, berating himself for bringing his sergeant, knowing he would have been much tougher on that bloody self-righteous bastard had DS Clark not been there.

He halted and pulled out his mobile. Janice answered straight away.

'Can you make your own way back to the station, Sergeant? I have business elsewhere.' McNab didn't wait for a reply before ringing off.

He strode along Sauchiehall Street towards the centre of town, entering the first pub he came to. The interior was empty apart from two guys in smart suits sitting in a corner, playing with their mobiles.

McNab approached the bar and ordered a double whisky. He observed it for a few moments, imagining what it would taste like. Then an internal voice reminded him that if he drank it, he would have to walk back to the police station. It wasn't far, but the absence of the car would be noticed, which would lead to talk.

In defiance of this thought, he took a mouthful. The spirit hit the back of his throat and fired down his chest, but for once left him cold. Who was he trying to kid? It wasn't being a DI that was shit. It was the way *he* was doing it.

McNab pushed the whisky away and exited, turning back in the direction he had come from. Minutes later he was re-entering the spiritualist building.

Patrick Menzies looked up in surprise as McNab walked in. The room had six other occupants now, seated in the circle. McNab ran his eye over the assembled company of four women and two men who regarded him back with a mixture of surprise and curiosity.

'Detective Inspector . . .' Menzies rose, flustered.

'We need to talk.'

'Of course.' Menzies turned to the group. 'Help yourself to coffee.' He indicated a tray laid out on a nearby table. 'I'll be right back.'

Menzies bustled his way across the hall to a glass door. 'We can speak in my office, Inspector.'

He led McNab into a small overstuffed room. Framed on the walls were rows of affidavits from satisfied customers. McNab studied them as Menzies closed the door.

'Please take a seat, Inspector.'

McNab turned and, ignoring the offer, came to stand a foot away from the medium. Menzies tried to step back but was obstructed by the closed door. McNab watched as beads of sweat broke out on the shiny skin. McNab stepped even closer. Now they were inches apart. At this distance he could smell the man's fear. The medium's breath was coming in short gasps, the sweat trickling down his face.

'Now we're alone, I want the truth,' McNab said.

8

The word 'post-mortem' struck fear into many hearts, police officers included. Attending one could reduce grown men to fainting bundles on the floor, even if they had attended the scene of the murder that had occasioned it.

The chaos of a murder scene was one thing; the methodical dismemberment of a body another. First-timers would look at the body on the slab, then at the instruments about to be used on it, and envisage a torture scene. It was, except that the victim could feel no pain.

If the audience made it to the next stage, the sound or smell usually finished them. Death had a scent all of its own. One you never got used to. Face masks did little to temper it. It permeated everything – your hair, your breath, your skin.

As for the sounds . . . Rhona had watched seasoned officers insert earplugs in an attempt to soften the noise of a drill or the high-pitched whine of a saw as it cut its way through a human skull. Then came the slicing open of the chest and abdomen. The visual image of the extraction of the major organs – heart, liver, kidneys – to be weighed, measured and examined. The cutting open of the stomach to reveal the victim's last meal – perhaps a half-digested McDonald's or Burger King, distinguishable one from the other by the way they sliced their gherkins.

Rhona was, like the pathologist, dispassionate, although the last-meal scenario always discomfited her, because knowing what a person had just eaten reminded you of how recently they had been a living, breathing human being. The rest was like a jigsaw puzzle. You examined the pieces to understand the whole.

McNab was bearing up well, despite being a little green about the gills. He didn't have to be at the PM; not all investigating officers chose to be. His former boss, DI Wilson, had always attended. It had been a ritual with him and Rhona. Standing side by side, listening to the pathologist Dr Sissons' pronouncements into the overhead mike. Discussing the findings together afterwards.

In this instance, she learned little more than she had deduced already. There were no signs of force on the body. No bruising before or after death. No needle marks, no abrasions. The hands had been removed post-mortem with a sharp implement, non-serrated. Possibly a hatchet or a machete. Prising the hands open had revealed nothing, which would disappoint Chrissy.

The victim had been healthy and in good physical shape. He had a runner's legs, with a muscled upper torso. Rhona imagined him playing basketball or football. He didn't have the thick neck of a rugby player. His lungs indicated that he wasn't a smoker. His heart appeared healthy, yet it had stopped. Exactly why, was undetermined.

Above the mask, McNab looked irritated by this. Rhona felt his frustration. Knowing exactly how someone died was the starting point for all investigations; discovery of the murder weapon an added bonus. As it was, they would have to await the results of a battery of tests and McNab was not a patient man.

They exited together, McNab pulling down the mask as soon as the door swung shut behind them. Rhona heard him mutter an expletive, but didn't react. His face was paler than usual, making his auburn stubble more pronounced. He shot her a look from those startlingly blue eyes.

'How the hell was he killed?'

'Maybe he wasn't killed,' she said. 'Maybe he simply died.'

'He went for a walk and just died?' he said sarcastically.

'It happens to fit young people. Sudden adult death.'

McNab raised his eyebrows, unconvinced. 'He heads for a coke stash, falls down dead, then someone comes along, chops off his hands and sticks a stone in his mouth.'

Put like that it did sound ridiculous. Nevertheless.

'If he was being threatened and had undiagnosed Long QT Syndrome—' Rhona began.

'You're saying he died of fright?'

'Stress, fright, overexertion.'

'Okay. Let's say he ran up the hill and fell down dead. Who the hell would kill his dog and chop off his hands, unless it's something to do with the coke?'

McNab was right. It did look gangland, even if they weren't sure exactly how the victim had died. But then there was the placing of the hands, and the stone in the mouth.

'What did the mother have to say?' she asked.

For a moment, McNab looked shifty. 'Just the usual. A model son. Never in trouble. A bit like myself,' he added, giving her his signature grin. 'Fancy a coffee before I call on the girlfriend?'

Rhona raised an eyebrow.

'Alan's girlfriend,' McNab said pointedly.

Rhona shook her head. 'I have to get back to the lab. There's a DI demanding test results ASAP.'

'Sounds like a bastard.'

'He is.'

McNab watched her walk away, imagining the outline of her body inside the shapeless forensic suit. Sparring with Rhona professionally, or otherwise, often made him hard. His own suit disguised it, thankfully. He wondered if she knew the effect she had on him, and suspected she did, although she never played on it.

She never played *with* it, either. McNab only wished she would. When he'd returned from the grave, she'd celebrated his resurrection with the best sex ever. He knew she didn't love him, but at times she did desire him. For his part, McNab loved and desired her all the time. In death and in life.

The only time he'd confessed to this was in the moments before his actual death. Lying on the pavement outside The Poker Club, blood pumping from his body, he'd said the words. He'd thought it was with his dying breath. Then he woke up in a hospital bed.

She had been told that he was dead, as they all had been, because it was safer for him that way. Chrissy had even organized his funeral. The full Catholic works and the police guard. He'd been laid to rest in a grave in a Glasgow Southside cemetery in a biting wind and a flurry of snow. Apparently, people had cried. McNab had been touched by that, even as he lived and breathed in a police safe house.

Death had protected him from reprisals until the Russian Kalinin's trial. It had freed him from his obsessions too. Now, officially alive again, they were back in full working order.

McNab tried to think about anything other than Rhona MacLeod in that changing room, stripping off her forensic suit and stepping naked into the shower. But all he could think of was burying his face between her breasts, in spite of the lingering scent of death.

He entered the men's section and stripped off. Luckily there was no one there to note his state of arousal. He stepped inside the shower cubicle and turned the dial to cold.

Rhona had felt his eyes on her back as she entered the changing room. McNab was always like this during an investigation. Every sense on high alert, his obsessions to the fore. That's what made him a good detective. He was raw and uncompromising and he saw things that others missed. She tried not to think about him now, in the neighbouring shower room.

She had seen him naked only once since the shooting. Then the scar had been red and angry, and she – who had seen much worse – had been moved to tears. The bullet wound would have faded now, but seeing it again, she knew, would bring back the night he was shot in all its terrible intensity.

He was gone by the time she emerged. Rhona had already made up her mind to ration their time together. Most of her work now would be performed in the lab and at her desk. She would meet McNab at strategy meetings, but they needn't be alone. It seemed better that way, for both their sakes.

9

Michael Joseph McNab had never been a student. His mother would have liked him to be and he had the grades, but he didn't want the debt. He and his mother had lived hand to mouth for too long by then. He'd contemplated the army, but the money was crap and they were still sending you out at seventeen to whatever front line they had going. McNab fancied living into his twenties, so he had opted for the police force instead.

He'd spent his teenage years in an area of Glasgow where you had to look after yourself. He'd carried a knife for a while, but worried he might eventually use it. So he tried out various self-defence classes, coming to the conclusion that the best method of self-defence was to run away very quickly.

This had saved him on a number of occasions. Most of those looking for a fight were drunk or high, so their reactions weren't a hundred per cent. If he clocked that he'd entered someone's radar, he would swiftly cross the road. If that didn't work, then he took off like a rocket, leaving his would-be assailants looking around them in surprise.

At the police college, he'd been surprised how soft many of the recruits were, especially those who had come there straight from a university education. With their eyes on the bigger prize of early promotion, they'd taken classes in sociology and psychology, and fancied themselves experts on the criminal brain, although they had never met a criminal.

One night he'd given an impromptu knife show, to demonstrate to his wide-eyed audience just what a guy with a chib was capable of. That had instigated the first of a series of reprimands, but had gained him some respect, and a reputation as a hard man. And reputations, as McNab knew, had to be lived up to, even at the level of detective inspector.

His former boss had come from similar origins. In the era between their respective childhoods, nothing much had changed in Glasgow. The weapon of choice had remained a blade, gangs still held territorial rights over the decaying inner city and the peripheral estates. Some areas had been spruced up, but the Thatcher era had decimated the industrial base that had given working men their pride, and started a trend in youth unemployment that carried on to this day. Unless, of course, you became a student.

It was reaching the Student Union that had led him to that train of thought. Having passed the handsome original granite building, McNab turned left and headed uphill into the grid of streets behind, where Alan MacKenzie had shared a student flat.

He'd evaded telling Rhona everything Mrs MacKenzie had said regarding her son's death. Despite his attempts at humour, it was pretty obvious from Rhona's expression that she'd registered his evasiveness. The likelihood was she would get the whole story from Chrissy anyway, Chrissy being the bush telegraph that linked the police station to the forensic lab.

If he'd revealed the story of the medium, he couldn't have avoided mentioning his own visit to the spiritualist church. Which would have led to the revelation that his DS believed in all that mumbo jumbo. Then there was the issue of his second interview with Menzies, which had produced fuck all. The man had been frightened, but not enough. Either McNab was losing his touch, or Menzies knew nothing more than he'd told them already.

The paint on the front door of number 21 was chipped and scratched, but the intercom functioned when McNab pressed the buzzer. It echoed through the building and a dog barked from the ground-floor flat. A small black terrier appeared at the window, the shadow of an elderly man behind. McNab made a mental note to speak to the occupier. Someone with a dog like that was bound to know the comings and goings at number 21.

A female voice answered.

'Jolene Hegarty?'

'Yes.'

'Detective Inspector McNab. I'd like to speak to you about Alan MacKenzie.'

A moment's hesitation. 'Have you found him?'

'Can you open the door, please?' The 'please' was more an order than a request.

There was a sharp buzzing sound and the lock sprang free. McNab entered. The close was clean, the faint scent of disinfectant still in the air from a previous wash. At the foot of the stairs, three padlocked bikes stood in a row.

He advanced to the second landing. A repeat of the well-worn outside door was enhanced by a pot plant, a little stringy as it grew towards the light of the cupola. For a moment McNab considered whether it might be cannabis, with no chance of survival in such conditions. He rapped the door a couple of times.

He heard an inner door open and pounding music escape, before it was shut. Footsteps came towards him. The front door opened a crack and a blonde-haired girl's face peeked through. McNab flashed his ID. When she didn't look as though she planned to open the door further, McNab said, 'I'd like to talk *inside*.'

The door was opened to reveal a fair-sized hall, with five doors leading off.

The pounding beat was coming from the door opposite. To McNab it resembled a traumatized heart on an operating table, rather than music – a sure sign he was getting old. In his youth he'd likened pounding music to having sex, each beat a further thrust, until the eventual climax. Now the *bump, bump, bump* just irritated him.

The girl gave the door in question a furtive glance and bit her lip. The look reminded McNab suddenly of Iona, and he was shocked to realize they were probably the same age.

He glanced around pointedly. 'Is there somewhere we can talk?'

She nodded and led him towards another door. Once opened, it revealed a kitchen, much like his own: full of dirty dishes and the smell of stale food.

She stood, unsure, so McNab gestured they should take a seat at the kitchen table.

At close quarters she was pretty, although her eyes were darkened by shadows. She'd either not been sleeping, or had been burning the candle at both ends.

'What's wrong? Is Alan okay?'

McNab ignored the question. 'Tell me about yesterday,' he said.

She studied his expression, trying to work out what the hell was going on. 'Alan's mother called around seven o'clock to ask if I'd seen him. I said not since that morning.'

'Did you know he was going home?'

'He usually did on a Sunday. He spent the day with his mum, walked the dog.'

'Are you and Alan an item?'

A flush crept over her cheek and her eyes darted towards the door as she answered. 'You mean do we sleep together? Occasionally. But we aren't exclusive,' she added defensively.

It sounded like the sort of excuse McNab would give about Iona, which made him mildly uncomfortable. He decided to change the subject.

'To your knowledge, was . . . is Alan involved in drugs?' he said, swearing inwardly at himself for messing up the tense.

She was immediately on to him. 'Has something happened to Alan?'

'Just answer the question,' McNab said sharply.

She searched his face, then said, 'Not really.'

'What does *not really* mean?'

'He smoked a joint now and again. That's it.'

'No cocaine, ecstasy, amphetamines . . .' McNab carried on with the all-too-familiar list.

'Alan is a serious guy. His father died when he was young. His mother worked hard to get him here. He appreciated that. He didn't want to mess up,' she finished.

Jolene was painting a similar picture to Alan's mother. Since they had never met, it rang true. But both of them could be lying. Alan's mother because she didn't know what her son got up to. Jolene because she didn't want McNab to know.

'Who else lives here apart from you and Alan?'

'Jamie and Helena, but she's away at the moment.'

'Is Jamie here?'

She hesitated, looking embarrassed. McNab, reading the expression, rose and walked swiftly through the hall to throw open the music room door. The pounding was coming from a docked iPod. McNab wondered how such a small object could generate so much noise. He removed it and silence fell.

The bedroom was obviously feminine and smelt a great deal better than the kitchen. A guy lay on the bed, the duvet pulled loosely over his naked body. He was in a deep sleep, mouth open, snoring softly. McNab barred the door from the fast-approaching Jolene, and swept the room with a practised eye, passing the two empty bottles of Spanish red and fastening on a dusting of white powder and empty sachet on a bedside table.

Behind McNab, Jolene protested. 'You have no right . . .'

McNab crossed to the bed and threw back the cover. The guy's penis uncurled and rose in welcome.

'Jo,' he slurred. 'Come back to bed, babe.'

McNab leaned over and shouted in his ear. 'Get up.'

The sound penetrated the stupor and the guy sat bolt upright, his eyes wide with shock.

'Who the fuck are you?'

'Police,' McNab said.

McNab watched as the forensic van pulled up outside. After calling the station, he'd taken a quick look in Alan's room, which was a great deal tidier than Jolene's. It was sparsely furnished with a double bed, a rail for clothes and a chest of drawers. A large flat screen stood on a computer desk with a keyboard. Below it, the main box blinked green. A nearby bookcase held a selection of paperback books and labelled folders with titles like *Soil Mechanics* and *Maths for Engineers*.

Helena's room had been locked and Jolene had insisted she didn't have a key. When McNab asked when Helena would return, Jolene said she expected her back by Wednesday.

Back in the hall, McNab greeted the two SOCOs and issued his instructions, then went to the kitchen to check on his detainees.

Their hushed conversation stopped abruptly when he opened the door. McNab hadn't allowed Jamie into his own room for his clothes, so he was sitting in his boxer shorts and a T-shirt, looking glum and definitely on a downer following his cocaine rush. Either that or he was worried what the forensic team would find in his room.

McNab observed them for a moment, then nodded at Jamie.

'Get dressed.'

'Then what?' Jamie said.

'Then come back here.'

Jamie slunk out and McNab turned to Jolene, who couldn't meet his eye.

'Who's your supplier?' he said sharply.

'It's just a guy, I don't know his name.'

'But you know his number?'

Jolene studied a coffee stain on the table.

McNab dropped his bomb. 'I regret to inform you that Alan MacKenzie's body was found on Sunday afternoon inside a stone circle on top of Cathkin Braes.'

Her face drained of colour.

McNab had led her on, seeking to gauge how much Jolene knew. Now he had his answer, to one question at least. Jolene had been too busy snorting and screwing to listen to the news. She hadn't known Alan was dead. Now she did, her brain, laced with fear, was working overtime.

McNab decided to add to that fear. 'His body was discovered near a stash of cocaine. Whoever killed him sliced the dog's throat, then chopped off Alan's hands and sat them on the standing stones.' Even as he said it, the image of the crime scene came into his head. The smell, the flies, the grotesque supplicant's pose.

Her hand flew to her mouth. She gagged and made for the sink.

McNab watched as murky red wine splattered the dirty dishes. In that moment, he decided it was time to clean up his own place.

She wiped her mouth on a grotty dish towel. Her face was as grey as the corpse he'd watched being cut open that morning.

'So, cocaine?' McNab said.

She anchored her hands on the edge of the sink, unwilling as yet to desert it.

'I told you, Alan didn't use cocaine.'

McNab sat back in the chair and folded his arms. 'But you and dickhead do?'

When she didn't respond, McNab gave her the ultimatum. 'Okay, Jolene, you give me the contact number of your supplier, or you and dickhead accompany me to the station.' It was a standard threat that worked on the innocent and guilty alike.

Something worse than fear invaded her eyes. 'What if they find out I gave you the number?'

'They?' McNab prompted.

She was gabbling now as though he held a knife to her throat. 'It's not always the same guy who delivers.'

'The number,' McNab repeated.

Jamie, now dressed in jeans and a different T-shirt, appeared at the door. At the sight of him, Jolene vomited again.

'See the effect you have on women,' McNab said drily.

Jolene collected herself and ran the cold tap, which only served to splash the vomit over a wider area. She wiped her hand across her mouth, looked at the dickhead, then at McNab.

'I'll give you the number,' Jolene said.

McNab's knock on the front door of the ground-floor flat set the terrier into a frenzy of barking. McNab wasn't a dog fan, but he appreciated their uses. He heard rapid scrabbling behind the door, then the slow, ponderous footsteps of its owner.

McNab checked the name on the old-fashioned brass plate then heard a guttural voice say, 'Back, Scout.' The dog gave a protest whine then apparently did what it was told, for the door opened.

McNab was ready with his ID. 'Mr Niven. I'm Detective Inspector McNab.'

The old guy squinted at the ID, then at him.

'I'd like to ask you a few questions.'

'What about?'

'The student flat upstairs.'

The old guy looked puzzled. 'I never complained.'

'It's not about a complaint.'

The man stood aside. 'You'd better come in then.'

The terrier eyed McNab's entrance with some concern until the old man said, 'It's okay, Scout.'

Mr Niven led him through to the sitting room. Immediately Scout took up his sentry position on the back of a seat near the window. Mr Niven waved McNab to one of two high-backed chairs that stood either side of a fireplace.

'So, Inspector,' he said, easing himself into the other seat.

McNab explained about Alan, leaving out the gory details. A shadow crossed the old man's face. 'The tall boy who was studying engineering?'

'You met him?'

'He took Scout out for a walk sometimes. Says he missed his own dog at home.' Mr Niven shook his head in disbelief. 'And this happened yesterday?'

McNab nodded.

'Why didn't the lassie tell me?'

'It wasn't confirmed as Alan until today.'

He shook his head again. 'I wondered why I hadn't seen him go in. Scout always makes a fuss when it's Alan.' He regarded McNab. 'How can I help?'

'Tell me everything you know about Alan and his flatmates. Who comes and goes. Stuff like that.'

Mr Niven nodded. 'I can do that.'

An hour later, McNab had learned a little, but not much more than he already knew. The lassie with the country and western name was nice enough, but didn't engage Mr Niven much in conversation. The young daft bloke played his music too loud, but since Mr Niven was a bit deaf, it didn't really bother him. There was another girl, he couldn't remember her name.

'Helena,' McNab had told him.

'Aye. Tall, slim, rides a bike.'

McNab asked about visitors.

'There's a bloke with a dog sometimes. An ugly brute. Scout hates it.' He'd shot a glance at McNab. 'I don't always sit at the window, you know,' he said defensively.

After that, McNab had thanked Mr Niven for his help and departed. All the occupants of the close would have to be interviewed, and the rest of the street, but he could leave that to the uniforms.

McNab contemplated a return to the station, then decided against it. Most of the team would have knocked off by now and headed for the pub. He realized joining them there was probably no longer an option. The boss had done so only on special occasions, knowing that his presence, much as they liked and respected him, would put a damper on the proceedings. It was a sobering thought, which made McNab want a drink even more.

Ten minutes later he was propping up the bar in the Thistle, waiting for his moment to ask about Alan, their part-time barman. The place was busy with fresh-faced students; even the ones behind the bar looked barely the age to drink, never mind serve.

McNab had ordered a pint, although he really wanted whisky. A pint would allow him to linger longer and get the feel of the place. He had made up his mind not to declare himself a policeman. There was a young woman serving behind the bar who had given him the eye. A chat to her might provide him with more information than a direct interview.

He finally got his chance when she checked the clock and indicated her shift was over. She served herself a Jack Daniel's and Coke and took it outside, smiling at McNab as she did so. He accepted her invitation and followed her with the remains of his second pint. The tables on the pavement were busy. She headed for a free one with a sign saying STAFF on it, and offered him a seat.

'Michael,' he said by way of introduction.

'Gemma,' she replied, lighting up a longed-for cigarette.

She was small, plump in all the right places and studying him with as much interest as he was her. McNab wondered what age she was and took a guess at nineteen or twenty. Another Iona.

'A student?' he said.

'Second year medicine.' She waved the cigarette in a gesture of irony. 'What about you?'

'A lifelong learner,' he said, which made her laugh.

McNab asked why she'd chosen medicine. The question was a productive one, keeping her chatting for a while, avoiding the possibility of McNab having to declare his own profession. He asked about the people she worked with here. That was when her face clouded over and she gave him a searching look.

'Are you a journalist?' she said warily.

He shook his head. 'Why?'

'We've had a couple in wanting to talk about Alan MacKenzie, the part-time barman.' She watched McNab's reaction.

'Alan MacKenzie?' he said in a neutral voice.

'They found his body on Cathkin Braes.'

McNab tried to look shocked.

She made an *Oh my God* face. 'Somebody said it might be drugs related.'

McNab let her continue without interruption, all the time wondering who the *somebody* was exactly. It only needed one member of the investigating team to blab.

'Alan wasn't into drugs,' she went on. 'Someone should tell the police that.'

'Maybe you,' McNab said, meeting her eye.

She was immediately on to him. 'You're a policeman,' she said accusingly.

'An off-duty one,' McNab said to placate her.

She swore under her breath. 'And I thought . . .' She stood up, the sentence unfinished.

'You thought right.' McNab gave her a lustful look, which didn't work.

'I don't fuck pigs,' she said loud enough for the neighbouring tables to hear.

McNab felt the cold wind of disapprobation, something he was used to. It seemed an appropriate time to leave, but not before he downed the rest of his pint.

Walking back to the flat, McNab contemplated whether Gemma would contact the station and complain about him. There was no rule that said off-duty policemen had to declare their profession while chatting up women, and her obvious distaste for the police suggested she would leave well alone.

But his brief encounter had proved something. As far as Gemma was concerned, Alan MacKenzie was an unlikely candidate for a drugs death.

He stopped en route and bought a bottle of whisky to replace what he'd consumed during his last session with Iona. The night air was warm and muggy. He heard a distant rumble of thunder and smelt moisture in the air. A jagged flash of light split the sky above the River Clyde. Seconds later, McNab felt a spit of rain on his face.

As he slipped the key in the lock, a black cloud descended on him. Entering the stuffy, silent flat only served to make it worse. He shut the door firmly behind him, crossed to the window and opened it a little. The sounds of the city drifted in, mingled with the smell of rain. Neither filled the emptiness.

This was what being a DI would be like. No more drinking after work with the team. No more whinging about management and bosses. DI Bill Wilson had a wife to go home to. A family to remind him there were other things in life besides madmen who chopped off hands and stuffed stones in dead people's mouths.

McNab looked at the dish-filled sink and quickly dismissed his earlier decision to deal with it. He rummaged around for a glass among the congealed plates and cutlery, and ran it clean under the tap.

Pouring himself a large measure of whisky, he promptly drank it, then carried the bottle and glass through to the bedroom.

Iona had gone as ordered, leaving only a rumpled bed. McNab sat where she had lain, and breathed in the scent of her and their coupling. Like the bloke in the flat, the memory of it brought a reaction from his own prick.

He tried to conjure up the delights of the previous night, but it wasn't Iona's face that swam before him. Frustrated and annoyed, he refilled his glass. Then he spotted the pair of earrings lying on the bedside table.

Iona had left him a get-out clause. The question was, would he use it?

10

Chrissy clicked her way through the crime-scene photographs, studying the victim's body from various angles and distances. Face down, arms outstretched, it reminded her strongly of a supplicant's pose in front of a high altar, as though asking forgiveness.

The image of sin and retribution was one Chrissy was familiar with. Raised in a Catholic family, her own experience of religion had rarely been positive, especially with regard to the female of the species who, as temptresses, had caused the fall from grace in the first place. That left them only two possible paths in life: wife and mother, or living in sin.

Her own mother had taken the first route. One she'd lived to regret. Chrissy's father was a drunk and a bully, and no amount of candlelit pleas to God had changed that. All Chrissy's brothers had followed their father's role model, except Patrick, Chrissy's favourite, who couldn't be more different if he'd tried. Kind, gentle, gay Patrick, who'd escaped the family home as soon as he was able.

Times had changed since then. Her mother had finally decided that God helped those who helped themselves. The crunch had come when Chrissy had fallen for a black man and had a baby boy by him. Her father had taken umbrage, realizing he hated blacks more than gays. He'd ordered Chrissy never to set foot in the house again, which was the tipping point for her mum.

Mrs McInsh now lived alone and happy in a one-bedroom flat and had her grandson Michael, named after McNab, to stay as often as she wanted, or as Chrissy needed.

Chrissy and McNab had never been lovers. He wasn't her type, nor he hers. They had, in fact, been sworn enemies at one time. Then he'd saved her life and that of her unborn child one dark rainy night outside a Glasgow poker club. Now whatever McNab did was all right by Chrissy.

Sam, the baby's father, had almost finished his training as a doctor and would head back to Nigeria soon. Chrissy knew she would not go with him. Sam did too, although they never spoke of it. She suspected Sam asked God to change her mind, at the Nigerian church where he worshipped every Sunday.

Chrissy's fear of displeasing Sam's God was far less than her fear that Sam might try and take his son back with him. For all his westernization, Sam was a Nigerian man. And in Nigeria, men owned their children and their wives. Chrissy had seen that plainly enough during the 'torso in the Clyde' investigation. Witchcraft, female circumcision and male superiority were as insidious in Sam's culture as homophobia, sectarianism and racism were in hers.

She and Sam had great sex, and laughed a lot, but Chrissy would sometimes catch his dark eyes looking at her when he thought she didn't realize. That look said what was in his heart. That she was his lover, but he knew she would never agree to become his wife. In all likelihood, once home in Nigeria, Sam would submit to his mother's wishes and marry a Fulani woman of intelligence and beauty. He would father many children, all of them as black as him and not the milk-chocolate colour of baby Michael.

This made Chrissy a little sad at times, but not downcast. She'd prepared herself for Sam's eventual departure. The flat was hers, she had her job. She had made a point of depositing Michael's passport in a safe place. Sam could not take him out of the country without it.

Chrissy's experience of the male of the species had taught her to trust only in herself. Life, she accepted, could be short, sometimes sweet, often very nasty. Her childhood had suggested this; her job confirmed it.

She had witnessed cruelty – both physical and mental – at home, but compared to many of the crime scenes she'd attended, her father and brothers had been angels. This had redeemed them somewhat in Chrissy's eyes, but not much.

Most murder scenes in Glasgow were random acts of violence. Vicious but unplanned attacks. The majority consisted of stabbings. Guns and crack cocaine tended to go hand in hand, as seen in cities south of the border. In Scotland, the old ways still held sway, although an influx of Eastern European hard men trading in drugs, guns and prostitution was changing the picture of crime north of the border. McNab's almost fatal brush with a Russian cartel had shown that.

The meticulous nature of her job fascinated Chrissy. A strong stomach allowed her to perform acts that would floor most people, including many police officers. Blood and bodily fluids did not offend her. The mess that accompanied death, the smell, the horror of it, she found herself able to cope with. She could see the waste, and feel sympathy for the victim, but without crime scenes she would be out of a job she loved.

Chrissy rose from the table and put on the coffee machine. Rhona would be back shortly from the PM and Chrissy was keen to know the outcome, the scene on Cathkin Braes having intrigued her. The scent of freshly brewed coffee was making her hungry, so Chrissy fetched the filled rolls she'd picked up at the bakers. If Rhona didn't turn up soon, she would get stuck into them herself.

As though on cue, she heard footsteps in the corridor and saw Rhona's outline through the glass. Her expression on entry was pensive. Chrissy knew that expression well. In Chrissy's opinion, her boss thought a great deal more about life in general than was good for her.

'Coffee?' Chrissy said by way of an opener.

Rhona regarded her with a look of surprise, as though she didn't expect to find her there, then smiled.

'Coffee would be good.'

'What about a filled roll?'

'Even better.'

Chrissy was keen to know what had happened, but concentrated on dealing with her hunger first. Rhona drank the coffee but ate only half of the roll. She clearly had something on her mind.

'Okay,' Chrissy said. 'What happened?'

'The PM was inconclusive.'

'Shit,' Chrissy said, disappointed.

Rhona explained about the tests for Long QT Syndrome and the possibility of fear or exertion being a factor.

'You're saying he died of fright?'

'McNab didn't like that explanation either.'

'I told you it was weird,' Chrissy said. 'And now all this stuff about the spirit world and a medium.'

'What medium?'

'McNab didn't tell you?' It was clear from Rhona's face that he had not, so Chrissy got stuck in with relish. 'At the briefing this morning, McNab asked if anyone knew anything about the spiritualist church on Sauchiehall Street. And,' she raised an eyebrow, 'DC Clark said she did. It turns out Mrs MacKenzie went there on Sunday morning and the medium told her that he had a message from Alan.' She paused to savour Rhona's reaction. 'Yep. Alan was already dead and trying to get in touch with his mum.'

Ten minutes later Rhona had the whole story, even details of McNab's reaction to the medium during the interview. No wonder McNab had had that shifty look when they'd spoken after the PM. If it wasn't so serious, it would be funny.

'You're telling me McNab went to a spiritualist church to interview a medium who knew Alan MacKenzie was dead before we found him?'

'He doesn't believe it, but DS Clark's mother is a member of the church and she says Alan's mother's story is true. Patrick Menzies, the medium, called out her name, which is Amy, and said he had a message from Alan, which meant he was dead. More than that. He died violently.'

Every word Chrissy uttered served to enhance Rhona's picture of McNab's reaction. McNab had no time for the mumbo jumbo of psychology; God knows how he would react to spiritualism being a part of his case.

'The medium said Alan had died violently?'

'Yes. Alan told his mother to go to the police because he had died violently,' Chrissy repeated for good measure. 'Sort of rules out the "died of fright" business,' she added.

The nagging suspicion that they were missing something had been with Rhona from the moment she had studied

the body in situ on Cathkin Braes. The post-mortem and
McNab's reaction had only served to strengthen that feeling.
Now all this about a medium. In the past she would have
called DI Wilson and chatted things through with him,
especially the stuff about the spiritualist church. Bill would
be circumspect, but non-judgemental. McNab, she suspected,
was smarting over his DS's apparent knowledge of the place,
maybe even her belief in it. His antagonism could close his
eyes to things he couldn't easily explain.

Chrissy seemed to be reading her face, and her mind.
'You could call Magnus. See what he thinks.'

'We'll stick to the forensic science first,' Rhona said.

11

Amy had forgotten what sleep was. After another night staring into darkness, she rose before dawn and went down to the kitchen. Alan had not lived in this house since he'd started at university, yet she had always felt his presence. Until now.

The house that had once been a home, now seemed to Amy to be a grave. Dark, cold and empty of life. Instead of conjuring up her beloved son's face, all she saw was the lifeless figure on the cold slab in the mortuary.

Looking down at Alan's body, she'd wanted to gather him in her arms as she had done when he was a child. To kiss the top of his head and promise him that everything would be all right, because she would make it so.

The police officer had allowed her a few moments alone with her dead son, but by then Amy knew she was staring at an empty shell. Alan had gone. Where, Amy had no idea.

Now she no longer said a prayer before the sleep that never came. Prayers and pleas for nineteen years had not kept her son safe. All the love and care she had bestowed on him, all her hopes and dreams for him, had come to nothing. And nothingness was now all her life consisted of.

She filled the kettle and set it to boil. Her body carried out everyday functions as though she were outside, looking on. What she saw was the empty shell of a middle-aged woman she didn't recognize. A woman who was merely putting in time until she too died and joined her son.

But would she join him? What if she took that step only to discover that death did not bring peace, but the continual and everlasting torment of his absence. Amy's brain agonized over such thoughts when it functioned at all. For the most part, grief took over. It consumed her, pouring her into a bottomless pit of despair and tears.

She did not even have a funeral to organize. The shell of her once-beautiful son hadn't been released for burial. It was being dissected and examined. Having been mutilated once by a madman, it was being mutilated again. Although she knew that Alan no longer inhabited that mound of cold flesh, Amy recoiled at the thought of his precious body being defiled.

Doreen called three times a day. Amy listened in silence to her friend's offers of help and company. She couldn't shake off the idea that if Doreen had not persuaded her to visit that church, then none of this would have happened.

Doreen's voice betrayed her own distress. They had been friends for thirty years, yet Amy doubted whether she could ever look on her friend again without remembering that moment in the church when Doreen had raised Amy's hand in the air. It seemed to Amy that Alan's life had ended then, as had her own.

Seated at the table, she registered that the kettle had boiled. She rose and made a pot of tea, recalling with a sharp pain how she'd chastised Alan when he wouldn't take the time to brew the tea in the teapot, but just dunked a teabag in a mug of hot water.

The memory of her irritation with him, the dripping

teabag marking the floor and the top of the bin as he disposed of it, stabbed her heart with regret. Why had she thought that mattered? Why had she moaned at him about it? Her mothering now seemed petty and restrictive, instead of full of care and concern.

She had been a bad mother. It must be her fault Alan was dead.

These thoughts whirled through her brain, along with ways she might have prevented Alan going out that Sunday. If only she had not gone to that church. They would have walked Barney together. Alan would have cut the grass and they would have sat together in the sunshine, the scent of new-mown grass in the air, she with a cup of tea, Alan with the cold beer she'd bought for him. Amy could see them now, Barney lying panting beside Alan's chair, her son's big hand ruffling the dog's ear.

The loss of Barney had been dwarfed by the greater loss of her son, but picturing the scene now brought the dog's death into sharp focus. They'd got Barney when Alan was five. He and the dog became inseparable. Amy knew how much Alan missed Barney when he moved out, but he would never have taken the dog because he knew that losing them both at the same time would have distressed her too much. So he'd come home every Sunday to walk his dog and give Amy time with 'both her boys'.

Sometime during the morning she'd washed and dressed. If she ate anything, she had no memory of it. She felt no hunger, except the gnawing hunger of loss. She sat at the window, watching and waiting, as she had that Sunday night. Still willing his tall figure to appear, Barney bounding at his side. Seeing her there, he would wave and smile, and Barney would bark.

Eventually someone did appear to open her gate and walk up the path. A man, shorter than Alan and with no dog at his side. Amy registered the shiny red cheeks, the plump body, the nervous manner.

It was her nemesis. The man who had pronounced her son dead.

The ring of the doorbell startled her, although she'd expected it. Her flailing hand knocked over the mug and cold tea spread across the table. Reaching the edge, it dripped onto the floor. Amy sat rigid as the bell rang again.

He had seen her at the window, she was sure of it. A third ring suggested he was in no mood to go away. When she still didn't respond, he rapped on the door, then shouted through the letterbox.

'Mrs MacKenzie. I have a message for you from Alan.'

He was sitting at her kitchen table. She had not offered him tea. It seemed to Amy that it was enough that she gave him house room.

When she'd finally opened the door, he'd appeared startled, then suddenly at a loss. Once again, Amy had felt a stab of pity for him. She wondered what drove him to do these things, whether he was mentally ill, or simply deluded.

Despite his obvious embarrassment, there was an underlying determination in his manner. Whatever he'd come to say was important enough to face her disgust, even her wrath.

Amy decided she would hear him out, then ask him to leave.

'Mrs MacKenzie,' he began, 'I know you are an unbeliever and I respect that. But when someone in the spirit world asks for my help, I cannot refuse.' He waited for a moment. 'Alan was most insistent that I come here, although he knew how you would react to my visit.'

Amy was aghast at this man who talked about her son as though he were alive. She opened her mouth to protest, then shut it again. If she allowed her anger to spill over, God knows what she would say or do.

'Messages from the spirit world are not always easy to interpret,' he said apologetically. 'Particularly in the case of a sudden and,' his voice dropped to a whisper, 'violent death.'

As Amy's anger bubbled over, she rose from the table and said in an ice-cold voice, 'I'd like you to get out now.'

He flinched as though she had hit him. For a moment Amy saw the boy Alan in the hurt, childlike expression. She stepped away from him, her anger turning to alarm.

'Get out of my house.' Her voice rose in fear.

'You must understand that Alan cannot rest until we help him.' His voice was insistent.

'Stop it,' she cried, tears running down her face. 'My son is dead.'

'Dead, but not yet at peace.'

Amy thought of the cold grey body on the slab and covered her face with her hands. It was as she had thought. In death, there was no peace.

He was suddenly beside her, urging her back to her seat. She slumped there, broken, her anger gone.

'Will you hear what I have to say?'

She looked up at the shiny cheeks, the eager eyes.

'For Alan's sake, at least?'

All the fight had left her body. *I have nothing to lose*, Amy thought, *because I have already lost everything.*

12

The summer days were long in Orkney, filling the evening with light. It was the time of year Magnus loved. His summer visits to his island home were precious and to be savoured. He would walk the beach at midnight, viewing the shadowed hump of Hoy across the waters of Scapa Flow, marvelling at the tricks the midnight sun played with the landscape. Sounds were different too and, most interesting of all, the summer solstice brought an intense energy and excitement, so that sleep seemed unnecessary. No wonder his forebears had built their worship around this magical time.

He had finished his walk and was now seated on the small jetty at the back of the house. He had contemplated taking the boat across to Hoy, camping in the ruins of the old Nissan camps and watching as the sun dropped below the horizon, to almost immediately rise again. Instead he'd opted to watch seals from the jetty and drink home-brewed beer as the longest day melted into the shortest night.

Although officially on holiday, he had been marking papers he'd set his psychology students during the summer term. Dispersed now, to work or travel during their recess, Magnus found it increasingly difficult to conjure up the eager faces he'd spent the previous academic year with. Other faces now filled his days. His neighbours and fellow

Orcadians, fishermen, farmers, shopkeepers and publicans. Many of them had known him since childhood, and were unfamiliar with his academic life in Glasgow or his dealings with the Scottish police force as a criminal profiler, except Erling Flett, who he'd gone to Kirkwall Grammar with, and who now, as detective inspector, headed up the small police team that served the isles from its Kirkwall base.

Magnus reached for the bottle of home brew and topped up his glass. The cloudy sweetish liquid was not designed to settle. The swirling sediment gave it its unique flavour and body. Orkney beer, like life in general, was never clear cut.

He had had no direct contact with the police since the Reborn case involving an inmate he'd been studying at the State Hospital. Free from police involvement, Magnus found himself studying earlier cases, going over previous profiling work of his own and of celebrated others.

Many detectives he'd worked with had accepted his help only because they were ordered to. They didn't hold with fancy notions of profiling, preferring to rely on years of experience of the criminal mind. Most of the time Magnus was inclined to agree with them. Psychology was, after all, intuition in action.

He lifted his glass and took a long cold swallow. The beer, his own make from a family recipe, was stored in a windowless outhouse with walls three foot thick, previously used for smoking fish. Hence its temperature. The house had been built below the high waterline by fishermen, because that land was free. When the tide came in, as it did now, the house was surrounded on three sides by water with a stone walkway to the front door. It was a bit like living on board a ship which didn't sway and heave, even in bad weather, although waves did spray his dining-room window at times.

Above him, the sky was a watercolour so rich in pinks, reds and oranges he felt he could reach up and smear the paint with his fingers. He thought how good it would have been to spend the night at one of the Neolithic sites on the island. The Ring of Brodgar, Skara Brae or even Maeshowe. To sit with his back against a stone sentinel, feel its energy, and watch the midnight sun as his ancestors had done. Still, he reminded himself, the dark shape of Hoy had dominated the landscape for longer than any of those ancient sites.

He yawned suddenly, his internal clock reminding him that humans needed sleep even if the sun never went down. He picked up the glass and empty bottle and left the jetty to climb the stairs to bed.

He was wide awake again at six, bright sunshine spilling in through the window that faced Scapa Flow. He rose to look out. Orkney, known for the strength and frequency of its wind, had forsaken its reputation, or was currently in the calm eye of a storm. Last night Scapa Flow had been ruffled with white lacy cuffs. Today it was flat calm with a glossy shine, suggesting it would be a fine day for a trip to Hoy.

After breakfast, Magnus set about gathering together his camping gear. This weather could last a day, or a week, or sometimes only a few hours. He planned to make good use of it.

He began by raiding the fridge and cupboards for provisions, stuffing them in his rucksack while he finished his coffee. If he left shortly he could have his camp set up on Hoy by mid morning, then maybe walk to Rackwick Bay. He was loading the boat when his mobile rang. His first instinct was to ignore it. Ten minutes later and he would have been out on the water chugging his way across Scapa Flow. He glanced at the screen and was pleased to see Erling's name. He'd mentioned to his friend that he hoped to cross to Hoy and spend a night in the old Nissan camp. They'd camped there as boys, trying to fish in the bay below until besieged by a family of seals whose presence had thwarted all hope of catching anything. Erling had promised to call if he managed to arrange time off.

'Hey, you just caught me. I've already loaded the boat, but I'm happy to wait for you,' Magnus offered.

'I can't get away, that's why I called.'

Magnus could tell by the tone of Erling's voice that something was wrong. 'What is it?'

'The attendant at Brodgar found the body of a young woman there this morning.'

'An accident?'

'Doesn't look like it.'

'Can I come up?'

'I thought you might want to. Head for the hotel. I'll get an officer to pick you up.'

As soon as he was in the car, Magnus switched on the radio. Extended coverage of *Orkney Today* came on at 7.30 a.m. The discovery of the body in the Ring of Brodgar was the main item, together with a request for people to keep away from the location. Orkney folk were no less curious than anyone else, and it wouldn't take many cars to block the Ness o'Brodgar, the narrow strip of road dividing the Loch of Stenness from the Loch of Harray, which led there.

The Ring had always held a fascination for Magnus,

from boyhood onwards. Set between the two lochs, Brodgar was only one of the many Neolithic sites that dotted the Orkney Mainland. It was a true circle, 104 metres in diameter. Thought to have housed sixty stones originally, only twenty-seven remained, with five of these fallen. Although the stones were not as tall as the group of four in the nearby field of Stenness, they were an undoubtedly impressive sight. Especially standing against the bruised sky of a midsummer dawn or sunset.

The remoteness of Brodgar had protected it from the attentions of the thousands of visitors that strove to celebrate the summer solstice at Stonehenge in England. But it still drew the hippy brigade, and its attendant, Douglas Clouston, who checked it every morning, had plenty of stories to tell of empty bottles, spliffs and used condoms he'd cleared from the site, particularly during the summer months.

When Magnus reached the car park at the Standing Stones Hotel, a police car was waiting for him. The driver was a man he knew from Stromness, Ivan Taylor. They exchanged a few words, but the officer knew nothing more than what Magnus had already heard. A girl's body had been found inside the Ring. 'One of those hippies that hang about up there,' was Ivan's opinion.

Erling was waiting for Magnus at the gated entrance to the site. They both donned white boiler suits before heading up the path towards the incident tent.

'We've asked central headquarters for help. They've contacted the team that covered the Sanday murder a couple of years back. They should be here by midday.'

Murders were as scarce as a heat wave in Orkney. Only two in the last thirty years. The most recent had involved a love triangle among incomers on the tiny island of

Sanday, population around five hundred. The body of the missing lover of the woman had been found battered to death, buried in the sand dunes by her previous partner and father of her child. R2S had been the team to collect the forensic evidence. It sounded as though they would be heading back here soon.

When they reached the tent, Erling stood aside to let Magnus enter first. As a boy, Magnus's acute sense of smell had often been a hindrance, nauseating him by the strength of it. As he'd grown older, he'd learned how to control it, even make good use of it in his work as a profiler.

He stood for a moment letting the smell inside the tent wash over him. The metallic scent of blood and the smell of gases associated with early decomposition were prevalent, but so too was the faint scent of cannabis. The young woman lay face down on the grass, fully dressed, arms and legs spreadeagled. Her head was turned towards him, her eyes closed. She might have been asleep, if it were not for her hands, each pinned to the ground by a long thin blade.

Magnus's first and immediate impression was that her killer was making a statement. The scene was orchestrated, the image carefully presented.

'Has a pathologist seen her?' Magnus asked.

Erling nodded. 'Dr MacLaren wouldn't or couldn't say exactly how she died, but he says her hands were likely impaled after death.'

'Do you know if she's local?'

'There was no ID on her, but the whole of Orkney knows about this. If anyone local is missing, we'll hear pretty soon.'

It was nearing the height of the tourist season when

the population of Mainland Orkney virtually doubled. The main access to the islands was via the Hamnavoe sailing from Scrabster to Stromness, but there were other routes. A ferry to St Margaret's Hope in the south, or a flight from the Scottish mainland into Kirkwall. There were also the cruise ships to consider. They docked in Kirkwall. Magnus didn't have to recite these thoughts out loud. Erling knew his patch.

'Why do you think she was laid out like that?' Erling said.

'I have no idea, although her arms are pointing south-east and south-west.'

'And that's significant?'

'Maybe for the person who laid her there,' Magnus said.

Erling's mobile rang. He glanced at the screen. 'The forensic team. I'd better go and make arrangements to meet them.'

'Mind if I stay here for a bit?' Magnus said.

'If you think it'll help.'

Magnus waited until Erling left, then slowly circled the body. The young woman looked to be in her late teens or early twenties. She wore no make-up, her dark hair was cropped short and she had been pretty in life. She wore jeans and a sweater-type shirt and light walking boots. He was reminded of the group of young archaeologists working on Orkney's latest Neolithic find nearby on the Ness of Brodgar. Might the victim be one of them? He knelt beside her and studied her mutilated hands. They were slim and fine-boned, the nails cut short and darkened by soil. He wondered if the knees on her jeans were dirty too.

Close up he could smell a faint perfume, something light and floral. She wore small silver crescent moons in her ears, and her nose held a stud, similar in shape. It was then Magnus noticed there was something in her mouth. He moved as close as he dared without disturbing the body. The mouth was partially open, as though in surprise. Beyond the teeth was something that looked like a stone.

Magnus gave up trying to decide if it was and stood up. The interior of the tent was warm and suffused with light. The summer solstice had rendered the islands free of wind, an unusual occurrence and not likely to last, even in midsummer, but he had the sudden impression he was standing in the quiet epicentre of a storm which had yet to break.

When he emerged from the tent, he spotted a police helicopter circling above them, as though choosing a place to land. It eventually dropped in a nearby field, where an incident van had already been parked. Magnus headed in that direction, keen to discover who the forensic team might be.

By the time he reached the spot, various equipment marked R2S had already been unloaded by two suited male figures, neither of whom Magnus recognized. He waited until the helicopter took off before approaching. Erling was already there, shaking hands with the men. He waved Magnus over and introduced him as Professor Pirie from Strathclyde University.

One of the men immediately recognized the name and mentioned their mutual acquaintance, Roy Hunter.

'Roy's at a murder scene on Cathkin Braes,' he said when Magnus asked. He glanced over at the Ring of Brodgar. 'It's a stone circle too. Not as impressive as this one though.'

Magnus was immediately intrigued. 'What happened?'

'The detective in charge thinks it's a gangland killing

over drugs. The hands were chopped off.' That was about the limit of the man's knowledge on the subject.

They moved to discuss the present crime. Dougie Simpson wasn't new to Orkney, having accompanied Roy Hunter on the Sanday murder. He remarked on how weird it was to be back so soon. 'Didn't expect to be here for another thirty years.'

Erling muttered something about changed days in Orkney and all three set off towards the tent with Magnus following. When Magnus re-entered, his place by the body had been taken by Dougie's colleague, Simon. Magnus watched as he began to take samples from the body, knowing the mouth would be somewhere on his list.

He didn't have long to wait before the mystery item was extracted.

It was a stone, just as he had thought.

'May I see that?' Magnus asked.

The stone was bagged in clear plastic and handed over.

Magnus held it up to the light. One side was blank, the other had a number scratched on it.

'I would say that was a four?' Magnus suggested and Simon nodded.

Dougie looked surprised. 'I've just remembered something Roy said. The victim on Cathkin Braes had a stone in his mouth. It had a five scratched on it.'

13

Magnus emerged to find the wind on the rise and flapping at the tent. He caught Erling's eye, realizing what his friend was thinking. The chances of the forensic tent being whipped away before the body was properly processed were high. There were few places on Orkney that weren't exposed to the transatlantic winds that swept the islands, and the Ring of Brodgar wasn't one of them. Had the victim been discovered in the Forest of Finstown, tucked down in the valley among its stunted trees, wind may not have been a major problem. Out here it most certainly was.

'I may have to call in an inflatable air shelter and generator,' Erling said as he observed the rushing clouds. 'Even that might not hang about for long. And it's noisy.'

The summer equinox had a history of producing high winds. Magnus could recall numerous stories, some amusing, others tragic, that focussed on this time of year. The previous summer a couple of German climbers had pitched their tent near the Yesnaby cliffs, planning to scale them. The wind had risen to gale force overnight and swept the tent and its sleeping inhabitants straight over the cliff and into the surging sea below. Had the climbers made their plans known to the locals, they would have been warned away from the cliff. Probably warned away from camping altogether, unless in someone's walled garden.

'So what do you think?' Erling said as they walked towards the gate.

Magnus wasn't sure he wanted to voice his thoughts yet. 'May I come to the strategy meeting?'

Erling gave him a penetrating look. 'We'll be glad of all the experience we can get. Murder isn't a speciality in Orkney. At least not since the Vikings.'

'I thought I'd give Glasgow a call. Check out Dougie's story about the victim on Cathkin Braes,' Magnus said.

They had reached the gate. On the other side the narrow road was lined with police vehicles and a queue of local traffic full of people desperately trying to go about their everyday business. Add the fact that the Ring of Brodgar was a natural heritage site, popular with summer tourists and cruise visitors, and Erling had his work cut out for him.

'Do you want a lift back to your car?'

Magnus shook his head. 'I'll walk, thanks.'

Erling nodded. 'I'll text you a time for tomorrow's meeting.'

Magnus set off along the narrow road, the roughened waters of the Loch of Harray on his left. He'd chosen to walk in order to call in at the latest excavations on the Neolithic temple complex that lay between the Rings of Stenness and Brodgar. A team of archaeologists worked it every summer when the weather allowed. Magnus had been following their progress since the first large flat slab had been revealed during ploughing some years before. Orcadians were used to living among ancient ruins, but this particular discovery, believed to pre-date Stonehenge and the Pyramids, had placed Orkney at the centre of Neolithic history.

Magnus turned up the path that led to the bungalow adjoining the site, now used for storage and a place to get out of the weather. Atop its small hill, it gave a grand view of the excavation stretching northwards to Brodgar.

The working group were on a coffee break or else had got together to discuss the revelation that a body had been found at the nearby Ring. When Magnus's tall figure appeared, it was immediately spotted by Jack Louden, the eminent young archaeologist currently in charge of the dig, who separated himself from the chatting group and approached Magnus, coffee mug in hand.

'Wondered when you'd appear.' Jack indicated the mug. 'Coffee?'

Magnus accepted and was ushered into the bungalow. The smell of freshly dug earth was as strong inside the kitchen as out, but Magnus also caught other scents: coffee, cigarettes and, again, the scent of cannabis.

Jack poured coffee from a large flask and handed Magnus a mug. 'You've been to the Ring?'

Magnus nodded. 'I take it you're not missing one of your female students?'

'Not at my last count. Although we do get hangers-on from time to time. Are you permitted to issue a description yet?'

Magnus was aware that the details would be on the news, likely within the hour. 'Dark hair, cut short. Late teens, early twenties. Dressed like your lot, jeans and boots, with dirt under her fingernails, and I detected the scent of cannabis from her clothes.'

Jack met his eye. 'She does sounds like one of ours, but the team's adamant they're all present and correct.' He took a mouthful of coffee. 'The Ring's a popular hangout this time of year for the young, both locals and visitors. Ancient site, long summer nights to party in.'

'Sex and drugs?' Magnus said.

Jack nodded. 'Much like our Neolithic ancestors, I suspect.'

Magnus cut to the chase. 'Do you know of a cannabis supplier on the island?'

Jack scrutinized him. 'You needing some for your ruminations?'

Magnus shook his head. 'I'm a home-brew man, myself.'

A flutter of concern crossed Jack's face. 'I don't want any of my lot getting into trouble.'

'Ask them in confidence and let me know?'

Jack thought about that, then indicated that he would.

Magnus finished his coffee and set the mug down. They headed outside. The group were back on their knees among the ancient stone ditches, slowly scraping away the earth. Painstaking forensic work, much like what would be happening at Brodgar.

Jack glanced up at the sky. In the far distance, black clouds clustered over Skaill Bay. 'We may have to cover up soon.'

Magnus thought of the forensic tent and the spread-eagled body of the young woman that lay inside. Heavy rain, common in all seasons in Orkney, would wash the wider crime scene clean. It wasn't only the wind that Erling had to worry about.

He waited until he was back at the Standing Stones Hotel and inside his car before he made the call. Walking along the open road in the wind, a mobile call had proved impossible.

Selecting Rhona's number, Magnus hesitated. He hadn't spoken to Rhona in some time. He'd wanted to, but was unsure whether his attentions would be welcome. He was also aware how his mind had quickly jumped on Dougie's story of the death on Cathkin Braes, seeing it as a reason to get in touch with her.

His psychological study of his feelings and reasons for action or inaction frequently irritated him, but he could do little to stop it. Magnus pressed the button and listened as it rang out. Rhona answered on the third ring. As soon as he heard her voice, Magnus was assailed by the memory of her scent. Not a chosen perfume, but the natural scent of her skin. It made him forget his carefully chosen words.

'Rhona?' he said to buy time.

'Yes?' She sounded mildly irritated.

'Magnus here.'

A short pause. 'Magnus, how strange. I was just about to call you.'

He found himself inordinately pleased by her confession even though he knew it would be a work-related call.

'Where are you?' she said.

'Orkney.'

'I thought you might be. No matter.'

Magnus convinced himself she sounded disappointed. 'What was it you wanted to speak about?'

'A murder on Cathkin Braes.'

'The victim with a stone in his mouth?'

He heard her intake of breath.

'How did you know about that?'

'An R2S team arrived here this morning with the news.'

'Why are R2S in Orkney?'

'A body was found in the Ring of Brodgar this morning. The victim had a flat stone marked with the number four in her mouth.'

14

Rhona listened intently as Magnus described the impaled hands, and the laying out of the body.

'I estimate her arms are pointing south-east and south-west,' he added.

'Any indication of how she died?' Rhona asked.

'Nothing obvious, but judging by the lack of blood, the hands were probably impaled after death.'

'How far on are Dougie and Simon with processing the scene?'

'Not sure, although the wind's rising here with the solstice, so he'll have to be quick.'

Rhona had planned to call Magnus to run her own scenario past him and was considerably thrown by the reversal of the situation.

'Do you know who the victim is?' she said.

'Not yet.'

'Can I get up there in time to take a look at the body in situ?'

'By helicopter, maybe.'

It was a long shot, especially since R2S were already there, but she could give it a go.

McNab wouldn't like this news one little bit, especially as it had come via Professor Magnus Pirie. 'I'll be in touch,' she said.

Rhona rang off and immediately called Roy Hunter's mobile. It took a few rings before he picked up. She heard his muffled voice, then his mask was removed and the words became clearer.

'Hi, Rhona. We're not quite finished here yet.'

'Thanks, Roy, but the call's about something else.'

She ran Magnus's news past him and was met with a stunned silence, then a long, low whistle. 'And you want to take a look yourself?'

'It might have to be via R2S.' She explained about the wind. 'I'd like to take a look myself before I confirm any similarity with DI McNab.'

'He's not a Professor Pirie fan, if I remember?'

'No, he's not.' An understatement.

'Okay. I'll request the Air Support Unit take you up as quickly as possible, because of the wind and danger to the crime scene. Can you get yourself over to the helipad at SECC?'

'I'll head there now.'

Chrissy appeared as she was disrobing.

'Where are you off to?'

'They've found a body in a stone circle on Orkney Mainland, impaled hands and a stone in her mouth.'

Chrissy wasn't often at a loss for words. When it did happen, it was worth seeing.

'I need you to carry on with the tests and to hold the fort for me.'

'And what do I tell Detective Inspector McNab?'

'That I've been called out on another case.'

'He'll ask where,' Chrissy warned her.

'Tell him Orkney, and leave it at that.'

'Does the handsome Viking feature in this?' Chrissy's eyes twinkled.

'It was Magnus that called me.' Rhona made for the door with Chrissy swiftly following, keen as always to have the last word.

'Shall I tell McNab *that* when I see him?'

'I'd leave Magnus out of it for the moment.'

Chrissy met Rhona's stern gaze, and her face fell. Baiting McNab was a full-time occupation for her, rendered even more fun by his recent promotion. Being denied such an opportunity was a blow. Chrissy bid her goodbye with a face forlorn enough to make a lesser mortal change their mind. Not Rhona.

All the same, Rhona couldn't suppress a smile as she exited the building and headed for the car. Chrissy may have been forbidden from mentioning Magnus to McNab, but her face would reveal it anyway.

She exited the university precinct and made for the river. Glasgow was basking in June sunshine, its citizens taking the opportunity to bare more flesh than was easy on the eye. The air in the city centre was thick with exhaust fumes as the one-way signs directed the cars endlessly round its grid system. Despite her familiarity with downtown Glasgow, it would still be easy to make a mistake and end up heading back the way she had come.

Reaching the river, Rhona turned west alongside the Clyde towards the Scottish Exhibition and Conference Centre and the nearby heliport where the Air Support Unit was based. A text arrived as she entered the car park. She drew up and checked her mobile. Roy had okayed her flight and they were waiting for her. She sent a message to Magnus, as promised, indicating she was on her way.

Removing her overnight bag and forensic case from the boot, she crossed the tarmac towards the distinctive black and yellow shape of the waiting helicopter. At her approach, a figure detached itself from the group of three and came towards her.

'Dr MacLeod? Neil Cameron. We're ready for you if you want to step aboard.' He took both cases from her. 'We're keen to get there and back before the wind steps up a notch.'

In the calm, simmering heat of Glasgow, it seemed strange to be talking about high winds. He read her expression. 'Warnings are out for gale-force winds and high seas around Orkney over the next twenty-four hours.'

Rhona thanked him, already wondering whether she'd be able to get back once she'd finished on site. But before that, she had to face the prospect of flying. Something she didn't relish. Despite her knowledge of physics and the scientific reasons why planes stayed up in the air, Rhona still regarded flying as a strange anomaly which could terminate at any moment. Flying commercially could be tempered by strong drink, usually a double whisky or brandy. Not a likely possibility in a police helicopter.

As it turned out, the noise was worse than the actual take-off. Rhona concentrated on that, her eyes half shut, not registering the rapid rise as Glasgow became the equivalent of a Google map below her. Then they were up, turned, and away, the city landscape swiftly replaced by deep dark lochs and mountain peaks, a patchwork of bright light and deep shadow.

Conversation verging on the impossible, Rhona eventually found if she dwelt on the magnificence of the landscape below her, she forgot to worry that there was nothing between her and those mountains but air.

The steady throb of the blades lulled her into a false sense of security as they beat their way across Caithness and its scattered abandoned townships. By the time they approached the Pentland Firth her anxiety was on the rise again. Buffeted by a rising wind, the officer who had welcomed her aboard signalled that she should hold on tight.

Below, a choppy sea swept through the deep water channel that divided Scotland from Hoy, the second biggest island in the Orkney group. Dark, heavy clouds swathed the western seaboard around Stromness, split by the sun's rays over the grey inland waterway she knew to be Scapa Flow.

Rhona concentrated on looking for Magnus's house on the northern shore, east of Stromness, and thought she spotted it next to the small local ferry terminal at Houton Bay. The sight of the stone house, part surrounded by water, generated sufficient memories to see her through to her destination.

Minutes later they were dropping into a field close to a circle of tall stones she knew to be Brodgar. Then she was back on solid ground, the noise fading to be replaced by a whistling wind.

With smiles, the co-pilot ushered Rhona and her bags wide of the blades, to immediately return to the helicopter. The noise rose to deafening levels once again and Rhona watched as the black and yellow shape took to the sky, grateful she was no longer aboard.

She waited in the blustering wind until it disappeared southwards before she took her bearings. No doubt someone had seen her arrive and would come looking for her. She picked up her bags and, head down against the wind, set off in the general direction of the Ring.

As she met the intervening road, lined with cars and police vehicles, a tall figure dressed in a forensic suit appeared in search of her. The height and build suggested Magnus, then Rhona noted the hair colour and facial features and realized it couldn't be.

The man approached, hand extended in welcome. 'Detective Inspector Erling Flett. You, I believe, are Dr Rhona MacLeod? R2S said you were coming. I'm very pleased you made it before we had to remove the body.'

'So quickly?'

'If we don't, the wind will.' He took her overnight case from her. 'We decided against erecting an air tent because of the forecast. It would mean dismantling what we have already. Better to use the time as best we can.'

He weaved his way among the parked vehicles. 'You can leave your overnight bag in the boot of my car for the moment.' He pressed the remote. The boot sprang open and he deposited her bag inside.

'I'm assuming you'll kit up here?'

Rhona had already begun. The wind, though strong, was warm, and once inside the suit she immediately felt the prickle of sweat on her skin. She struggled into the boots then pulled on gloves, taping them first to the suit, before pulling on a second pair. The hood in place, her hair no longer whipped at her eyes.

'Ready?'

She gave a quick nod.

'This way.'

Rhona followed the tall figure to a revolving metal gate.

Fattened by the bulky suit, she squeezed herself through. DI Flett ignored the gate and used his long legs to leap the fence.

In front of Rhona lay a gentle incline, traversed by a grassy path. The incident tape had indicated an outer cordon beginning at the gate. A second cordon had been erected just past a three-foot ditch that encircled the Ring. Her first impression was of the difficulty of the location, the extent of the crime scene, and its importance in the tourist life of Orkney. It was the island equivalent of discovering a midsummer murder victim in Edinburgh Castle.

Walking in a forensic suit wasn't easy, especially over rough ground. DI Flett waited for her to catch up.

'We'd better stick to the long way round and avoid the heather.'

The stones stood in a trimmed grass circle, which differed in width, while the central area was mostly heather-covered. Difficult to walk through and even more difficult to forensically search.

Rhona nodded her agreement and followed him as he entered the Ring and headed right. A little higher now and more exposed, she could feel the full force of the west wind that churned the surfaces of both lochs.

The forensic tent had been anchored down as much as possible. Despite this, it billowed in and out, snapping its desire to be free. The hum of a small generator indicated the presence of arc lights.

'The R2S team are at the station, preparing the forensic material for transit. So you're on your own.'

Erling glanced westwards where a blanket of grey-black cloud hung in waiting. 'According to the weather forecast

we have a couple of hours maximum before that lot
reaches us,' DI Flett told her as he held back the tent flap.

Rhona raised her mask, checked her hair was tucked
under her hood and entered.

15

She stood for a moment, partially blinded by the arc lights' blaze. Shutting her eyes, she focussed initially on the smell. However long you worked with the dead, the scent of death always hit with the same power. Pervasive, encompassing, it invaded your clothes and your senses. Shielded from the wind, the interior of the tent was almost balmy. Perfect conditions for decomposition, which was underway.

Rhona studied the layout of the body before approach, recalling Magnus's brief description as she did so. Unlike Magnus, she had viewed the body on Cathkin Braes and her immediate impression was of similarity. Premeditated murder was thought out and planned, the method and the delivery. A random act of violence was chaotic, surprising, often followed by panic, resulting in attempts to hide the body, or by simply running away. Whoever killed this girl had neither panicked in the aftermath nor immediately made a run for it. Care had been taken to display the killer's handiwork, to indicate his ownership of the result.

Rhona moved closer and hunkered down beside the body. Rigor mortis, or the temporary rigidity of the muscles after death, had begun, visible in the face, jaw and neck muscles, extending into the arms and trunk. Pressed sideways to the ground, hypostasis had darkened the lower half as gravity drew the blood downwards. As a rough guideline, the state of the body suggested she'd died where she lay sometime during the night.

Rhona set to work, the moan of the wind and the hum of the generator fading into the background. She was determined not to check the time, nor worry that DI Flett would announce their imminent departure. She would concentrate only on the woman who lay before her.

The face was young and make-up free. Her eyes were open and unmarked by petechiae. A decision had been made not to remove the clothes and bag them to preserve evidence. Rhona wondered if that had been wise, but understood that pressure of time had dictated the decision. The stone had been extracted from her mouth and doubt-less was now stored in the evidence room back in Kirkwall police station.

Rhona bent close to the face and sniffed, catching the sweet, musty smell of cannabis. She sampled the mouth, finding no evidence of semen, then the hands. The finger-nails were dirty, as though the victim had been digging recently or had clawed at the earth in her death throes. The idea of poison presented itself as a possible mode of death. Or perhaps a drug overdose? But why lay out the body in such a manner, unless those present at the time had also been high?

She was sampling the clothes when DI Flett reappeared.

'I'm sorry, we need to remove the body now.'

Rhona stood up, suddenly registering how high the wind had become. A squall of rain hit the roof as two stretcher-bearers entered and began to bag the body, turning it to expose the underside.

Rhona halted them before they could zip up the bag,

using the time to take some photographs and further samples from the clothing. Minutes later they were carrying it out and struggling down the path to a waiting ambulance.

'Can I work the ground under the body before you dismantle the tent?'

'The tent might remove itself from over your head soon,' DI Flett warned.

'I'll take that chance,' Rhona said.

'Ten minutes, then we need to take down the arc lights, before they get damaged.'

Rhona got down on her knees again. The grass below the body was flattened, but not bloodstained. She took a sequence of photographs, knowing this was one spot R2S could not have reached. There were two noticeable indentations on the flattened grass. The dirty marks on the front of the victim's jeans suggested she had been kneeling here, prior to her death.

Rhona spotted something in the grass. She extracted the end of the roll-up with tweezers and bagged it. As she rose to her feet, DI Flett appeared with a couple of officers to dismantle and remove the lights.

'Okay?'

Rhona acquiesced, lifted her forensic case and followed him out.

The sky was a seething cauldron of cloud, the long summer day darkened by it. Droplets of rain met her face as she followed DI Flett down the path towards the waiting vehicles. She squeezed through the gate, just as the rain came on in earnest. The downpour caused a flurried retreat to the waiting cars that lined the road. The grey Loch of Harray beat against its narrow shoreline. The summer solstice had brought its promised storm.

Rhona got into DI Flett's car, still suited, and began to disrobe with difficulty.

'If you hang on a minute, I'll run you to the Standing Stones Hotel. You can get rid of the suit there.'

Rhona nodded and, having freed her hands, feet and head at least, gave up the struggle. DI Flett turned the car with some difficulty on the narrow strip of tarmac and set off in a southerly direction.

Although Rhona had spent a weekend in Orkney with Magnus, she had no real sense of the layout of the island. She was aware that Stromness was on the western side, Kirkwall on the east and the large island of Hoy to the south. The roads that wove round the coast and across the main island, serving the fertile farms and hamlets, were unfamiliar to her. A few minutes later DI Flett turned left and drove a short distance along a busy main road, to enter the car park of a reasonably sized hotel.

The squall was still at its peak as they made their way to the front door, DI Flett carrying the bags. Once inside reception, he stripped off his forensic suit while she did the same.

Now she could observe the detective in the flesh, Rhona realized why she had thought at first he might be Magnus. Same height and build, first impressions again suggested Norse blood. The thought made her check her mobile, only to discover a message from the other Viking suggesting they meet at the Standing Stones Hotel when she'd finished on site.

'I have to go,' DI Flett said. 'They'll feed and water you here.'

'I suppose there's not much chance of getting back to Glasgow?'

'Tomorrow, maybe. This should blow itself out by then.'

As soon as he'd left, Rhona rang the bell on reception. A young woman answered and promised food in the lounge, but no chance of a room.

'I'm sorry. We're booked out with tourists this time of year. I could ring round, see if I can find space anywhere, but since all these policemen have been shipped in to deal with the murder . . .'

'You can stay with me,' a male voice said.

The young woman's eyes lit up as she viewed Magnus over Rhona's shoulder. Rhona was reminded of Chrissy's facial expression when she looked on Professor Pirie.

Rhona braced herself and turned.

They hadn't met or spoken since the Reborn case, in which Magnus's profiling ability had played a substantial part. McNab, then a detective sergeant, had treated his boss's decision to involve a forensic psychologist with antagonism and suspicion, which had only worsened when the two men had met. Nothing had changed since then. Now that DI Wilson was on extended leave, because of his wife Margaret's illness, the newly appointed McNab could chose to use Magnus's undoubted skills – or not. Rhona suspected the latter would be the case.

'Magnus.' She smiled and saw the return smile in his eyes.

'You've been to the Ring?' he said.

'I have, and managed some time there before the wind took over.'

'Shall we get a drink and talk?' He led her through to the bar. 'First a whisky, then some food?'

She nodded and took a seat, already questioning the wisdom of taking up Magnus's offer of staying with him at Houton Bay. Magnus and she had history. She had history with McNab too, but he was less liable to take it seriously. Magnus analysed everything and everyone. Useful when profiling a murderer, less comfortable in matters of the heart.

He was back, setting two measures of whisky and a small jug of water on the table. They each added a little water, swirled the whisky round the glass and breathed in the scent.

'Peat and heather,' Rhona said. 'The peat on Orkney is quite unique,' she quoted Magnus from a previous whisky encounter. 'It has very little wood content. Because of the wind, the heather is deep-rooted and resilient. Highland Park's aromas reflect where it was made.'

He smiled. 'You remembered.'

'A connoisseur once told me I have a good nose,' she reminded him. She took a mouthful, happier now that they had established contact again, if a little awkwardly. Her relief was short-lived.

'I thought we might eat at the house,' Magnus suggested. 'I can muster fresh scallops and home brew, or white wine if you prefer?'

Rhona met his eye. She did want to talk to him about the victim in the Ring of Brodgar and she needed somewhere to stay, and most definitely a shower. If she could smell death on her clothes, hair and skin, Magnus's keen nose undoubtedly could.

'Okay,' she conceded and watched his eyes light up.

On the way to Houton, Magnus turned on the radio. Above the wind and rain they listened to BBC Scotland's broadcast on the suspicious death at a prominent Neolithic site in Orkney. Glasgow's murder victim was referred to as possibly gang related.

The wind had reached gale force when they drew up outside the grey stone house. Rhona's last visit had also been in summer. Then she had sailed down Scapa Flow in Magnus's boat on mirror-like water. Not today. White-crested waves broke over the nearby jetty and swept round the stone plinth on which the house stood.

He parked close to the front door and they made a dash for it. Once inside the thick stone walls, the wind descended to a whisper.

Magnus handed her the bags. 'You know where to find your room?' He indicated the narrow staircase. 'And the bathroom? I'll fetch in some home brew.'

The scent of the sea permeated the house. Rhona breathed it in and remembered. Stopping at a window in the upstairs corridor, she looked out on a stormy Scapa Flow, the towering shadow of Hoy behind. She knew a squall like this was common in Orkney whatever the season. Chances were tomorrow would be flat calm and she could head back to Glasgow. The post-mortem on the Orkney victim would likely take place in Inverness or Aberdeen. She wondered whether she should attend.

She heard the back door bang and watched as Magnus made a dive for the home-brew shed to emerge with a couple of bottles. She would have to be careful, his home brew was sweet but strong.

She stripped off in the bathroom and stuffed her clothes into a plastic bag, knotting the top. Stepping under the hot shower, she soaked her hair and looked about for shampoo. She lathered it on, then set about soaping her body.

Dressed in fresh clothes, and feeling a lot better, she

headed downstairs to be greeted by the scent of garlic and ginger frying in the kitchen. Rhona stood for a moment watching Magnus's tall figure at work. A keen cook, he was completely absorbed and unaware of her presence. Then he caught her scent and turned.

'Supermarket brand shampoo,' he said apologetically.

'I like it,' Rhona said.

'A starter?' He pointed to a plate of olive-oil-soaked croutons topped with fresh basil and chopped tomato.

Rhona selected one and popped it in her mouth, suddenly realizing how hungry she was. It tasted delicious.

'Home brew or wine?'

'Home brew.'

Magnus seemed pleased by her request. He opened the fridge and extracted a bottle and tipped the cloudy liquid into a glass.

'This year's. See what you think.'

A mouthful of the golden liquid brought a sudden rush of memory of her previous visit, all of it pleasant.

'Very good,' she said.

'I've lit the fire in the dining room. I know it's June, but it's behaving like November. Take the starter with you.'

Rhona settled by the fire, and glanced around the room. It looked exactly the way she remembered, although with a few new driftwood carvings added to Magnus's collection.

She found herself at ease in these surroundings. Despite the wildness of the weather which beat at the window, in here tranquillity reigned. She suddenly remembered what or who was missing and called through to the kitchen.

'Do you still have Olaf?' Olaf was a large grey tomcat who caught his own fish, making him an easy house guest when he chose to stay.

Magnus appeared with the bottle to top up her glass. 'He still deigns to visit now and again. Although I fear he's found a girlfriend in a new house further along the shore and is being kept busy.'

They ate the delicate and delicious scallops in companionable silence at the dining table, with the patter of rain on the window. Afterwards they took a softer seat near the fire, wine glasses in hand, and Rhona raised the subject of her visit.

'Tell me what you think,' she urged Magnus.

He considered her request for a moment. 'Whoever killed her had thought it through. The impaled hands. Their careful placing. The marked stone in her mouth.'

Rhona nodded. 'There was no evidence of sexual activity. Soil marks on her jeans suggest she had been kneeling prior to her death. I also found a roll-up under the body.'

Magnus nodded. 'I could smell cannabis. What about the Cathkin Braes victim?'

'No evidence of sexual activity. A young male, similarly laid out, but with the hands chopped off and displayed on the stones. And he had a pebble in his mouth with the number five scratched on it.' Rhona observed Magnus's surprised reaction.

'I'd heard about the pebble, but the hands . . .' He looked perplexed. 'A copycat killing?'

'The full details on the Cathkin Braes murder haven't been released to the press yet.'

Magnus absorbed the significance of this.

'When was the body discovered?' he said.

'Sunday afternoon.'

'What about the post-mortem?'

'Inconclusive. McNab thinks it was drugs related. There was a report of a stash of cocaine nearby.'

'Drugs are everywhere. Orkney, Shetland, the Western Isles.'

Magnus was right. Drug cartels operated throughout Scotland, its mainland and islands. Orkney and Shetland, with their oil money, were ripe pickings for dealers.

'There's a strategy meeting tomorrow,' Magnus said. 'Would it be useful for you to come along?'

'I'll check with DI McNab first and decide in the morning.'

Magnus looked surprised. 'McNab's been promoted?'

'Party was at the weekend,' Rhona said. 'He's still recovering. From the shock and the alcohol.'

'McNab's instinct and intuition are first class,' Magnus said swiftly. 'He'll make a good inspector.'

Both were lost in thought for a moment, Rhona conscious of Magnus's proximity, the quiet power of his presence. He kept his glance averted, staring at the fire with an intensity that unnerved her.

'If you don't mind, I'm a bit tired.' She rose. 'Thanks for the meal. The food was delicious, as always.' She knew she sounded stiff and formal, but the glowing fire, the beer followed by wine, were lowering her defences.

If Magnus was disappointed at her imminent departure for bed, he covered it well.

By the time she reached her room, Rhona already regretted her brusque withdrawal. She liked Magnus, found his company entertaining, and at times enticing. Maybe too enticing.

She admonished herself as she brought up McNab's number and listened to it ring out.

*

Cursing, McNab exited the bed. He found his shirt soon enough, but his trousers eluded him. A sudden image of Iona unbuttoning his fly reminded him where they were. He skirted the bed, where she lay sleeping, and found them on the floor next to her.

He grabbed the mobile from the back pocket and checked the screen. Expecting the police station, he saw Rhona's name instead. He hesitated for a split second before answering. Keeping his voice low, he headed for the sitting room.

'Dr MacLeod. You're up late.' He closed the door quietly behind him.

'Did I wake you?'

'Let's say you got me out of bed.'

'Then my apologies to your companion,' she said, sounding less fazed than he'd hoped by his remark.

'Who says I have a companion?'

'My guess is you're standing stark naked in the sitting room, with the door closed,' she laughed. 'You only answered because it might have been the station.'

'I only answered because it was you. What's up?'

'The Orkney murder looks a lot like the Glasgow one. The body was laid out in a similar fashion, a stone in her mouth with the number four on it.'

'What?'

'In this instance, the victim is a young woman and her hands were impaled, not chopped off.'

'You're suggesting a connection?'

'I'm saying I don't believe in coincidence and,' she paused for a moment, 'neither did Bill.'

McNab gritted his teeth. If she was going to cast DI Wilson up at him at every opportunity . . .

LIN ANDERSON

When he didn't immediately reply, Rhona continued. 'Have you ever found a murder victim with a stone in their mouth, with a number scratched on it?'

'No,' he conceded.

'Now we have two in the space of two days.'

'You need to stop telling me how to do my job, Dr MacLeod,' he said more sharply than intended.

'I'll send you the photos and you can take a look yourself.'

'Thanks,' he said and rang off. He stood for a moment, a cold draught shrivelling his balls. He glanced at the bedroom door. What the hell was he thinking inviting Iona back? Rhona had known when she'd challenged him who he was in bed with – a lassie half his age.

He couldn't chuck Iona out now, not after what they'd just done, but he had no desire to climb back into bed with her. McNab fetched a sleeping bag from the hall cupboard and settled down on the couch. Tomorrow Iona would leave, and for good this time.

Rhona threw the mobile on the bed. The tranquillity of her surroundings had dissipated, her irritation at McNab replacing it. She knew he was worried by his new position, even threatened by it. It was okay to be a maverick DS when you had the wise counsel and guidance of a DI like Bill Wilson, always supportive, always on your side. But Bill was no longer there, and there would be plenty who would be watching and waiting for McNab to screw up. Including herself.

She took out her laptop and sent a selection of her images to McNab's official email address, then went to the window and looked out. The wind had dropped, and the sky, no

112

longer full of angry clouds, was bright with a midnight sun. Sounds of Magnus moving about below were followed by the back door opening. Rhona watched as he emerged, bottle and glass in hand, to sit on the jetty. She recalled sitting there with him on the previous occasion, admiring the outline of Hoy against a similar sky.

Rhona abandoned her dark thoughts and the possibility of sleep, and went out to join him.

As she emerged, Magnus looked surprised and pleased. 'Can't sleep?'

'It's as light as morning.'

She settled herself on the wall, while Magnus fetched her a glass. Watching as he poured, she found herself anticipating the sweet, cloudy taste. Her promise to avoid too much home brew seemed to be evaporating.

'Did you manage to contact McNab?'

'I did, and he wasn't happy about the possible connection.'

'This is his first murder enquiry as DI?'

When Rhona indicated it was, Magnus looked sympathetic. 'A straightforward gangland murder would be easier to deal with.'

'McNab never likes things straightforward or easy,' Rhona reminded him.

Magnus gave her a wry smile. 'Nor does he like the involvement of criminal profilers.'

'He may have to, if it turns out the murders are connected.' Rhona was silent for a moment. 'The body with the stone marked with a five was found inside a Neolithic ring of five stones. Chrissy immediately pounced on the significance of that. Now we have a body identified by a four, but in a much larger stone circle. Can you think of any connection between the two sites other than they're Neolithic?'

'Nothing immediately springs to mind, but I can check with my learned friends digging at the Ness of Brodgar.'

'How many stones circles are there around Scotland?' she asked, anticipating the answer before he gave it.

'A great many more than five.'

16

'Coffee and toast or would you prefer something cooked?'
Magnus offered when Rhona appeared at the kitchen door
next morning.

'Coffee's fine.'

The home brew had left her unscathed, proving
Magnus's claim that with no additives it was unlikely to
cause a hangover. He poured her a mug and pushed some
buttered toast towards her. Rhona, not used to food first
thing, regarded it with suspicion.

'I'll have something after the meeting.'

She carried her coffee onto the jetty and went back to
her spot of the previous night. The water was calm, the sky
clear. The wind for which Orkney was famous had dissipated,
making it difficult to recall the squall which had attacked
the tent while she'd taken her forensic samples.

Magnus followed her out.

'I've been considering the positioning of the body,' he
said. 'Do you want to take a look?'

He led her into the dining room where a map of Scotland,
including the Orkney Islands, had been spread out on the
table.

'A line directionally south runs close to the ring on
Cathkin Braes.' He pointed to a marker. 'That's your Neolithic
circle of five stones.'

He indicated a line drawn from the Ring of Brodgar heading south-east. 'This one slices off a triangle just north of Aberdeen. Nothing significant on that line, as far as I know. However, the western one hits land here.' He pointed to the Outer Hebrides. 'Close to another major stone circle, Callanish, on the Isle of Lewis.'

Rhona challenged him with a look. 'You're assuming the direction of the arms is significant. What if the positioning of the body is more about supplication than direction?'

'You're right.' Magnus glanced at his watch. 'We'd better head for Kirkwall.'

They passed the journey in silence, each deep in thought. It was easy to let your imagination run wild when faced with the phenomenon of similar deaths in such strange surroundings. But just because both deaths involved Neolithic sites needn't mean McNab's theory wasn't right and that the deaths weren't drugs related.

Erling was waiting for them in the incident room. Rhona nodded to Dougie and Simon as she took her seat. R2S had set up an interactive screen to show the assembled team what had been captured at the deposition site.

Dougie ran them through the 360-degree images of the crime scene and then of the wider area. Close-ups on the body from a variety of angles as well as from above simply reinforced the fact that the victim had been very carefully positioned.

At the end of the presentation, Erling asked Professor Magnus Pirie to come forward and present his thoughts.

It was obvious from the smiles of acknowledgement from the local force members that Magnus was well known. The R2S boys were also aware who he was. That only left those drafted in from the mainland, who observed Magnus approach the front of the room with interest.

His tall figure looked impressive, his manner serious. Rhona recognized the concentration and remembered the first time she'd observed him in action. She'd had reservations about using a criminal profiler. They all had, McNab the most. Magnus had screwed up on his first case, putting more than himself in danger. Two young women had died during the investigation. Their deaths had marked Magnus. They had marked Rhona too, because of her own involvement in the case.

Magnus glanced briefly in Rhona's direction before addressing the assembled company.

'The location chosen by an organized killer – and I believe the perpetrator to be organized – is as important as the modus operandi. We don't know yet how exactly the victim died. However, the signature of the killer is the most important aspect of all, and the two, MO and signature, are not the same. In this case the manner used to display the victim – the impaled hands, the arranging of the body and the stone placed in her mouth – constitute a signature.' Here he paused. 'One which had already been seen forty-eight hours previously in Glasgow.' There was surprise at this revelation. Magnus indicated to Erling that they should hear from Rhona.

At Erling's invitation, Rhona rose and joined Magnus at the front. She described the last forty-eight hours, and the similarities and differences between the two crime scenes.

The Orkney team was agog now. The thought that the killer might be local had shocked them. The suggestion that the death might be linked to Glasgow was easier to deal with.

A young DC with weather-beaten cheeks asked the first question.

'Did the Glasgow stone have a number on it?'

'Yes,' Rhona said. 'A five.'

That gave them all food for thought. It wasn't long before someone asked, 'Does that mean we can expect three more?'

A shocked ripple went through the group.

'We have no idea what the numbers mean. Or how exactly either victim died. Or why both bodies were laid out as they were,' Rhona said truthfully.

Erling took over then, thanking them both for their contributions.

'Our first job is to identify the Orkney victim. It seems increasingly unlikely she's local. I need to know who she is and when she arrived on the island.' He began to hand out tasks. Magnus and Rhona departed, their contribution over.

'Ready for food now?' Magnus said.

'Definitely.'

'We'll leave the car here and head for the main street.'

Minutes later they were seated in a cafe within sight of St Magnus Cathedral. As they waited for the bacon rolls to arrive, Rhona asked why Magnus hadn't mentioned his Callanish theory.

'I spoke to Dougie. He's going to plot it out accurately first.' He hesitated. 'I asked if he'd do the same for the Cathkin case. Is that all right?'

'McNab won't like it either way.'

'Are you and he . . .?' Magnus began.

'McNab and I have never been together,' she said honestly.

'But I thought after the Russian trial . . .?' Magnus ground to an embarrassed halt again.

'I thought McNab was dead. We all did. Then he rose from the grave.' She smiled. 'McNab appreciated my joy at his resurrection. As you would expect.' Rhona changed the subject. 'The post-mortem's in Inverness later today. I'm going to hitch a lift with R2S. After that I'll head back to Glasgow.' She paused. 'I assume you're here for the summer?'

Magnus indicated he was. 'Although I'm happy to come south if required.'

'I'll see if we can both have access to the crime-scene software. That way you can see how we're progressing.' Her mobile rang. She glanced at the screen to find Chrissy's name.

'Any word on the QT test?' Rhona immediately asked.

'Nothing so far. When are you back?'

'Later today.' Rhona explained about the Inverness trip.

'Will Magnus be with you?' Chrissy said sweetly.

'No.'

'Pity.'

Rhona rang off to find Magnus regarding her quizzically.

'We're awaiting the results on Long QT Syndrome. You probably know it as sudden adult death.'

'Where young sports people suddenly collapse and die in dressing rooms?'

She nodded. 'A genetic abnormality of the heart where the time taken to recharge the electrical system after each heartbeat is longer than normal. The heart doesn't pump oxygen, the brain is deprived and the person loses consciousness and dies,' she continued. 'The condition often manifests itself in pre-teens or teenagers. Our victim was nineteen. High emotion or stress can trigger an attack.'

'He died of fright?'

'Fear may have been a contributing factor.' Rhona hesitated, knowing this was the moment she should mention what had happened to Alan's mother. 'There's another reason McNab should involve you.'

'Really, what?'

Magnus listened intently as Rhona explained what had happened at the spiritualist church service.

'And no one knew of Alan's death before this happened?'

'Apart from whoever chopped off his hands, no,' Rhona said.

'That's fascinating.'

'McNab doesn't think so.'

'I'd like to speak to the medium,' Magnus said.

'Let me work on McNab first.'

'Okay,' he conceded.

They made their way back to the car. Rhona had arranged to meet R2S at the field next to Brodgar at 2 p.m., from where the helicopter would take them to Raigmore Hospital. She didn't relish another helicopter ride. In fact, two more rides. But her curiosity was greater than her fear.

Magnus gave her a warm embrace and a peck on the cheek as they said goodbye.

'Give Chrissy my love.'

'That would only encourage her,' Rhona told him.

'Let me know what happens?'

'I will.' She lifted her bags and made her way across the grass, wet from last night's rain. The cordons round the Ring were still in place and the hillside was dotted with white-suited personnel combing the area, but the tent had gone.

Rhona dipped her head under the blades of the helicopter and, with a helping hand, climbed aboard. Dougie was already inside. Noise made conversation difficult but he indicated he would be attending the post-mortem with a view to constructing a body map of the victim with the pathologist, Dr Emily Sinclair.

They rose, hovering briefly above the field. From here the circle of stones was a manageable size. Its close connection via the Ness of Brodgar to the Stones of Stenness and, in the near distance, the hump of Maeshowe, was clearly visible.

Then they were heading towards the stormy strip of water between the islands and mainland Scotland.

17

Magnus turned away as the helicopter swept over the dark hump of Hoy and disappeared. He had been right to contact Rhona. The cases were too similar in signature not to be connected. However, that didn't mean drugs weren't involved or that they weren't the prime reason for the killings. Gangs often used signature methods of dispensing with those who stepped out of line. Although, he reminded himself, they rarely chose Neolithic sites to do so.

On that thought, Magnus made the decision to go back to the dig and seek out Jack Louden. If Jack had discovered contact details for the local pusher, he was unlikely to supply them via his mobile.

Clear skies had brought out the excavation team. The trenches were alive with volunteers, small trowels carefully brushing soil away from history. Magnus was in awe of their dedication in what was definitely back-breaking work. He found Jack directing operations in the northern area, closest to Brodgar.

Jack suggested Magnus go and put the kettle on, he would be along shortly.

The common room was empty. Magnus located the kettle, filled it and set it to boil, then checked for clean mugs, of which there were none. He chose a couple from the table and washed them at the sink under cold water. Locating an open carton of milk, he sniffed it, and decided it was fresh enough.

He spooned instant coffee into the now-clean mugs, noting that the scent of cannabis in the room had dissipated. Magnus wondered if news of his request had frightened the smokers away.

There was a row of hooks near the door, hung with coats, jackets and waterproof trousers. Beneath stood a row of muddy boots and backpacks. Magnus thought again of the boots the victim had been wearing, the casual clothes, the dirt under her nails. He went closer, trying to pick up the scent of cannabis from the clothes. Smokers never realized just how obvious their habit was, especially to someone with a strong sense of smell. However, the clothes smelt predominantly of damp peat and heather.

Jack entered to end his investigation.

'I was planning on giving you a call.' He poured boiling water into the mugs and the scent of coffee filled the air. 'Milk?'

Magnus shook his head.

Jack spurned the milk too, but added two heaped spoonfuls of sugar from a battered packet.

After stirring and tasting, he sat down opposite Magnus, withdrew a piece of paper from his pocket and pushed it across the table.

Magnus glanced down to find a mobile number.

'When you call, just say "Tanya".'

'Who's Tanya?'

'No idea.'

Magnus pocketed the paper. 'Can I ask who gave you this number?'

'You can ask, but I won't tell.' Jack scrutinized him. 'And I don't want the police involved. I don't want anyone here getting into trouble. Okay?'

Magnus indicated he understood, despite feeling uncomfortable about such a promise. If he found out anything that might help in the murder investigation, he was obliged to inform the police. He let that go, for the moment.

'I'd like to ask you an archaeological question, but whatever we discuss has to stay between us.'

Jack looked interested. 'Fire away.'

Magnus briefly described both crime scenes, including the careful layout of the bodies and the stones placed in the mouths.

This was obviously news to Jack. Intriguing news.

'And you thought it might be a re-enactment of a Neolithic ritual?' he guessed.

Magnus nodded.

Jack looked thoughtful. 'We're pretty sure the Ness buildings we're excavating offered a ritual passageway from life at the Stenness site to death at Brodgar. So the body is in the correct Neolithic location for death.' He paused. 'I'm not familiar with the Glasgow site. Can I think about this and get back to you?'

'Of course.'

Jack finished his coffee. 'I'd better encourage the troops while the weather's good.' He abandoned the mug with the battalion of others. 'Fancy a pint in Stromness later?'

They arranged to meet at the Stromness Hotel around nine. Magnus hoped by then he would have met his mobile contact. He waited until Jack had gone back to the trenches, then headed outside to make the call. The mobile rang out three times before it was answered.

'Tanya?' Magnus said, following Jack's instructions.

A female voice with a faint Orcadian accent said she would get back to him, then rang off. When he tried again, the call went unanswered. Defeated and disappointed, Magnus made his way back to the car. He wondered about contacting Erling to see if there had been any new developments, but had to accept that Erling too would be in touch when, or if, it was necessary.

The drive home should have lifted his spirits. The sun shone on Scapa Flow and the wind had dropped to a whisper. The midsummer light was playing its usual tricks with the landscape, giving the impression that the shimmering island of Hoy was floating on top of the waters of the Flow. Magnus had seen such a mirage before, but then he had been on Raasay looking towards the Cuillins of Skye.

When he reached home and opened the front door, he was immediately aware someone had been in the house. The scent was female, possibly perfume, perhaps soap or deodorant. He entered quietly and followed the scent, coming to the conclusion that the visitor had been in all the downstairs rooms but hadn't ventured upstairs. Since he rarely locked up, it wasn't unusual to get a visitor when out, usually one of his neighbours from the other houses that lined the bay, but this scent wasn't one he was familiar with.

The scent eventually led him to the back door. She was sitting on the wall, enticing a seagull with a piece of bannock taken from his bread bin. It was a dangerous endeavour. The gull, eyes protruding with desire, screeched above her. It finally swooped and she flapped it away. It dived again, more determined this time. Before the beak met the bread, she had thrown it into the water. She ducked as the gull swooped past her, the beak barely missing her head.

A risk taker, Magnus thought, but it didn't need a psychologist to work that one out.

Suddenly bored with her play, she threw the remainder of the bannock into the water and three more gulls arrived to fight over it. Angry, threatening squawks, fury-filled eyes and pecking beaks followed her action, causing a satisfied smile.

'Hello?' Magnus said.

She took time to turn, although it was obvious she'd heard him. When she did, Magnus saw a heavily made-up face, long straight black hair, a nose ring and pale pink lips. The effect in the darkness of a club might have been attractive. In bright June sunshine she had the look of a pretty clown.

Now *she* was examining *him*. His face first, then his upper body, finally fastening her intent gaze on his crotch. Psychopaths, Magnus could deal with. Sexually blatant young women he found more of a challenge. He refrained from shielding his privates from her exploratory stare, but with some difficulty.

Eventually her eyes rose to his face, to check if she had unnerved him. Magnus strove to assure her by his expression that she had not, with some success. Annoyance clouded her eyes and her mouth formed a petulant pout.

'Can I help you?' Magnus offered.

She slid off the wall and sidled towards him. Dressed in skin-tight jeans and a short top, further piercings became evident. Under the make-up, he judged her to be in her late teens. She came close enough to make him want to step back. Magnus chose not to. He was a great deal taller than she was, which put her head mid chest.

She ran her finger up his left thigh. Just in time, Magnus caught her thin wrist in his large hand.

'What's going on?' he said.

She tried to free herself and Magnus tightened his grip. 'Well?'

She sagged and her eyes misted with tears. Fearing he may have hurt her, Magnus let go.

At this, she gave a triumphant laugh and strutted back to the wall, rubbing her wrist. Settling herself on top, she pulled out a joint and lit it. The pungent smell wafted towards Magnus. He had a sudden image of his elderly neighbour, Mrs Clouston, coming in for a visit, to find him here with a pot-smoking teenager.

'So are you going to tell me why you're here?' he said.

She regarded him for a moment, then seemed to come to a decision.

'The girl at Brodgar. How did she die?'

'Did you know her?' Magnus asked.

'I want to know how she died,' she repeated.

'They're not sure,' Magnus said quietly. 'But if you think you know who she is—'

She cut him off before he could finish. 'I know she was a stupid bitch,' she spat at him.

'Why was she stupid?'

'She meddled in things she shouldn't have.' A flicker of fear crossed her face.

'What sort of things?'

She contemplated him for a moment then nipped the joint and stuck it in her pocket, and slid off the wall.

Magnus realized she was about to leave and he'd learned nothing. He stepped in front of her.

'Did Tanya send you?'

She looked blank. 'Who's Tanya?'

Something in her tone said she was telling the truth. Magnus stood aside. He fired his final shot as she reached the gate that led to the road.

'I want to find out who killed the girl. Will you help me?'

At first he thought she hadn't heard him, or else was ignoring his request. Then she paused and turned.

'Why do you care?' she said.

'Because no one deserves to die like that.'

She observed him for a moment, her eyes wide with fright, then she opened the gate, slipped quickly through and was gone.

Magnus wasted precious moments wondering what her visit might mean before realizing he had no idea how the girl had got there. Hurrying through the house, he threw open the front door. There was no sign of her on the single-track road that curved round the bay. Yards away, the vehicle ferry was boarding for Hoy. He searched the passengers, looking for her dark head, but couldn't spot it. A car was heading swiftly up the track towards the main Orphir road, but it was already too far away for him to tell if she was in it.

Back on the jetty, he contemplated why the girl had sought him out, why he had been tested, and whether she did know something about the dead girl. He ran the entire scene over again in his mind and came to the conclusion she had come here to tell him something. Something that frightened her more than baiting a seagull.

18

The victim was slim but not overtly thin, her hair glossy, her face clear. In life she would have been a healthy, pretty young woman. The only blemishes were the ugly wounds in her hands, exposed now with removal of the two spikes.

Rhona listened as the pathologist recorded the state of the body, making the same judgement as herself. The hands had been pierced after death. How the victim had died was not outwardly obvious. No evidence of bruising, even round the wrists. It seemed the young woman had met her end, in whatever form, without a fight.

Dr Sinclair raised the right arm to check underneath, then the left, this time exposing a tattoo. She motioned Rhona to take a look.

A tattoo was a very personal adornment, especially those hidden from common view. Rhona recognized the symbol almost immediately, having seen it on a young man she'd examined, who'd been washed ashore after a fishing accident.

It was a beautifully fashioned white eagle, with a golden beak and talons, wearing a gold crown, all set within a red shield. The angel wings on either side were elaborate and more feminine than those found on her fisherman, but it was undoubtedly the Polish coat of arms. Below were the words *To ja napisze zakonczeme mojej historii*, which Rhona couldn't translate.

Dr Sinclair looked at Rhona over her mask.

'You recognize the tattoo?'

Rhona explained what it was.

'Do you know what the words mean?'

'No.'

'We have Polish staff in the hospital, including one in the mortuary. Let's see if we can find out.'

Dr Sinclair waved through the glass at an assistant and requested that Antoni come in. Minutes later a young man appeared.

Dr Sinclair indicated the tattoo.

'The Polish coat of arms,' he said immediately.

'And the inscription?'

He studied it for a moment. 'Roughly translated, it means "In my story, I write my own ending".'

Not in this case, Rhona thought sadly.

Two hours later she had learned that the girl had not had sex prior to her death. That she had died sometime during the night before she'd been found. Her stomach contents consisted of fish and chips, much of which wasn't digested. The internal organs appeared healthy, yet her heart had failed. Heart failure was a mechanism for death in broad terms, but it didn't indicate the underlying pathology and therefore wasn't an acceptable cause of death. So the PM was negative and they would test for Long QT, just as in the Glasgow case.

'We send samples of the skeletal muscle to the Molecular Genetics department at Aberdeen Royal,' Dr Sinclair told her. 'They'll look for the faulty genes associated with Long

QT. Toxicology samples go to their Clinical Biochemistry department.'

One young death from Long QT might be a possibility, but two, in similar locations, with a similar signature, didn't seem possible or probable, unless the perpetrator had worked out how to scare people to death. Which meant they would have to look to toxicology for an explanation.

Once de-robed, Rhona gave McNab a call.

'Dr MacLeod. I thought you were lost.'

Rhona ignored the jibe. 'I've just come out of the PM on the Orkney victim.'

She could sense McNab's impatience as he waited for her to go on.

'Her hands were pierced after death. There were no other signs of violence. She hadn't had sex and she was laid out just like the Glasgow victim. This time the hands were arranged to point due south-west and south-east, and she had a stone in her mouth with the number four on it.'

Rhona heard McNab's muttered 'Fuck's sake' under his breath.

'How did she die?'

'The PM was negative. They're going to check for Long QT and look at toxicology.'

'Just how common is this Long QT?'

'Last report I read suggested it could be one in two thousand in that age group, but it doesn't always lead to sudden adult death. That's usually brought on by stress, extreme sport or shock.' She didn't use the word terror, but it would have been just as apt.

'When are you back?' McNab said.

'Tonight.'

'Let's talk tomorrow.'

McNab rang off, mention of Magnus conspicuous by its absence. If McNab chose not to involve Magnus, there was little she could do about it.

The police helicopter had been summoned to an emergency. Dougie had opted to go with it, but Rhona decided to catch the train back to Glasgow. The carriage was busy with summer visitors, which rendered the prospect of working impossible, so she spent the time watching the highland landscape pass her by, this time at ground level.

The journey reminded her how long it had been since she'd ventured north and west. Her holiday trips to Skye had ended abruptly with her father's death and she'd visited the island only once since then on official business. Forensic experts weren't in great demand in the remote parts of Scotland, at least not until now.

A call came in from Chrissy as the train entered Drumochter Pass, but it was quickly cut off by the encircling mountains, much to the annoyance of Rhona's neighbours who were deep in their own mobile conversations, loud and mundane for the most part.

How much of our lives was recorded on mobiles, Rhona thought. Which was probably why the perpetrator had made certain one wasn't found on the Orkney victim.

A text pinged as the train drew into Perth station. It was an order framed as a request. Chrissy wanted Rhona to come to the jazz club as soon as she got off the train. Rhona said a silent goodbye to a shower and a Chinese takeaway, knowing she would learn more from Chrissy in half an hour than if she read every report written in her absence.

She caught the subway from Buchanan Street to Byres Road, grateful she only had a small overnight case to carry up and down the stairs. Glasgow was enjoying similar weather to Orkney. A clear sky, still bright with midsummer light. Its residents were making the most of it. The outside tables on Ashton Lane were packed, with little standing room on the narrow street. The sandwiches had run out on the train and she had blunted her hunger with crisps and coffee. The smell of food from the various eateries reminded her of how empty her stomach was.

The cool shadow of the basement was in direct contrast to the late sunshine. Rhona stood for a moment at the back of the cavern-like room. All eyes and ears were on Sean and his saxophone. It was a sound and a sight she was used to, yet it often reminded her of the first time she'd watched him play. It had been at a police party in the club to celebrate DI Bill Wilson's fiftieth birthday. Bill was a big jazz fan, Rhona most definitely not, but she had taken a shine to the saxophonist, as he had to her.

Sean Maguire, part owner of the club, had sought her out during the break, bringing a bottle of red wine to her table and two glasses. Rhona had made no attempt to resist his Irish charm. Sean had walked her home. And the rest was history.

Catching sight of her now, Sean brought the piece to an end and immediately launched into 'Misty', a number he knew she liked. Rhona smiled over her thanks.

Chrissy was at the bar, a cocktail glass containing a bright pink concoction in front of her. Quick to recognize the change in melody and the reason for it, she turned to acknowledge Rhona's arrival. 'About time,' she declared.

Rhona ignored the reprimand and ordered a large glass of white wine and another packet of crisps, real food having become a distant dream.

'Well?' Chrissy said.

'Well what?'

Chrissy sighed in exasperation. 'How did the Orkney one die?'

'The PM was inconclusive. They're testing for Long QT.'

'Seems to be an epidemic of that. I wonder if our medium foresaw that one.' She lowered her voice. 'Word is McNab went back to the church alone. Gave Menzies a hard time. So bad he called Janice.'

'Did he register a complaint?'

'Patrick Menzies knows Janice and her mother. He didn't want to make a fuss.'

'Has McNab referred to the Orkney case yet at any of the team meetings?' Rhona said.

'No, but DC Watt knew about it anyway,' Chrissy informed her. 'He comes from Kirkwall.'

So the cat was out of the bag. Maybe when she talked to McNab tomorrow, she could bring up the topic of Magnus. Three glasses of wine and two packets of crisps later, Rhona declared herself tired, hungry and intent on heading home. Chrissy was unperturbed, having divulged all her news, stated her opinion on both cases and asked when to expect Magnus's arrival.

As Rhona carried her bags to the door, Sean appeared.

'Leaving already?'

'I need to eat something other than crisps.'

He took the bags. 'We're two minutes away from my flat and food.'

'I was—'

'Going to order a Chinese takeaway?' he finished for her. 'I'll have food in front of you quicker than that.'

The offer was tempting. Of all the men who had entered

and exited her life, Sean had been the best cook. She missed that about him. That, and other things.

Sean led the way upstairs and along the road. Five minutes later she was under a hot shower, anticipating the meal whose aroma she could already smell. This was what her life had been like when she and Sean had been together. Coming home after work, the anticipation of good food, wine and company dispelling whatever crime she had pored over during the day.

Rhona turned off the water and stepped out, burying her head in a large towel, reminding herself that telling Sean to move out of her flat had been the right choice, and that she preferred living alone. As she dressed, she nevertheless found herself examining the toiletries and being strangely pleased to find no evidence of a current female resident in his domain.

The table had been set. A bottle of wine stood open, taking the air. Sean proudly showed her the label. Rhona feigned surprise and delight. Sean, the wine connoisseur, smiled, knowing full well the name meant nothing to her. He poured her a glass. Rhona took a sip and declared it delicious, which seemed to satisfy him.

'Take a seat. I'll dish up.'

Moments later she was gulping down the freshly cooked pasta with garlic and broccoli as though she feared he would remove her plate.

'Good?' Sean asked.

'Mmm.'

'It's an old Sicilian recipe, which featured on *Montalbano*.' When Rhona looked blank, Sean explained. 'An Italian cop programme. Inspector Montalbano loves his food.'

He had made her laugh. It was a trick of his. One of

the things Rhona liked about him, along with his blue eyes, dark hair and . . .

'What are you thinking about?' he said.

Rhona shook her head to dispel the image of Sean naked in her kitchen, whistling an Irish tune while making their morning coffee.

'Nothing much.'

He accepted her non-committal reply. 'Coffee? Whiskey?'

Rhona nodded, wondering if she was past refusing any delight Sean might offer tonight.

He sent her to sit on the couch while he prepared the coffee, fully clothed this time. Rhona glanced about the room, remembering the night Sean had brought her here after the cinema murder. How he had soothed her fears about her son Liam. What had happened afterwards.

He placed a bottle of Irish whiskey on the coffee table with two glasses. 'Help yourself.'

Rhona eyed the bottle, knowing what might happen if she drank any more. She poured one anyway. The whiskey tasted strong after the mellowness of the wine.

'How's Magnus?'

Sean's question caught her off guard.

'Fine,' she said cautiously. Sean, like McNab, was not a fan of the Orcadian professor, his reason being personal and a lot to do with her. Rhona expected Sean to continue, but he seemed to think the better of it. He suddenly set his glass on the table, glanced at his watch and rose.

'I'm afraid I have to get back to the club.'

'I was just about to call a cab,' Rhona said promptly.

Sean looked down, a smile playing his lips. 'And here's me thinking you were planning on staying the night.'

'You wish,' she retorted, already on her feet. She retrieved her mobile and brought up the taxi number, irritated with herself for relaxing her guard. Sean was playing her, like he always did. And she'd almost succumbed, seduced by good food and too much wine.

'It'll be here soon. I'll wait outside.' Rhona made for the door.

Sean followed her into the hall and retrieved her bags.

'I can manage,' Rhona insisted.

'We can leave together,' he said in answer to her look.

When they reached the street, Rhona urged him to go. 'The taxi'll be here any minute.'

Sean looked as though he would say something further, then shrugged. 'See you.'

'See you.'

Rhona didn't watch him walk away, but sensed nevertheless when he turned to look back. She kept her eyes firmly forward. With Magnus and McNab she always felt she had the upper hand. That had never been true of her relationship with Sean Maguire, which was why it must never be rekindled.

19

Stromness was a long town, traversed by a narrow street that weaved its way along the shoreline. On the seaward edge, fisher houses stood side on, each with their own small jetty. On the northern side, the ground rose steeply. Ancient narrow flagstone lanes with intriguing names like Khyber Pass divided front-facing houses, leading you to the top of a sizeable hill. Sheltered from the main force of the Atlantic winds, Stromness, also known by its older name of Hamnavoe, offered a safe haven for its inhabitants, and for the main ferry service that ploughed its way between here and Scrabster on the mainland.

Although Magnus admired the bigger town of Kirkwall with its splendid St Magnus Cathedral, Hamnavoe was by far his favourite. With less room to spread out, it had retained its fisher town character. The main street was open to cars travelling in both directions, despite being single track, and you could still park your car in the wider bits. On this occasion, Magnus chose to leave the car down by the harbour. The *MV Hamnavoe* was already berthed, having made her last trip to and from the mainland for the day.

The Stromness Hotel was a tall building facing the harbour, its main door reached by a set of wide steps. On the left, at street level, was the wee bar he was headed for. Jack was already inside, a locally brewed beer before him.

'What are you having?' he offered.

'The same,' Magnus said.

They took time to savour the beer, before Jack suggested they head to one of the outside tables. He had something to show Magnus. The sun wouldn't drop below the horizon for three hours at least, before it swiftly came back up. It was a perfect night to sit outside, still and mild, though not exactly warm.

When they'd settled down, Jack produced a map and spread it out on the table. It was a map of Scotland and its islands, but not one Magnus had seen before. The most prominent features were not the major cities and routes in between, but Neolithic sites. Jack had drawn a series of straight lines connecting a number of these together.

Jack began his explanation. 'We don't know for certain why stone rings like Brodgar were built, or why they were built in specific places. But there is no doubt that those who built them chose their location carefully.

'The sun was an important part of their worship,' he continued. 'You probably already know about the rays of the midsummer and midwinter sun and the entrance to Maeshowe?'

Magnus nodded.

'As to whether human sacrifice was part of any ritual, we don't know. So I can't help you on the spiked hands and the stone in the mouth. As for the direction of the hands, that, I must admit, intrigued me. Have you heard of ley lines?'

'My father used to douse to find field drains on the farm,' Magnus told him.

'Dousing locates disturbed ground. It's used to locate buried bodies, or underground water courses. Ley lines are similar. They appear to suggest an energy change in the earth's surface. You use the same method to locate them. Two L-shaped metal rods will do. When you cross a ley line, the rods move towards one another and cross, just like in dousing. Marker stones such as the one on the drive leading to the house we use at the Ness are on them. These lines appear to link Neolithic sites. The physics of dousing and ley lines is unexplained, so scientists tend to dismiss them. Non-scientists like your father just use them in a practical way, because they work.'

Magnus nodded in agreement. Plenty of scientists didn't believe in psychology either.

Jack pointed at the Ring of Brodgar's position on the map. There were three prominent lines radiating from it. One due south, one south-west, the third south-east. Jack ran his finger along the south-west line. Magnus knew where it was headed before Jack got there.

'Callanish,' he said.

'You'd spotted that already?'

Magnus nodded.

'The south-east one looks as though it might run through what was once a triangle of three stones at Skelmuir Hill in Aberdeenshire. There's only one stone still standing there, as far as I'm aware.'

'And the hands at Cathkin Braes?'

'You'll need an exact compass reading to check them out.'

'R2S, the forensic team, are mapping an accurate layout.'

Jack nodded and lifted his pint. He took a long swallow while Magnus continued to study the mesh of lines crisscrossing the map. There were scores of marked sites, many of them clustered near the lines. And no way they could determine an exact fit.

'Another one?' Jack offered.

Magnus rose. 'I'll get it.'

There were only a couple of people in the tiny bar, the clientele taking advantage of one of the few summer evenings they could sit outside. Magnus headed for the Gents, while the barman poured his order. As he entered the empty toilet, he was conscious of someone coming in behind him and the door shutting. He turned to find a hooded man barring the doorway. He fired Magnus an expectant look, and held out his hand.

Magnus had never encountered a beggar in Orkney, and his surprise resulted in silence. The guy produced a small sachet from his pocket and waved it at Magnus.

Now Magnus understood. 'How much?'

'Twenty.'

Magnus handed over a note and received the bag. As the man opened the door, Magnus used his bigger bulk to push it shut again.

'I need some information.'

The guy shook his head. 'No questions,' he said in a thick accent. Magnus took a guess and repeated his request in his limited Polish.

The man's eyes registered surprise. He muttered what sounded like a curse, and pulled a metal object from his pocket. With an ominous clicking sound, a blade appeared. Short and sharp. He used it to wave Magnus away from the door.

Magnus immediately obliged and in seconds the man was gone.

Magnus stood, his need to use the urinal surpassed by the surreal nature of the encounter. Eventually he pocketed the cannabis, used the facilities and went to collect the beers.

Jack was watching for him. 'I wondered where you'd got to,' he said.

Magnus, keeping his voice low, gave a brief résumé of the encounter. 'How did he know who I was, and where I'd be? I never gave my name when I called Tanya,' he said.

'It doesn't take a cop to work that one out. You and I talk. I ask the team for a contact, obviously on your behalf. We come here for a pint tonight.' Jack shrugged.

'There's no chance one of your lot knows who the victim is, and is keeping quiet about it?' Magnus said.

'They told the police they didn't. I have to believe that.'

Magnus let it go, accepting Jack's need to protect his team. The cannabis connection had always been a tenuous one. Even if the elusive Tanya knew the victim, she was unlikely to reveal it to Magnus, or the police.

'So,' Jack said. 'What next for our investigation?'

'We await developments.'

Jack, looking disappointed, began to fold the map.

'Can I hold on to that for the moment?' Magnus said. 'At least until R2S come up with the compass readings.'

'Okay,' Jack replied reluctantly.

After his strange visitor, Magnus had decided to lock the house when he'd set out for Stromness. That fact irritated him now, as he searched for his key. He eventually found it in a rarely used pocket and slipped it in the lock.

The silence on entry seemed profound. It was a silence rarely experienced in Orkney, or at his flat in Glasgow.

Here, the wind and sea were in perpetual motion. In Glasgow it was the traffic. Magnus stood for a moment in the hall, subconsciously scenting the air, registering the fact that no one had been there since he'd left.

Although it was late, he had no desire for sleep. The midnight sun had reset his internal clock as it always did. Insomnia was the price you paid for long summer days this far north.

Magnus headed for his study and opened the window a little. Now the silence was broken by the soft lapping of water against the jetty. Across the Flow, the humpback of Hoy loomed inky black against a red and purple sky.

He located the bottle of Highland Park he kept on the bookcase and poured himself a shot, then spread the map out on the table near the window. The map bothered Magnus in ways he could not yet put into words.

His job as a profiler was to try and interpret the signature of a killer. To build up a picture of the person who committed such an act. Everything was done for a reason, which may have no rationale to the observer, but nonetheless was clear to the perpetrator.

The perpetrator had a reason for positioning the hands. A reason for the stone in the mouth. A reason for the number on the stone. What the hell was it?

Magnus drank down the whisky and poured himself another.

He knew he should stop thinking now, and try to get some sleep, but he couldn't get the questions out of his head. It was always like this. The crime followed by a fog. Then a deluge of thoughts. A bombardment of ideas. A maze of possible paths. The majority of them leading to a dead end.

And doubt. Doubt that the psychological theories were valid. Doubt that he could apply them correctly. Doubt that he believed the stories he told himself.

McNab, on the other hand, operated in reality. He wasn't interested in playing with psychology. McNab had to take ultimate responsibility for his every move.

That was why McNab doubted and questioned. To a detective, everyone was capable of lying. Everyone *was* lying, until proved otherwise.

Magnus confronted the next uncomfortable thought, that there was a distinct possibility they were being set up. By the layout of the body, by the manner of death, by the symbolic nature of it. A possibility that the perpetrator was playing with them. That they were the pawns in his game.

The light had finally faded, rendering the room full of long and ominous shadows.

Magnus felt suddenly chilled, inside and out. He closed the window and carried the whisky up to his room. Tomorrow he would contact Erling and find out whether the link between the two deaths was officially established. Then he would plan his journey south.

20

She'd fucked up by coming on to him. He hadn't liked it. That had surprised her because it usually worked and gave her the upper hand. She rubbed her wrist, remembering his reaction, the look in his eye as he pushed her away. That had unnerved her and she'd stupidly lit the joint.

Normally that would have calmed her down, so she could speak to him. But combined with what she'd taken earlier, it had made her head weird. On the ferry back she'd felt sick.

Looking across the Flow, she could picture his house by the shore and the jetty where she'd waited for him. She'd had it all planned and still she'd fucked up.

She fingered the stud in her nose, pulling at it until she felt it weep. The scent of the seepage brought three flies almost instantaneously to investigate. It made her think about the stupid bitch lying in the Ring. The flies buzzing round, filling her eyes and mouth.

Why had the woman been there? It was *her* location. She, Morvan, had won her location fair and square. Months it had taken her. But what if she *had* got there first? Would she be the one in the mortuary?

A cloud of midges found her. She would have to move or she'd be eaten alive. She stood and walked over to the concrete slab and free-standing chimney, all that was left of the Second World War Nissen hut. Below her, Scapa Flow glistened under a full moon.

Since the stupid bitch was dead, did that mean she was safe?

She took out her phone, and looked at it. She shouldn't go online. It was too risky. But what if something happened to the others?

She didn't really know them anyway. They weren't her responsibility.

Guilt swept over her. Shouldn't she warn them just in case? Hey, maybe she was wrong and what had happened had nothing to do with the game. It wasn't as though it was a war game.

Then why had the girl died?

She set the mobile down, her hand trembling. Fear was still stabbing at her despite the effects of the joint. She would light another if need be. Otherwise she would get no sleep. She rolled one, her hand shaking. Once lit, the glow calmed her a little.

Before she'd come here, she'd read about this place where grown men had been driven insane, not by the war they fought, but by being eaten alive by midges. The aromatic smoke enveloped her, shielding her from the more voracious biters. She would have lit a fire in the chimney, but hadn't wanted to make her presence known.

She would pack up camp and leave tomorrow. Catch the morning ferry south. Then the train. She'd be back in the city by nightfall. No one knew what she looked like. No one knew who she really was. Now the other girl was dead, she was safe. That thought helped her drift off into sleep.

She awoke suddenly and with a start. Her mouth felt

dry and crusty with dead midges, her head still swimming with the effects of the drug. She tried to sit up, feeling woozy. The slap and suck of water on the rocks below suggested Scapa Flow had woken as she had slept. She felt about for her mobile to light the way, but it was no longer where she thought she'd laid it. She stumbled to her feet, and into the rising wind. Nearby she heard her tent flap and wondered why she hadn't crept inside before falling asleep.

The wind rustled the surrounding heather. Tinder dry in the sustained warm spell, it sounded like a crackling fire. Somewhere, the horn of a boat hooted like an owl in woods. *But there are no woods here*, she thought, *no trees*.

As she approached the tent, she thought she heard her game name, 'Morvan', like a whisper on the wind.

She stopped short, unnerved and listening. This had been happening recently. She was smoking too much grass. She forced herself forward. There was a knife in the tent and a torch. Holding them would make her feel safer.

But she never reached the tent.

From behind, a hand pushed her and she stumbled forward, falling onto the concrete. For a moment she was too shocked to move, then she managed to drag herself to her knees. Immediately hands forced her back down.

Her head was wrenched back, then slammed down to crack against the concrete. Stunned, she couldn't resist as she was dragged by the hair, then rolled inside the tent. She scrabbled about, trying to find the knife as the tent collapsed about her and she was rolled in an ever-tightening cocoon, then lifted.

She heard a scattering of stones. They rumbled forward and fell to bounce off the cliff below. Suddenly she knew what was about to happen. Her scream, prevented from escape by the nylon gag, drove backwards and down her throat.

And then she was launched.

The first time she hit the cliff face, her jaw smashed, driving her teeth upwards and inwards.

The second bounce shattered the bones in her right leg and shoulder.

The third sent a rib to pierce a lung.

By the time she met the rocks that rose above the now-seething waters of the Flow, she wasn't yet dead, until a sharp pinnacle pierced the nylon cocoon to enter her left eye and then her brain.

Above, her attacker listened to each slam of the descending body, counting them, hoping there would be five.

21

'And then there were three,' McNab said ironically.

'That's not funny,' Rhona said.

McNab turned on her. 'I know it's not fucking funny. It's you who's suggesting it.'

'I didn't suggest . . .' She paused.

'No, but you implied.'

McNab was on edge and, she suspected, hung over. She didn't feel that good herself after the wine last night at the jazz club, then at Sean's. Rhona winced at the memory.

'We can't ignore the similarities,' she said quietly.

'No one's ignoring them,' McNab said tersely. 'I'm in contact with the DI in charge up there.'

'And?'

'We're awaiting results from both PMs *and* from forensic,' he added pointedly.

'What about this spiritual church business?'

He shot her a look fit to kill. 'Chrissy been blabbing again?'

'The whole team's been blabbing.'

'You and I both know that the mumbo-jumbo stuff is just that. Mumbo jumbo.'

'So Patrick Menzies isn't a suspect?' she said.

'A prospect for the funny farm, maybe.'

'He didn't mention Orkney?'

'Definitely not.'

Rhona decided to wade in. Sometimes it was the best way with McNab.

'Magnus took compass readings. The victim's hands at Brodgar were placed to point south-east and south-west.' She carried on despite the glint in McNab's eye. 'The westward line passes through Callanish on Lewis, the second largest stone circle in Scotland.'

McNab held up his hand. 'Stop right there.' He looked askance at her. 'And I thought you were a scientist, Dr MacLeod.'

They were in McNab's office and their raised voices were no doubt being noted in the incident room. The next strategy meeting was due to begin in five minutes. This time it would be key personnel only, including the senior officer in charge, Superintendent Sutherland. A man McNab had failed to impress on a number of occasions, which might have had something to do with his combative attitude.

Rhona was about to come back at McNab with a further piece of news, when there was a tentative knock on the door.

McNab bellowed, 'What?'

DS Clark looked in warily. 'They're ready for you now, sir.'

The strategy meeting was proceeding more smoothly than Rhona had expected. Roy Hunter of R2S had just completed his demo of the online crime-scene mapping of the Cathkin Braes site, together with the evidence collected. The PM results, or lack of them, had been discussed. McNab had handled everything up to now with aplomb. Now it was Rhona's turn to speak.

She gave details of the body in situ, emphasizing the layout and positioning, the samples she took and why. She then brought up the subject of the stone. They all knew about the number scratched on it, but there was one detail they didn't know. Something she would have told McNab, had she been allowed to before the meeting.

Rhona indicated Roy should bring up her images and detailed analysis. Then she began.

'A forensic examination of the stone in the victim's mouth indicated it wasn't local. In fact, the stone in question is the geological equivalent of the stones used to build the Ring of Brodgar in Orkney.' She paused for a moment, aware that Superintendent Sutherland was listening intently. 'The stone in the mouth of the young woman found in the Ring of Brodgar in similar circumstances some forty-eight hours after our crime, doesn't belong to Orkney, but has been identified as similar to that of the stones found on Cathkin Braes.' She paused briefly before adding what had to be said. 'After visiting the Orkney locus on the invitation of Professor Magnus Pirie, who has worked with us on a number of cases, and seeing the body in situ, it is my forensic opinion that the two crimes are linked and may therefore have been committed by the same perpetrator.'

They were back in McNab's office and if the atmosphere had been cool before, it was arctic now.

'What the fuck do you think you're doing springing that one on me?' McNab said in a quietly ominous voice.

'You didn't give me a chance before,' Rhona began.

'You made me look like a prick.'

'You can do that all by yourself,' she countered, even though she knew he was right. She should have found a way to tell him about the stones before the meeting. And throwing in Magnus had been like a red rag to a bull. She had compromised McNab in front of his commanding officer and he had every right to be angry.

Rhona was formulating an apology when McNab said quietly, 'I can't work with you any more, Dr MacLeod.'

His words were like a slap in the face. She'd expected a bust-up. She and McNab were good at that. She hadn't expected what amounted to a dismissal. McNab couldn't order her off the case, but he didn't have to confer with her personally about it. Their relationship had always been spiky, but good teamwork needed trust, and she, it seemed, had betrayed his.

'Okay,' she said. 'I'll pass the reporting work on to someone else to do.'

McNab didn't look up from his desk when Rhona left. She had shafted him with the geological info on the stone, but it was, he had to admit, partly his own fault. He'd been unnerved by the 'where are the hands pointing' routine. That and her mention of Patrick Menzies. He'd mocked her concerns and cut off any chance she had of giving him details of the stones before the meeting. The truth was he had a bad feeling about this case and being in charge seemed to be messing with his brain. But he was hardly going to admit that to Rhona or anyone else.

He tried to look on the bright side. With Dr MacLeod out of the picture, he would be feeding one less obsession. As if on cue, his mobile rang. McNab glanced at the screen to find Iona's name. He didn't answer and a few seconds later a text pinged in.

Opening the bottom drawer of his desk, McNab felt at

the back for the half-bottle and shot glass. Like an illicit smoker, he'd become obsessed about someone smelling whisky on his breath in the office. DI Wilson had always kept a bottle of whisky in the filing cabinet, but for celebratory purposes only and he was quick to bring it out if he thought that any member of his team deserved praise.

On that thought, McNab slammed the drawer shut.

He lifted the internal phone and called the Tech department. It was the new guy who answered. He sounded as young as he looked. McNab wondered when they'd started employing twelve-year-olds.

'DI McNab. I was about to call you. We've found something on Alan MacKenzie's computer that might be of interest.'

'I'll be right there.'

McNab sat for a moment. He knew what he had to do, but it stuck in his craw. He eventually lifted the phone and dialled the number.

22

Kirkwall and its airport were swathed in a thick blanket of fog. The sea haar had rolled in on the town in the wake of the unusually warm summer weather. At times like this, you wished for the return of the wind. The western mainland had been basking in sunshine, Houton included, when Magnus left for Kirkwall. He'd met the creeping haar at Waulkmill Bay. The tide was out and the image of its glorious sands reminded Magnus of the first time he'd been asked to use his psychological skills in his island home.

He had been nervous about agreeing and aware that although he had the qualifications, he had yet to acquire the experience. Erling, a neighbour of the people involved, had been so persuasive, Magnus had at last conceded to his request. The case was a fascinating one. An incoming family had come to live in a remote farmhouse at Waulkmill Bay. To people used to the noise and thrust of London life, Waulkmill was a quiet haven of tranquillity. The parents certainly thought so. As did their seven-year-old son. At first all was well, until the boy began having shattering nightmares. His pleasure in his new home diminished to the point of almost complete withdrawal. From being frightened by night, he became frightened by day too, hardly venturing outside, when before he had spent most of his days wandering the shore.

Magnus had finally worked out what was making the boy so withdrawn and repressed. The boy's subconscious simply couldn't deal with the silence and the emptiness. A high wind could not replace the noise of traffic. Screaming seagulls could not replace the background sounds of a city of millions.

They'd tried various remedies, mostly involving recorded city sounds to fill the emptiness. It had helped a little, but not enough. Eventually the family had moved back south to the hustle and bustle, and the boy had recovered and thrived. The consolation for his parents was to spend short holidays on the island they'd fallen in love with, but could not live on.

As he entered Kirkwall, Magnus heard the fog horns blare from the port. He recalled hearing one the previous night as he'd eventually drifted off to sleep and realized that this fog was what it had foretold.

As he parked, he reminded himself what he planned to tell Erling. He'd decided not to mention the cannabis incident in the pub, but just to stress that he smelt cannabis on the victim's clothing and leave it at that. He did intend to mention the strange girl who had come to see him. She hadn't had an Orcadian accent, although nowadays that wasn't unusual. There were plenty incomers and plenty accents, from all over the UK and further afield. An email from Rhona this morning had given details of the PM on the Orkney victim. Doubtless Erling would know about the Polish tattoo and the geology of the stone in the victim's mouth.

They were all in the meeting room above the office. The windows that normally had a view towards the harbour, now looked out on grey soup. As a consequence, despite it being a midsummer morning, the overhead lights were on.

Magnus slipped in quietly and took a seat. The discussion was focussing on the recent discovery of the geological origins of the stones and the strengthening of the links between the two cases. With the advent of a single Scottish police force, the practice of sharing expertise had become the norm, sending in specialized teams wherever they were needed. The problem was incorporating local knowledge on the ground, and avoiding the unspoken suggestion that local officers just weren't good enough for the big cases, even on their own turf.

Sharing data through systems set up by R2S was straightforward. Anyone involved in investigating interconnected murders would be given authorized access to the online data. Magnus was not, as yet, official, although he hoped soon to be, courtesy of Erling and the Orkney case.

He wasn't sure how much he wanted to say about his discussions with Jack Louden. Police officers were pragmatic on the whole, and the theories he and Jack discussed would sound like fairy stories to most of those in the room. Having said that, myths and legends were part of Orkney folklore and they often had quite rational reasons behind them. Magnus sincerely hoped any thoughts he'd had about other possible locations were unfounded. Better, he decided, to stick to the facts they had now and hope that none of his wilder theories came to pass. He tuned in to what Erling was saying.

'I can confirm that I've spoken to Detective Inspector McNab, who is in charge of the Glasgow investigation. Due to the discovery of evidence of a cocaine stash close to the victim, he would like us to consider the possibility that both deaths may be drug related. We have conferred on all similarities and Dr Rhona MacLeod, the forensic expert who was here on site yesterday, has co-ordinated forensic details on both loci,' Erling said. 'We have as yet no confirmation of the identity of our victim, although we are pursuing the possibility that she is a Polish national, or connected to the Polish community. The Glasgow victim has been identified as Alan MacKenzie, a nineteen-year-old student. We are unaware of any link between the two victims. Clarifying this must be a priority.'

Having ended the session, Erling indicated he wanted to talk to Magnus in private. The team dispersed with a sense of purpose. The chance of working on a murder enquiry in Orkney didn't come along very often. Most police work here was routine, with increasingly drugs and social problems as the focus.

Erling ushered Magnus along the corridor and into his office.

'I'm assuming you want to be part of this?'

Magnus indicated that he did, but felt compelled to enlighten Erling on the possible problems that might bring.

'I've worked with DI McNab when he was a DS. We didn't exactly hit it off.'

'I know.'

Magnus was surprised.

'DI McNab made it clear that if I chose to have you on board, that was my business.' Erling raised an eyebrow. 'What did you do to piss him off?'

'He doesn't hold with psychologists trying to tell the police how to do their job. And he's been proved right in the past.'

Erling considered this. 'I don't promise to act on what

you say. But I will listen. And I'll authorize that you be given access to the online material. That way you'll know what's happening on both cases, without having to approach DI McNab.'

'Sounds good to me,' Magnus said gratefully.

Magnus brought up the subject of his young visitor and related what she'd had to say about the victim. 'I think she may have caught the ferry from Houton, but can't be sure. A smallish black car, make and number unknown, was heading swiftly for the main road at the same time as the ferry left.'

Erling asked for a description which Magnus supplied. 'She was pretty forward,' he added.

Erling smiled at his friend. 'I take it you don't frequent Kirkwall clubs when you're here. The social etiquette of teenagers is not the same as when we were that age.'

'We had our moments,' Magnus replied.

'Most of them behind the village hall with a half-bottle of whisky.'

That reminded Magnus to mention the scent of cannabis on the victim's clothing.

Erling wasn't surprised. 'There were deposits of resin on her clothes mentioned in the forensic report. Also evidence she'd been handling patons.'

'She was packing crab at the fish factory?'

'There's a number of Polish workers there doing the twelve-hour shifts no Orcadian wants,' Erling said. 'We're checking if she was one of them. So, are you staying on here or going south?'

'I thought I might head to Glasgow for a couple of days,' Magnus admitted before posing the question that had been preying on his mind. 'Can I ask if DI McNab mentioned anything about a prior warning of Alan MacKenzie's death?'

'What warning?'

Magnus explained about the medium, Patrick Menzies.

Erling's expression was highly sceptical. 'Clairvoyants are not encouraged in police work. I'm with DI McNab on that,' he said.

'But you don't mind me checking it out?'

'That's up to you.'

Magnus glanced at his watch as he drew away from the police station. He had half an hour before he needed to check in for the flight south. The mist had dissipated, increasing the likelihood that his flight to Glasgow would take off. He'd locked up properly before leaving Houton, and left a note for his nearest neighbour saying he would be away for a couple of days at least.

Kirkwall airport lay over the hill to the south of the town. On reaching the brow, the car emerged into bright sunshine. The contrast dazzled Magnus's eyes. The rolling fields were a glistening green. The cattle that provided the south with the famous Orkney beef dotted the fields.

The rich fertility of Orkney was always a surprise to first-time visitors, especially if they'd envisaged a landscape similar to that of Shetland. Orkney was the home of farmers who did a little fishing, while Shetland was the other way round. Oil had changed both sets of islands, but probably the Shetland Isles more than his home.

Magnus thought again about his visitor. If she'd caught the ferry, she could have been en route to Lyness on Hoy, or the island of Flotta, grown in population by its oil terminal facilities. Hoy, in contrast, was mostly uninhabited, though popular with visitors because of the beauty of the westward-facing Rackwick Bay and the Old Man of Hoy. The girl hadn't struck him as a walker or climber. Maybe she was working in one of the canteens on Flotta.

Waiting in the cafe for his flight call, Magnus went over her words to him again. She'd given the impression that the victim had interfered in something and this had brought about her death. But what? A drugs delivery? He had no doubt his visitor was a user of cannabis and maybe more. Her agitation and lack of control suggested amphetamines or cocaine. She'd wanted to tell him something. Magnus only wished Rhona had been there. Her presence might have made the difference.

He tried to think positively. He was officially on the case now, thanks to McNab. Something he hadn't reckoned with.

23

McNab hated being in the Tech department. If he were honest it was because he didn't understand any of it. Forensic was bad enough, but at least the experts weren't kids. In here was like being back at school with the swots and nerds who knew the answer to everything. It was their version of willie waving, or so McNab liked to think. Even when they tried to explain things in terms they believed an idiot like him would understand, he found himself tuning out mid sentence, in case he was infected by the weird digital insanity of it all.

He'd been in a bad mood when he arrived, having made the call to Orkney. He'd tried to congratulate himself for a wise and sensible move, but hearing DI Flett's accent had immediately reminded him of Pirie, and he'd made it plain he didn't want to work with that particular Orcadian. To give him his due, Flett had been unfazed by that and had offered a compromise McNab could just about put up with.

So now, having parked two of his obsessions for the moment, he should have been a happy man. But the ridiculously young face sitting in front of a large computer screen, displaying what looked like a game, was seriously pissing him off. McNab registered that once again he'd been focussing on his negative thoughts rather than what the boy wonder was saying.

'Run that past me one more time,' McNab said.

'From where?' The youthful voice sounded eager and not the least bit irritated by McNab's inattention.

'From the beginning.'

'Okay. Briefly, the victim was a keen online gamer. He played most of the popular ones and ranked high on all their charts.'

The word 'boring' resounded in McNab's head, but he managed not to voice it and nodded to go on.

'However, in a hidden and passworded area, I found another game.'

McNab's immediate thought was that it was pornographic, but that was quickly squashed.

'It's a Druid-themed game currently being played, I think, by five people.' He brought up a stylized map of what looked like the UK. On it were a number of crosses. McNab ran an eye over them.

'There're twenty-five crosses,' the boy wonder was saying. 'I think they mark Neolithic or Druid sites . . . like this one.' He pointed to Orkney.

McNab had already spotted that one and the one due south of Glasgow. He muttered 'Jesus' under his breath.

'Who's playing this game?'

'Their avatars are all Druid in origin. Myrrdin, Caylum, Erwen, Morvan and Moonroth.'

'What's an avatar?'

The boy wonder looked startled and a little fearful at McNab's tone.

'Their online persona,' he said. 'A name, usually accompanied by a stylized image of the person they're pretending to be.'

'What's this game about?'

'I haven't been able to engage with it yet and I can't find any mention of it on any of the discussion boards.'

'So why the hell summon me here?' McNab snapped.

The Tech guy flushed, making him look even younger.

I'm bullying a child, whose name I don't even know, McNab thought.

'What's your name?'

'Ollie.'

Fuck, what kind of handle was that? Thank God he wasn't wearing specs. He looked enough like Harry Potter as it was. 'Okay, Ollie, I need you to locate and identify these gamesters for me as quickly as you can,' McNab said in a softer tone.

The flush faded to be replaced by a determined look.

'And get back to me if you find anything, no matter how small. Okay?'

'Right, sir.'

McNab decided he had to know. 'What age are you, Ollie?'

'Twenty-four.'

Had he looked that young at twenty-four? A picture of Iona reared up in his mind. This was the age of the guy she should be screwing, but somehow he didn't think Ollie would appeal. Not unless he had a couple of death-defying scars as collateral.

'Anything on the computer apart from games?'

'Mostly university work. Maths problems, which I don't understand.' He gave a wry smile.

'Emails?' McNab tried.

'He had a uni account for his lectures etc., and a personal account. There's nothing in the personal account that mentions the game.'

'So a mystery, eh?'

'That's half the fun. As well as not knowing who you're up against.'

McNab thought it sounded like his job, if you omitted the fun part.

On leaving the Tech department, he decided it was time to get away from the police station. There was one job he couldn't hand over to anyone else, not even his DS.

McNab picked up his car and headed south. The continuing sunshine that bathed his city in a mellow glow seemed to mock him, suggesting that Glasgow had no shadowland, no places where evil flourished and dark deeds were done. McNab knew better. Behind closed doors, bad things were happening, even as he passed them by. Some he might get to hear about. Many, he never would. Even if he kept his ear to the ground and had his team of black ops out there, ever keen to exchange information for a monetary award.

McNab had never understood his hidden troops. Being a spy had never appealed, unless while watching James Bond's latest outing. The snitches he knew weren't handsome, and they weren't babe magnets either. The majority were so close to the ground that those they informed on had probably stepped on them already without even noticing.

Still, he needed them as much as they needed him.

The drive out gave him time and space to mull over what had happened in the last few days. Much of which he didn't like. His theory of a gang-related killing on Cathkin Braes was developing more holes than a sieve. Yet he couldn't shake off the feeling that the buried cocaine stash was somehow involved. DI Flett had indicated they'd found traces of cannabis resin on the Orkney victim and confirmed that they had a real problem with all types of drugs getting into Orkney. Flett hadn't been averse to connecting this to the death of his island victim.

McNab forced himself to consider the alternative: that the deaths were linked by the game that Ollie – he winced again at the name – had discovered on Alan MacKenzie's computer. Surely it was too much of a coincidence that he'd been playing a game with four others, which involved the Neolithic site he'd died on? And what about the stones and the decreasing numbers? He'd been sharp with Rhona about that, but she'd been right to consider it, just as she'd been right to study the geology of the stones. Something he hadn't thought of.

McNab allowed himself to consider another uncomfortable question. What the hell did Patrick Menzies have to do with it all, if anything? McNab was a natural and committed sceptic. Death was death. The end of. Kaput. There were no voices from beyond the grave. No messages. Menzies was a trickster, a fraud who tortured bereaved people with nonsense about the afterlife. In that he was no different from other religious nutters.

But the Druid game had to be thought about, whether he liked it or not.

McNab considered what Ollie had said about gamers. How they loved their secrets and their mysteries, and the fun of not knowing who or what they were up against. He had a sudden image of himself as a participant in one of those games. Only he was the one the rest were whispering about behind his back. The one being set up for a fall.

*

The plane wasn't as tiny as the Loganair that served the smaller northern and western islands, but it wasn't big enough for Magnus's tall body. He was in the single row seats on the left of the aircraft, so at least he could ease his long legs in the aisle now and again. Thankfully, the journey was only fifty minutes so he'd be back in his waterfront apartment within the hour.

He'd used the time in transit to check out details on the spiritualist church and Patrick Menzies. As far as believers were concerned, Menzies had a formidable reputation, despite the little-boy-lost look in the accompanying photograph. Testimonials were numerous and complimentary. He gave the bereaved what they sought, which didn't mean much in Magnus's eyes. Grief was a powerful emotion that could lead to experiences little short of psychosis. Meeting with the dead while asleep. Talking to them. Walking with them. Asking forgiveness for wrongs done and words left unsaid was a normal part of grieving, even though it did resemble mental illness at times.

Magnus had a great deal of time for the subconscious. He often relied on his own to work while he slept and present him with the solution to a problem when he awoke. If the brain was left to its own devices, it was capable of extraordinary bursts of insight. However, communing with the dead was not, in Magnus's opinion, one of them.

He took a taxi from the airport and, changing his mind, asked to be taken to Glasgow University instead of to his flat. Rhona, in a return text, had indicated she was at the lab. It seemed important to speak to her in person as soon as possible.

When the receptionist called up to Rhona's lab, he was asked to wait and told she would be down directly. Magnus felt a little guilty arriving unannounced and guessed Rhona would immediately think something was wrong.

The concerned look on her face as she emerged from the lift confirmed this.

'Has something happened?'

Magnus quickly assured her. 'I'd like a word. Do you have time to talk?'

She hesitated. 'Okay, but it'll have to be quick.'

She led him along a corridor to a room with a coffee machine. It was empty apart from a young woman in a lab coat in the far corner, absorbed in a copy of *The List*. On their arrival, she seemed to realize she'd been there long enough. She abandoned the magazine and exited, paper cup in hand.

Rhona indicated the machine. 'Coffee?'

Magnus shook his head. 'I don't want to keep you.'

'Okay, let's sit.' She chose a place near the window.

Magnus began by telling her he was now officially on the case, courtesy of DI McNab.

That astonished her. 'McNab okayed it?'

'Provided I keep out of his way.'

She gave a small laugh. 'Much like myself.' She paused. 'So what next?'

'I plan to check out Menzies and the spiritualist church.'

'Good luck with that.' Rhona glanced at her watch. 'I should get back before Chrissy blows a fuse.'

'There's one more thing. I had a visitor at Houton. A teenage girl.' Magnus gave a brief summary of his encounter, omitting the sexual aspect.

Rhona was reading his expression. 'She knew the victim?'

'She said she was a stupid bitch who meddled in things she shouldn't have.'

'And that meddling caused her death?'

'That's what she implied.'

'Did she mention Alan or Cathkin Braes?'

Magnus said no. 'Although she was definitely strung out on something, so McNab could be right and the Orkney death is drug related.'

'She's the first real lead we've had,' Rhona said. 'Let's hope they find her.'

24

Visiting divers often took their best memories from Burra Sound. That's what he'd been told when he'd signed up for a week's diving in Scapa Flow. It had been a magic week so far. Great diving during the day, and plenty of fun in the pubs of Stromness in the evening. Ashley was really sorry to be heading back home to Manchester and work tomorrow.

But he still had today and Burra Sound to look forward to.

Chugging out from Stromness this morning, he'd almost convinced himself he could move to Orkney. He would have to find a job, of course, though the island appeared pretty buoyant even in a recession. But could he live without the Manchester club scene? And what he'd heard about the winter weather, not to mention the long hours of darkness, did quell his enthusiasm somewhat.

Still, darkness and bad weather wasn't an issue today. After the high winds of the summer solstice, the weather had settled into mild and calm. Burra Sound, he knew, was pretty tidal and dives could only be made at slack water, but according to Mike, their dive leader, that meant the visibility was exceptional. And one of the dives today featured the *Tabarka*, a 2,642-ton merchant ship lying in 12 to 18 metres of water, recently voted 'Scotland's best scenic dive' by *Diver Magazine*.

LIN ANDERSON

He'd come alone for the week, his city dive buddies otherwise engaged. It was always a bit tricky when you came solo and were paired with a new and untried partner, but he liked Debbie. She knew her stuff, even if she was a bit on the cautious side. Better that, he reminded himself, than the gung-ho guy he'd had to deal with on a South of France trip a couple of years ago.

They'd had a lot of fun, on the dives and afterwards, but they'd kept sex strictly out of the equation, even though he'd been sorely tempted at times. Debbie was attractive in a healthy sort of a way and nothing like his usual dance-club conquests. No make-up, no short skirts and high heels, but he liked her trim, muscled body. Wearing a dry suit, they all looked like the Michelin man, but once the kit was off and she was into jeans and a T-shirt, she was worth a second glance. He didn't do sex with a dive buddy, though, because it invariably complicated things when you just wanted them to watch your back.

So he'd fantasized about Debbie, but kept his dick in his pants. That didn't mean he'd had a lean week. Two days in he'd met a student working on an archaeological dig outside of town. She was from Manchester too and they'd hit it off . . . on the bed, against the wall, in the shower, on the floor. Ashley smiled at the memory.

'Hey, a penny for them,' Debbie said.

'Too graphic, even for you,' he joked.

She smiled, then turned abruptly away.

'You okay?' Ashley asked.

'Just a little sad to be going home,' she admitted.

'Me too.' Ashley wondered at that moment whether he should ask for her mobile number, whether she would

170

want him to. He suddenly realized tonight could be the night. The buddy relationship would be over after today's dive. He caught her eye and gave her what he hoped was an encouraging smile. She laughed in return, but Ashley wasn't sure whether it was *at* him or *with* him. That was the problem with girls who weren't obvious. How the hell did you know if they fancied you?

He was saved from further ruminations by the boat slowing down and Mike signalling that they should step off into the water. Debbie was first in, followed by him, then the other two pairs. They all headed for the buoy above the wreck. When they got there, he and Debbie exchanged signals and began their descent.

The old merchant ship, sunk originally elsewhere in the Flow and later dragged here by the Royal Navy, was lying upside down. A strong tidal stream had stripped her clean of silt. Sunlight filtering down through the water danced like a million star drops on her bulk. No wonder they called ships 'she', Ashley thought. To his eye, the majestic hulk resembled a glistening Pre-Raphaelite woman stretched out along the seabed.

The dive would be predominantly inside the body of the ship. From an entry point in the stern, there followed two layers to explore, ending with the engine rooms, much of the machinery still identifiable. Mike had indicated that natural light entered all along her length, so a torch wouldn't be needed.

As they approached the kelp and barnacle-encrusted hull, they were suddenly surrounded by a cloud of tiny transparent ghost shrimp being grazed by a shoal of fish. Ashley recognized them as pollack, common in these waters. Greenish black above a silver lateral line, with a white underbelly, the pollack darted around the divers, intent only on the annihilation of as many shrimp as possible.

They were at the stern now, where two openings had been blown for access. Ashley watched as their fellow divers entered the lower opening, then signalled to Debbie that they should head for the upper level. Once inside they would be almost completely enclosed. He okayed Debbie to take the lead, knowing that would please her.

Entry proved straightforward. They'd been told this particular dive spot was a giant underwater playground and first impressions suggested that was true. That and the promised image of a cathedral, light pouring in through the various openings like stained-glass windows.

From the outside, the wreck had looked promising. Inside, it was a veritable Aladdin's cave. Ashley immediately headed for a cluster of jewel anemones. A kaleidoscope of florid pinks, lime greens and yellow gemstones, cushioned in delicate maerl algae, they resembled a display in a gaudy jeweller's shop window.

He signalled to Debbie that he wanted to stop and take some photos. She okayed him, as mesmerized as he was by the vision before them. He took a 360-degree video, then settled on single images, already planning on sharing them with fellow divers on Flickr.

They finned their way slowly towards the bow, constantly tapping one another on the shoulder when they found something interesting to study or photograph. Down here, among all this wonder and beauty, breathing oxygen-charged air, Ashley came to a decision. He would ask for Debbie's number. Maybe it was time he went for a less obvious girl. One who could share his passion for diving, rather than clubbing.

They would soon be at the bow. Debbie slowed, waiting for him. Again he indicated she should take the lead, knowing she liked that. The way out was narrow and, they'd been warned, a little tricky. Care had to be taken not to get caught on the jagged, encrusted metal or, once outside, to be caught in a tidal surge and separated.

Emerging successfully, they paused to watch a rising bubble of air as the sun's rays caught and painted it all the colours of the rainbow. The bubble expanded as the water pressure lessened, flattening itself into the shape of an upturned saucer, rotating, refracting sunlight. Ashley and Debbie exchanged glances, dive buddies, appreciating what they, together, had just seen.

The bubble was followed by another, and another. A shoal of tiny fish darted amongst the bubbles, grazing on some microscopic food. Ashley spotted a crab perched on a metal strut, feeders tipped red, scooping the same source of food into its open mouth.

A further cluster of bubbles escaped from below and rose up. Ashley decided one of their fellow divers must be emerging from the lower layer of the wreck, but when he looked there was no sign of dry suits and air tanks.

Curious now, he indicated he planned to descend deeper to investigate and Debbie followed. A little dimmer here, he tracked the escaping bubbles to what looked like a dark blue cylinder, a few metres long. His first thought was that it might be a rolled sail, lost overboard from a passing yacht.

The rule was never to touch things found in or around wrecks, especially here in Scapa Flow where some wrecks were designated graveyards, but the *Tabarka* had been a merchant ship and deliberately sunk and Ashley could see no issue with a sail. He tapped Debbie on the shoulder, indicating he wanted to approach for a better look.

They moved forward together.

Closer now, he realized the material wasn't sailcloth but blue nylon, anchored in place by a cord that had become caught in the jagged metal of the hull. His immediate reaction was to reach out and touch the object. What happened next was completely unexpected. The roll of nylon began to writhe as though filled with life. Ashley finned back, startled, as more gas escaped in a cloud of bubbles, followed by small darting fish and another crab. Ashley glanced at Debbie, seeing the laughter in her eyes suddenly changing to shock.

The movement had freed the cord from its metal restraint. The obstacle rolled in the current and they were presented with its underside. It took seconds for them to register what they were looking at. It was a face, the eyes, cheeks and lips of which were pulsating with scores of voraciously feeding tiny fish.

Debbie screamed, the sound swallowed by her mouthpiece, then suddenly the body was whisked away from them in the current. Ashley acted instinctively, grabbing the cord, wrapping it round his wrist.

Now the corpse and Ashley were one, bound together until he could rise to the surface, dragging death behind him.

25

The pub hadn't changed. It was still sporting a big, somewhat frayed Union Jack above the bar, reminding McNab that he was a left footer in a right-footed establishment. Thoughts on independence for Scotland hadn't crossed this threshold. Neither had thoughts of supporting a rival football team, despite the recent financial struggles of their own.

But there had been one change. The clientele was no longer uniformly white, although the areas of the bar they chose seemed to have demarcation lines. McNab wondered too at the Polish voices, as he'd assumed that the majority of Poles were Catholic. As for the Turks and Romanians, he had no idea which religious flavour they preferred.

The text he'd sent from the car had remained unanswered, but he was hopeful his contact would appear. Money was always short here. Money for drink, money for drugs, for the rent, especially now that they had to pay up front for that extra room. And he'd indicated he was willing to pay a substantial amount for information that would lead to his enlightenment on that cocaine stash.

McNab ordered a pint and took it over to a corner table, marked by cigarette burns but no longer sporting an ashtray, full or otherwise. In all honesty, he'd preferred the smoke-filled version of the place – back then, meetings were less obvious.

He was an inch from finishing his drink when Big Davy walked in. Broad rather than tall, he carried himself with confidence and a sense of belonging. Davy wouldn't cower in the corner like McNab, hoping no one would notice his presence. He didn't glance McNab's way, but he'd sussed him nonetheless. McNab carried on reading the beer-stained copy of the *Daily Record* he'd found on the seat. It was yesterday's edition, but the doom and gloom were the same. Davy ordered a pint and drank a half of it like a man with a thirst, then he took out his fag packet and headed outside.

McNab, knowing the drill, followed. Smoking was another obsession he'd managed to shake off, until he'd ended up in the police safe house, where death at Russian hands had begun to look better than the crushing boredom. So he'd reawakened the habit to pass the time. A mistake he was still paying for.

Davy was standing on his own, inhaling a few swift draws to take the edge off his craving. He didn't turn when McNab lit up beside him. McNab tried not to inhale and failed.

'Been up the Braes recently?' McNab said by way of entry to the conversation.

Davy made a sound that might have been a laugh. 'What's up there then?'

'A snowfall.'

Davy took another draw. McNab tried not to.

Eventually Davy came back with, 'I heard it didn't lie long.'

'True, but when it went, it left something behind.'

Davy remained silent, working his cigarette until he'd sucked it dry. He dropped the end and ground it out underfoot. McNab forced himself to do the same.

'The snowman had nothing to do with that,' Davy said.

'So no connection between the snow and the deposit in the stone circle?' McNab said to make sure.

Through the smoke, Davy's cold eye fastened on McNab. 'Didn't I just say?' he spat at him.

'So where's the snow now?' McNab tried.

Davy smiled. 'Falling all over the place.'

'Orkney?'

Davy grunted. 'Who knows and who the fuck cares?' He held out his hand. 'Got a spare smoke, *Inspector*?'

McNab handed him the packet, sorrier to see the cigarettes go than the money he'd tucked inside. Davy headed back in. From the doorway, McNab saw him order up another pint, this time accompanied by a whisky chaser. Davy was spending his earnings already.

McNab stood for a moment, wishing he'd handed over the money inside the copy of the *Daily Record* instead. He licked his lips. Even that slight encounter with nicotine was buzzing his blood and his brain. Giving up fags was harder than celibacy. He'd certainly thought about smoking, dreamt about it, at least as often as sex.

He spat the taste out of his mouth and tried to focus on what he'd got, which wasn't much. Davy had intimated that the body and the coke were unrelated. That could be a lie, but who would draw attention to a stash by leaving a body behind? Then again, they didn't know that someone would dig up the stash and call the cops. If just the body had been found, there wouldn't have been a connection.

As far as a fucking game was concerned, McNab decided, he was definitely on Level 1, assuming there was nothing lower than that.

He'd parked the car round the back. It looked lonely

sitting there on the crumbled asphalt. As he slipped in and started up the engine, a big black Mercedes tank with a heavy metal grille up front, swept in to keep him company.

Very close company.

So close McNab could no longer open the driver's door, even if he'd wanted to. The buzzing in his brain upped tempo as nicotine met with a sudden surge of adrenaline.

McNab hit reverse and roared back, spraying stones. The tank went into reverse too, right across his path. McNab slammed on the brakes and caught a whiff of smoke, rubber-scented this time, as the back of his car pinged against the tank's grille.

He forced the stick into first and, foot on the accelerator, ramped up to third and took off, just as the tank gave him a shove. Now he was flying forward towards a sagging fence. He swerved right at the last moment as the tank roared in from behind. With its heavy metal grille it cared less about hitting the fence than about squashing him.

McNab screeched a circle, smoke coming from his wheels in a black cloud as he left his treads behind. He cursed himself for lingering, for not leaving the car out on the main road, ready to jump into. He was definitely losing his touch. Or else deliberately courting trouble in search of excitement or a hard-on.

A glance in the rear-view mirror showed that the tank had turned and was on its way, burning as much rubber as he had. When McNab swivelled to the front again, he found three masked youths, hoods up, standing across the exit, each holding a machete.

'Shit!'

He pressed his foot to the floor. The one in the middle

was the last to abandon ship, but not before hurling his machete at the windscreen. It hit with a crack and flew off as McNab bounced the car via the intervening pavement and onto the road. He swerved left, aiming for the nearest main thoroughfare, knowing he had more than one back street to reconnoitre before then.

The posse was waiting at the T-junction. Another trio of machetes, suggesting they must be buying them bulk order. His one consolation was the absence of guns.

So far.

The tank was back on his tail, bearing down on him like Spielberg's truck in *Duel*. McNab decided to take no prisoners and mowed into the triplets, sending them flying. No one threw a weapon this time, but a shower of stones hit his rear window. He took another left at the junction, passing a wide-eyed woman with a pram, praying that the truck would miss her too.

Then he was out and onto the main road, squeezing himself between a bus and a pissed-off Volkswagen, whose driver blared his horn.

McNab gave him the finger.

Once clear, he contemplated calling in to report that the natives were restless in the area of the Union bar, but decided against it. By the time a couple of cars had reached their destination, all would be quiet on the western front. He'd gone snooping and someone had taken offence.

He headed for the flat, in need of a drink – more than one, in fact – and there was the safest place to indulge. When he pulled up outside, he checked his face in the mirror to find a bloody cut where his head had slammed into the windscreen. He wiped it clean with his arm. It wouldn't do to scare the neighbours.

The flat, on entry, seemed different. He sniffed the air. Where was that familiar fusty smell of dirty dishes and unwashed clothes? He opened the inner door and looked about in surprise. The room was clean. No piles of dishes in the sink. No clothes lying around.

Iona!

He marched into the bedroom. There was no one there, but the bed had been changed, something he couldn't remember when he'd last done.

McNab swore very loudly and slammed the door shut again.

Back in the kitchen, he went in search of the whisky. She'd washed all the glasses and put them in a cupboard along with the bottle. He poured himself a large glass and drank it. Being in a room that didn't smell, he could suddenly smell himself, a mixture of sweat and fear. He poured another shot and headed to the shower.

Undressed, he examined himself in the mirror. If they'd pulled him out of the car, what would he look like now? McNab had a sudden flashback to his hours tied to the chair under examination, Russian style. He'd ridden the pain then with ever-increasing anger. Eventually he'd come to embrace it, even welcome it, because it had pissed off his torturer so much. If you can't frighten with the promise of pain, what the hell can you do?

He'd begun to understand then what sadomasochists sought. The way in which pain and pleasure became linked. How whipping and being tightly bound could bring blood surging to the surface, making anticipation of what was to follow both exquisite agony . . . and ecstasy.

He was pumped up like that now. He let himself imagine finding Iona here and what he would have done to her, partly from anger, partly from relief that he had outwitted his attackers – Mercedes man and the hooded wee punks.

He caught tight to the sink and let the feeling wash over him.

The ring of his mobile brought him back to the here and now. Glancing at the screen, he found Iona's name.

Serendipity.

26

Everyday actions can quickly dislodge items of trace evidence indicating where you've been, and who you've had contact with.

Unless, of course, you die.

From the moment of death, assuming your body is left in situ, the rate of loss decreases rapidly. Which means evidence of your killer is on you. As you are on your killer.

The problem lay in identifying those traces and finding a match. It was a problem Rhona relished. At times like this it seemed that there was a mountain to climb, but then again she liked climbing mountains.

She'd already prepared her report on the tool used to remove the hands. Chopping wounds were created by hatchets, axes, machetes, meat cleavers or swords. The weight of which might render even thin, unsharpened edges effective. Occasionally the sharpened edges could transect the bone with little effort. Sometimes she saw trench-like fractures with comminuted edges, where the bone was powdered by the impact.

In this case, the weapon, which she believed to have been a machete, had been ultra sharp and used cleanly. The style, shape and metal, she was still working on, but it hadn't been a painted or patterned blade, so no weird

Samurai ancient metal forged in history like a Hollywood movie. Any of the popular machetes might match it. Sharp, decisive, honed to perfection, whoever had wielded it had known their trade.

From his stomach contents, she'd deduced that Alan's final meal had consisted of a plain bagel with peanut butter, and black coffee, consumed a couple of hours before his death and not fully digested. There were no toxic substances that might have indicated he'd been poisoned. In fact, none of the forensic work so far had revealed why the heart of a fit young male had suddenly stopped beating.

Until the recent arrival of the toxicology report.

The PM had found no evidence of needle marks on the body, no external or internal evidence that suggested Alan was a regular drug user. But it required only one point of entry for an overdose. In this case, a combination of heroin and cocaine, in substantial quantities, had been injected directly into a vein. Cocaine would have sent his heart racing. Heroin would have slowed it down. The rapid change in heart rate was the most common cause of overdose amongst speedball users.

So McNab had been right. The death had been drug related, but not, she thought, gang related. Rhona considered calling McNab to see if he'd seen the report, then remembered he didn't want to work with her any more. From now on Chrissy had to be the go-between. Chrissy had accepted the role, but only after she'd grilled Rhona about the reasons for it.

'Okay, I'll do it. If only to keep the peace,' she'd added nobly.

'I remember a time you and McNab weren't on speaking terms.'

Chrissy had chosen to ignore that reminder and they'd left it at that.

Rhona experienced a pang of regret, tinged with frustration. Whenever McNab felt threatened he acted like a piss artist, which is why they could never be an item. She recalled his young admirer at the party and hoped he'd had the sense to check her actual age before bedding her. Maybe his love life, or lack of it, was the reason he was so on edge? Such thoughts led back to memories of her last brush with Sean. Not somewhere she wanted to go.

She brought up the images of the body at post-mortem. The most popular injection site was the crook of the arm. After that, the forearm. As sites became infected or veins collapsed, addicts went for trickier places such as the thin veins on the back of the hands, or the fingers, all of which could prove painful and required finer needles. The femoral vein in the thigh came next. Dangerous if you missed the vein and hit an artery.

Alan wasn't an addict and had been wearing shorts and a T-shirt, so plenty of sites available and easily accessible. Assuming he hadn't administered the injection himself, how had it been accomplished and where?

Rhona revisited the images she'd taken of the body in situ. Alan had been lying face down in a supplicant's pose. From the state of the body, he'd lain in that position since death. Perhaps he'd been lying like that when the drug had been administered?

Her eyes went to the neck. Injecting into the neck was a no-no for most addicts. They usually needed help or a mirror to achieve it. There was also the danger they would hit an artery and bleed to death. But if you wanted someone dead, whether they bled to death from your attempts at injection or died from the overdose wouldn't much matter.

Rhona magnified her images of the neck for a closer look.

Five minutes later she called the mortuary.

Dr Sissons listened to her in silence. Not the easiest of men, he didn't like his work questioned. The fact that he didn't interrupt with a dismissal suggested he was at least intrigued by her suggestion.

'I'll take another look,' was his short reply.

Rhona, pleased, settled back to examining the material she'd taped from the clothes and body. If the killer had administered the drug from behind, he'd made contact with the clothes and the body while doing so.

Magnus took a seat at the rear of the room, which was swiftly filling up. The Thursday medium session was proving popular. The audience was predominantly women, mostly middle-aged to elderly. There was a scattering of couples, but very few people looked younger than mid thirties. Magnus guessed it went with the territory. You had to have experienced the death of someone close to you and the older you got the more likely that became. A man his age stood out from the crowd, when he really wanted to blend in. That had been his reason for considering inviting Rhona to accompany him here. They would have looked like a couple, perhaps mourning the death of an elderly parent, or even a child.

After failing to ask her during their meeting, he'd later sent a text, giving the time and suggesting she come along. The spiritualist church was a five-minute walk from her flat on top of the hill that rose behind this section of

Sauchiehall Street, though she probably hadn't been aware of its presence until now.

There had been no response from his text, so he'd come in alone.

Tonight there wasn't a service prior to the mediumship. Magnus was glad about that. He wasn't a churchgoer, except for attendance at island funerals or special services held in St Magnus Cathedral, and would have felt an even bigger fraud singing hymns under these circumstances.

At the allotted time, the door to his left swung open. Sensing the medium's arrival, the crowd hushed and turned in his direction. Menzies was short, a little plump, with an air of hesitancy. For a moment he stood as though paralysed by those stares, then he turned and looked directly at Magnus. They locked eyes for a moment, then Menzies walked down the aisle towards the front.

Magnus studied the expressions on the faces of the audience as Menzies passed them by. On some, he would have described it as close to rapture. Whatever Magnus thought, these people believed in what this man was about to say. Magnus strove to clear his mind. If he was to evaluate, he must do so as a psychologist. He was not here to mock, but to try and understand.

Menzies had gained the stage. He took up his place in the centre and gazed out across the room, packed with people waiting to hang on to his every word. The atmosphere was tense and full of expectation. His audience was there because they had lost someone they loved and wanted them back, even in the guise of a few words from beyond the grave. Even if those words were simply lies.

Menzies appeared ill at ease, as though what was about to happen was not of his choosing. Magnus wondered how much of that was for show. The medium eventually welcomed the audience in a halting voice, his eyes sweeping the room, pausing now and again to note the presence of a recognized face with a small smile and a nod. The frequency of these interchanges showed Magnus just how many members of tonight's audience were regulars.

Then he felt the medium's eyes rest upon him. The look was both questioning and, at the same time, encouraging. Magnus realized he was, with that look, being welcomed into the congregation, as a believer or unbeliever.

Menzies now offered up a small prayer for guidance before becoming very still, his eyes closed. Silence fell like a soft, enveloping blanket. A few moments passed, then Menzies began to speak as though to some disembodied voice at his shoulder. A shiver ran through Magnus. His senses on high alert, he became prey to the numerous scents surrounding him. Anxiety, fear, hope and grief. To his right a woman sat forward, her body rigid, her mouth moving silently. Magnus lip-read the repeated words, 'Please, God, please'.

In his pocket, his mobile vibrated an incoming call just as the medium opened his eyes and looked directly at Magnus. His gaze rested there a moment, then swept to the right.

'I have a message for Betty. Is there a Betty in the room?'

Three hands went up, including Magnus's desperate neighbour.

'The message is from Jim.'

Two hands were lowered, but not that of his neighbour.

She was on her feet now. 'I know a Jim,' she shouted as all eyes turned towards her. 'My husband.'

Menzies nodded and began a whispered conversation via his left shoulder, finishing with the words, 'God Bless'.

'Jim wants you to know that he is fine, Betty, and you've not to worry. He will always be with you.'

The woman gave a small sob of relief, and a ripple of approbation went through the crowd. Magnus felt a surge of anger at what appeared to him to be a charade. But his neighbour didn't think so. Sensing Magnus's eyes on her, she turned and gave him a watery smile. Any words of anger melted on his tongue.

The mobile vibrated again. This time he took it out and glanced at the screen to find Erling's name.

Magnus rose and made his way to the exit as Menzies made his second call. He didn't wait to hear who it was for.

'Erling?' he said as soon as the door swung shut behind him.

'A couple of divers found the body of a female, wrapped in a tent, in the wreck of the *Tabarka*. Someone had been camping at the Nissan huts on Hoy the day that young woman visited you.'

'And you think it's her?'

'It could be. The general description you gave matches, although there's not much left of her face. And no ID on the remains.'

'You want me to take a look?'

'If you would.'

'I'll catch an early flight tomorrow.'

Magnus stood in the brightly lit hallway. From beyond closed doors came the sound of clapping as Menzies continued to commune with the dead.

27

Rhona pushed open the flat door with a tired sigh of relief. A few seconds later Tom was at her side, his loud purring indicative of his pleasure at her arrival. Since her return from Orkney, he'd been especially affectionate. Her neighbour was happy to top up his food and water, but Tom liked company, especially of an evening.

Late sun washed the kitchen in a warm light. This was her favourite room, with its intimate view of the convent garden, an oasis of peace, which she retreated to at times – if not in body, then in spirit. The statue of the Virgin Mary stood in pride of place on the manicured lawn, cared for with love by the resident gardener. The two of them were acquaintances, although distant ones who resorted to smiles and waves to maintain their friendship.

City life was like that. A few firm friends and an ocean of others who, while not knowing you personally, were also part of your existence in small ways. The guy in the Italian shop where she bought her fresh pasta. The girl on the stand she bought her morning coffee from. The doorman at the forensic lab.

Rural life was different. There you belonged. Even though you might have moved away, you were always one of their own. She felt that about Skye, just the same way Magnus felt about Orkney. It was something they both understood.

Despite the circumstances, she'd enjoyed her return to the island. And things had gone okay with Magnus too. On that thought, she checked her mobile and found his message asking her to meet him at the spiritualist church. Not something she wanted to do at this moment in time.

She kicked off her shoes as though that decided things for her.

A shower then something to eat was her preference. Despite this, she did go through to the front room. Magnus had indicated that the church building was on the section of Sauchiehall Street not far from the steps that led down from the flat. It was a route she'd often taken on walks, although generally turning right before she met the main thoroughfare, choosing the streets that bordered the park or along by the Kelvin.

Curiosity suggested she ask Magnus to drop by after he'd spoken to Patrick Menzies. She decided to make up her mind after she'd had a shower and eaten. If he'd already talked to Menzies and gone home, then fate had played its hand and she was free to relax.

She ordered up a pizza, checked Tom's bowls had the requisite amount of food and water, then took herself off to the shower. By the time she was dried and dressed, the buzzer was heralding the arrival of her meal.

She opened her front door in anticipation, only to find not the pizza delivery man but McNab. Rhona stared at him in amazement.

'Aren't you going to invite me in?'

'Only if you're here to deliver pizza.'

'I hope you ordered a large one,' he said, pushing past.

Rhona followed him into the kitchen, wondering what

on earth had changed his mind about having anything to do with her.

'Whisky?' he said.

'Top cupboard along with the glasses.'

He retrieved the bottle. 'Are you having one?'

'I haven't eaten yet.'

'You'll need it when you see what I've got to show you.'

'That sounds ominous.'

'Fetch your laptop.'

'Why?'

'Because someone has blown our cover.' He glared at Rhona, suggesting he might be referring to her.

'What are you talking about?'

'Get the laptop,' he ordered.

Rhona fetched her bag from the hall and set up the laptop. She logged on, then McNab took charge. In a few minutes, she was presented with a basic outline map of the UK with a number of crosses on it. One of them rested on the main island of Orkney, another just south of where Glasgow would lie.

'According to the Techies, Alan was playing an exclusive game with only five players, which involved Druid sites around the UK. Until an hour ago, only myself and the Tech department were aware of this map. Now it's trending on Twitter.'

McNab was right, this was bad news. The police relied on help from the public and the media, but sensationalizing a case could greatly hamper the investigation.

'Does the Tech department have any idea who put the map online?'

'It wasn't us, that's for sure.' McNab threw her a look

that spoke volumes. 'Last I heard, Pirie was showing you a map of possible locations.'

Rhona wanted to deny this, but couldn't outright. 'Magnus and I discussed the direction of the hands and possible linked locations, which I urged you to consider. You chose not to,' she reminded him sharply.

McNab's retort was cut short by the sound of the buzzer.

Rhona went to answer it. The long-awaited pizza had arrived along with a second and probably unfortunate visitor. Rhona paid for the pizza, then ushered Magnus into the hall, motioning him to silence.

'McNab's here,' she said quietly.

'I'm sorry.' He looked embarrassed. 'I didn't mean to intrude.'

'He's after *your* blood, not *my* body.' She indicated the kitchen door and let Magnus enter first.

McNab's expression when she'd followed Magnus in brought the term 'stags at bay' to mind. If she'd had her mobile handy she would have taken a picture and sent it to Chrissy.

A bristling silence ensued for some time, probably because neither man wanted to concede any ground. McNab presented many of the characteristics of a high-testosterone male. Magnus was more subtle, but the need to control and to win was just as strong. They could have made a powerful combination, but that would require concessions on both sides, which wasn't happening at the moment.

Rhona ignored the stand-off, preferring to serve the pizza. She cut it into three slices, making hers the largest.

'I suggest we eat first and talk after.'

Her intervention appeared to break the stalemate.

McNab helped himself to another whisky, then set about his pizza slice. Magnus declined his portion, muttering that he'd already eaten, but he poured himself a whisky. Rhona finished her helping and eyed the third slice, before retrieving the knife and dividing it in two, pointedly taking the larger piece again. If McNab noticed, he didn't comment, but polished off what he was offered.

The box empty, Rhona put it in the recycling beside three more, making a mental note to switch to Indian or Chinese next time for a change. She replenished her own glass, added some water in view of the previous evening's proceedings, then drew Magnus's attention to the laptop, whose screen had switched off in the intervening meal break. His reaction when the map appeared was fairly dramatic.

'Where did you get this?' he demanded.

McNab was immediately in there. 'You recognize this map?'

'It looks similar to one Jack Loudon showed me.'

'Who the fuck's Jack Loudon?' McNab said.

'He's in charge of the dig on the Ness near the Ring of Brodgar.'

'You discussed the case with him?' McNab said in disbelief.

Magnus looked slightly uncomfortable. 'We discussed the layout of the bodies and any link that might have with their Neolithic locations.'

'Like what?'

'Whether they resembled Neolithic sacrifices.'

'And did they?'

'He couldn't say, but he did point out the significance of the hands.'

McNab had heard this line before, too often for his liking.

He held up his own hand to silence Magnus. It worked, but Magnus wasn't pleased at the reprimand. Rhona moved in before things got any warmer. She explained about the game.

'This map is associated with an online game Alan was playing with four others. Until now that wasn't common knowledge.'

'Now it's all over the internet,' McNab said.

Magnus looked aghast. 'And you think that has something to do with me?'

When McNab didn't answer, Magnus continued. 'First of all, I said it was similar, not the same. Jack's map was true to scale, unlike this one. Secondly, it only covered Scotland and a small portion of the north of England. There were a lot more sites marked, and they had ley lines between them.'

'What the hell's a ley line?' McNab said.

Rhona came in. 'An energy line, probably magnetic. Ancient civilizations built near or on them. You said there were five participants in this game. What if the Orkney victim was also playing it? And that's what connects the two deaths?'

Before McNab could answer, Magnus intervened. 'I don't think the Brodgar victim was involved in the game.'

He had McNab's attention now and his silence.

'I had a visit from a girl who I think was the intended victim at that location.' Magnus described his frightened visitor and their conversation.

'So we find *her*,' McNab interrupted. 'It can't be difficult in a place the size of Orkney. I thought everyone knew everyone else.'

'That's why I'm here. A couple of divers found what

they believe to be her body trapped in the wreck of the *Tabarka* off Hoy in Scapa Flow. DI Flett called me a short while ago. I'm headed up tomorrow to ID her.'

McNab's tenseness was replaced by fury. He rose and walked to the window, which was as far away from Magnus as was possible in the room. Rhona sensed he seriously wanted to smack Magnus in the face. It was time for her to intervene with her own news, which she suspected McNab wasn't yet aware of.

'The toxicology report revealed that Alan died from an injection of heroin and cocaine, probably administered in the neck.'

McNab turned to face them. 'I knew that bloody stash was involved somehow.'

'The girl who visited me was high on something,' Magnus added, as though to smooth the waters between himself and McNab.

'We don't know yet how the Orkney victim died,' Rhona reminded them, then voiced what she thought was the most important question. 'How soon before we find out the identities of the players in this game?'

'Ollie's working on it,' McNab said. 'He may look twelve, but I think he knows what he's doing.'

Rhona thought for a moment. 'What if it was the perpetrator who put the map online?'

Both men took time to digest this.

'You mean to up the stakes?' Magnus said.

McNab looked irritated. 'You're assuming the game is what this is all about.'

'No. But it's a line of enquiry we can't ignore,' Rhona said.

McNab shot her a withering look. 'Your job is to ask

questions of the crime scene, Dr MacLeod, not direct the investigation.'

Rhona realized McNab was back in defence mode, which generally ended in attack.

'I'd like you both to leave now,' she said firmly.

The two men regarded her in surprise.

'But we haven't finished—' McNab began.

'I have.' Rhona indicated the door.

They exited like two recalcitrant schoolboys.

Rhona watched them descend in angry silence. It almost made her want to laugh, if the reason for both their visits hadn't been so disturbing.

28

Now that his body had been released for burial, the reality of Alan's death had to be faced. Until today, Amy could periodically fool herself that everything that had happened had been a dream. That on Sunday, Alan would arrive as normal. To this end she'd bought a chicken as usual, and some of the beer he liked. She'd also topped up on dog food for Barney.

Her vigil at the window had continued. Lack of sleep and regular food had placed her in a semi-comatose state, prone to occasional hallucination. She heard Alan's voice as regularly as she heard Barney's bark. She caught Alan's fleeting shadow as he moved about the house, heard his music playing in his room. All of which she clung to as reality.

She did not eat Doreen's heart-warming stews and soups, or give in to her constant urging to come out for a coffee. She had let Doreen into the house, but her stays were curtailed and the conversation one-sided. Amy had not revealed her visit from the medium and had no intention of doing so.

When the female police officer had called, she'd let her in too, because somewhere in her grief-befuddled brain she knew she must. The news that Alan's body was at the undertaker's in preparation for burial she'd accepted without comment. She could not imagine burying her son, or cremating him, because she couldn't believe he was dead. And the visit from the medium had only served to reinforce this.

Her initial anger at Patrick Menzies had been replaced with a desire to be in his presence, because it made her feel closer to her son. They spoke on the phone regularly. It was Patrick who had arranged the undertaker for her. It would be he who took her there shortly to view the body of her son. She could accept this because she knew the body was only a shell and that Alan was still here with her.

Patrick was also trying to persuade her to speak to the detective on the case. He wanted her to relay the messages she was receiving from Alan. To set Alan free, he said.

Amy hadn't agreed to this. Not because she didn't want to help the police but because she was frightened that if she did so, Alan would leave and she would be truly alone. Finally and forever.

The doorbell sounded. Amy imagined Barney's bark in answer. She rose and went to open the door.

Patrick smiled in at her. 'Are you ready, Amy?'

She nodded.

'Then let's go.'

His car was small, very clean and smelt of lemons. Amy relaxed back into the seat. Being in Patrick's presence made her feel safe, as if Alan sat between them. Although it would be squashed in here with her big son. Amy smiled at the thought. They didn't talk on the way. Patrick never tried to get her to talk. It was as though they spoke silently to one another. He turned and gave her a soft look. Even his looks were kind.

She was dozing when they reached the funeral home and he had to touch her arm to waken her.

'We're here, Amy.'

For a moment she was paralysed by fear. 'I can't . . .'

He took her hand. 'You can.'

She gathered what little was left of her strength, and got out of the car. She noted nothing of the place on entry, spending all her time and effort putting one foot in front of the other. Patrick spoke to someone, a man, she thought, although she kept her head down. Then they were ushered into a room where soft music played. *This isn't Alan's music,* she thought. *We're in the wrong room.* She hesitated and Patrick took hold of her hand again.

'Come,' he said and led her to the coffin.

She looked down on her baby, man-size now, but still her baby. She reached over and touched his hair, thick and glossy as ever. How could his hair feel so alive?

'It's important to say goodbye,' Patrick said.

'He's not gone,' she reminded him.

'His spirit no, but this part of him, yes.'

Amy kissed her fingertips and touched the cold lips. 'Goodbye, my baby, my boy, my fine young man.'

She didn't register being led away, nor being placed in the car. Her next memory was Patrick getting in beside her.

'We have to speak to Detective Inspector McNab now,' Patrick said gently. 'Alan wants us to.'

29

Today had not begun well, just as yesterday had ended badly. Having ejected Iona when the news came through about the map going viral, he had similarly been ejected, along with Pirie, from Rhona's presence.

McNab had a feeling he was about to be ejected again. This time from the case, or from his role in it. The summons had been waiting for him when he'd arrived this morning. Returning home last night, he had slept very little and worried a lot. The map going viral was more than just a setback. It made the case UK news, and had already attracted international attention.

And it was drawing nutters like flies to a corpse.

An early visit to the Tech department had found a big-eyed Ollie with his eyes resembling those of his namesake. He'd been playing the night owl, and been bamboozled by how swiftly the map had captured the imagination of the digital community. He had also made some progress on the game.

'There are five levels.'

'Now there's a surprise,' McNab had said wearily.

'When you reach the fifth, you attain a higher level of consciousness, become something else . . .'

'Dead?'

Ollie obviously didn't do sarcasm. 'I think you attain a

new persona, get gold stars or something. Although it's supposed to be Druid-like, it only uses some of the real Druid stuff.'

The words 'real' and 'Druid' didn't belong in the same sentence, but McNab refrained from saying so.

'The Order of Bards, Ovates and Druids is a trilogy so doesn't match the pattern of five.'

McNab felt a wash of irritated disinterest sweep over him. 'Ollie,' he held up his hand. 'I need to know who's playing the game.'

'But if we understand the game, we could pinpoint where the next location will be.' He noted McNab's puzzled expression. 'If they reach level five, they're sent somewhere.'

'But they won't keep playing, not when they wake up to the fact that two of them are dead!'

Ollie was the puzzled one now. 'The game isn't out there yet. Only the map.'

McNab was seized by an idea. 'Why don't we expose the game and ask the players to come forward?'

Ollie shook his head in disbelief. 'You'll be inundated with nutters who say they're playing it and hackers trying to play it.'

With that worrying thought, McNab had departed, minus an answer for his commanding officer which either of them would like, or even understand.

The meeting with Superintendent Sutherland was scheduled for ten o'clock. McNab had the caffeine buzz by nine thirty in anticipation. That's when he got the message that Mrs MacKenzie was here, wanting to speak to him. What the front desk didn't mention was that she was accompanied by Patrick Menzies. McNab discovered this when DS Clark showed them into his office.

McNab threw his sergeant a look that suggested he would deal with her later, but it appeared to have little effect on her demeanour. McNab questioned once again if he was losing his touch.

He welcomed Mrs MacKenzie and offered her a seat, then was forced to shake Menzies' hand. That accomplished, he focussed on the woman. As far as McNab was aware, Alan's mother had not taken to Menzies. Now, from the manner in which she checked with him before speaking, that situation had changed.

'Detective Inspector,' she began. 'Alan . . .'

When she hesitated, McNab came in. 'His body has been released for burial?'

She nodded.

'And our liaison officer explained how we believe he died?'

She nodded again.

'I'm very sorry, Mrs Mackenzie, for your loss. I assure you we're doing everything we can to find who did this to your son.'

She glanced at Menzies and he gave her an encouraging look.

'I think I can help you with that,' she said, more strongly now.

'Have you remembered something that might help?' McNab said.

'No, but I've received messages about Alan . . .' She ground to a halt.

Menzies looked as though he might intervene, but didn't.

McNab's suspicions grew and began to flower. 'Messages? Like text messages, emails?'

'No, they come via Patrick.' She glanced again at Menzies. 'But they're from my son.'

McNab lifted the polystyrene cup and swallowed the remaining double-strength coffee to avoid an immediate response. Within seconds the caffeine buzz was back.

'Your son is dead, Mrs MacKenzie,' McNab said gently. 'Dead men don't send messages.'

'He wanted me to tell you he was playing a game. There were five of them. He's worried about the others.' Her hands trembled in her lap. Menzies reached over and patted her arm reassuringly.

McNab felt the hair on the back of his neck rise. 'What sort of game?'

She looked to Menzies again, who then said, 'I think a computer game over the internet.'

The hairs on the back of McNab's neck were still standing to attention. He ignored Menzies, who was leaning towards him, and concentrated on the woman.

'Do you know who else was playing this game with Alan?' McNab said.

She shook her head. 'We don't know, so we can't warn them.' Her voice trembled a little.

'Alan believes whoever set up the game intends their death,' Menzies said.

McNab glanced at the medium, resenting his intervention. 'And when exactly did this message from Alan arrive?'

'The first was on Monday night,' Menzies said. 'Alan has been in touch a number of times since, urging his mother to come and speak to you.' He hesitated. 'He has also tried to impart other information but,' he looked distressed, 'communication with those on the other side is not always clear, Inspector.'

McNab forced himself not to add 'because they're fucking dead'.

The office phone rang shrilly.

'Excuse me for a moment,' McNab said, grateful for the interruption, until he heard Janice's voice.

'You were due in with the super five minutes ago, sir.'

'I'd like you to take a statement, Sergeant, from Mrs MacKenzie and Mr Menzies about messages from Alan,' he said, and put the phone down.

'I apologize, Mrs MacKenzie. I have a meeting with my commanding officer about your son's case. DS Clark will take a statement from you.' McNab studiously avoided another Menzies handshake. The truth was he couldn't look at the medium without showing his distaste.

Once out of sight, McNab composed himself. Whatever happened, he had to give the impression he was on top of the case – notwithstanding voices from the dead and viral maps. He approached the super's room and knocked on the door.

He had never liked Superintendent Sutherland. Most people didn't like their boss, but he had been lucky with DI Wilson, whom he both liked and respected. Sutherland, to McNab's mind, was like a career politician, in the job for self-aggrandizement, rather than public service. The advent of the single police force had seen a mad scramble for the fewer higher echelon positions on offer. Sutherland had scrambled as hard as the next man, but hadn't reached pay-off and was thus a bit miffed. He still played golf with the great and the good according to office gossip, but that wasn't enough compensation for more power.

McNab suspected he was regarded by Sutherland on a good day as an irritant. On a bad day, as a scourge. Today was a bad day. McNab was reminded of a former head-master of his. When called to his study, you were required to stand as remote from his desk as possible, thus rendering you a small and distant fly in the headmaster's ointment. One that could be flailed at a distance by the whip-like strength of the master's tongue.

Here, McNab also remained at the door, although not so distant that he couldn't see the twitching nerve to the right of Sutherland's mouth, nor the rigidity of the muscles in his neck.

'I'd like an explanation, Detective Inspector.'

'About what exactly, sir?' McNab strove to keep his tone deferential.

'About how you're handling this case.'

'We are progressing, but it is a complex case involving two diverse locations. We've established how the Glasgow victim died and expect results on the Orkney victim shortly. We believe they may be connected via an online game which the Technical department is currently studying. There are five players, four of whose identities we have yet to confirm. My Glasgow sources tell me the cocaine find and the body are not connected.' He took a break as Sutherland held up his hand. McNab felt as irritated as Pirie had looked last night, when he'd done the same.

'How did this map and its implied connection to the case get online?'

'That we don't know, sir.'

'You realize we are in danger of instigating copycat killings?'

'I do, sir,' McNab said, although until that moment he hadn't, too intent had he been on the possibility that there might be three more potential victims.

'I want a shut-down as far as the media is concerned. I alone will be interviewed. No one on the case is permitted to discuss it outside these walls. Not in the pub. Not online. Not at home. Not to anyone. Is that clear?'

'Yes, sir.'

'I want the identities of the other gamers found and found quickly.' He paused. 'You have forty-eight hours to get on top of this, Inspector.' He did not specify what would happen if he didn't.

McNab departed.

The sudden silence as he entered the incident room was palpable. McNab was surprised to see Janice back at her desk. He motioned for her to follow him into his office.

'I want everyone here at two p.m. with whatever they have, including the Tech guys. From this moment on no one is to discuss the case outside the station. Sutherland's orders.'

'Right, sir.'

'Now, what the hell happened with Menzies?'

'He had a written statement prepared, sir, giving details of Alan's messages.'

'And what do these messages say exactly?'

'It isn't clear.'

'Mumbo-fucking-jumbo?'

'Professor Pirie might make sense of them. He managed to decipher the victim's diary on the Reborn case.'

McNab caught the pleading tone in her voice.

'That was maths, Sergeant, not messages from the dead.'

'Mr Menzies knew about the game, sir.'

That, McNab could not dispute, although he dearly wanted to know how the medium had got wind of it.

Janice, taking advantage of his silence, went on. 'The

Tech department could check his statement in case it has something to do with the game.'

McNab tried to behave like his former boss would have done.

'Send it over, Sergeant. I'll take a look.'

30

The T-shirt was a blue marl crew neck consisting of 65% polyester and 35% cotton, sporting a slightly faded Topshop label. The shorts were checked blue denim and had been purchased from the same company. His boxers were from Marks & Spencer, as were the socks. The trainers were black plimsolls, well worn.

Close examination had revealed a spot of blood on the neckline of the T-shirt, which proved to be Alan's and probably occasioned when his neck had been injected.

Rhona had recovered a number of fibres from the clothing, of various origins and composition: animal hairs that matched the family dog; vegetable in the form of leaves and grass from the surrounding area. She had also identified two unique human hairs, neither of which were Alan's, and a number of man-made fibres not belonging to the clothes he was wearing.

The underwear held traces of semen which matched their owner's DNA and a blonde hair sample whose morphology was pubic. A smearing of vaginal fluid in the opening on the boxers suggested Alan had had sex sometime prior to his death, but there was no evidence that semen had been spilt where he'd died.

McNab had mentioned that Alan and a female flatmate were an occasional sexual item. Rhona imagined a

Saturday-night or Sunday-morning coupling, after which Alan had set off to visit his mum. If he'd arranged to meet someone at the stone circle, she didn't believe he'd thought himself in any danger. From the evidence at the crime scene, Alan had lain down in the circle willingly.

And what about the stone? It had turned out to provide both a question and a partial answer.

Any surface that was as smooth as the miniature ridges on a finger could potentially bear identifiable latent finger-prints. Because of the flexibility of finger skin, she'd retrieved prints from cigarettes, paper, fruit, crumpled cans, bed sheets, rubbish bags and dead bodies.

In this case, the stone, not the body, had provided her with one, from the Cathkin Braes victim at least. She hadn't been so lucky with the Orkney stone, retrieving only a partial print which proved insufficient to match the two. Nevertheless, it was something, although if the perpe-trator wasn't on the database then they required a suspect before it could be used.

Rhona went online and checked whether the crime-scene software had been brought up to date. The geologic-al make-up of the stones was there, plus notification that a print had been retrieved, but no matches were indicated on the database search. That didn't mean they wouldn't yet generate one. Everything required time, resources and money. Especially money.

She took a break and made some coffee. Chrissy was absent, attending a court appearance on another and quite different case, regarding a break-in. Rhona missed her company, having wanted to talk through last night's proceedings with her forensic assistant.

While drinking her coffee, she went online again to

check for any further spread of the map story and found #stonedead still trending on Twitter. Rhona read some of the wild suppositions about where it would happen next, Stonehenge proving the most popular, probably because it was the one the majority of people had heard of. The eye of the public seemed to have moved south, which McNab would be happy about. She was momentarily grateful the map featured the entire mainland and not just the northern section of it.

The call came through from Magnus just after midday. She'd been expecting him to get in contact despite the manner in which the previous evening had ended. Magnus wasn't one to hold a grudge, unlike McNab.

'It was the girl who came to see me at Houton,' he confirmed. 'Although I had to go mainly by the piercings, and the clothes.'

'Are they any further forward on the Brodgar victim's identity?'

'Her name is Adelina Bacha, she arrived from Poland a week ago and started work at the local fish factory.'

'Why was she at Brodgar?'

'The police don't know why or how she went there, although I suspect one of Jack's team might. Most of them have transport and live in Stromness where the factory is, but I'll leave Erling to find that out.'

'Are you planning to stay up there?'

'No. I want to talk about the map. I've had an idea.' He didn't elaborate and she didn't ask him to. 'I'll catch an afternoon flight. Are you free to come over tonight?' When Rhona didn't immediately answer, he added, 'Patrick Menzies gave a statement which contained messages he alleged came from Alan. DI McNab sent me a copy and asked if I could decipher them. I think they might refer to the map.'

Rhona, covering her surprise at this turn of events, told Magnus she'd text to confirm later and rang off. It sounded as though a truce had been called between the two men. Even more amazing was McNab giving the time of day to the medium's contribution.

The room was packed. McNab ran his eye over the assembled group, who appeared tense and engaged. He contemplated for a moment that they might think he was about to announce his re-assignment, after his summons to the super's office, so he gave them a grim smile to reassure them. If they were relieved it wasn't immediately obvious.

McNab had a sudden and startling out-of-body experience where he was part of that audience looking back at himself, standing up there, waiting to pontificate on something he knew fuck all about. He, like them, stood on the outskirts of a maze. Plenty of possible paths to follow, with no guarantee of reaching the centre. They had all been given specific jobs, sometimes boring, but which at least gave them a sense of purpose and direction. He, on the other hand, had to determine those jobs. He had spent the time since the meeting with the super working out what his next step should be, all the while worried that he was missing something important.

He'd done what DS Clark had asked regarding Menzies' statement, although it had stuck in his craw. Nutters like Menzies often cropped up in murder cases, inveigling their way in, sometimes claiming to have evidence, sometimes even admitting to the crime. Attention seekers and minor psychopaths. McNab suspected Menzies was a bit of both.

But he had fooled the mother. That's what worried McNab. That and the fact that his detective sergeant appeared to give credence to what the medium had to say.

He dragged his thoughts back to the present and called for attention. He brought them up to date regarding the Orkney case, then set the ball in motion by handing the floor over to the boy wonder.

Ollie, for all his youthful appearance, looked unperturbed as he approached the front. Touching the screen, he brought up an image of a stone circle. Above it was the name STONEWARRIOR.

So now we know the name of the game, McNab thought.

'The game, I believe, is on five levels, all of which appear to require an in-depth knowledge of Druidism and important sites both Druidic and Neolithic. A sort of Mastermind game. Unlike other warrior games, it's not about fighting, but about gaining knowledge and solving puzzles.'

Ollie brought up a series of images. One looked like a three-circled labyrinth. Another, an ancient gnarled oak tree. A third, a set of standing stones linked by lines with mathematical symbols. 'I think the players were probably selected from one or more sites associated with Druidism and gaming, such as *World of Druids*, *World of Warcraft* and *Druids Grove*. They are unlikely to know one another except by their avatar.'

Ollie continued: 'In Druidism the number three is significant. Their philosophy is built on reverence for the earth, the ancestors and the gods. Land, sea and sky. Normally those seeking knowledge begin training as a Bard, who holds the knowledge of the stories and myths of the belief system. Then they become Ovate, who have the gift of prophecy and can converse with the spirits, a bit like clairvoyants today. The third and highest level is that of a Druid priest. As such, the game resembles this, but doesn't mirror it. I think when a fifth level is reached there's a ceremony, which involves a stone circle. A stone circle is regarded as a potent energy source. However, I've yet to break the password for full entry, so much of this is guesswork.'

McNab looked at the bemused faces of his team, although one or two of the men had nodded when certain games had been mentioned. They were obviously far more aware of the gaming world than he was.

When Ollie stood down, McNab resumed his place at the front.

'As you are aware, a map of twenty-five stone circle sites has been released online, linking it to this case. Interest in this has sparked it trending on Twitter as #stonedead. This complicates the investigation. I have no doubt we'll be besieged with calls offering help or information. Most of it will be unhelpful, much will be rubbish, but we'll have to treat each call seriously.' He paused for a moment. 'Superintendent Sutherland wants nothing said about the case outside these walls. Not in the pub to one another, or to partners at home. Do I make myself clear?'

McNab had been putting off mentioning the medium, but it had to happen, whether he liked it or not. He brought up a copy of the statement on the screen.

'The medium Patrick Menzies claims to be in touch with the Cathkin Braes victim regarding this game. He states that the victim is concerned for the well-being of the other players and is attempting to help us locate them.'

The hush was deafening.

'I couldn't help but notice that a number of those present seem familiar with the world of games. If any of you recognize anything in this statement that might help the investigation, then I want you to come to me.'

McNab took himself out after the meeting. As a DS he'd walked and driven the streets of Glasgow regularly. As DI he'd been spending too much time in the office contemplating the possibility of failure. It was time he acted on instinct.

31

Signature characteristics were more likely to be associated with a particular offender than their modus operandi. The two stone circle deaths matched in signature, via the careful layout and positioning of the bodies. One set of hands had been pierced, the other chopped off, which might indicate picquerism, where the perpetrator gained sexual pleasure from cutting or stabbing their victims.

Modus operandi referred to the particular way by which the perpetrator carried out the task of killing his victims, which could change depending on circumstance. In the infamous Jack the Ripper case, the more privacy the killer got, the more time he took to mutilate the body. There was some controversy as to just how many killings were involved in the Jack the Ripper murders. Consensus said five, but an analysis in the *Journal of Investigative Psychology* suggested that on the basis of signature and modus operandi, Jack the Ripper had been responsible for six deaths. From his own research into the case, Magnus was inclined to agree.

As for the unknown girl on Hoy, her death bore no resemblance to the two killed within the stone circles, and could not be determined as murder. Yet all Magnus's instincts told him she shared the same killer and only the circumstances of her death were different. His visitor had suggested that Adelina Bacha had died at Brodgar in her stead. If that was true, then the girl who'd turned up on his doorstep had been right to be afraid. Had she not come to Magnus, her death might have been deemed an accident most likely caused by high winds, like the climbers on Yesnaby.

Magnus had gone willingly to identify the body, but it hadn't been an easy task. In normal circumstances, one quick look would have sufficed. In this case, there had been very little left of the pretty, overly made-up face he'd encountered on his jetty.

According to Erling, they hadn't recovered any belongings or mobile on the body, or in the vicinity of where they believed the tent had been pitched. The police were currently interviewing the residents of Hoy, but it was high summer and there had been a considerable number of day trippers, many of whom had already departed. Added to that, a cruise ship anchored off Kirkwall had disgorged a large number of visitors on the days leading up to her death.

Meanwhile, the body had been flown to Inverness for the post-mortem.

On the cloudless flight back to Glasgow, Magnus had had a good view of the landscape. In his mind's eye, he saw the marked map Jack had given him. Luring a victim to any one of the locations via the game would be easy, and for the majority, the prospect of discovery as remote as the location.

But from his reading of the perpetrator, an undiscovered body was not what was desired. Apart from the unnamed victim on Hoy. Perhaps because she'd broken the rules of the game?

The ping of the microwave indicated his evening meal was ready. Magnus extracted the plate and, sweeping aside the material he'd been working on, sat down to eat. Afterwards, he took the remains of his glass of wine onto the balcony.

Below him, the waters of the Clyde glistened in the early evening sunshine, smooth and untroubled, unlike his thoughts. Over the last few hours Magnus had come to the unwelcome conclusion that they were dealing with a well-organized and highly motivated perpetrator, whose plan of action included testing those who sought to find him. The map's release and the trending on Twitter, Magnus suspected, were both part of that plan.

The question was, what would happen next?

He fetched the printout of the medium's statement and sat down to study it. His visit to the spiritualist church had done nothing to convince him that Menzies was anything other than a charlatan, well-meaning possibly, but emotionally dangerous to those who were grieving. And yet he'd appeared to know about the existence of the online game Alan was involved in even before the authorities had. And he'd announced Alan's death prior to it being discovered.

The police were often plagued by people who believed they could help in high-profile murder cases, despite having no true knowledge of them. Such witnesses offered sightings of possible perpetrators, or gave spurious evidence, to gain attention or to feel part of the investigation. Clairvoyants featured predominantly in cases of missing bodies, offering to pinpoint possible locations, but as far as Magnus was aware, no bodies had ever been located with the help of a clairvoyant.

Logic, therefore, determined that Patrick Menzies was deluded, openly lying and manipulating, or that he'd known where Alan was going to be the morning he was killed, and why. Magnus was inclined to believe the former.

The case was also ripe for copycat killings such as in the Ripper murders, or false confessions. Magnus didn't envy the newly promoted McNab his role or his responsibility. Being out of the spotlight was a more comfortable position, although when Magnus was convinced he had important information which might help an enquiry, he'd often found it difficult to persuade those in power to believe him.

He'd watched McNab's intuition in action, and had been impressed by it. McNab read situations with an innate intelligence and insight that didn't require psychological research to prove him correct. Maybe that was why McNab pissed him off so much.

It was an uncomfortable thought, which Magnus quickly dispensed with. He finished his wine and went to check his mobile. There was no sign of a text yet from Rhona. He was aware she might choose not to come, but he was hoping curiosity would drive her here. And he would welcome her scientific brain on the material he'd collected.

He cleared away the dishes, brought out a bottle of Highland Park and poured himself a glass, then settled down with the statement and the map.

32

'How much further?' she said, wiping a trickle of sweat from her cheek.

He checked his bearings, then pointed due east. 'It should be over there.'

She shielded her eyes and took a look in that direction. As far as she was concerned it was a long way to trek for a shag. She wasn't averse, particularly since he'd brought some good shit to smoke when they got there, but the hike was killing the anticipation.

'There it is. See, the big grey stone.'

She tried to focus, but the sun was in her eyes and the rolling farmland seemed to shimmer and move like a restless sea. When he'd first suggested coming here, they'd been listening to the Police singing 'Fields of Gold'. She'd pictured herself walking through ripened barley, and what they would do there. That image and the dope they'd smoked had set the scene perfectly. But like most fantasies, it hadn't quite matched her expectations yet.

He was striding ahead, having apparently spotted his phallic symbol. According to him, midsummer was a potent time to indulge in sex at such a spot. Something to do with the power of energy lines. Well, she hoped he had enough energy left for the both of them when they finally got there.

He'd stopped now beside what looked like a long grey lump of fallen stone. The image of a collapsed phallic symbol didn't bode well. She felt a giggle rise in her throat, then stifled it when she saw his expression.

'There used to be three in a circle, but some bastard knocked them down.' Anger flashed in his eyes.

He looked so serious, she felt the desire to laugh building again, so she said, 'I need to pee.'

Irritation replaced the anger. 'We're almost there,' he said.

'Walk on, I'll catch you up.'

When his striding figure was ten feet away, she hitched up the floaty dress she'd thought would match the occasion and squatted, glad she'd already removed her pants in anticipation of what was to follow.

When she stood up again, she realized he was waiting with his back turned. His good manners endeared him to her again and she felt the stirring of desire return.

This could be good, after all, she thought.

As she reached him, he took her hand and, leaning down, kissed her full on the mouth. When she felt him stir against her, she broke free and, dragging him along, shouted, 'Come on, let's hurry.'

As they ran, she felt her bare breasts jump against the cotton. Her heart rate rose and her face flushed. A beat of desire found her groin. She laughed with joy. This was what she'd imagined when she'd listened to the song.

They crested a small mound and saw the upright stone before them.

Panting, her heart crashing, she pounded down the intervening grass as a curlew rose to bleat above them. The sudden appearance of the bird startled her. She didn't like swooping birds or fluttering wings and covered her head with her arms.

'It's okay. It's only a curlew protecting its nest.'

He drew her into his arms and lifted her lightly, placing her back against the stone.

Now they were in shadow, yet the stone felt warm through the thin cotton of her dress. Her skin prickled, through heat or anticipation.

'Can you feel it?' he whispered in her ear. 'The energy in the stone?'

He slipped his hand up and under her dress. Tracing his finger up her inner thigh, he found entry. She gasped as his other hand grabbed her hair, tipping her head back. Now she was looking up into the sun, and the heat was all about and inside her. His finger retracted and she was suddenly empty again.

'Now,' she urged, but he used her hair to turn her head and she yelped at the sudden discomfort.

'Face the stone,' he said.

She did as asked, bracing her palms against its roughness. Her body sang with desire as the stored warmth found her palms this time, radiating up her arms and down through her torso.

She gave a cry as he entered her, welcoming the pounding rhythm that pressed her forehead against the roughness of the stone. The satisfying beat of it seemed to go on forever. She felt a trickle of sweat descend her face and seep into her open mouth. It tasted of salt and blood.

The curlew was back, swooping and crying above them as he reached climax. She sagged a little as he extracted himself, then she felt his arm encircle her waist and lower her gently to the ground.

The grass smelt cool and sweet. She thought how right he had been to bring her here.

His fingers found the pulse in her neck and stroked it. She wanted to stay here, her face in the sweet-smelling grass. She wanted more of him, until the sun finally sank over the horizon. She felt him straddle her back and realized it was about to begin again.

A fly buzzed round her head, smelling her sweat and the trickle of blood from the scratch on her forehead. She felt a sharp pinprick in her neck. At first she thought the fly had bitten her and tried to slap it away, but he took both her hands and placed them on the ground. She smiled as a wave of euphoria claimed her. Her body felt as soft as a cloud. She knew if he let go of her she would float up above the tall grey stone.

He left her as the sun sank below the horizon. The sky was a deep red over the fields as he walked back. This time had been the best. Almost perfection. More time, more pleasure. And she'd enjoyed it too. Even as he'd laid her out, she'd been smiling. He hadn't stabbed the hands this time, just cupped them closed. It would look the same, but not quite. Keep them guessing. He'd chosen the best image he'd taken and uploaded it before he left the site. It would be out there now. How soon before they worked out where she was?

Not before he was well away.

There was a ditch by the side of the road, fed by a field drain. He wiped the mobile clean of prints and dropped it in, covering it in a mixture of mud and slurry. Then he headed for the van.

33

McNab took out the piece of paper Jolene had given him and dialled the number. As before, it rang out unanswered. He suspected she'd deliberately given him a wrong number, or that this particular pay-as-you-go mobile had already been discarded. Probably because she'd warned her supplier.

He couldn't blame her. Maybe he would have done the same at her age and in her circumstances. Fear was a strong motivator. And she was right to be afraid of pissing off those who supplied what she needed to get high.

The long warm spell continued unabated, with plenty of young flesh on display in the university precincts and along Ashton Lane. McNab tried not to be distracted by it as he bought a pint and muscled himself onto an outside table. He must have radiated 'cop', because the two resident guys took themselves off pretty quickly. McNab supped his lager and kept an eye open for her.

Their phone conversation had been stilted, but she hadn't openly refused to meet him. Maybe the public venue helped or maybe she was just relieved that he hadn't suggested she come down to the station.

Either way, there she was.

McNab stood up to make himself more visible. She clocked him and headed his way. She was wearing shorts, and a top that exposed her midriff. McNab kept his eyes firmly on her face.

'Jolene. Can I get you a drink?'

She eyed his pint. 'I take it you're off duty?'

He glanced at his watch for effect. 'Off duty and off the record.'

'Then I'll have the same as you.' She settled herself down on the chair, grimacing as the hot metal met her thighs.

McNab shouldered his way to the bar and placed his order, stocking up on another for himself to avoid a return journey. When he got back she had lit up a cigarette. McNab contemplated suggesting they move inside so she would have to put it out, or just asking her for one.

Both constituted failure, so he concentrated on his pint instead.

She sipped at her own between drags. Her fingers were long and slim and black-tipped, and they were trembling a little. She was unnerved and unsure. Just where he wanted her to be.

Eventually she could wait no longer.

'Why am I here?'

He pushed the piece of paper across the table. She glanced down, recognizing what it was. A flush crept up her cheek, just as the colour drained away from the rest of her face.

'No one home,' McNab said in a surprised voice.

'I told you, it changes.'

'So what's the call number now?'

She didn't reply.

'Forensic tell me that Alan had sex the morning he died. Was it with you?' He met her eye.

She'd been gearing herself for an explanation as to why

she didn't have a new supplier number, so the sudden change of subject threw her.

'I . . . we . . .'

'We have a DNA sample that will tell us anyway,' McNab said.

'But you have no right—'

He swiftly cut her off with the question he really wanted to ask. 'Alan was playing an online game. Do you know anything about that?'

She'd been marshalling further indignation on the sex question, and was nonplussed.

'What has a game got to do with anything?'

'It was a Druid-type game. There were five players. Did Alan mention any of them?'

'Why?'

'Because they might die, like Alan.'

His pronouncement shocked and frightened her. 'Alan died because he was playing a game?'

'Did Alan ever mention an online Druid game?'

She thought for a moment. 'No, but he might have talked to Helena about it.'

'Why Helena?'

'Because she's into all that stuff. Earth, sea and sky. She took a course to become a Bard.'

Bard, Ovate then Priest. If *Stonewarrior* involved progression through Druid knowledge, surely Alan would have quizzed his knowledgeable flatmate about the game?

'Is Helena back from her travels?'

Jolene shook her head. 'No.'

'You said she would be back by Wednesday.'

'She should have been.'

'Where is she exactly?'

'She went to celebrate the summer solstice somewhere. That's all I know.'

McNab's heart sank. 'Call her,' he ordered.

'I have. She doesn't answer.'

McNab looked round Helena's room, annoyed with himself for not insisting they see it when they were checking out the rest of the flat. Jolene was right. Helena was definitely into the world of Druidism, as evidenced by the various posters that dotted the walls and the collection of books on the shelves. She was also a postgraduate student at Glasgow University, doing an MLitt in Celtic and Scottish Studies. Just the person to solve puzzles posed by *Stonewarrior*.

The room smelt stuffy in the heat, but it was clean and tidy. According to Jolene, Helena had a laptop which she had most likely taken with her. It certainly wasn't on view in the room. Jolene had also given McNab Helena's mobile number, but like Jolene, all his attempts at calling her had gone straight to voicemail, so the Tech guys were trying to pinpoint the mobile's location now. Further conversations with Jolene suggested that Helena might have gone south, maybe even as far as Stonehenge.

'So she didn't head for Orkney or the Western Isles?'

Jolene had looked blank at that, until McNab explained about the major stone circles there. It seemed ironic that he, who had started out ignorant of such things, was now assuming the role of an expert.

After Jolene, McNab had fastened on a fidgeting Jamie who, in a bout of verbal diarrhoea, admitted to being big into computer games, especially *World of Warcraft*, but denied that Alan had ever mentioned playing *Stonewarrior*.

'Have you seen the latest?' Jamie was as excited and

wide-eyed as a lottery winner. He pulled out his mobile and flicked the screen about for a bit, then handed it to McNab.

'There's been another one. Look, you can just see the standing stone in the background.'

The girl might have fallen asleep, face down in the sunshine. There was no obvious sign of a struggle. Her face, turned sideways to the camera, was pretty and calm, bearing what looked like the trace of a smile. But she'd been arranged, the arms stretched out, the fingers pointing.

'When did you see this?' McNab said.

'About an hour ago.'

McNab felt sick and in need of a drink at the same time. He vacated the room and the flat, heading down to the street, where he checked his own phone. Two missed calls, both from his DS.

Janice answered his return call immediately. 'Sir, have you seen the image?'

'Yes. Do we know the location?'

'No, sir, but Ollie thinks he can work it out given time. Something to do with the size of the stone, distant landmarks and the position of the sun.'

'If anyone finds her before that, I want to know. Right away.'

McNab pocketed the mobile. One step forward. Three fucking steps back. If that was a real victim, then the perpetrator was pissing on them. If it was a copycat killing, they were being pissed on by some other nutter. If it was a set-up, they were being pissed on by everyone.

The sick feeling was now replaced entirely by a need for whisky.

He contemplated the nearby pub where Alan had

worked before his demise, then decided against it. He was prepared to be an outcast, but he just didn't want to be called a pig at the moment.

He needed to think long and hard about his next move. As he walked swiftly home in the fading light, he recalled a programme he'd watched on one of his home-alone nights, when he hadn't succumbed to calling Iona. It was a BBC take on a possible mega tsunami caused by a collapse of rock into the sea from an eruption on one of the smaller Canary Islands. What had struck him most was that the warnings of the impending disaster would travel more swiftly through Twitter and social networking sites than anything the authorities could offer.

The Twittersphere was way ahead of them on this too, either by accident or design. Routine policing didn't work in this world and his skills were insufficient to the job. Let's face it. He was drowning in a sea of digital shit.

He made a stop at the off-licence at the end of the street, promising himself to phone for a pizza and eat it before he opened the bottle. And no Iona tonight. Another promise just waiting to be broken.

34

Rhona tried McNab's number but it went to voicemail after three rings. She then tried DS Clark. The background noise when Janice answered suggested she was at the pub. Not surprising considering how late it was. Rhona asked if McNab was there.

'He doesn't come with us since his promotion,' Janice said.

There was only one thing worse than getting drunk with colleagues, and that was getting drunk alone.

'Have you any idea where he is?' Rhona said.

'He had an interview with the super about the case, told us not to discuss it outside the station, then left.' Janice's tone suggested the interview had not gone well.

'Does McNab know about the photograph that's currently up online?'

Janice hesitated, as though remembering McNab's orders, then answered. 'He called and asked if the Tech department could place the location.'

'And could they?'

'Not so far. They're not even sure if it's real,' Janice said.

Rhona thanked her and rang off, before she voiced her own opinion.

She'd been working late at the lab when the news of

the possible third *Stonewarrior* victim had arrived. Downloading and studying the image had led her to believe there was a distinct possibility the female in the photograph was a victim and not a copycat killing or a stunt, the reason being that the hands had been arranged to point in two distinct directions, just like the other victims. Although the press had made mileage of a 'ritual' pose at Cathkin Braes and Brodgar, they'd not had access to the full details.

Crime-scene details did seep out on occasion, sometimes accidentally, more often on purpose. Tabloid hacks were willing to pay for juicy material to keep their readers happy, and there were always moles in the police service willing to supply information at a price. Just as the police had their paid snitches in the underworld.

But, as far as Rhona was aware, only she, Magnus and McNab had discussed the possible connection between the directional layout of the hands and other Neolithic sites. True, McNab had dismissed any such links, but things had changed in the interim.

She decided to check out McNab's flat first. If he wasn't at home, then she would go on to Magnus's place. That determined, she tidied up, brought her lab notes up to date and left.

Despite the late hour, dusk had barely fallen over the university grounds as she emerged from the building and made for her car. Before setting off she tried calling McNab one more time, with no success. She then texted Magnus to say she would be over later. Somewhere in between, she decided, she would need to pick up something to eat.

Rhona had never been to McNab's flat, even when they'd been on better terms. McNab, on the other hand, wasn't averse to turning up on her doorstep unannounced, as witnessed by the other night. If he saw this visit as Dr MacLeod 'trying to tell him how to do his job again', things could turn sour. If he refused to listen to what she had to say regarding the photograph, she would go over his head and McNab would have to take the consequences.

With such fighting thoughts in her mind she drew into a parking place yards from his block and switched off the engine. Five minutes later, having decided not to forewarn McNab of her arrival, she'd gained access to the close via the common buzzer.

Now at his door, Rhona stood for a moment, then gave a firm knock. When there was no response, she tried again, louder this time. McNab might be holed up inside with a bottle, but surely curiosity would demand he check who was at the door?

Then she heard it. A rustle of movement. McNab was in there. Rhona waited impatiently for footsteps to approach. They didn't.

Had McNab seen her from the window? Is that why he wouldn't answer?

Irritated by the thought, she prised open the letter box.

'McNab? Are you in there? Open the door. We need to talk.'

Her demand went unanswered.

Other than break down the door, she had no option but to leave, which Rhona proceeded to do. The door was opened as she reached the lower landing. She glanced up to find McNab looking down on her.

'What's your problem, Dr MacLeod?

McNab indicated the large pizza he'd been eating. 'Want a slice?'

Pride suggested Rhona said no, but hunger won out, so she accepted.

McNab waved her to a seat, fetched a knife and a plate, cut her a decent-sized piece and handed it over. Suddenly seized by hunger, Rhona decided to eat first and talk later. A few mouthfuls in, she relaxed a little, and took a look round the room. There were no signs that McNab had been at the bottle. The space was clean and tidy, with no dirty dishes littering the sink. On entry to the flat, she hadn't picked up the smell of alcohol, but she had caught a female fragrance. A door to what looked like the bedroom stood a little ajar.

McNab spotted her swift glance in that direction. 'Iona isn't here,' he said. When Rhona didn't respond, he continued with what could only be described as a glint in his eye. 'But she did clean up. And changed the sheets.'

Rhona tried to look disinterested and concentrated on her pizza. When she'd finished, she set the plate on the table. It was time to get down to the real reason she was here.

'The photograph released online—' she began, before he cut her off.

'I'm dealing with it,' he said.

Rhona carried on regardless. 'I think there's a good chance it is our next victim. I also believe I know where it was taken.'

He met her eye. 'Really? Where?' he said warily.

'The ley line running from the right hand of the Brodgar victim meets a Neolithic site in Aberdeenshire at Skelmuir Hill. There's only one stone still standing, just like in the photograph.'

McNab looked at her askance. 'That's it? That's your proof?'

'It's worth considering.'

'If you believe in Pirie's magic lines,' he said sarcastically.

Rhona bit back a retort, recognizing that they were entering troubled waters.

McNab tossed the empty pizza box on the coffee table and sat back, regarding her with a belligerent eye. After a moment he said, 'Why do you think the photograph might be genuine?'

Now was her chance and she took it. 'The media were aware that there was a ritualistic pose in each of the crime scenes. But no one knew we were questioning the directional aspect of the hands, except you, me and Magnus.'

'Does this Skelmuir Hill feature on the online map?'

'The map doesn't have a scale. It's not clear where any of the crosses are. That's why it's been posted online. To confuse the police and generate speculation.'

McNab shot her an exasperated look. 'The same could be said about the photograph.'

'We should search Skelmuir Hill,' she insisted.

'And what if there's another photo online tomorrow? And the day after that. How many stone circles are there? Most of them in remote locations. When we've wasted resources running around all the Scottish ones, do we move south of the border?'

McNab was right. You couldn't waste money and resources on hunches. Yet . . .

He'd noted her worried expression and made a small concession in her favour. 'I'll think about it, okay?'

It was all she was liable to achieve tonight.

LIN ANDERSON

McNab deposited the pizza box in the bin and produced a bottle of whisky and two glasses.

'No thanks. I'm driving,' Rhona said.

'Take a taxi. We need to talk.' He proceeded to open the bottle and pour two drams, despite her refusal. Annoyed by the display of his usual arrogance, Rhona rose.

'Where are you going?' McNab said.

'Magnus has a theory about the statement Menzies gave you.'

McNab glanced pointedly at his watch. 'And you're headed to his place at this late hour to discuss it?'

'I came here at this late hour, didn't I?' she shot back. 'I'll let you know if we come up with anything.'

'You do that, Dr MacLeod.'

A frosty silence accompanied her exit. Rhona imagined McNab heading back to the whisky bottle and wished she hadn't been so abrupt when he'd suggested she stay and talk. Should she go back in? Call a truce? Hear what else he had to say?

As Rhona hesitated on the landing, she heard someone buzz McNab's flat. A female voice spoke and McNab invited her up. Rhona hadn't seen Iona since McNab's promotion party. On that occasion, she'd watched Iona size McNab up and make her play. At first he hadn't seemed interested, but Iona didn't give up easily. Every time McNab had gone to the bar, she'd made a point of giving him a look that suggested she was keen and available.

Then McNab had made his move, but on Rhona, which hadn't pleased Iona. Rhona had turned him down, the way she usually did. Making a joke of it. Trying to show she liked him, but it just didn't work that way between them. McNab had seemed more stung than usual that night. And so Iona had got what she wanted.

They passed on the stairs, neither woman acknowledging the other. Rhona didn't need to see Iona's face to know how displeased she was to find Rhona there. The feeling was mutual.

'Idiot,' Rhona muttered as the front door swung shut behind her, not sure if she was referring to McNab or herself. No wonder he'd been so keen to get her to stay. She wondered which of the two women he'd wanted to annoy the most.

Rhona got into the car and slammed the door. If McNab was set on screwing someone young enough to be his daughter, she would leave him to it.

McNab watched the car take off. Iona's arrival hadn't been by invitation. When the buzzer sounded, he'd imagined, or hoped, Rhona had changed her mind about staying. When he'd heard Iona's voice, he'd realized the two women were bound to meet at the front door. He hadn't wanted to argue with Iona within earshot of Rhona, so he'd buzzed her in.

Now she was standing in front of him, eyes ablaze with indignation.

'You have to leave,' he repeated.

'But I've only just got here.'

'I didn't ask you to come.'

'Ask? It's usually an order, Detective Inspector.'

'Go home, Iona. I'm working.'

'So that's what you two were doing?'

McNab sighed. This was where his prick had led him. To a jealous nineteen-year-old.

'Leave, Iona,' he tried again in a weary voice.

When she shook her head, McNab decided he was past argument. He headed for the door himself. 'Be gone when I get back,' he ordered.

A litany of profanities followed him out, most of them referring to his sexual inadequacies, of which, it appeared, there were many.

Once outside, McNab glanced up at the window. He was taking a chance leaving Iona there in that frame of mind. Who knew what she would do in retaliation for his rejection? He certainly didn't think it would be more housework. McNab had an image of a wrecked room and wished he'd taken the whisky bottle with him.

He consoled himself with the fact that he'd kept both promises he'd made himself tonight. He'd eaten before he opened the whisky, and he hadn't called Iona and asked her to come over. Despite that, the evening hadn't quite worked out as planned.

35

When she rang the buzzer, Magnus answered immediately, relief obvious in his voice.

'It's very late,' she apologized as he ushered her in.

'Is it?' He looked preoccupied. The blond hair he'd worn long when first they'd met, was cut short now. Rhona remembered how he had first fitted her image of a Viking. Despite being Orcadian, given an outfit, axe and helmet, Magnus would have been an excellent participant in the Shetland Festival of Up Helly Aa. Now, beardless, shorn and agitated, he had more of the look of a soldier just returned from Afghanistan.

Magnus waved her into the sitting room. The French windows stood open, letting in the lights of Glasgow and the sound of the river beneath. It wasn't surprising Magnus had chosen to live here. The flat might be in the centre of the city, but he was as close to a wide expanse of water as he was in Houton Bay.

His desk was covered with evidence of his attempts to make sense of Menzies' statement. Books littered the couch, the coffee table and the floor. A digital whiteboard had been set up. It was covered with notes, questions and symbols in a variety of colours, projected from Magnus's laptop.

'It won't make any sense,' he said as she ran her eye

over the notes. 'Until I explain.' He handed her a printout of what appeared to be the police statement.

'Can I get you a drink or a coffee while you read it?'

'Just water, thanks.'

Magnus headed for the kitchen. She heard the water run and the coffee machine start up. Magnus's agitated state suggested this wouldn't be his first cup of coffee of the evening.

Rhona glanced over the paper. The statement was short, about half a page, and read almost like a stream of consciousness. There were sentences, but they didn't seem to string together. There were also numerical references and some formulae, which looked geometric. The number five figured a lot. And there were some poorly sketched symbols. One like a triple spiral, another like a tree.

Magnus was back with her water and a mug of coffee, the smell of which made her want one. She forced herself not to ask and drank the water instead.

'You need to be aware of a couple of things. First of all, I don't rate Patrick Menzies. In that, McNab and I agree.'

'So the statement is nonsense?'

'I don't think these are the words of a dead person. I do think, though, that it might have bearing on the case.'

'How?'

'The perpetrator appears to be preoccupied by Druidism and stone circles. Both of which, I think, Menzies is also interested in. I believe the statement is his theory about what will happen next.'

'So how did he know that Alan was dead before his body was discovered?'

'There's a lot about life and death we don't understand. Premonition being one of them. People often know instinctively if a person close to them is in danger, or has just died. It seems at its most powerful if that person is your own child. Maybe Menzies picked up on a concern Mrs MacKenzie had for the welfare of her son and used it in his act.'

'That's cruel.'

'No more cruel than relaying messages from the dead, such as, "Don't worry. I'll always be with you."'

Rhona didn't believe in life after death either, but she also didn't want to think that Patrick Menzies was tricking people every time he held a service.

'So how does his statement help?' she said.

'In it he mentions the sacred geometry of Scotland and the pattern of five. The spirals and tree of life are in there too – symbols associated with Druidry. I looked back at Jack's map and, combining things, came up with this.'

Magnus went over to his laptop, which controlled the screen.

'The numbers I think refer to the structure of a geometric shape.'

A familiar image of a man appeared, arms and legs outstretched within a circle. Lines from the head, feet and hands criss-crossed to make a five-pointed star.

'The star symbolizes, among other things, Jesus's death on the cross,' Magnus said, 'his head, pierced hands and feet being the points on the circumference. In the Christian tradition the single point must always be at the top. If inverted it's regarded as Satanic.'

He made an adjustment. Now the figure, the star and its circle lay inside the borders of a pentagram.

'A five-sided figure.'

'Which looks a bit like Jack's map,' Rhona said.

Magnus nodded. 'Now, if we add in a detailed map of Scotland, we get what is sometimes called the sacred pentagram of Scotland.'

It was a stunning image. The pentagram stretched as far north as Orkney, and south to just below Glasgow. Westward as far as the Outer Hebrides, eastward to Aberdeenshire.

'The apex is Brodgar,' Magnus said. 'The centre point of the baseline is the Cathkin Braes circle.'

'Is the upper right Skelmuir Hill?' Rhona asked.

'It's not the only standing stone in the vicinity. We'd have to confirm with a GPS reading.' He went on, 'The upper left is most certainly the stone circle at Callanish. Then things change somewhat. The baseline when extended meets the island of Iona to the west, and Lindisfarne off the north-eastern coast of England. Both are sacred sites, but Christian rather than Neolithic.'

'Another photograph has appeared online of a possible victim. A girl lying near a standing stone,' Rhona said.

Magnus looked aghast. 'When?'

'Earlier tonight.'

He was already at the laptop. It took him seconds to find it. 'I was too engrossed in the statement. I didn't realize this had happened.' He studied the image closely.

'McNab thinks it's a hoax,' Rhona said. 'I'm not so sure. Look at the way the hands are placed. And the stone behind her. Is there a chance it could be Skelmuir?'

'There are single marker stones all over Scotland,' Magnus said.

'I asked McNab to check out Skelmuir Hill. He said he couldn't spend money and resources on every hunch we have.'

'He's right. And the perpetrator knows it.'

36

Neil Cameron had always wanted to fly choppers, although it had taken him time, effort and a substantial personal investment to gain his licence. Afterwards, the most lucrative way to use his newly gained skills had been to service the North Sea oil rigs, ferrying the workers to and from the platforms in all weathers. He'd done that for a while, but quickly grew bored by the monotony of it. Wild weather and high seas had been a challenge at times, but not enough to hold his interest. The money itself, once his debt was repaid, offered opportunities to heighten excitement, but the way riggers burned money wasn't for him.

Flying a police helicopter had proved to be what he wanted. Plenty of variety in the job. No two days the same and not short on excitement and sometimes even mystery.

Like tonight.

They had taken off from Oban, having been sent there from Glasgow earlier in the day. A boat suspected of carrying drugs had been reported in coastal waters off the ferry port. When it had docked, the team he'd brought north had been waiting. A sizeable amount of cocaine had been swiftly located by the sniffer dog. Everyone was happy, except the boat's crew, at least two of whom appeared shocked by the discovery. Cameron's opinion

241

was that they had been set up to take the rap should the cargo be discovered, but that was for others to sort out.

As he and Fergus had prepared to head for home base on the Clyde, a call had come through, sending them eastwards instead. The flight across the Cairngorms had been spectacular. Nearing midnight, and at midsummer this far north, the sun still danced on the mountaintops and played in the deep east–west pass of the Lairig Ghru. Gazing further north, the distant islands of Orkney were still bathed in daylight. They wouldn't see darkness before three o'clock in the morning. A darkness that would dissipate with the rising sun, two hours later at five.

Cameron checked his instruments. They were fast approaching the GPS reading given by headquarters. Having traversed the mountain range, the chopper now beat its way over Aberdeenshire fields, dotted by farmsteads, where pinpoints of light indicated their residents were still up and about, despite the late hour.

The time spent in the air with this job had taught him more about Scotland than any history or geography book ever could. From above he'd viewed the results of the Ice Age in the scoured-out mountain corries, the Neolithic history in the shape of stone circles and burial mounds, and evidence of the highland clearances in the deserted townships and abandoned crofts, where people had been forced to make way for sheep.

Below him now was evidence of the richness of the farmland that encircled the lights of Scotland's new industrial base, the granite city of Aberdeen, anchored firmly facing the North Sea and its black gold.

One thought always struck him in these crossings from mainland to islands, north and south, east and west. This was an empty land, a great wilderness at its centre. An easy place in which to disappear.

Fergus, his co-pilot, was pointing below, indicating they should be directly over the location now. Cameron switched on the spotlights. The beams traversed a grassy mound, illuminating the stone sentinel that stood at its centre.

Cameron controlled their descent while Fergus used his night goggles to take a closer look.

'See anything?'

Fergus craned his head, and Cameron dropped a little lower in response, swinging the chopper round for a better view beyond the stone.

'There's something there,' Fergus said.

The moon, hidden behind a cloud until then, suddenly emerged, bathing the standing stone in silvery light.

'Fuck!' Fergus said as a black cloud rose towards them.

'What is it?' Cameron shouted, seeing his shocked expression.

'Bluebottles. Fucking hundreds of them.'

A swarm found their way inside the cockpit and tried to commit suicide against the windscreen.

Fergus signalled that they should land.

Cameron swung westward by two hundred yards and began to set down. As the blades slowed, their erstwhile visitors took leave of them and headed back towards the grey shadow of the stone.

Fergus's face looked white and strained. 'They were feasting on something. Let's hope it's dead mutton.'

Cameron handed Fergus a high-powered torch and jumped down.

The air was hot and heavy with no wind. In the still

air, the buzzing grew so intense, it sounded like the flies were inside his head. As they moved towards the shadowy shape, the cloud rose again, exposing their meal.

37

Weary, McNab was now thinking of his bed and the bottle of whisky he'd left behind. He'd hung around outside the flat for a while hoping Iona would leave, but when she hadn't, he'd gone walkabout while trying to avoid becoming one of the many Glaswegians inebriated by a heady mix of summer weather and booze.

The walk had turned out to be fruitful. Free to think without interruption, he'd come to his senses and responded to the online photograph by asking the Air Support Unit to take a look at the Skelmuir site on their way back from a drugs recce in the west.

That had been well over an hour ago and there had been no response as yet. Whether that was good or bad, he wasn't sure. He didn't want another victim, but he also didn't want to look a fool. Thus, neither outcome was satisfactory.

The sun had finally sunk behind the horizon, which meant it should have grown cooler, but the stone buildings and tarred pavements seemed to radiate heat. The clammy air heralded a thunderstorm, brewing in dark clouds over Cathkin Braes.

Sweat trickled down his back under his shirt. He thought about a cool shower. He thought about ice clinking in his whisky. He thought about Rhona and Magnus supping Highland Park together, discussing his case, without him.

He should have gone with her to Magnus's. Behaved like a detective rather than acting the big man.

He glanced up at the darkened window of his flat. Iona had either left or gone to bed. He hoped for once the former was true. He had well and truly conquered his Iona obsession. It seemed she had too, judging by the way she'd described his efforts at sex. McNab felt a little aggrieved at the memory, then reassured himself that Iona wouldn't have returned as often as she had if his performance had been that bad.

When he reached the front door, he found it standing half open. His first reaction was relief at the thought that she'd gone. The second was annoyance that she'd left the place unlocked. When McNab pushed the door wide, the smell hit him.

Shit. It was definitely the smell of shit.

It wasn't the first time McNab had entered somewhere to find the previous illegal visitor had left his mark. McNab had developed the knack of closing his nostrils and turning off his olfactory sense if necessary. The worst thing you could do to contaminate a crime scene was to vomit all over it.

Nevertheless, he grabbed a towel from the bathroom as he passed and covered his nose and mouth before stepping into the main room.

The mess had been distributed, suggesting the delivery man or woman had excellent control over their bowels. There was some on the settee. A further deposit on the coffee table where he'd recently eaten his pizza. Urine had been sprayed along a lower wall. On the kitchen surface someone had spent time cutting white powder, leaving thin lines of it.

McNab took all this in, without moving from his place in the doorway. A forensic team would get plenty from this, if he chose to call one in, but if it was Iona's work, did he want to?

He considered the sprayed line of urine. Whoever had done that could take aim, suggesting the culprit was either a man or a large dog. McNab considered the possibility that Iona had had an accomplice. Someone she'd called in to help her enact her revenge.

Having checked the wreckage of this room, he noted that the bedroom door was closed. He made his way carefully across the intervening carpet and turned the handle.

It opened without difficulty.

There was no further onslaught of bad smells and a quick glance round indicated defecation had not reached the bedroom. The duvet, however, was heaped up, suggesting there was something or someone below it. McNab caught a corner of the cover and flipped it back.

Rhona climbed wearily into bed. Despite her avoidance of caffeine, sleep did not come easily. Her conversations with McNab, then Magnus, began to merge with her own forensic work to create a psychotic dream state in which understanding lay frustratingly out of reach. Sometimes the solution was in her lab, which she could no longer locate in the university buildings. Sometimes within a maze, built like a triple spiral, the centre impossible to find. Sometimes it lay at the top of a tree which she could not climb.

Wearily she tossed and turned, until the sound of the buzzer infiltrated her nightmare. Bemused, she saw from her mobile that only an hour had passed since she'd gone to bed. Her first thought was that someone had pressed the wrong buzzer. A second blast, extended this time, suggested she was wrong.

She rose, worry already taking over from the bad dream.

McNab's voice sounded slurred, as though he might be drunk.

'Can I come up?'

'No.'

'I need a place to sleep.'

She couldn't resist a dig. 'Iona throw you out?'

'Can I come up?'

The desire to gloat won. Rhona released the door.

McNab looked rough, she was pleased to note. Rough, smelling of whisky, but not drunk. She wanted to know what had happened, but didn't want to appear too keen.

'Thanks,' he said when she indicated the spare room. 'My place is crawling with SOCOs.'

He launched himself onto the bed, fully clothed, and immediately shut his eyes. What he'd just said suddenly struck Rhona. 'Why is there a forensic team in your flat?'

McNab mumbled something unintelligible. Rhona sat beside him and repeated the question as a soft snore sounded. She gave McNab a shake. He pulled himself free and turned his back on her. The snore became louder. Rhona stood up. She'd seen McNab in a deep sleep before. Nothing would wake him now, short of an all-out attack.

She opened the window a little, but the outside clammy air failed to remove the smell of heat and sweat that emanated from McNab. Rhona departed, shutting the door behind her. If sleep had been tricky before, it would be even more elusive now, with McNab's mysterious arrival.

The storm broke shortly before dawn. The rain fell with a vengeance, pounding the window ledge, heavy drops jumping in through the open window to patter on the wooden floor. Rhona made no effort to rise and close it, grateful for the cool freshness of the rain's arrival.

After that she slept.

When she awoke, McNab had disappeared, only a slightly rumpled bed suggesting Rhona hadn't dreamt his presence. She made a pot of coffee, poured a large mug of it and phoned Chrissy. It was obviously family breakfast time in the McInsh household. Rhona could hear Michael's baby yells and Sam's dulcet tones as he soothed his son.

'What's up, boss?' Chrissy said.

'What the hell happened at McNab's flat?'

There was a moment's silence as Chrissy digested the question.

'I don't know. You tell me,' she said, sounding intrigued.

'McNab's had a break-in.'

'First I've heard of it.'

A small slither of suspicion entered Rhona's mind. Chrissy was always first to know. She had an army of spies with fast-texting fingers. One of her fellow SOCOs should have contacted her by now.

'McNab arrived here late last night. Asked for a place to sleep. Said his place was swarming with SOCOs, then conked out,' Rhona said.

There was a noise that sounded like a snort of derision.

'And you fell for that story? More likely Lolita threw him out.'

Rhona rang off before she made a bigger fool of herself than she already had.

38

McNab surveyed the room. At least the smell had gone, but he could do little for the urine trail on the wall. The powder on the kitchen surface had been cocaine. He'd tested it on his lips to make sure, and there was no mistaking the tingling sensation.

He'd been wrong about bodily waste being absent from the bedroom. Removal of the duvet had revealed that. The bedclothes were in the washing machine, tumbling round with his clothes from last night.

He surveyed his handiwork, already questioning why he hadn't just called in the SOCOs, as he'd told Rhona. The reason, of course, was Iona. His dalliance with her hadn't been wise. If this was her handiwork, assisted or otherwise, he didn't want it broadcast.

He thought back to what he'd believed to be whisky-fuelled sex sessions and suspected that, had he examined her eyes more closely, he may well have found dilated pupils.

His memory of their first meeting at the party came back to him. Had she been high then? And why had she come on to him?

His irresistible charm?

Another scenario presented itself, the word 'set-up' featuring strongly. Iona had been hell-bent on accompanying him home that night, and very keen to return. She was well aware he was a cop, which put a lot of women off, but not Iona.

McNab cursed himself for a fool.

Detectives were taught to believe everyone a liar until proved otherwise. It went with the territory. Why hadn't he followed the golden rule with Iona? He had a sudden image of himself sleeping and Iona checking his mobile . . . the numbers, the calls, the emails.

Jesus, what had he been thinking?

If Iona had indeed been a plant, who had planted her?

His glance went to the kitchen surface. She'd had access to cocaine. Had snorted it while trashing his place, probably in the company of at least one male. They'd made no effort to hide the fact.

A thought suddenly occurred. They hadn't located the cocaine stash, so the police had assumed its owners had collected it. But maybe they'd assumed wrongly? Maybe its owners were looking for it too? Maybe they needed to know if the police had it?

McNab cast his mind back over the few conversations he'd had with Iona. They hadn't amounted to much and focussed mostly on sex. But what about when he'd slept? He was a deep sleeper, especially after booze and sex. Iona would have had any amount of time to check out his phone. And his text to Big Davy was in there.

Was that why he'd been cornered at the Union bar?

His eyes roamed the room, replaying its state when he'd returned last night. What was he expected to do on his return? Call in the troops? Look for clues? Take forensic samples? Or clear up and hide the fact that it had happened?

He of all people knew that however clean it looked now, forensically it was anything but. Even the cocaine he'd washed from the surface could still be detected. And what about the blood on the bedclothes? There hadn't been much and he'd wondered whether it was menstrual blood, or a deposit from a previous energetic coupling. He'd laundered the sheets anyway.

What he should have done was show the flat to Rhona. Ask her to take samples and store them, in case he should need them later.

Instead, he'd acted in haste, maybe to repent at leisure.

His mobile rang. McNab glanced at the screen.

'Sergeant?'

'The Air Support Unit have reported a body in the location you identified, sir. It looks like the girl in the photograph.'

Cameron's initial images taken immediately after touch down weren't best quality, but there was no disputing that a body lay on the ground in front of the standing stone, nor that it was female.

R2S's arrival had produced more detailed photographs, now part of a collage on the screen in the incident room. Alongside was the image circulated on the internet. They certainly looked the same – the floral dress worn by both females, the layout of the body and, most importantly, the face.

Whoever had posted the image online had been at the crime scene, and not long after the girl had died.

McNab had already spoken with the crime-scene manager. According to the SOCO sent to examine the body, there had been nothing in the victim's mouth except flies. So no stone, and therefore no indication whether this was game victim number three – or number four, if Pirie's theory about his Houton visitor was correct.

McNab wasn't happy that his order to check Skelmuir Hill had been the right one. At that moment, he wished he'd been made to look a fool. He wished the online photo had been a hoax. Instead he had another murder victim on his hands. Was it a copycat killing, instigated by the online frenzy of interest, or the latest from the same perpetrator?

The signature looked similar, but it wasn't the same. There was no stone in the mouth. Like the positioning of the hands, that feature hadn't been made known to the general public. Yet there was no doubt the hands in this case had been positioned, as Rhona had pointed out when she'd urged him to check the location.

Linkage denial – the inability to see that crimes were connected and have the same perpetrator. Was he suffering from that, or was he just being bloody-minded because Pirie was involved?

He'd been summoned to Sutherland's office on arrival. The meeting had played out much as before. Sutherland had suggested he didn't have a grip on the case. McNab pointed out that it was he who had sent the chopper to Skelmuir Hill. When asked why, McNab, for his sins, had given the impression that he had been the one to deduce the location from the online photograph. That had silenced Sutherland's criticisms, albeit briefly.

'When will we know the identity of anyone else playing this game?'

'Very soon,' McNab had lied.

But they had made some progress, although McNab

had chosen not to mention it. The search party at Skelmuir Hill had found a mobile. It had been dropped in a muddy ditch near the locus. Tech was examining the mobile now. McNab's gut instinct told him it would be the phone used to send the photograph. He hoped his hunch was as good as Rhona's had been.

Walking into the computer room depressed McNab. There was something about all that equipment, the sterile airless nature of the place. It reminded him of the mortuary, apart from the fact it didn't smell of dead bodies and disinfectant. He didn't like Rhona's lab either, too clinical, all shiny and full of stuff he didn't understand, which is what he felt in here.

Ollie, wearing outsize earphones, was sitting in front of a large touch screen. Beside him on the table lay an untouched bacon baguette and a can of Irn Bru. McNab's stomach groaned at the sight of it. He'd left Rhona's before breakfast, hoping she might think she'd merely dreamt his visit and his mention of SOCOs the previous night. Eating had been furthest from his mind while cleaning the flat. Now hunger was back with a vengeance. McNab eyed the baguette like an addict eyeing a line of coke. Ollie, absorbed in whatever he was doing, seemed to have forgotten his food. McNab wondered if he'd miss a bite.

Then Ollie, with that sixth sense that someone was watching him, turned, exposing a line of words on the screen.

Tune in, turn on, play hard, Live or Die by the Game.

'What are you doing?'

Ollie, catching McNab's venomous expression, looked puzzled and took off his earphones.

'What did you say?'

'I said what the fuck are you doing?'

'I'm playing the game.'

'You're playing a game?' McNab said incredulously.

Ollie looked offended. 'No. I'm playing *the* game.'

McNab's starved brain finally cottoned on to what was being said. 'You've figured it out?'

'Enough to make a start.'

A box suddenly opened in the bottom right-hand corner of the screen and a stream of letters appeared, which at first glance didn't make any sense.

'Someone's whispering to me,' Ollie said. 'That's good.'

Ollie typed a reply, which also didn't make sense. Then the screen froze. The string of expletives that emerged from Ollie's young mouth would have put McNab to shame.

'I'm out,' Ollie said by way of an explanation.

'Why?'

'I guess the puppetmaster didn't like me.'

Ollie's use of the word 'puppetmaster' caused McNab's heart to sink into his empty stomach. He reached for the baguette and broke it in two. He waved a half at Ollie. 'Mind?'

'Go ahead.'

'Any coffee?'

When Ollie nodded, McNab ordered it black.

Fifteen minutes later he was up to speed, on some of the terms at least. The game being played was an ARG, an Alternative Reality Game, controlled by a puppetmaster who lived behind a curtain. Players were recruited via rabbit holes. They were selected by the puppetmaster depending on how they answered a set of questions. The game consisted of clues in the shape of puzzles and information-gathering online and at physical sites, which if solved led the player to a 'treasure'. The players could be contacted in various ways, by phone, email, social media messages and online sites.

'I think he recruited them via chat sites for game players,' Ollie said. 'Then he selected a group of applicants.'

'Five?'

'Initially, yes.' Ollie looked worried.

'What do you mean, initially?' McNab said.

'I think the map and the photograph were put online to draw other participants into the game.'

'They were rabbit holes?' McNab said, trying to get his head round it.

'They're also clues.'

'Clues to what?'

'Who the killer is. Who's next to die, and where.'

'Jesus Christ,' McNab hissed.

Ollie brought up a screen. 'This is what comes up after you send in answers to the initial questions.'

McNab read the words.

Entity
Your test results have been received.
Stonewarrior is a cutting-edge alternate reality experience.
DO NOT ATTEMPT TO CONTACT THE STONEWARRIOR CORE.
Ignore communications from anyone seeking
information about the Game.
Tune in, turn on, play hard, Live or Die by the Game.

McNab pulled up a chair. 'My turn.'

39

'He's doing what?' Rhona said in disbelief.

The last fifteen minutes had consisted of a forensic interrogation by Chrissy about McNab's mythical break-in, followed by news that a body had been found at Skelmuir by an Air Support Team sent there by McNab. Something he'd definitely failed to say he would do the previous night. Now he was apparently playing a game.

'Can you get him for me? It's important.'

'He doesn't want to be disturbed,' DS Clark said apologetically.

Now Rhona was the one in an alternative reality.

'What's up?' Chrissy said, seeing her startled expression as she hung up.

'It seems McNab is trying to engage with the online game.'

Chrissy didn't look put out by that. 'Good,' was her response. 'The R2S crime-scene photographs of Skelmuir Hill are up,' she said. 'Come and take a look.'

They adjourned to Chrissy's laptop and Rhona observed as Chrissy slowly flicked through them.

'It's the same girl, no doubt about that. The layout of the body too. But no impaled hands. And no stone in the mouth,' Chrissy said.

Despite the differences, the images did echo those taken

on Cathkin Braes and at the Ring of Brodgar. Rhona said as much.

'It could be copycat,' Chrissy said. 'After all the material that's online about the killings.'

'What are you talking about?'

'Remember the Boston marathon case, how everybody posted on the Reddit site, supposedly trying to help. Amateur internet detectives nearly fucked everything up. They set up a subreddit called FindBostonBombers? Well the same's happening here.'

Chrissy brought up a screen with the headline that read 'WhostheStonewarrior?'.

Rhona read it with a sense of dismay.

'Mind you, the tabloids aren't much better. And it's going to get a lot worse if a body appears south of the border,' Chrissy foretold.

Rhona made a quick departure to write up various detailed reports on her findings, leaving Chrissy mid-sentence. It was the only tactic likely to work. Judging by Chrissy's expression through the glass, which resembled not a goldfish with its mouth open, but a piranha deprived of its meal, the interrogation wasn't over yet.

And Chrissy was right. The whole episode regarding McNab's supposed break-in was odd, but she would have to wait until he was available to speak to about that and about Magnus's deliberations the previous night.

Rhona turned her attention to her report on the Brodgar victim. Toxicology had identified a large quantity of cocaine and heroin in the body, strongly linking it to the Cathkin Braes killing. The vagina and other orifices were found to be free of semen. A presumptive test for saliva had proved positive. Adults made about 1.0 to 1.5 litres of saliva a day. It wasn't unusual for saliva to turn up at crime scenes. The girl's neck, ears and mouth had held traces, the DNA of which had matched traces on the roll-up found in the grass. The victim's saliva was also on the roll-up, suggesting she'd shared it with someone prior to her death. Rhona pictured the girl necking with someone, sharing a joint. Had that person been the one to kill her?

And now they had another victim.

Her desire to visit the latest locus was strong. Despite R2S's detailed record of the event, there was nothing to compare with being on site. The victim had been located in the early hours of that morning. Ideally the body would be in situ for twelve hours. There was still time.

She thought of Magnus. He too would want to visit the locus if possible. If a chopper wasn't available, they could share a car, although it was a three-hour drive to Aberdeen.

Rhona began making the necessary calls.

40

According to the Wild Wisdom of the Order of Bards, Ovates and Druids, the biggest problem of the present day was that humans had separated themselves from nature – so much so that they may not survive as a species. And so Helena had chosen to go wild over midsummer: camping in remote places, interacting more with nature, forsaking the real world. She'd forgotten that when she finally did want to reconnect, she might not be able to. Helena glanced down at her dead mobile, then out of the bus window. The scenery was fantastic, suggesting that even if the battery still had power, she would be unlikely to find a signal.

She abandoned her mobile and concentrated on the view. She hadn't intended on venturing this far, but the last message she'd received was too intriguing. Calling herself Caylum had led the puppetmaster to assume she was male. That in itself had made the interchange interesting. Meeting him in person would be even better.

She'd got involved via the Druid website. Having completed her course, it seemed the perfect way to test her knowledge. It had proved challenging, and she was aware she was pitted against others. How many she wasn't sure. She didn't normally play online games. They were for geeks who liked to kill things. But this game had been different. It had expanded her knowledge, intrigued and satisfied her. She was keen to meet its originator.

She'd intended heading to Stonehenge for midsummer. Then the message arrived. It had been too good to ignore. She'd never really considered this location as being all that important. Although mentioned, it certainly hadn't featured prominently in her studies. She wondered if it was within walking distance of the bus stop. Whether she would be able to find it, especially if her mobile wasn't working.

The warmth of the sun on the window was making her drowsy. Her eyes drifted shut and she entered the comfort zone between sleeping and waking, where thoughts become colourful and confused. She saw herself walking through bright green grass, blue cloudless sky above, the sun warm on her shoulders. She saw the marker stone laying its long cool shadow along the ground to meet her. She saw the puppetmaster, young, good-looking and definitely fanciable, walking towards her.

A fantasy, but a nice one.

The rhythm of the bus wheels on tarmac, the smooth rounding of corners and the soft sound of the air conditioning won over wakefulness and she slept.

She was wakened by rain beating the glass and the rumble of thunder. Startled, she forgot for a moment where she was and why. The bus had pulled up in front of a small hotel. There was only herself and the driver left on board.

'This is the end of the line,' he said. 'Hope you brought your brolly.'

'I was heading for the stone circle.'

The driver indicated the sheets of rain through which the hotel was just visible.

'It's a two-mile hike and no shelter when you get there.

261

Better to wait until this lot eases off, which, according to the forecast, might not be until tomorrow.'

The bus door swished back to reveal the power and ferocity of the thunderstorm.

Seeing her forlorn expression, he said, 'Megan will give you a bed for the night. She has a couple of rooms.'

Helena had planned on erecting her one-person tent near the circle, but there was little chance of that happening at the moment. She thanked the driver and, as suggested, made a beeline for the hotel entrance.

Once inside, the noise of the storm abated. Helena stood, unsure, in what was obviously the reception and bar rolled into one. A wood fire burned in a large fireplace; a big clock that looked as old as the wooden beams that criss-crossed the ceiling ticked with reassuring firmness against the wind and rain that beat the small windows. Outside might be a watery Armageddon but in here peace reigned.

She heard soft footsteps, then a young woman appeared behind the bar. Helena gave her a smile, which was quickly returned.

'The bus driver,' Helena began.

'Iain.'

'Said you might have a room?'

'We do.'

'I was planning on camping, but—'

They both looked up as a clap of thunder boomed above them.

'It'll clear by tomorrow,' her host suggested in a positive voice. 'My name's Megan. Follow me and I'll show you the room.'

Helena wanted to ask the price first but felt too embarrassed to do so. Perhaps sensing this, Megan mentioned a sum for dinner, bed and breakfast that sounded less than Helena had imagined and she nodded, relieved.

The attic room was small but more than adequate for a night's stay and the bed looked comfortable. Helena asked if Wi-Fi was available. Megan shook her head.

'And there's no signal on mobiles either. You'll have to walk up the glen road for half a mile, then you'll get one. We have a landline if you need to make a call.'

Helena nodded her thanks and Megan left.

She plonked herself down on the bed, grateful she had somewhere dry and comfortable to spend the night even if she was cut off from the outside world, and the puppetmaster.

What would happen when he couldn't reach her to give the final instructions? She was assuming she was in the right place and that the stone circle she'd identified was the correct one. She hadn't got it wrong up to now, but there was always a chance.

The thought unsettled her. She checked the sky for any hopeful signs and found none, then plugged in her mobile to charge it up.

When the rain eased she would walk out as directed and pick up a signal. Check if there was any further communication from the puppetmaster. Until then, she would have to wait.

41

McNab stared at the screen in disbelief. The questions had appeared straightforward. He hadn't even needed Ollie to interpret them. He was pretty sure his answers were correct, although his opinion was sought more often than a factual reply. The session had reminded him of a police interview, only in this case he'd been the one being questioned.

Regardless of all that, he was out.

Beside him, he could feel Ollie's tenseness. McNab threw the chair back and stood up.

'You lot are supposed to be able to trace things. If he's interacting with mobiles and digital devices you should be able to fucking find him.'

Ollie opened and shut his mouth. If he'd been about to explain how difficult that was proving to be, he'd decided against it. McNab turned heel and walked out. If this had been a terrorism call, it would be all systems go to find the participants. If it had been a serving soldier or policeman lying dead in a Neolithic circle, MI5 would have been all over it like a rash. But resources, effort and time were all limited when you were dealing with the deaths of computer geeks and game players. Especially if they were dying north of the border.

He headed for the coffee machine and chose a double espresso, drank it swiftly, then repeated the action, carrying this one through to his office. DS Clark rose from her desk as though to follow him in, but he waved her away and shut the door firmly behind him.

He had barely sat down when his mobile vibrated an incoming text.

He checked the screen but the number had been shielded, which could mean it came from one of his informants. McNab opened it.

Welcome to Stonewarrior. Await instructions.
DO NOT ATTEMPT TO CONTACT THE STONEWARRIOR CORE.
Ignore communications from anyone seeking information about the Game.
Tune in, turn on, play hard, Live or Die by the Game.

McNab rose, his first instinct to head back to the Tech department and have the text traced. His second instinct was the opposite. He sat back down, two questions prominent in his mind.

How the hell had they got his mobile number? And if he attempted to trace the call, would this – their only contact with the game – be broken?

Gut instinct told him to wait and do nothing, yet. Despite his misgivings, he felt a surge of excitement. He was *in*, whatever that meant. The puppetmaster, not content with playing them from afar, now wanted to make it personal.

His first big mistake.

McNab sat back in the chair and savoured his double espresso. The caffeine was good but not good enough. He took the paper cup to the filing cabinet and tipped in a good measure from the bottle kept for celebratory occasions, which this definitely was.

McNab savoured the whisky and the moment.

The puppetmaster had made the first move in this new game. Now it was McNab's turn.

An incoming text interrupted Rhona's attempt to call R2S and check out the availability of a helicopter. Viewing Skelmuir Hill on Google Earth had shown a veritable maze of rural roads. Add getting lost to a three-hour drive and the Air Support method seemed the better bet.

She checked the sender of the text and, seeing McNab's name, decided to read it first. It turned out to be a terse command ordering her to meet him as soon as possible at his flat and to bring her forensic bag. Rhona tried returning the call but got no answer.

She contemplated contacting him via DS Clark then decided against it. Whatever was going on, McNab definitely didn't want it official or Chrissy would have known well in advance. Rhona glanced through the glass to find Chrissy hunched over a microscope. The first problem would be exiting the lab without engaging in a further conversation with her forensic assistant.

But what about her planned trip north?

She swithered. McNab wouldn't ask her unless it was important. Last she'd heard he'd been playing the Druid game. What had become more important than that?

42

The downpour hadn't ceased, but it had definitely lessened. Helena had been dozing on the bed. Having camped for a succession of nights, the luxury of a mattress had proved too enticing for her aching limbs.

As the thick cloud parted, a shaft of sunlight had invaded her room and woken her. Rising from the bed, she'd surveyed the weather prospects, deciding that a walk as far as a signal was now a possibility, if not as far as the stones themselves.

She retrieved her mobile and headed downstairs.

Megan spotted her descent. 'When do you want to eat?'

'I was just going to check my mobile. When I get back?'

'Fish and chips do? Fish freshly caught this morning.'

'Sounds great.' And it did. Helena's stomach rumbled in anticipation. At the price she'd been quoted, she could add on a pint of lager.

She took herself down the road following Megan's directions, keeping an eye on her mobile screen. The road ahead rose to top a hill with a great view of a deep glen heading west. Higher hills rose to either side, explaining the blocked signals. But here she had a couple of bars, possibly enough.

A series of pings suggested she was right.

Helena scanned the list eagerly, but none of them were

from the puppetmaster. However, there were a couple of missed calls from her flatmate Jolene and a text.

Helena clicked it open.

Call me.

Helena was pretty sure it would be about the rent. She'd told Jolene she would be back on Wednesday and would pay it then. So, she was three days late. What was the big deal?

She flicked through the others, but there was nothing worth reading.

A surge of guilty conscience made her write a swift reply to Jolene.

Back Sunday. No worries.

That should keep Jolene off her back.

She stood for a bit, silently wishing that another more interesting message would arrive. Eventually she gave up. She would head back and eat, then try a little later. As though to urge her on, another sweep of rain was heading her way. The glen was no longer visible, it and the neighbouring mountains swathed in black cloud.

Helena turned and made her way swiftly back towards the hotel.

43

Rhona tried the communal button. If McNab was here he wasn't answering his buzzer. The main door clicked open and Rhona headed up the stairs. McNab's door was off the latch, obviously in anticipation of her arrival. She called his name as she stepped into the hall, then waited for his reply.

It never came.

'McNab?' she tried again.

There were no forensic treads set out in the hall. No evidence that any examination had taken place. It wasn't that unusual for a police officer's home to be targeted, but if it was, the matter was taken seriously. No one wanted their address to be common knowledge, or their phone number. McNab had been responsible for putting away a lot of criminals. Men and women he'd had banged up were often back on the streets all too quickly. And McNab wasn't one to disguise his role in any conviction he was responsible for, which meant his profile was always at its maximum.

Rhona listened for sounds of anyone in the flat. There were none.

She pushed open the sitting-room door.

The first thing she noticed was the acrid smell. McNab had been cleaning, or at least spraying a great deal of bleach about. Then she spotted the arc-shaped yellow stain on the wall, which looked suspiciously like a urine trail. Someone had had a go at the mark, but had only succeeded in whitening the wallpaper.

They'd been at the carpet too. The proof being a couple of colourless patches in the pattern. Even the coffee table hadn't escaped the frenzy, the varnish lifted in a circle in the centre.

McNab wasn't the cleaning type. According to him the tidy nature of the flat on her previous visit had been down to Iona. But this wasn't basic housekeeping. This was something else entirely. This is what you found when people wanted to remove forensic evidence.

What the hell had he been trying to clean up?

McNab was a loose cannon at times, hence her fear for him in his new post, but removing evidence was not something he would do. But evidence of what?

She'd been there a good five minutes and McNab still hadn't appeared, despite the door being left off the latch. Rhona checked her mobile. There were no further texts. When she tried calling him, she got the messaging service.

The only sensible explanation was that he'd been called away, so had left the door open in expectation of her imminent arrival. Which meant he'd assumed she would respond to his order. The thought rankled, but she set about checking the rest of the flat anyway.

The bed had been stripped, the washed and still-wet sheets in the washing machine. The wardrobe doors were open and it looked as though McNab had been rummaging in there. There were a few empty hangers and an open drawer.

Had this been a suspect's flat she would have made the

assumption that the bird had flown the coop. Rhona tried to recall last night's events. McNab hadn't been carrying any luggage when he arrived. Not even a backpack.

So why the missing clothes?

In the bathroom, McNab's shaving utensils were conspicuous by their absence, which suggested that he had in fact decamped and probably to Iona's. The thought irritated Rhona, plus the suspicion that having ordered her here, McNab had had no intention of being here himself.

Not for the first time did she call herself a fool for her response.

What she should do now, was leave. That's what her rising anger told her. Concern gave her a different message. Something had happened here. Something that worried McNab. He'd broached the subject the previous night then fallen asleep before elaborating on what it was. He'd contacted her this morning and asked for her professional help.

Despite the circumstances, that's what she was here for.

Rhona donned the regulation boiler suit, shoes, mask and gloves. If there was something to find, then she would discover it, despite the obvious attempts to clean up.

Two hours later she had a forensic picture of the room before the cleaning frenzy. It was a troubling one, especially the presence of cocaine on the work surface and the bloodstains on the sheets. Whoever had put them in to wash had set the water temperature too low to remove the marks. The stained wallpaper had turned out to be urine as she'd thought. The bleach attack on the carpet hadn't managed to remove all traces of human faeces.

LIN ANDERSON

Different scenarios played out in her head, none of them good, and all of them involving Iona, which was probably why McNab had chosen to keep it off the record. If a crime had been committed here and Rhona failed to report it, then she became an accessory.

She went back through each room, standing long enough to ask herself what she had sampled and why. The bathroom came last. She dusted the toilet seat for prints, just in case an intruder had used it, although if he'd urinated against the wall that was unlikely.

That's when she saw the wire just under the lip of the cistern. She laid down her dusting equipment and lifted the lid. The orange balloon was attached to the ballcock. Rhona untied it and lifted it out. If it contained what she thought, there would be others. She put the filled balloon into an evidence bag.

This time her search wasn't for traces of an intruder, but for teabags of cocaine. The rifled wardrobe produced three of them, one from a shirt pocket, two inside rolled-up socks.

A fourth bag she found taped behind the poster on the wall above the fireplace. All juvenile places to hide your stash, she told herself. Therefore more likely done by Iona. The question was did McNab know his girlfriend was using and hiding the stash in his flat?

Rhona tried not to think the unthinkable. That McNab was the one who was using.

She packed up her samples and stripped off the boiler suit. During her sojourn at the flat she'd made three attempts to contact McNab, all of them fruitless.

When she left she pulled the front door firmly shut behind her.

272

She would store all the evidence she'd collected at the lab, then she would locate McNab and sort out this mess before things got any worse.

44

McNab flung the bag in the back of the car. He would have preferred to wait for Rhona but the instructions had been very specific and time was of the essence. He was taking a chance, but his instinct told him this was what he had to do if they were to have any prospect of catching the perpetrator.

If it all went wrong, he didn't want Rhona to be involved, but he did want her to know the truth. Using the mobile was now out of the question. He would need to get word to her another way.

The jazz club was quiet, with just a scattering of lunchtime visitors. McNab did a quick check to make sure none of his colleagues were there before heading for Sean's office. Sean and he might be love rivals but McNab had reason to trust the Irishman.

'McNab, what brings you here?' Sean said in surprise at his entry.

'Rhona.'

Sean immediately rose from the seat in concern. 'What's happened?'

Not for the first time did McNab recognize just how deep were the ties that bound Rhona and Sean together. 'Nothing,' he said swiftly. 'I need you to deliver something to her. If necessary,' he added.

Sean examined him closely. 'Okay.' He resumed his seat. 'And how will I know if it's necessary?'

'You'll know.'

'You in trouble?' Sean didn't say 'again', although he might have.

'I have a little undercover job to do. I'll be out of contact for a while.'

'How long exactly?'

'Twenty-four hours.'

'And I deliver whatever it is if . . .'

'I don't come back for it,' McNab finished for him. He laid the mobile down on the desk.

Sean looked down at the phone, then up at McNab. 'I hope you have someone watching your back?'

McNab didn't answer. 'Twenty-four hours,' he repeated. 'No longer.'

Sean called something in Irish as McNab departed. McNab hoped he'd wished him good luck.

DS Clark was used to McNab's way of working when he'd been the DS and she the detective constable. But the next rung up the ladder had changed things for both of them.

Their relationship had always been prickly, because McNab didn't take rejection very well. Like every other female in the office, Janice had been tempted by the roguish smile, but the thought of being swiftly dropped was worse than the prospect of the encounter, so she'd turned him down. McNab hadn't given up easily. After the third time, he'd made a remark that had seen him called into DI Wilson's office. Whatever had been said in there had put an end to things. Janice had been pleased and sorry at the same time.

Since McNab had taken on the role of inspector, Janice had watched him fight his old self, while trying to become a version of DI Wilson. It would never work and Janice knew it. No two DIs operated in the same way, despite carrying the same title. McNab needed to stay his own man if he was ever to be as successful as he had been at DS level. She would, of course, never tell him this. Her plan had been to take the sarcasm, the blame and the sudden reversal of decisions on the chin, until McNab found his true way.

Janice didn't doubt that this would happen, but she knew he needed someone to watch his back in the interim. In the absence of DI Wilson, that role fell to her.

McNab had been out of contact now for four hours and there were things he needed to know, the first one being that the geocaching guy who'd seen the cocaine stash had been located and was willing to speak to someone about it. The second, and even more important development, had come from Dr MacLeod.

Of the two hairs found on Alan MacKenzie's clothing, one had been identified as belonging to Alan's flatmate, Jamie. DNA from the other had produced two partial matches when run through the database, which indicated both were related to the hair's owner, and both had been convicted of a crime. One of the two was a man of seventy who had committed a series of burglaries over a period of ten years. Angus Patterson was now living in a care home in Paisley and was suffering from dementia. The other partial match belonged to Isabel Kearney who'd been convicted of manslaughter, having stabbed her abusive husband to death. Her story was an uncomfortable read. She'd been sent to prison five years ago, but had only served six months of her sentence before finding an opportunity to hang herself.

Janice entered McNab's empty office and laid the report on his desk next to the paper espresso cup. She lifted the cup to throw it in the bin and caught the whiff of whisky. McNab had returned from the Tech department with a face like thunder. Her attempt to speak to him had been thwarted when he'd disappeared in here and shut the door in her face. Whatever had happened when he'd tried to play the online game had made him so angry he'd resorted to drinking on duty.

Something that Sutherland would just love to find out.

Janice gave a quick glance round, wondering if the bottle was still in here somewhere. The top drawer of the filing cabinet stood partially open. She walked over as though to shut it, but really to see if that was the hiding place.

It was, and the bottle, two-thirds consumed, was still there.

Janice closed and locked the cabinet and slipped the key into the desk drawer. McNab would go mad when he found out she'd been snooping, but she could cope with that. On her way out Janice picked up the paper cup and took it to the ladies toilet where she rinsed it clean of the smell of whisky, crushed it and threw it in the bin.

Once back at her desk, she gave Dr MacLeod a ring.

Rhona listened to Janice's story, without reciting her own. 'And you've no idea where he might have gone?' Rhona said.

'No, apart from the fact his mobile's either switched off or out of range.' Janice hesitated, which suggested there was more.

'What else?' Rhona said.

Janice's voice dropped to a whisper. 'I found a bottle of whisky in his office.'

'He's drinking on duty?'

Janice's silence was enough answer.

'Does he know about the familial DNA matches?'

'No. The report arrived after he'd gone out.'

Rhona hesitated. 'The woman he's been seeing. Her name's Iona. He met her in the pub the night of his party. Any chance you can locate her?'

A moment's silence, then Janice said, 'I'll ask around. See if anyone knows her.'

Rhona rang off without mentioning her visit to McNab's flat, which, she acknowledged, was her first step on the wrong path.

She threw down the phone. Damn and blast McNab for putting her in this position. She should have known he wouldn't handle being a DI. He always thought only he could figure things out.

The labelling of the trace evidence from the flat had caused her some problems, the main one being Chrissy. She stored them out of Chrissy's immediate view, but it was unlikely they would go unmarked for long. What exactly she would say to Chrissy, Rhona had no idea. Lying wouldn't work. Chrissy was a veritable lie detector, being so good at avoiding the truth herself.

Rhona made a coffee and sat down to think.

McNab had disappeared off the radar and he wasn't answering his phone. Those two things worried her even more than the state of his flat and the cocaine stash.

'Coffee time?' Chrissy's expression was inscrutable. She busied herself pouring a mug and scrabbling about in the biscuit tin. When she emerged, she got straight to the point.

'So what does McNab think about the familial matches?'

'No idea.'

'But you were on the phone to Janice. I heard you.'

Jesus. Could Chrissy hear through walls?

'McNab's out. He hasn't seen the report we sent yet.'

Chrissy made a sound that suggested she was on to Rhona. 'Didn't you call him?'

'He's out of range, or his mobile's switched off.' Rhona tried to sound unconcerned.

'Mmm.' Chrissy attacked a Jaffa Cake.

Rhona thought it symbolized going in for the kill. She was right.

'He's gone awol, hasn't he?'

'What makes you say that?' said Rhona indignantly.

'Remember the time he took me to The Poker Club and you wanted to come? We wouldn't let you, because you are incapable of bluffing. Your face is an open book. Where's McNab?'

'I have no idea,' Rhona said.

'Now, I believe you.' Chrissy helped herself to another biscuit. The second Jaffa Cake was swiftly demolished.

'I think McNab's fucked up big time.' She observed Rhona. 'Want to tell me how?'

45

DS Clark stood outside the interview room, collecting herself before she went in. It wasn't as though she hadn't done this before. A million times. It was just that . . .

Before she thought any further, she opened the door.

The guy was sitting just as she'd left him. The room smelt of male sweat mingled with strong aftershave. An unappealing combination. She found herself making judgements on the occupant. Judgements she wasn't comfortable with. Such as he wasn't fanciable, because he sweated too much and didn't use deodorant.

It was cruel. She knew it and disliked herself for it. It was also unprofessional.

On the other hand, the guy didn't seem to care that being smelly might make things difficult for those around him. Especially in the close confines of an interview room.

If she was assessing him, he was also assessing her. Janice was used to such looks from men, especially in her capacity as a female police officer. Phrases such as 'obviously a dyke', 'tits too small', 'doesn't get it often enough', 'frigid bitch' and 'cunt on legs' sprang to mind.

'Mr Munro,' she said quickly to stop that train of thought. 'Detective Inspector McNab isn't available to speak to you—'

'I'd rather talk to you.'

'But I thought you asked to speak to him?'

'I told them I *didn't* want to speak to him. *Anyone* but him.'

Janice wondered if he'd met McNab before and didn't fancy a second round. 'I understand you want to make a statement?'

He nodded. A trickle of sweat descended his cheek. He made no attempt to wipe it away.

'I saw him, that detective, take the cocaine.'

If Steve Munro had declared his undying love for her, it would have surprised Janice less.

'Sorry . . .'

He interrupted her. 'Is this recording? I want it recorded. I went back to see if the holdall was still there. I saw him dig it up and take it away.'

Janice almost laughed, it was so ridiculous.

'You say you saw Detective Inspector McNab remove a holdall you claim held cocaine, which was buried on Cathkin Braes?'

'I saw a guy remove it. I didn't know then it was the detective. Then I saw him on the news. It was him all right.'

Janice ignored that for the moment. 'When exactly did you see someone remove the cocaine?'

'Late Sunday night.'

Janice tried to remember when McNab had first mentioned the report of the cocaine stash. It had been on Monday at the strategy meeting.

'When did you first report finding the buried cocaine?'

'On Sunday, after I saw the body.'

'You reported the body and the cocaine at the same time?'

He shook his head wildly. 'No. I wasn't sure about mentioning the cocaine in case someone had seen me with it. I called back later and they put me through to the detective.'

'But you saw it removed on Sunday night?'

He looked puzzled as though she had gone off script and he couldn't remember his lines. 'I thought it was one of them who'd taken it. Then I saw him on the telly. It was definitely him. The detective.'

The guy was talking bullshit, but she couldn't stop him if he wanted to give a statement, and once he did that it had to be dealt with.

Allegations against police personnel occurred with monotonous regularity, usually with respect to assault. McNab had been involved in an assault charge on more than one occasion, and cleared, mostly down to his commanding officer at the time, DI Wilson.

Janice wished DI Wilson was here now. She cleared her throat.

'You want to make a statement regarding DI McNab?'

He nodded, then repeated his assertion. 'I saw him take the cocaine from the hiding place on Cathkin Braes on Sunday night.'

'When the area was thick with police officers?'

He shot her an angry look. 'They'd mostly gone by midnight. Any left were inside the tent.'

That was true. Too true to be comfortable.

Janice tried to remember when she'd last seen McNab up there, then stopped herself. This was ridiculous. McNab didn't remove a stash of cocaine. The guy was making it up.

His cheeks and forehead were slick with sweat, his

eyeballs darting about. He was obviously shitting himself, but he was here and prepared to make a statement that would put him and McNab under scrutiny.

'Would you like a mug of tea, Mr Munro?'

'Why?' he said suspiciously.

'We usually offer people tea when they're making a statement.'

'I'd rather have coffee,' he said grudgingly.

Janice nodded and stood up. 'I'll fetch paper and a pen, and a cup of coffee.'

He sat back, looking relieved. Mission accomplished, he wiped his forehead of sweat.

Janice exited and shut the door, her hand trembling. McNab had disappeared, leaving a trail of unanswered questions in his wake. Now this?

She calmed herself. Remember the rule of the detective. Everyone was lying until proved otherwise. A small voice questioned whether that included McNab.

'Okay,' Chrissy said. 'This is how we play it. I sign the evidence bags that came from McNab's. I do the standard tests. We keep everything in house, until he's back and we can speak to him and find out what happened.'

'What about the cocaine?'

'I test it against the trace samples we took from Cathkin Braes.'

It was what Rhona had intended doing herself. 'And if it's a match?'

'McNab's not using,' Chrissy said. 'But the daft bitch he was screwing probably is, which is why we have to find her.'

Rhona explained about her conversation with DS Clark.

Chrissy shook her head. 'I'll speak to Janice. It's better if I look for Lolita unofficially. That way we keep the relationship under wraps.' She shook her head. 'This is all your fault, boss. If you'd taken McNab up on his offer the night of the party, Iona would never have got her claws into him.'

Rhona opened her mouth to protest, but Chrissy had already deposited her mug and was on her way out. The door shut with a bang.

Rhona glanced skywards. 'Where the hell are you, McNab?'

46

McNab pulled into the petrol station. According to the sign this was the last chance to fill up before he hit the wasteland. McNab didn't like wide open spaces, nor the scent of things growing. The mean streets of Glasgow, even the area round the Union bar, were sweet in comparison to what lay around him.

Mountains, emptiness and silence.

Still stiff from the long drive, and his overnight sleep on the back seat, he eased himself out of the car, filled up and went to the kiosk, taking out the pay-as-you-go mobile and checking it as he entered.

'No signal here, pal,' a Glasgow voice informed him from behind the counter. 'The mountains,' he added by way of explanation.

'No signal? *Anywhere?*' McNab said, aghast.

'Hit and miss most of the time. Where you headed?'

'West,' McNab said.

'It gets better when you hit the coast.'

McNab gathered a selection of snacks and a bottle of Irn Bru and paid for them along with the petrol.

'Hope you booked a bed ahead. It's busy this time of year with tourists.'

The word *busy* didn't work for McNab, not surrounded by emptiness.

'How long before I meet the sea?'

'Three hours, give or take a caravan or two.'

Jesus, three more hours of this.

'Don't bother with the sat nav. It'll send you the wrong way,' his advisor threw after him in a sarcastic voice as he departed.

McNab started up the engine and drove away. In the rear mirror, the Glaswegian who'd bizarrely departed the city to live in this wilderness watched him leave.

McNab turned on the car radio. The result was a hiss of indecipherable words, regardless of which station he sought. So no radio reception either. McNab didn't do music plugged into his ears, so he would have to travel in silence.

As a result his brain replayed the scenario that had brought him here.

He'd initially failed the entry test to the game, then received a message via his mobile, declaring him a player. That had suggested the puppetmaster had been aware of his identity. Not only that, he'd also got hold of McNab's number.

McNab thought back to the trashed flat and the suspicion that his mobile had been compromised. Maybe he'd been wrong about Iona. Maybe she hadn't been stalking him because of the cocaine stash. Maybe she had something to do with *Stonewarrior*.

He briefly considered that possibility, but didn't wear it. Nothing she'd said or done suggested any link with the game. But that didn't mean she hadn't sold his number on to whoever sought it.

Another possible explanation was that there was a mole at the police station, maybe even in the Tech department. Personnel were vetted for both the force and the support staff, but it needed a techie to play the game, and what better if you played it from the inside?

Iona, Ollie, Big Davy. How many more people couldn't he trust?

An image of Rhona came to mind. He'd asked her to forensically examine the flat without an explanation. What would she do when she found out what he'd tried to clean up, as she undoubtedly would? If she suspected a crime had been committed, it was her professional duty to report it. Her first instinct, he thought, would be to try to talk to him. He glanced down at the silent mobile. And that wasn't a possibility until the twenty-four hours were up.

As for DS Clark, he'd dumped her in more shit than had been spread about his flat. His sergeant, McNab was certain, would try to protect him as long as she could. Something he didn't deserve.

The road had narrowed to a single track, weaving through an expanse of bog, interspersed with rocky outcrops and stagnant pools. Ahead of him, a camper van trundled, obviously in no hurry. McNab put his foot on the brake, cursing. Stuck behind a tourist would see a three-hour journey extend to four.

He blasted the horn.

His demand bore fruit, sending the van into the next passing place to allow him to overtake. McNab signalled his thanks by raising his hand. A young male watched McNab sail past.

Ten minutes later he emerged from the valley, and the pay-as-you-go on the passenger seat lit up a possible signal. The puppetmaster's instructions had been clear. Any communication from McNab en route to their meeting place and he would forfeit the game. Since he had a trace on McNab's mobile, he would know if it was being used. McNab had chosen to believe him, and left his mobile with Sean. But he wasn't fool enough not to have a back-up.

At that moment the 'no signal' message appeared again on the screen. *Some back-up.*

The sun had moved behind the mountain range, casting the road valley in deep shadow. McNab shivered and took his eye briefly from the road to switch off the air conditioner. Checking the rear-view mirror, he caught a glimpse of the camper he'd passed a while back, coming up behind him at high speed.

So he *had* pissed the driver off and now it was his turn to be tail-gated.

McNab contemplated the fast-approaching passing place, then decided against it. If the driver of the shagging wagon wanted a rally, who was he to deny him?

McNab put his foot down. The car sprang forward, like a horse kicked in the flank, leaving camper boy way behind. McNab smiled. Maybe single-track roads weren't so boring after all.

But his challenger wasn't giving up that easily, and whatever was under the camper's bonnet had plenty of horsepower. Plus, it was obvious by the way he took corners that he was familiar with the road. This wasn't going to be a one-horse race.

The road had left the bog and now wound its way through a ravine. To the right a fall of scree ended in a riverbed. To the left rose a wall of rock. McNab took the first two corners too wide, and got a brief glimpse of how far he had to fall, should he make a mistake third time round.

'Don't be a stupid bastard for once,' he told himself.

This wasn't the place for a race, especially against someone who was familiar with the terrain.

First passing place, and he was in it.

Two bends later, one appeared. McNab braked and began to draw in, happy to acknowledge defeat by giving the thumbs-up to his erstwhile racing companion. He never got the chance.

The camper van hit his boot straight on, thrusting it forward. McNab felt the snap as his neck whiplashed back and forth in quick succession. Before he could gather his wits, the van hit again. McNab, stunned by the impact, lost control of the wheel and the car took an abrupt turn to the right. He'd been travelling at twenty, the van much faster. Their combined speed sent him hurtling towards the bank of scree. McNab hit the brakes, while simultaneously pulling on the handbrake. There was a sickening screech as the car tried to obey. Smoke rose in nauseous waves as the wheels grabbed frantically at the tarmac. The car slithered onwards, albeit slower.

The van had blasted into reverse and was coming at him again.

It hit the passenger door this time, causing McNab's head to strike the side window with a crack. He had to get out of the car before the bastard sent him over the edge. Eyes watering from the impact, McNab managed to release the seatbelt and scrabbled with the door.

It flew open and he fell out, the back of his head taking the impact this time.

A figure appeared to block McNab's watery view of the sky.

His last thought before blackness overtook him . . . who the fuck was this guy?

47

He pocketed the mobile and removed everything from the boot and the glove compartment. Then he set about pushing the car over the edge. The bank was steep enough for it to go alone once it was on the move. But he had to be swift. There was little traffic on this road, but it was the tourist season and someone would eventually come along.

The car resisted at first, its chassis twisted by the impact, but his strength was more than enough to get it going. Sweat erupted all over his body, making his hands slippery. He wiped them on his jeans and gave one last concentrated effort as a cloud of midges arrived in search of his salt and blood.

With a grunt it went over. There were no boulders to block its path, only the sliding scree to aid its descent. It slithered downwards, bending small saplings in its wake, speeding up as it reached halfway. He heard the splash as it rolled into the river. The water soon found it, rearing up and over the bonnet and roof.

He stood for a brief moment, acknowledging his success, then turned back to the van. He did a quick check for damage. The grille he'd fitted to the front had borne the most impact. It looked none the worse for it. He climbed into the driver's seat, took a swift look behind him, did a three-point turn and headed back the way he had come.

48

Janice read the statement one more time. It was ridiculous, and implausible, but nevertheless it had to be checked. She was sure, if she could speak to McNab, that he would be able to blow it out of the water. She imagined the look he would give her. Quailed under its imagined scorn.

She laid the paper down on McNab's desk beside the report on the familial connection. This would all be sorted out when McNab reappeared. Meanwhile, they would carry on as normal. She contemplated calling Dr MacLeod, but was unwilling to divulge this new development. She tried to imagine why Steve Munro had made such an accusation. Fear seemed foremost in his mind, which suggested he may have been leaned on. If he had been the anonymous tip-off, as he'd claimed, why divulge his identity now?

No matter which way she looked at it, it was not good news for the DI. She made a decision and slipped the statement into the desk drawer. The report she would make a point of dealing with. Maybe even have something concrete when McNab reappeared, as he would surely do tomorrow.

Janice checked the phone number of the nursing home. She would give them a call and arrange to speak to Angus Patterson, assuming he was still capable of talking at all.

*

Rhona stood for a moment to admire the front garden. Margaret had always been a keen gardener, as evidenced by the display on show. Rhona, on the other hand, was an expert at killing houseplants. When Sean and she had lived together, he had cultivated a selection of herbs in a kitchen window box. Parsley, rocket, thyme and rosemary. She knew the names, could even distinguish between them. Unfortunately, the plants rebelled when Sean left. The thyme had lasted the longest, but even it chose to go eventually. Death being preferable to living with her.

It wasn't a pleasant thought and led to other thoughts of death. Margaret had survived breast cancer, only to see it return. The second prognosis was good, but Bill had decided that, this time round, they would face the surgery and chemo together. Margaret had tried to discourage him from taking leave, believing he was better concentrating on a case than fussing round her, but she'd eventually relented.

Rhona pushed open the gate and walked up the path to the front door. She hadn't warned Bill she was coming, because she hadn't been sure she would carry it through. She pressed the bell before she could change her mind.

It was Margaret who opened the door. Rhona tried not to examine her for signs of illness, but as a scientist that was verging on the impossible. It took a couple of seconds to assure herself that Margaret looked tanned and well. Her hair was cut close to her head, but it looked glossy and she hadn't lost any weight since the last time they'd met.

'Rhona. What a nice surprise. Come through. We're in the back garden. I've got Bill spraying the tomatoes. Blasted greenfly gets worse with the better weather.'

He was in the greenhouse, doing as instructed. DI Bill Wilson, her friend and mentor. At the sight of his tall figure, Rhona realized with a jolt how much she had missed him.

He turned and, seeing her arrival, swiftly abandoned the greenfly spray and came to greet her.

As she had studied Margaret, Bill now subjected Rhona to the same scrutiny. Intuition was simply psychology in action, Magnus liked to say. One look would tell Bill that she was here for more than just a social visit, despite her attempts to appear otherwise.

It seemed Margaret had already sussed that out. 'I'll fetch some tea.'

Bill waved Rhona towards the path that ran between the lawn and the flower beds.

They strolled along it for some moments before he spoke. 'How's he doing?'

'Struggling a bit, I think.'

Bill nodded. 'Everyone does when handed more power and responsibility.' He stopped to study her. 'Want to tell me more?'

Rhona gave Bill a brief résumé about Iona and the mess at the flat.

'You think this girl was a plant?'

'I think she may have been. The holdall of cocaine hasn't been located. We assumed the gang had taken it. Maybe they hadn't.'

'And she was set the task of finding out?'

Rhona nodded.

'And this game that's being played out online?' Bill said.

'You've been following it?'

'Trust McNab to get that for his first case as DI.' Bill gave a wry smile. 'He hates computers.'

'Almost as much as he hates psychologists.' Rhona paused. 'The internet interest has made it even more difficult for him. Sutherland's on his back a lot and . . .'

'And?' Bill said.

'Apparently McNab tried engaging with the game, and failed. He left the Tech department in a fury. Next we know he marches out of the police station. Nobody's been able to get hold of him since.'

Bill waved her to a seat. They settled there, looking back across the green expanse of lawn at the house. Rhona spotted Margaret checking on them from the French windows and deciding the time for tea had not yet come.

'Tell me everything you have on the case.'

It took twenty minutes. When Rhona eventually reached the familial matches to DNA found at the scene of crime, Bill stopped her and asked her to repeat the names.

'Angus Patterson and Isabel Kearney.'

'They're brother and sister. Angus was a lot older than Isabel.'

'You knew them?'

Bill nodded. 'Angus was a housebreaker and petty criminal. Disappeared off the radar a while back.'

'He's in a nursing home, suffering from dementia. Isabel Kearney—'

'Took her own life in prison. The man she stabbed was her husband, Derek Kearney. Kearney had no previous convictions, so wouldn't be on the database, but he was a bastard. Raped her at knifepoint, God knows how many times. She would never press charges, because of the boy.'

'She had a child?'

'Josh. He was fourteen when it happened. We thought at the time it might have been Josh who stabbed Derek, but Isabel always insisted it was her and her DNA was all over the knife.'

Rhona waited, knowing there was more.

'Shortly after she died, the boy disappeared from care. We never found him.' He paused. 'It was McNab's first case as DS.'

49

Josh Kearney was born at midnight on a kitchen floor that swam with his mother's blood. It was a speedy birth brought on by a punch to the stomach. Derek Kearney had returned from a visit to the pub and took umbrage when Isabel felt less than keen to have sex. Derek had always made a point of hitting Isabel where the bruises would not be seen. Her pregnancy had made this more challenging, because her belly had become a focus of attention. Thus he had taken to fucking her anally, so as not to arouse suspicion.

It was not often she resisted. In this case she had, and bore the brunt of his anger and frustration. He'd left almost immediately afterwards, realizing that she had gone into labour, something he had no wish to view or take part in.

The birth was swift and occurred before the ambulance arrived. They found Isabel lying on the floor, the baby, cord uncut, resting in her arms. Josh was bloody and bruised, like his mother, but alive.

Josh had, of course, no memory of his beginnings, but of what played out afterwards he was very clear. His father never hit him, but continued to torture his mother. Josh observed and absorbed this, even learned from it. By five, he was trying out some of his father's actions on children smaller than himself. He pinched them, bit them, poked them with sharp objects, but made himself scarce when someone came to answer their cries for help.

Josh was never referred to a social worker. He was fed and housed and his mother gave him love, which seemed strangely at odds with his perception of human relationships. His mother acted as though the way they lived was the norm, but she didn't invite friends or other children to the house, except his uncle Angus.

Angus was always old. Old and cunning. He brought the boy presents. Toys, DVDs. He took the ten-year-old shopping and showed him how to acquire similar items, warning him never to tell his mother.

Angus liked the ladies. He invited Josh to observe what fun the boy could have when older. Josh was hidden in a cupboard when one was due to arrive at Angus's place, the door left open for him to watch.

It was nothing like what went on in his own house.

There was no screaming or crying during these encounters, but subservience was required, and paid for. The females were invariably young. Josh liked watching them undress and seeing them naked, although he felt sickened by Angus's wrinkled rump bumping up and down against their smooth young skin. Or when he thrust himself into their painted mouths. Josh took to working himself while he watched and even now a memory of those childhood scenes could bring him to climax.

As he grew older, he learned to be out of the house whenever his father was at home. Then he didn't have to see or hear what played out between his parents. His father had invited him to watch once, excited by drink and the possibility of an audience. Josh, who had gone along with so much, found himself appalled by such an offer, and left the house, the image of his mother's expression of fearful compliance a permanent fixture in his memory.

At fourteen, he'd acquired a girlfriend who permitted him easy access, which strangely Josh found he did not want, so he dumped her. At this time, his father had begun to find himself unsatisfied by the sexual torture of Josh's mother. The rules by which he had fulfilled his desires seemed too restrictive. The need to hide evidence of it, no longer important.

Josh knew his father was continually testing his mother's limits of endurance, her continuing submission fuelling an even greater need for control.

Then one night in the same kitchen it had all come to an end.

Derek had her pinned face down on a kitchen unit, a knife nestled to her throat, when Josh walked in. Derek had ignored his son's arrival and continued his relentless violent thrusts. Blood trickled down his mother's neck.

Josh stood silent as his father finished, wiped himself on his mother's skirt, then offered his son the option of going next.

Had his mother screamed at him not to, had she cried, maybe things would have played out differently. But she didn't. She stayed where she was, her face pleading with Josh not to make his father angry.

Josh had approached as though willing, and his father, pleased, had slapped him on the back.

'Your turn,' had been his words.

Josh had taken the knife from his father's hand and shoved it in his father's belly. His face had been a picture.

Paths of the Dead

Josh gripped the wheel a little tighter as a scrapbook of images presented themselves. Like any good story, the end had reflected the beginning. He had come into this world, a product of his father, exactly where his father's life had been ended, by him.

Although, he reminded himself, it didn't really end there, because she, as always, had taken the blame. A martyr to the end, his mother had removed the knife from his hand, wiped it, then proceeded to stab his father relentlessly. She hadn't done it from anger, but from love, something Josh would never understand.

Even as he thought this, a hand moved to the driving wheel to touch his own.

'Where are we going?' she said.

'You'll see. Soon.'

She looked pretty, the warm glow of the evening sky painting her cheeks pink. He pulled out his mobile and took a photograph.

50

It was a matter of opinion whether Angus Patterson was alive or not. A heart still beat in his chest, although feebly. His body was present in this world, emaciated and grey, despite their efforts to get him to eat. His mind, however, was frequently absent.

A project to help dementia patients to remember, which consisted of presenting them with photographs and music from World War Two, would send him into a paroxysm of rage. Whereas page three of the *Scottish Sun* brought a leery smile to his countenance.

He was infamous in the nursing home for trying to squeeze female buttocks whenever he had the chance, going even further if a skirt was worn. At times, nurses would spot a small limp white sausage exposed in his lap. They would promptly shove it back in and zip him up, which was what he'd wanted them to do all along.

When he was aware of his surroundings, he conceded that life had dealt him a reasonable end. Surrounded by women, most of them young, many of them pretty, wasn't a bad way to end your days. They washed and fed him. All of which meant he had their hands engage with his body. And he didn't have to pay for it either.

At this moment, he was seated in the day room, sun streaming through the glass, a pretty woman by his side.

She was plump, which he liked, her breasts straining the shirt she wore. Although his wits and memory deserted him at times, his sense of smell never had. And he could smell skirt. Young skirt.

'Mr Patterson. I wanted to ask you about your family,' the pretty mouth was saying.

Angus licked his lips.

'Have you any family? Nieces or nephews? Grand-children?' She smiled her encouragement.

Angus thought about other painted lips. Of all the colours worn, he'd always like red the best.

'Have you any family, Mr Patterson?' she said again.

'Give us a fuck.'

She sat back, surprise on her face.

'I'll pay,' he promised, his hand reaching for his zip.

She stood up and retreated.

Anger swept over him. What was wrong with the bitch? He'd offered to pay, hadn't he?

A couple of figures rushed in. One came towards him and told him to stop swearing like that. The other swept the skirt away. Fury exploded in Angus's brain and everything turned red. He was frightened by the red mist. It made him think of hell.

'I'm sorry about that,' the attendant said when they reached the hall.

Janice waved her concerns away. 'In my line of work, you hear much worse than that,' she said.

'You were asking about his family?'

'Yes.'

'He has a photograph in his room in a drawer. Of a woman and small boy. He told me once it was his sister.'

'May I see it?'

The woman led her along a corridor lined with doors. Noises drifted out. Weeping, muttering, odd-sounding laughter. It reminded Janice of prison. Only in here the inmates were imprisoned by their minds and not by bars.

They had reached a door with ANGUS PATTERSON, 117 on it. The attendant slipped a key in the lock and turned it.

'If we don't lock the rooms, people get muddled and go in the wrong one. It causes problems.'

She stood aside to let Janice enter.

Angus's room was simply furnished. In a corner was a pile of *Sun* newspapers, some yellow with age. The woman opened a drawer and brought out a photograph.

Isabel Kearney wore a frightened look, as though something evil lurked just beyond the camera. She was with a dark-haired boy, with large empty eyes. He was almost as tall as his mother, gangly, big-footed, with the promise of more growth to come. Janice guessed he was about ten. Was he the possible link they were looking for?

'Angus has moments of lucidity. We know about his criminal background and *all* about his sex life.' The attendant pulled a face. 'This is the only relative he's ever mentioned.'

'Does anyone visit him?'

'Not as far as I know, but I can check our records and get back to you.' She paused. 'Is this in connection with an old crime?'

'I'm not at liberty to say, although I do need to take this and get a copy made. I can get it back to you by tomorrow,' Janice said to allay the woman's obvious concern.

Janice tried McNab's mobile again before she started up the car.

She didn't expect him to answer and he didn't. McNab was renowned for going it alone, so this wasn't that unusual, but he was a DI now. Something he should remember.

The mobile rang as she engaged gear. She went back to neutral and answered.

'Janice? It's Patrick Menzies here. Any chance we could talk? It's urgent.'

'What's it about?'

'Another victim.'

51

Enlisting the help of everyone who was there, Chrissy had collected eighteen mobile photographs taken during McNab's party. Iona featured in quite a few, especially when she'd hooked up with the newly promoted DI. There was a wistful one taken as McNab watched Rhona leave and one where they stood laughing together. Not for the first time did Chrissy wish Rhona had taken him home with her.

No one she'd spoken to had admitted to knowing Iona. Most thought she'd simply been in the pub and had joined in the fun. Initially Chrissy had thought the same. Not any more.

One photograph had caught her eye in particular. In it, Iona was deep in conversation with a bloke and they looked *very* friendly. Yet, shortly afterwards, Iona had abandoned the boyfriend and made a play for McNab. Chrissy could understand why women fancied McNab, even though she didn't herself. He'd been in good form that night, telling stories, making people laugh. He *was* the man. Definitely. So Iona had switched allegiances.

Chrissy didn't buy that version of the story. The more she thought about it, the more it looked like a set-up. And one that involved the boyfriend. Talking to the bar staff confirmed her suspicions. Apparently Iona had told one of them she was there for the police party, despite no one knowing who she was.

So confirming why she was there had been easy. Finding her had proved more problematic, until Chrissy had shown the photograph in a pub further down the road. It seemed Iona had worked there for a couple of months, so they had her contact details, including her address. They hadn't been keen on giving them out, until Chrissy explained who she was, laying the emphasis on the word 'police' rather than 'forensic'.

So here she was, gazing up at a set of flats, one of which was Iona's.

Chrissy tried not to imagine what might be going on behind the closed curtains. If McNab was in there, he would be less than happy to discover her on the doorstep.

Chrissy pressed the buzzer. Nothing happened. Neither did anyone pull back the curtain to check who wanted entry. She pressed again, holding it on this time. Still nothing.

Just then the door sprang open for someone to exit. A bloke, wearing earphones, tried to pass, but Chrissy brought him to a halt. She flashed her ID, and articulated the word 'police', then showed him the photograph and asked if Iona lived there.

He looked relieved to find it had nothing to do with him then shouted above his music, 'Second floor, middle door. I think she's away, though. Haven't seen her recently.'

'Does she live alone?'

He shrugged. 'As far as I know.' Satisfied he'd done his bit, he replaced the sound system and headed off.

Chrissy, her toe in the door, let him leave before she went into the close. The middle door on level two was badly in need of a paint job. Chrissy stood for a moment listening, but like the neighbour said, it didn't sound as though there was anyone inside. She checked out the locks. An upper mortice and a lower Yale. If the mortice wasn't on, entry would be easy. She put her eye to the crack to find that the Yale was the only thing keeping her outside. Seconds later she was in, courtesy of her specially designed lock breaker, fashioned from a plastic milk carton.

The narrow hallway had three doors leading off. The first led to a small toilet and shower, the second to a combined kitchen and sitting room. Dust motes danced in the sunlight that filtered through the closed curtains. On her entry a couple of flies rose from the remnants of a meal on the coffee table, then resettled to continue gorging and laying their eggs. An empty vodka bottle lay on the floor next to the table. The room smelt stale, even unpleasant. Chrissy traced the worst of the smell to an open carton of milk on the kitchen surface. The milk was going off, but hadn't yet reached the stage where it smelt like a decomposing body, although in this heat it wouldn't be long before it did.

She went to take a quick look in the bedroom. There was always a chance that Iona would return, so she didn't want to hang around too long. Chrissy wrinkled her nose. The putrid smell was in here too, maybe even stronger. By the time anyone came back, this place would be as stinking as McNab's flat.

She glanced around the shadowy room, making out a double bed, a wardrobe and what looked like a dressing table. The curtains were thicker than in the sitting room and blocked out all light.

Chrissy reached for the switch, just as her eye caught sight of what looked like a foot sticking out from under the duvet. Shock rooted her to the spot.

Jesus. Iona *was* here.

She took a step backwards, as quietly as possible, then halted.

Something wasn't right. The foot was pale, but filtered light from the hallway suggested a mottled pattern on the underside. Chrissy switched on the light.

The heaped duvet on the bed didn't move. She caught the corner and slowly raised it. The second foot appeared, followed by the legs and buttocks, all bearing the early signs of decomposition. Chrissy let the duvet fall back down, then walked round to the head of the bed and lifted the duvet again.

And there she was. Naked and dead, an empty syringe clasped in her right hand.

Chrissy let the cover fall back down as the scent of death brought the resident flies through from the sitting room.

Once in the hall, she gathered herself together. There was no way to keep this under wraps, not like the trashed flat. McNab was in the shit, whatever she did.

Chrissy pulled out her mobile and made a call.

52

'Her name was Iona Stewart. She was nineteen, according to her ID card.' Chrissy flourished it in Rhona's direction. 'Well, at least she wasn't under age.' Her tone was a mixture of sarcasm and relief. McNab was in enough trouble as it was.

Chrissy's call had brought Rhona here from Bill's house. His decision to accompany her had been made in an instant. Rhona had watched as he'd explained to Margaret. Margaret's reaction had been one of concern but she didn't seem remotely put out by her husband's departure.

As she'd wished Rhona goodbye, she'd quietly thanked her. 'He's had enough of killing greenfly. You're doing me a favour,' she'd added.

In the drive over, Rhona had filled in the details she'd missed in her earlier explanation. Bill had listened in grim silence, the full enormity of McNab's situation becoming apparent.

'How long has he been off the radar?'

'I saw him in the early hours of Saturday morning, when he turned up at the flat. The last time I saw Iona was at his place late Friday evening. She arrived as I left. I received a text from him the next morning, ordering me round to his flat with my forensic bag.' Rhona had described the scene she found there.

'So he tried to clean up, then thought the better of it?' Bill had said.

'It looked like that.'

'McNab wouldn't stay out of contact this long.'

'I agree.'

'So we start looking for him.'

It was a decision she couldn't make, but Bill certainly could. She listened as he put a call in to the station.

'Sergeant Clark is out interviewing Angus Patterson,' Bill told her when he'd hung up. 'And we're trying to trace McNab's mobile.'

It was a start.

The last time she had seen Iona she had been very much alive. Alive and angry. Rhona had been angry too. And the cause of both their anger had been McNab. The body that lay on the bed was identifiable as Iona, but it wasn't the young girl who had marched past her, her eyes flashing her annoyance.

The eyes staring blindly at her now were opaque, a clouded mirror of what they had been. The lithe body that had flounced up the stairs had become stiff through the natural process of rigor mortis and was now dissipating into flaccidness once more.

During life, her body's core temperature had been 37 degrees. Death stopped the core mechanisms that regulated that temperature, and the body moved towards the temperature of its environment. With the warm weather, the temperature under the duvet had been warm and constant, but the state of the body and the eyes were not enough to determine the time of death accurately.

Chrissy was reading Rhona's thoughts.

'Did she die before, or after, McNab disappeared?'

'She died sometime between Friday at ten when I saw her and today when you found her,' Rhona said firmly.

'Which puts McNab in the timeframe,' Chrissy said.

'We can't avoid that.'

Chrissy looked worried.

Rhona tried to reassure her. 'Bill's back. He'll sort this mess out.'

'If Sutherland lets him,' Chrissy said ominously.

The syringe held the remnants of a speedball cocktail. If Iona wasn't a heroin user, the quantity of heroin alone might have killed her. When Rhona examined the body she could find no evidence that Iona had been injecting. Not in obvious places like the forearms or hidden spots between the fingers and toes. Her neck showed finger bruising, suggesting she had been forcibly gripped there, perhaps to administer the drug. If that was the case, then she hadn't been a willing supplicant like the others who had died in a similar manner.

There was no evidence of sexual assault, although semen from previous recent encounters would still be retrievable from the vagina, no doubt some of it matching McNab's stored profile. Iona's nasal passages had provided traces of cocaine which matched the mix from samples taken from the burial site on Cathkin Braes.

McNab's initial assessment that Alan's death had been related to the cocaine stash was not yet disproved.

She scraped under Iona's fingernails, conscious that every sample she took from her body might implicate McNab. Having sex with someone didn't mean that you'd killed them. But the question kept returning despite all her attempts to subdue it. Why had McNab disappeared without explanation to either her, or his detective sergeant?

She had almost completed her forensic examination of the body when her mobile rang. Rhona checked the screen and saw Sean's name. When she failed to answer, it stopped, only to start again seconds later. On his third attempt she answered because Sean would never call her incessantly without a reason.

'Sean?'

'It's McNab,' he said.

53

The image on the screen was of a smiling young woman. The background suggested she was in the passenger seat of a vehicle, probably some sort of van. It had been posted online by Stonewarrior at midday today, Sunday. The female had been identified as Helena Watters, flatmate of Alan MacKenzie and student of Druidry. According to Jolene, another flatmate, Helena had sent a text to say she would return on Sunday. The location of the mobile when the text was sent was being traced. Exactly when the photograph had been taken could not be established. So, Helena could be alive, or she could already be dead.

The entire team was assembled. Superintendent Sutherland stood on Bill's left, DS Clark on his right. Rhona stood at the back of the room with Magnus. It felt like old times, she thought. The bad old times when McNab had been missing, presumed dead.

Bill spoke first, indicating that McNab's mobile had been located and that he'd told a friend he was going undercover and if he didn't return within twenty-four hours, the friend should contact Dr Rhona MacLeod and hand over the mobile.

'The mobile has revealed a text conversation between Detective Inspector McNab and someone we believe is the perpetrator. We think Detective McNab received verbal instructions to visit a location, although that is not certain. We therefore must assume McNab chose to follow those instructions without reference to his commanding officer.' Bill's voice was heavy with condemnation, which Sutherland acknowledged.

'When the perpetrator uploaded this photograph he also issued a challenge to his online followers, who have been trying to predict his next move in the game he calls *Stonewarrior*. According to reports, considerable numbers of people have responded and are making their way to various Neolithic sites, believing they've identified the fifth point in the game. We must assume that any evidence of heightened police activity will be duly noted and posted online, exacerbating the problem.'

A photograph now appeared on the screen of a woman and a boy of about ten, which Rhona had not seen before.

'Dr MacLeod identified a familial link between the perpetrator and Isabel Kearney. Mrs Kearney took her own life five years ago while in prison for the murder of her husband. Her son, seen in the photograph, would be nineteen by now. It is vital we locate Josh Kearney.'

There was a ripple of conversation, silenced once again by Bill's voice as he asked Magnus to come to the front.

Rhona thought that Magnus appeared nervous. Delivering scientific data, she decided, was much preferable to trying to offer psychological insight into what they were dealing with. Yet it had to be done. How the perpetrator was thinking at this point was vital to deciding their next move.

Magnus began by reminding those present about the signature and modus operandi of the perpetrator, then he concentrated on the way the mode of operation had altered and developed as he'd gained in success and was not apprehended.

'He is obviously highly skilled in game playing and in using the internet. It may be he has studied at a university, or he may have simply developed his skills independently. I would argue that he also has a mathematical knowledge of theoretical game playing in a psychological sense. So we're looking for a highly intelligent person with the technical abilities of a computer hacker and the psychological insight to anticipate his opponent's next move, rather like a highly skilled chess player. As in any game, there are levels. The victims were tested and their success meant, not a reward, but death. The puppetmaster does not like anyone to challenge his knowledge or authority. Having established Detective McNab's position in the investigation, he strove to have him enter the game, in order to defeat him.'

A hushed silence followed this announcement. Rhona glanced at Superintendent Sutherland's face and saw only controlled anger. The image on the screen changed. Now it was the map overlaid with the pentagram.

'The game has five levels and shows a repeated pattern of five. Four bodies have been found, three associated with the game, but only three Neolithic locations have been used.' Magnus pointed to Brodgar, Skelmuir and Cathkin Braes. 'If the young woman in the image is a prospective victim, she will be number five. Whether he will continue to use the five-sided figure as a symbol of the game remains to be seen. If we continue to use the pentagram as reference we have two possible locations.' He pointed to the map.

'Callanish, on the Isle of Lewis, and the island of Iona

are possibilities. However, we may be mistaken regarding the pattern. Many of the parties posting online disagree with our interpretation and have mapped the locations using the bigger frame of the UK, resulting in gamers descending on locations such as Stonehenge.'

Bill interrupted to ask if Magnus thought that this was a possibility. Magnus considered the question for a moment. 'I'm not sure of anything,' he said honestly.

His departure from the front caused a second wave of discussion. Bill motioned them into silence.

'We believe the Brodgar victim was a case of mistaken identity and that the game's victim was in fact the young woman found in Scapa Flow. The mobile which was discovered at the Skelmuir Hill locus was the one used to send the photograph of the Skelmuir victim, which fits with that theory. According to the Technical department, there were five players, known as Morvan, Caylum, Myrrdin, Moonroth and Erwen. Myrrdin, we believe, was Alan's avatar and Morvan, the Hoy victim, has been established as Jessica Samson. Erwen is possibly the female identified as Alisha Morrison, an Aberdeen university student, whose body was discovered at Skelmuir. Which leaves Caylum and Moonroth as the remaining players. Our IT department suggest there is a possibility that either Moonroth or Caylum may be the avatar of the puppetmaster himself.'

Bill asked Detective Sergeant Clark to speak next. If Magnus had looked unsure, Janice looked positively sick with trepidation. Rhona suspected it wasn't talking to her colleagues that was the problem, but what she was about to say.

'We've taken a further statement from Patrick Menzies, the medium who foretold the death of Alan MacKenzie

LIN ANDERSON

during a spiritualist service. Mr Menzies maintains there's been a further death, the location of which he can't pinpoint, but it involves water. The victim, he says, is male.'

316

54

So, this is what it felt like to drown.

He'd helped drag bodies from the River Clyde, sat in on their post-mortems. He'd listened to what they had gone through in the moments before their death, but he'd never tried to imagine what it must have felt like. Now he knew.

In those few moments, he was surprised to find a series of images of his life flash before his eyes. He relived his childhood fear of enclosed spaces, of the terror of the dark, of monsters under the bed. He replayed the gunshot that had exploded inside his body, shattering his internal organs. He saw again Chrissy's terrified expression as he shielded her and her unborn child, then Rhona's as she'd held him to her, trying desperately to stem the blood. It had all been in vain, because death had let him go only to return to claim his prize.

Drowning encompassed all his fears. In the thick darkness, the monster that was water pressed on him from all sides, his breathing space a tiny portion of what he needed. It caged him in a claustrophobic metal shell. It compressed his chest, crushing all attempts to take in air.

As he drifted into unconsciousness he realized that being shot had been easier, kinder and infinitely quicker.

*

LIN ANDERSON

To Megan, travelling the road in her beat-up Volkswagen, the river looked its normal self, if a little swollen by the recent rain. She wasn't looking for an accident, she was searching for a young girl who had set out and not returned. It was Megan who had advised her how to reach the standing stones. Therefore she felt responsible for her visitor.

She headed for a passing place as the blue dot of a neighbour's van came into view. As she drew in, she realized something had happened at this spot. Glass littered the road, skid marks gleamed darkly against the tar. This was a tricky stretch for the unwary. Tourists needed to stay close to the rock wall, but afraid of hitting it, they often strayed out, too near the scree.

She came to a halt and stepped out of the vehicle. She gave the passing van a wave, then crossed the road and looked down. The skid marks met the edge, but did not swerve back.

Megan examined the bank of scree and noted the bent saplings. She shaded her eyes and checked the foot of the bank and found nothing. She stretched her gaze towards the river.

Then she did see something. The sun caught metal and flashed it back at her, like a mirror signal. The water was tumbling over something and it wasn't a rock.

Fear took her over the edge. She slithered downwards on her bottom, propelling herself with her hands. It wasn't the first time a car had gone over at this spot, and the previous occupant hadn't lived to tell the tale.

Reaching the foot of the bank, she rose shakily to her feet and hurried across the rough grass. Down here it was clear that a vehicle had come this way and that it had entered the water.

Lying a couple of metres from the edge, the vehicle sat wedged behind a rock, which had prevented it from being swept downstream. For the most part the flow of water parted behind the obstruction, with an occasional eddy breaking across the roof.

Megan edged further in.

The water was thigh high now and dragging her feet from under her. She knew she should turn and go back, call for assistance. She also knew that there was no signal at this spot, which meant she would have to drive until she picked one up, further down the glen.

And there might be someone trapped inside the car.

Megan grabbed hold of a branch of a nearby alder bush to steady her passage and kept going. She had almost reached the vehicle when she spotted a man's head. It was bent backwards, the neck arched, his nose periodically above the water. She saw an explosion of bubbles and realized he was trying to take a breath from the pocket of air trapped in the underside of the roof.

Megan let go of the branch and grabbed for the door handle, just as the door swung open and the man launched himself out.

They immediately became entangled and were swept downstream, like jammed branches, flailing, surfacing, choking and sinking again in the swift current.

McNab's feet found ground first. He grabbed at a sharp rock protruding above the surface and dragged himself ashore. As he dropped to his knees, a hand caught hold of his ankle. McNab kicked back sharply in response and heard a crack as his heel hit bone.

Megan, gasping in pain, lost her own footing and submerged, swallowing water. Stunned by the impact of

McNab's blow, she rolled. Now her face was under water and she had no strength left to right herself.

McNab turned in a fury. If the mad guy in the camper van wanted rid of him, he would have to try harder than this. Then he caught sight of the slim female body, face down in the river.

Christ!

McNab flung himself back into the water as the current swirled her from him. He grabbed for a leg and caught the hem of her jeans, but the flow fought back, keen now to whisk its prey away. McNab's strength was ebbing, his grasp weakening. He was going to lose her. He half dived, half flung himself at her retreating form, wrapping his arms round her legs. They were swept away again, entwined but no longer fighting.

McNab tried to find the bottom. Careering like a drunk man, he stumbled across stones, the swift flow defying his attempts to get a foothold. He changed tack and dragged himself up her body. When he reached her shoulders, he rolled her over and caught her with one arm against him, exposing her bloodied face to fresh air, then, cradling her against his chest, he kicked them both shorewards.

His heel had opened the skin on her cheek, maybe even fractured the bone. McNab pressed his mouth to hers and blew in a breath. There was no response. He blew in again, her mouth soft and cold under his lips.

He pounded her chest, then blew once more. There was a long moment when he convinced himself he'd killed her, then she coughed. Bloodied water spouted from her mouth. She coughed and more spurted out. McNab gave her time to clear her lungs, then gently rolled her onto her side to recover, and sat down next to her.

She was in her twenties, he guessed. Slim, probably fit by the way she had fought him and the water. Her face was beginning to swell from his kick, but the gash was no longer seeping blood. He was horrified by the damage he'd done, but his last memory was the onslaught of the van, and looking up as van man's boot had descended on his face.

After that his world had taken off on a nightmare ride of screeching metal and crunching stones. Then the cold rush of water and the desperate need to take in sufficient air to help him force the door open and escape the car.

When the hands had grabbed him from behind, he'd assumed his foe had come to make certain his end, so had fought back.

And this is what he'd done.

Her eyes flickered open. They were brown. She looked startled and unsure.

'It's okay. You're okay,' he said in what he hoped was a reassuring voice. 'I'm sorry I kicked you.'

Confusion was replaced by memory. She struggled to sit up. McNab helped her.

'You were in the car,' she said.

'Yes.'

Her body moved into shock and she shivered violently.

'Where's your transport?' McNab said.

'Up where your car went over.'

He helped her to her feet. 'Can you make it?'

'If you can, so can I,' she said firmly.

They hobbled together along the shore towards the bank of scree. Every bone and sinew in his body screamed in complaint. Her eye was already shutting and her cheek had puffed up. By her occasional concerned glance at him, he guessed he didn't look any better, and probably a lot worse.

'Do you have a mobile?'

'Yes, but there's no signal here.' Catching his expression, she added, 'There's a landline at my hotel about ten minutes away.'

The scree proved the worse part of the journey. Sliding down was easy in comparison to scrambling up. He reached the top first and gave her a helping hand. They lay panting on the top. Far below he could see the glinting metal of his car.

'If it had been raining, I would never have seen you,' she said. She was shivering violently now. McNab offered to drive and she accepted.

He got her in the passenger side first. There was a rug on the back seat and he wrapped it round her.

'Which direction?'

She pointed back the way he had come.

McNab made a very careful three-point turn. There was no way he wanted to descend that scree again. She indicated a turn-off that he'd passed en route. Ten minutes later they arrived outside a small hotel. He helped her out of the vehicle.

'You need to get off the wet clothes and get into bed. Have you got anyone that can help you do that?'

She shook her head. 'I'll manage,' she said through chattering teeth. She opened the front door and pointed out the phone, then went upstairs.

McNab strode quickly to the phone, then hesitated. Who exactly should he call and how much should he reveal? As soon as he'd engaged with the game, this had become personal. He had no doubt that the dark-haired guy in the van was the one who'd communicated with him. And now as far as the puppetmaster was concerned, he was dead, which was to his advantage. Van man couldn't have gone far, not on these roads. McNab could of course blow the whistle and have everyone out looking for him, but that would alert him. Alternatively, he could try to track him down himself, then call in the troops.

As DI, the first option should be his chosen one, but then again, he was unlikely to remain DI after this. Even DS status looked remote.

Now that the twenty-four hours were up, Sean would hand over his mobile. Then the shit would truly hit the fan. By then, he might well have located the puppetmaster and taken him into custody.

He heard a crash like someone falling. McNab took the stairs two at a time. His Good Samaritan, whose name he did not yet know, was sprawled on the bathroom floor, the shower hissing hot behind her, the room full of steam. It appeared she'd managed to undress and take a shower before passing out. McNab scooped her up and carried her to the nearest bedroom, pulled back the duvet and laid her down. He tucked the cover round her, then checked the pulse in her neck, which beat strongly. He prodded the bruised cheek and decided the bone wasn't broken. She would come to with a black eye and bodily bruising, but would definitely live, no thanks to him.

McNab looked in the wardrobe for a change of clothes, but it appeared she didn't live with a male companion. The other two doors on that landing were locked, so he assumed they were the letting rooms. He headed downstairs. The lower level consisted of a comfortable, if old-fashioned, sitting room kitted out for guests. No television, probably

323

because of a poor signal, but plenty of books and magazines. The fire in the hearth was set but unlit. A large kitchen out back was warmed by an oil-fired range. Off it was a cellar and an interconnecting door leading to the bar. It was compact and looked as though it hadn't had its decor changed in decades, if not longer.

McNab surveyed the ample selection of whiskies and finally settled for a Jura. He poured himself a sizeable glass and tossed half of it back. The descending liquid was the only warmth in his body. He waited until the effect hit his bloodstream then drank the rest.

'I'll have one myself. Large,' a female voice said from the doorway.

His erstwhile saviour was up and dressed, with a little colour back in her cheeks.

McNab selected a glass and did as he was bid. She accepted it with a wry smile and knocked it back, much like he had done.

'I'll get you a change of clothes. My brother leaves a store here for when he comes to stay. You look roughly the same size.'

McNab didn't care what size the clothes were, as long as they were dry. He said so. She disappeared and came back a short while later with a pair of jeans, a shirt and a sweater. She handed them over.

'Shoe size?'

'Ten and a half.'

'Scott's feet are bigger, but a couple of pairs of socks and you could wear his walking boots.'

She suggested he had a hot shower. 'You know where it is,' she said, acknowledging his role in putting her to bed. McNab nodded, making no comment. He had no desire to make her feel embarrassed, considering the injury he'd already inflicted on her.

McNab headed upstairs with his bundle. In the over-the-sink mirror he examined the results of his 'accident'. The face was more gargoyle than man. His chest was developing a patchwork of bruises interspersed with long and occasionally deep scratches he had no memory of getting.

The shower was both pleasure and torture as it heated his body while stinging his cuts and bruises. He made it quick, then stepped out and dabbed himself dry. The clothes fitted reasonably well. The jeans were a little long, the shirt a little big. He pulled on the double socks and eased his feet into the summer walking boots and laced them up tightly.

Back downstairs, he found her in the kitchen making coffee.

'Megan,' she said, when he asked her name.

'Michael,' he told her, leaving out the DI part.

She handed him a mug and indicated he should take a seat at the table. McNab, having made up his mind in the shower what his next move would be, was ready when she posed her question.

'What happened back there?'

'A camper van drove me off the road.'

She looked shocked. 'On purpose?'

'On purpose.'

'We'd better call the police.'

'I am the police,' McNab said. 'I need to find that van. Can I use your pick-up?'

'Yes, of course, but . . .' She hesitated. 'I need to look for Helena.'

The name rang a shrill bell in McNab's brain. 'Who's Helena?'

'She's a guest. She arrived yesterday off the bus. She set off for the stone circle but . . .'

'She hasn't come back?'

'No—' She halted, having seen McNab's face. 'You think she's in danger?'

McNab was on his feet. 'Let's go.'

55

They were in McNab's office, temporarily occupied by Bill.
Rhona had just told him that she thought she'd seen Josh
Kearney during McNab's party.

'Chrissy collected mobile images taken that night. There
was one of Iona talking to a guy who may be the boy
in the photograph with Isabel Kearney. I can't be sure,
but . . .'

'So Iona and Josh Kearney may be acquainted?'

'The meeting looks more intimate than just an acquaintance.'

Rhona realized by Bill's expression that their thoughts
were progressing along the same lines.

'Iona was used to get access to McNab,' Bill said.

'I think he was beginning to suspect that, especially
after the flat was trashed.'

'The question is, why?'

Bill sat down at the desk and pulled open a drawer.
He pushed a piece of paper over to Rhona. 'Read that.'

It didn't take long to read the half-page scrawl and every
word filled her with anger. She pushed it back at him.

'That's rubbish. I was in the tent until late. McNab left
before me.'

'Are you sure?'

She wasn't and it probably showed on her face. She had

stayed late in the tent, communing with the dead, writing up her notes. The mortuary team had been there when she finally emerged. She'd declined their offer of a helicopter descent and chosen to walk down to the car park, the long summer day having not yet descended into darkness. She'd last spoken to McNab more than an hour before that, when he'd asked when they could remove the body. Could he have still been on site? McNab hadn't mentioned cocaine until the Monday strategy meeting. He hadn't said anything to her about it when they'd spoken at the crime scene.

Bill interrupted her flow of thought. 'What the statement says is physically possible, just not probable.'

Rhona didn't believe the accusation, but having Bill reinforce that belief, despite the mess McNab had created, was reassuring.

'If Josh Kearney was close to Iona, he would also be in the frame for her murder. Assuming it was murder,' Bill went on.

'The prints on the syringe are hers, but there's evidence of bruising round her neck which definitely occurred before death.'

'What about sex games? How old were the bruises?'

Rhona knew where this was going. 'There was no evidence that she'd had sex in the lead-up to her death.'

'But McNab's semen will still be there?'

'If he didn't use a condom. Yes.'

'Can you get a print from the neck?'

She'd tried, unsuccessfully, and said so. Bill looked disappointed.

He glanced at his watch. 'Time to speak to Mr Munro again.'

*

'You should have told me,' Rhona said accusingly.

'He asked me not to,' Sean replied calmly. 'McNab said it was undercover work and required twenty-four hours. As soon as the time was up, I told you.'

Rhona had come straight to the jazz club from the police station. Their earlier meeting, when Sean had handed over the mobile, hadn't lasted long enough for her to vent her anger at his actions – or inactions.

'You realize he might be dead?' she said.

'I don't think so.'

'So now you have the second sight?' she said sarcastically.

'No, but I do know that McNab seems to have more lives than a cat. He had a plan he was following. He appeared confident.'

'Arrogant, you mean?'

'That too,' Sean acknowledged. 'Look, if this maniac who's posting photographs of his victims online *had* killed him, wouldn't we have seen evidence of it by now?'

Sean was right. Had McNab been killed, the puppet-master, as described by Magnus, would have relished broadcasting it. Then again . . .

'I'm not so sure,' she said.

'Why?'

'If, as Magnus believes, the Brodgar victim was a case of mistaken identity, there are two victims still to go.' She paused. 'Helena . . .'

Sean uttered the words Rhona didn't want to say. 'And McNab.'

Bill indicated that DS Clark should accompany him to the interview room. He could tell by her expression she was discomfited by the prospect. He understood her reluctance, but in this job you had to face your demons, and he was keen to see how Steve Munro reacted with her there.

The interview room was airless and too hot. Normal Scottish weather precluded any need for air conditioning. The central heating was switched on on the first of October and switched off on the first of May, whatever the weather. A heat wave didn't feature anywhere in the building's construction, hence the temperature of the room.

Bill introduced himself and DS Clark. Munro shot the sergeant a poisonous look as though it was her fault he was back here.

'I told her everything already,' he said.

Bill ignored that and asked Janice to set up the tape, then laid the earlier statement out on the desk. Munro gave it a cursory glance. 'See, that's what I told her.'

'And you stand by your statement?'

'I do,' Munro said, sounding anything but certain.

Sixty seconds passed. Munro began to squirm under Bill's steady stare. Then another sixty, during which Munro's expression moved through a number of guises. Bill gave it a further minute then suddenly leaned forward, so that his face was inches away from Munro's.

'Who told you to tell us such a bunch of lies?'

A startled Munro drew back as though a dog had tried to bite him. He eventually managed to utter, 'Nobody.'

Bill eased a printout from the folder in front of him and slid it across the table. 'Was it this man?'

Munro's eyes wanted to go there, but he wouldn't let them.

'Look at it,' Bill ordered.

The eyes slid down, recognition blooming, although he was trying desperately to hide it.

'Never seen him before,' Munro said.

'What about the girl with him?'

Munro shook his head. 'Her neither.'

'So you didn't have sex with her?'

Munro looked genuinely aghast. 'No way.'

Bill extracted a photograph of Iona's dead body and pushed it across.

Munro's eyes flickered towards it and were held there in horrible fascination as he realized what he was looking at. Bill pointed at the neck.

'Did you squeeze her throat a bit to help you come?'

Munro gagged. Bill thought he might throw up, but chose to ignore it.

'We can match prints, you know? Even from bruises.'

Munro's voice emerged in a hoarse whisper. 'I didn't touch her.'

'But you met her?'

'Only once.'

The flood gates were opening. Bill helped them on a bit. 'The guy in the photograph, what about him?'

Munro shook his head.

Bill stabbed at the picture. 'If he could do that to his girlfriend, what d'you think he'll do to you?'

He watched as the remark hit the bullseye and the flood gates were gone. Words tripped over one another in an effort to get out. The girl had contacted Munro. How she'd got his number he had no idea. She'd said she was into geocaching and wanted to talk about it. When they met up, the guy appeared. Told him to give the statement about the detective, or . . .

'The gang who buried the stash would know I was the one who told the police about it.' Munro was shaking with fear. 'I saw what they did to that guy on Cathkin Braes.'

Bill didn't enlighten him as to who the real perpetrator had been.

'Do you have a contact number for either of them?'

Munro shook his head.

'So the guy in the photo doesn't know you were recalled for questioning?'

Munro didn't like that idea. 'He seems to know everything.'

56

She was ripe and ready. Keen and willing. He realized he'd kept the best to the last. She wasn't yet a supplicant, but would be soon. The newspapers had called him 'the monster among us'. Yet he'd killed kindly. No pain, just pleasure. He'd only fucked the Skelmuir girl, and she'd asked for it, enjoyed it. He'd used violence on no one before death, except the detective.

The detective hadn't changed. Back then, he'd been just as arrogant. He'd walked into their home, their lives, with no knowledge or understanding of the game that had played out in that house. He didn't know how each level had been reached. How many fights had been lost and won. How the end had become inevitable. He, Josh, had tried to explain, but his explanation had been dismissed. Supplication had been the essence of the game. Like Christ on the cross, his mother had died for his sins, despite his own admission of guilt.

Josh wondered what would have happened if he'd done as instructed that day. If he'd raped his mother and let his father watch. Would she still be alive?

'It's beautiful here.'

Her voice brought him back, if reluctantly, to the present. Finding her waiting patiently for him as instructed, had irritated him initially, just as success at thwarting an

LIN ANDERSON

opponent in a game, caused him to lose respect for the
loser.

She was intelligent, that was obvious. If she'd beaten
him, would he have spared her? Even now he questioned
whether he would kill her. The dose he used need not
necessarily kill. Maybe she would take the pleasure he
offered and survive.

The thought enticed him. It took root beside his earlier
thought about his mother. That maybe she would have
lived had he made a different choice.

'Between the devil and the deep blue sea,' she used to
say. As a child it was the devil Josh feared, and not the
deep blue sea.

As they approached the circle he began to feel its energy.
A stone circle wasn't built on one energy line, but on a
crossroads. Some people felt that energy, others were oblivi-
ous to it. He watched as she crossed into its realm.

She stopped and looked at him.

'Do you feel that?'

'What?' he said as though he didn't know.

'A tingling.' She might have been talking about sexual
desire, apart from the puzzled expression.

'It's the energy from the stones.'

She ran to the centre and stood, arms outstretched. His
reaction was not something he recognized. Emotions so long
buried rose in a jumble of memories. A slideshow of fast-
moving pictures. His own arms outstretched. His mother
picking him up. Soft words and caresses. The scent of her
skin, her cheek pressed against his. Then the scent of blood,
the smell of fear, the stink of sweat and sex.

'Are you okay?'

Her concern irritated him. He forced a smile. 'Great. What do you think? Was it worth all the tasks?'

'I loved them,' she said with a broad smile. 'I called myself Caylum. Did you think I was a boy?'

'I knew you were female,' he said. It hadn't been because of her answers, but because he'd traced her IP address, then intercepted her mail, hacked into her webcam. He'd know everything about her before he let her join in the game.

'What shall we do?' she was saying. 'Dance round the circle naked like in the *Wicker Man*?'

'We can if you want to.'

She thought for a moment. 'Why not?' She caught his eye. 'But you have to go first.'

Her order, for that is what it was, discomfited him. If he refused, she might become difficult. But if he did strip off, she would see his desire. A horrible memory swamped him. The kitchen. His father's bared buttocks. The relentless pounding and grinding. How his father had wiped himself on his mother's skirt.

'Ladies first,' he tried.

She eyed him. 'You're embarrassed.'

He didn't countermand this, sensing she liked the idea.

One moment she was dressed, the next she stood naked before him. She was tall and slim, the shadows of her hip bones visible. Her breasts were small and shaped like pears. He was moved by the freshness and ripeness of her. In that moment he wondered whether he might be capable of love. The anger that had consumed him for so long evaporated and he re-imagined himself as her lover. The moment was fleeting and over as soon as she spoke.

'Your go,' she said.

The worm inside him turned.

57

Before leaving the hotel, Megan had made a brief phone call. McNab caught the words 'camper van' in the conversation, which hadn't pleased him. He'd challenged her about it when she hung up.

'I don't want him to know I'm alive. And he will if it's obvious we're searching for him,' he'd said sharply.

She seemed unfazed by his anger. 'The neighbour says he passed a camper van heading up the glen road. I let him think it's a guest who missed the turn-off.'

McNab nodded, somewhat mollified.

'Helena borrowed my bike, but she would have to walk the last part.'

This time Megan drove. She took the bends with ease and at great speed. McNab found himself gripping the seat, which produced a wry smile.

Ten minutes of hairpin bends later, she braked and turned right, drawing up in front of a padlocked gate, on the other side of which a dirt path headed into the hills.

'We walk from here.'

'*I* walk from here,' McNab said firmly.

'But you don't know where you're going.'

'Then tell me.'

He was out of the pick-up now and preparing to vault

336

the gate. Once over, he awaited her instructions. She was thinking about arguing with him.

'This is police business,' he said.

She acquiesced. 'Keep on this path until you reach the brow of the hill. From there you should be able to make out the stone circle, due north-west on a neighbouring hill.'

'Thanks.'

'You should catch a signal once you get higher,' she called after him.

McNab took off at a jog. Stiff from the crash, his legs complained bitterly at first, but then began to loosen. The boots were at least one size too big and he could feel the heels rubbing through the double socks, but blisters were the least of his worries.

He ran for twenty, walked for twenty, moving to more walking as the gradient increased. Soon sweat was trickling down his back and chest, its stinging salt reminding him of his other injuries. Once on the brow of the hill, he shaded his eyes and looked in the direction she'd indicated. The sun was on the wane, causing a patchwork of light and shadow on the surrounding hills. At first he couldn't see the stones, then the outer rim of the sun re-emerged and shone on them. At this distance they were small in stature, nothing like the images he'd seen of the Ring of Brodgar. Neither could he make out if anyone was there.

Suddenly aware of his prominent location, he dropped to the ground. The last thing he wanted was to make his presence known, although the fact that someone was in the vicinity might dissuade the puppetmaster from carrying out his plan.

He solved the dilemma by swiftly moving downhill in the general direction of the stones. The path had narrowed to little more than a sheep track between heather, the long spell of dry weather rendering it so brittle, it crackled against his legs.

At the foot of the hill he found himself suddenly in a bog and in danger of losing the oversized boots. Not for the first time did McNab remind himself how much he hated the countryside.

Eventually gaining dry ground, he was now close enough to see the stones above him. If there were people up there, they weren't visible from this angle. He began his ascent. Halfway up, he caught sight of a splash of colour. Breathing heavily and eaten alive by the dusk-descending midges, he crowned the hill.

He was right. There was something colourful amidst the stones. His chest heaving, his breath coming in gasps, he ran towards the circle. The bundle lay in the very centre. The closer he got, the more human in shape it became.

He knew it was Helena before he reached it. He had never seen the tall, slim girl who the old man downstairs had described, but he had stood in her room and smelt her scent. McNab stumbled into the circle just as the sun's rays hit the largest of the stones, lighting it up like a beacon among the growing shadows.

Megan was right. There was a signal up here. McNab watched the row of bars grow, then selected the name and dialled the number.

Her voice was tentative. She had no idea who was calling from this number.

'Rhona,' he said.

A brief hesitation before she registered his voice. 'Michael?'

Her use of his first name pleased him.

'Can you get me out of here?'

'Where's here?' she said immediately.

'The Old Forge Inn.' He gave her rough co-ordinates.

'Why are you there?'

'I'll explain when I see you.'

'What about your car?'

'A write-off.'

She mentioned the Air Support Unit. 'I'll call you when I've sorted something out.'

'Use the inn's landline. The signal around here is shite.'

She wanted to tell him something, but was hesitant. So he helped her along. 'I'm in big trouble, I know.'

'It's not that,' she said.

'What, then?'

She told him about Iona.

McNab walked back inside the ring. The energy he'd felt the first time was even stronger now. A tingle ran up his spine. He had a sense of being watched and ran his eyes over the neighbouring hilltops, but saw nothing. God, how he hated this emptiness.

He'd been wrong about the bundle on the ground. Pulled back, the torn coloured throw had revealed only a mound of heather, as though someone had fashioned a bed to lie on and look up at the night sky. McNab had searched the ring thoroughly for any other signs of visitation, but found only hoof marks and droppings from the sheep that dotted the hillside.

Before he deserted the ring, he called Megan and she said she would pick him up at the gate. McNab made his way back as the sun began to set. As he walked, he thought of Iona. Her inviting smile. Her laughter, which had seemed genuine at the time, but now replayed as false. He pictured her cocaine-bright eyes. The open red mouth. The piercings that had brought her pleasure and which seemed to him to mar her beauty. Rhona had explained about Iona's connection with someone called Josh Kearney. How he had been DS when Kearney's mother had killed his father. How a single hair found on Alan MacKenzie's clothes had led Rhona to the woman he'd put in prison for murder.

The sky was a fiery red as he picked his way through the bog, then retraced his steps via the first hill, finally regaining the original track. Looking up at the bruised sky, he recalled the blood-soaked floor of a kitchen. The man lying there, his chest stabbed in a frenzied attack. There were, according to the post-mortem, forty-three stab holes, some of them having been pierced more than once.

The wife had been seated at the kitchen table when he'd walked in, a large kitchen knife in her hand, the front of her clothes splattered red. She'd told him her husband had raped her, so she'd killed him. The teenage boy who'd opened the door to him had disagreed. He'd insisted that he had been the one to kill his father, because he caught him raping his mother.

The woman had dismissed her son's attempts to take the blame. McNab had ignored his own suspicions that the boy might be telling the truth and testified in court against the woman. It was his first murder case as DS and he'd been pleased by his success.

McNab now recalled how the boy's eyes had turned on him in court and flashed their hatred as his mother had been sentenced. Six months later, Isabel Kearney had been found hanging in her cell. The son had run away from numerous foster homes by then and was no longer on the radar. They'd hoped he might reappear for his mother's funeral. When he hadn't McNab had assumed her son didn't know about his mother's death, or didn't care.

It seemed he'd been wrong.

McNab was almost at the gate now, beyond which stood the pick-up. He found himself longing for another shower, no matter how much it stung, some food and definitely some whisky. He began to hope that the helicopter wouldn't come for him until tomorrow. That he might fall into a bed at the inn tonight.

Megan's smile when he opened the passenger door lifted his spirits a little. As did the words that followed.

'A woman called on the landline. She said the Air Support Unit would pick you up at nine tomorrow.'

McNab groaned as pulled himself onto the seat.

Megan performed a nifty three-point turn, and set off on her speedy way again.

'Had she been there?' Megan asked.

'I don't think so.'

'I haven't seen the bike I loaned her anywhere on the road either.'

The bike. He'd forgotten about the bike.

'What do you think has happened to her?'

He thought Helena was already dead, and that her photograph would appear online soon, but he couldn't say that.

When he didn't reply, she said, 'The man in the van. Is that who they're calling Stonewarrior?'

He glanced swiftly at her.

'I don't have the internet, or much of a TV signal, but word travels fast in rural communities.'

There was no point in lying. 'Yes, that's him.'

'And he has Helena?'

'Probably.'

He assumed an expression that suggested he was unwilling to continue the conversation, because he knew she would ask what happened next. And he didn't have an answer.

They heard the helicopter as they approached the hotel. Its lights picked them out as the beam swept the surroundings, looking for a place to land.

'Shit!'

'They said not until the morning.' Megan looked disappointed.

She brought the pick-up to a halt and McNab eased himself out. The last thing he wanted was to appear hurt anywhere other than his face. He strode across, trying not to wince, and ducked under the slowing blades. Neil Cameron gave him a long hard look.

'Been in the wars?'

'Car accident. You're early.'

'We were called back from Callanish. They're keen to have you home.'

McNab was immediately on the alert. 'Callanish. What happened there?'

'Nothing, but DI Wilson wasn't taking any chances.'

Bill was back then, which meant he was out. A mixture of relief and anger swept through McNab. *Fuck it*, he thought. *It was always going to happen, anyway.*

Behind Neil, the radio crackled into life. Neil adjusted

his headset and listened in, then said, 'You got anything
to collect before we get going?'

McNab shook his head. He glanced back to where
Megan still stood by the pick-up.

'Give me a minute.'

The wind from the blades was whipping her hair across
her face, covering the damage he'd done.

McNab reached out his hand, then thought the better
of it. They were way past the hand-shaking stage.

'Thanks,' he shouted above the noise. 'And sorry about
your cheek.'

She nodded, sweeping her hair behind her ear. 'Come
back sometime.'

'I'm not one for the wild open spaces. If you're ever
in Glasgow . . .'

'What should I do about Helena's things?'

'She left stuff here?'

'A laptop and a mobile. She needed to recharge them.'

McNab signalled to Neil that he would be back in five
and followed Megan to the hotel.

She lifted a key from a rack in the kitchen and led him
upstairs.

Inside the room was a scattering of clothes, a small
rucksack and a laptop. Plugged into the laptop was a mobile
phone.

McNab put everything inside the bag.

'What happens if – *when* she comes back?'

'Call me.' McNab gave her the station name and
number, knowing it sounded impersonal.

It was an awkward goodbye. As he climbed into the
helicopter he couldn't help but think how differently things

might have worked out had Megan been at the party that night.

As they rose, the lights of the inn blinked back at them from what seemed to McNab to be an ocean of darkness.

58

His beams picked out an empty road ahead. As he took a sharp bend, the lights suddenly caught a figure in the midst of crossing. He made out the reflection of eyes and the bristling shape of antlers before the stag bounded across and disappeared up the left-hand slope. The near collision startled him out of his reverie.

She was asleep, her head nestled against the backrest. He could smell her scent, a little musky with the heat in the van. He'd set the air to cool, but the fan had continued to blow warm air at them, so he'd finally settled for putting it off and opening his window. The incoming breeze ruffled her hair. She was dreaming, her eyes moving behind the lids.

He'd been surprised when he'd found her waiting for him, surmising that she might have taken fright and not come. That had been the danger of publicizing *Stonewarrior*. But out here there was no signal and she'd remained ignorant of what had happened to the other participants.

She'd asked him to take her to the hotel she'd stayed in to collect her things, but he'd managed to dissuade her. She could call the hotel when he picked up a signal, explain she'd be back later to collect them. She'd seemed content with that. For the moment.

He'd expected to feel the same with this one as he had

with the others, but didn't. Maybe the death of the policeman had changed things? A wave of pleasure swept through him at that thought. The bastard hadn't looked so cocky, lying there on the road, knowing he was about to die. An image of Iona came to mind. She too had failed him. She'd gone along with all his demands, until the last and most important one.

Framing McNab and ruining his career were acceptable to her, especially after what the detective had done to Josh's mother. Even more so after he'd rejected her. But Iona had gone as far as she was willing in their game. She would not agree to McNab's death.

So Iona had died instead.

Helena stirred and shifted in her drug-induced sleep. Her head found his shoulder. Her warmth flowed into him. He had a brief memory of being cradled against his mother, and her warmth.

Josh felt himself stir and pushed her head away.

The game was reaching its finale and there was no one to stop him now. By the time they traced him it would be over. He had challenged them and found them wanting. He had reached level five, unhindered.

It was time for the game to be played out to its end.

59

'We believe this is the man we're looking for.'

All eyes turned to the screen. It was the photograph from the party, Josh and Iona deep in conversation, with only his profile in view.

'Josh Kearney. Nineteen years of age. Highly intelligent, an avid gamester and a skilled hacker. Trace evidence from Alan MacKenzie's clothes led to a familial link on the database.'

Bill pulled up the photograph of a younger Josh with his mother. Rhona was struck again by the child's empty eyes and his mother's frightened ones.

'Josh is the son of Isabel Kearney, who was jailed for the murder of her husband when the boy was fourteen. DI McNab was in charge of the case.'

All eyes turned briefly to McNab. His face was a mess and from the way he moved it was obvious the body beneath the shirt was equally bruised and beaten. McNab and she had had no opportunity to talk before the meeting. In fact, Rhona suspected he was doing his best to avoid her.

Bill continued. 'DNA saliva samples taken from the neck of the Brodgar victim and semen collected from the Skelmuir victim indicate Kearney as having been with both women prior to their deaths.' He paused.

LIN ANDERSON

The online image of a smiling Helena Watters in the passenger seat of a vehicle appeared next.

'Helena Watters may be victim number five. DI McNab describes the vehicle she's travelling in as a converted camper van, dark green in colour.' He quoted the number plate. 'The perpetrator is unaware that we have identified this vehicle, which is to our advantage.' He paused. 'You'll know by now that the other sites indicated as possible loci by Professor Pirie are being watched. Online interest has generated unprecedented numbers of visitors to these sites, which is what the perpetrator intended. This has put pressure on police resources, as was also intended. He has his fifth victim, that much we know. Where he intends taking her, we have no idea. If we ask the general public to help find the van, he will be alerted to that fact and may kill her before he reaches his destination.'

Bill gave out instructions and dismissed the team, then gestured to Rhona and McNab to join him in his office.

Magnus was already in there, something that surprised McNab, although he covered it well. There was a detailed ordnance survey map spread out on the desk. The points on the pentagram and the ley lines between were clearly marked in red. Magnus appeared drawn, as though deprived of sleep.

'Where did you last see the van?' Bill said.

McNab approached the desk. As he bent to study the map, Rhona noted him wince in pain. He pointed to a remote single-track road.

'Which way was the van heading?' Magnus said.

'North.'

'There's a small stone circle—'

McNab cut Magnus off. 'They didn't go there. I checked.' A nerve twitched at the corner of his mouth.

Magnus studied the map again. 'There's nothing else of significance in that area.' He sounded frustrated.

'Did he give any indication of a location other than that stone circle?' Bill said.

'I had one message. One set of co-ordinates. They're on my mobile.'

'And you didn't speak to him directly?'

McNab looked irritated at being asked. 'No,' he said shortly.

Rhona's immediate thought was that he was lying, or at least side-stepping the truth. Instinct told her he had spoken directly to Josh Kearney, or had a hunch where the van might be headed. But if so, why deny it? McNab was as desperate as the rest of them to catch Kearney.

Moments later, there was a knock at the door. It was Bill who called 'Enter', while the expression on McNab's face spoke volumes.

The look exchanged between DS Clark, Bill and McNab needed no explanation.

When the door closed behind McNab, Rhona said, 'What'll happen?'

'Superintendent Sutherland will suspend him pending the investigation into Iona's death,' Bill said.

'What about the *Stonewarrior* investigation?' Rhona said.

'McNab's no longer directly involved.'

'But he knows more about it than any of us,' Magnus said.

'We'll have to manage without him.'

By the end of the meeting they were no further forward. Magnus appeared distracted and indecisive, and Rhona could contribute nothing more than she had already. She also felt, as she thought Bill did, that McNab's loss to the investigation was a serious one. The sense that they had no way of preventing the death of the fifth victim pervaded their discussion. Without an idea of where Josh was headed, they would have to rely on a sighting of the van. It looked as though Bill would take the decision to release its description and thereby warn Josh that they were on to him, which might hasten Helena's death. It was a decision Rhona was glad she didn't have to make. Magnus's last offering was that the psychology of the perpetrator suggested he would play the game to the end, whatever the consequences.

When Magnus departed, Bill asked for coffee to be brought in for both of them before settling down at the desk. This had been Bill's room before McNab had been promoted, yet he now looked out of place and uncomfortable. She thought it might be the missing swivel chair, removed into storage until he returned from compassionate leave.

Bill read her thoughts. 'This one doesn't turn, and turning in that old chair helped me think. That and the view from this window.' He was silent for a moment. 'Let's talk about Iona now,' he said. 'How does it look for McNab?'

'Not good,' Rhona said honestly. 'Saliva from the neck area is his. Also semen retrieved from high up in the vaginal track. I couldn't find anything of Josh Kearney on her.'

'The finger marks on her neck?'

'I couldn't get a print.'

'Shape and size of the hand?'

'Medium-size male, at a guess.'

'So they could belong to McNab?'

Rhona didn't want to admit that, but had to. 'It might be difficult to disprove.'

'Have we established how she died?'

'Post-mortem report confirms a heroin overdose. Her prints are on the syringe, but judging by their location, I believe it was placed in her hand after the event.'

'The prosecution could mount a case against McNab using the forensic evidence alone,' Bill said worriedly. 'According to McNab, he asked Iona to leave the night he stayed at yours. She refused, so he walked out and eventually turned up at your place. When he went back next morning the flat was trashed. Our detective inspector is well known for his temper. The prosecution could use that as a motive.'

'Josh Kearney helped trash McNab's flat.'

Surprised, Bill waited for Rhona's explanation.

'MDNA,' she said. 'From the faeces.'

MDNA was carried in tiny structures, mitochondria, that lived inside cells. When the egg was fertilized by the sperm, the male mitochondrial DNA was destroyed, which meant only the female MDNA was passed on. And MDNA was preserved in faecal matter.

The traces of faeces McNab had failed to bleach away had led again to Isabel Kearney. It was her son, Josh, who'd defecated in McNab's flat.

Bill gave a grim smile at her news.

60

The helicopter had set down just after midnight and a cop car had driven him home. He'd ignored the bed, fearing memories of Iona, and, dosing himself up on paracetamol and whisky, he'd lain down on the couch instead. The scent of bleach still lingered in the room. He couldn't smell the shit, but imagined he could anyway. Sleep had eluded him, replaced by a desperate need to form a plan of action for tomorrow. He had no intention of revealing the murder attempt. The fact that Kearney believed him dead was to his advantage, but McNab cared less about the attempt on his own life than that Kearney, having used Iona to set him up, had then disposed of her.

And how long had Kearney been planning his death? Had the *Stonewarrior* game been formulated with that thought in mind? Or was it just serendipity that he turned out to be the officer in charge when the game began?

He'd eventually drifted off into a nightmare of drowning and had woken drenched in sweat. The reek of his body was more than he could stomach, so he'd taken a shower, cold enough to thrust him back into life.

Examining himself in the bathroom mirror, he'd realized that most of the discomfort came from a gash below his left arm. Initially he'd believed all the cuts to be minor, but this one throbbed and was now emitting a bloody pus.

McNab had bathed it clean, then checked the cabinet for something to dress it with. A depleted first-aid kit had provided a dressing and tape, but no antiseptic ointment.

By the time he'd finished, the sun had risen and the day of reckoning had begun.

Sutherland had been swift and to the point. Nothing he'd said had caused any surprise. McNab was off the case, and off work pending an investigation into his handling of it. He was also required to provide a formal statement in the case of the unexplained death of Iona Craig, a nineteen-year-old female he'd reportedly been having a relationship with.

McNab's interruption at this point to say, 'We had sex. We were not in a relationship,' didn't go down well. The vow he'd made in the dark hours of the night to zip his lip had proved impossible to keep.

There was also, Sutherland had revealed, the statement given by Steve Munro regarding McNab removing a holdall of cocaine from a location on Cathkin Braes. That had been news to McNab and he'd referred to the accusation as 'fucking lies'.

The meeting had ended abruptly at that, with Sutherland ordering him to go to an interview room and provide a statement regarding his *relationship* with Iona Craig.

McNab had made the statement as brief as possible. In a series of blunt sentences he'd said how they'd met. Given the number of times they'd had sex, and where. Described how he'd asked her to leave. She'd taken it badly and refused. He'd walked out, only to return to a trashed flat, which he'd asked Dr MacLeod to process forensically as he believed a male had helped her do it. He stated he was

LIN ANDERSON

certain his mobile had been compromised, probably while he'd slept.

He then signed it and left.

Now outside the station and a free agent for the foreseeable future, perhaps forever, McNab felt only a sense of relief. Kearney had done him a favour and he was about to repay it big time.

Ollie had agreed to meet, although with a certain amount of trepidation. Outside his usual high-tech environment, he looked forlorn, like a child who'd just had a toy taken away. They were sitting in one of the numerous Glasgow coffee shops. McNab's need to visit a bar had diminished from the moment he'd been suspended, caffeine having taken the place of whisky as his drug of choice.

Ollie hadn't touched the latte he'd ordered and was shifting in his seat. McNab had already drunk his double espresso and was considering what persuasive technique might be used on the man-boy to get what he wanted.

'As you know, I'm off the case,' McNab said evenly. His remark seemed to ease Ollie's trepidation a little, until the one that followed brought his apprehension swiftly back.

'But I believe,' McNab said, 'that you and I can catch the puppetmaster.'

Ollie opened and shut his mouth as McNab continued. 'You are not a police officer and for the moment neither am I. We are Joe Public and as such are free to engage with Stonewarrior.'

One look at Ollie's face suggested he might be using the wrong method of persuasion, so McNab played his first reserve card. 'I have already met with the puppetmaster.'

'You actually met? But I thought—'

354

McNab held up his hand to prevent further interruptions. 'We met at the location he sent me. That's how I was able to describe the van.'

Ollie was all ears now.

'He also tried to kill me *and* almost succeeded.' McNab gave a grim smile, which he hoped made his gargoyle face look worse, then shifted painfully in his seat to indicate further, not so obvious, injuries.

Ollie's owl-like eyes grew even bigger. Time for another card.

'So much so, that he believes I *am* dead –' McNab paused – 'which puts *us* at a distinct advantage.'

The use of the word *us* had had some impact. McNab watched as Ollie processed this, then continued.

'He jeopardized the game and his own safety to kill me, which suggests my demise was high on his to-do list. If he realizes I'm still alive . . .'

Ollie knew where McNab was headed, so McNab played the final card.

'And anything we can do to distract him from his fifth victim must be good. Right?'

Ollie didn't want the girl to die, that much was obvious. If there was a way his knowledge and expertise could prevent this, he would do it.

'Okay, but we have to work from my place.'

McNab nodded. 'Let's go.'

Ollie lived in two rooms, one of which resembled his place of work. A variety of flat screens, numerous keyboards and a continuous hum of power flowing and processors working greeted their entrance, obviously continuing to operate whether he was present or not.

Once inside, Ollie seemed to relax. Like a pilot in a cockpit, he was home.

McNab unpacked Helena's bag, revealing her laptop and mobile.

'These belong to Helena Watters. She left them charging at the hotel she was staying in.'

Ollie looked startled. 'Shouldn't you have handed them in?'

McNab tried to look contrite. 'I forgot the bag this morning. Too much on my mind. I'll hand it in after you take a look.'

61

A deer crossing the road, McNab swerving to avoid it. The car ending up at the foot of a bank. Being picked up by a local hotelier. All sounded plausible, because a good detective knew that the best way to tell a lie was to embed it in the truth.

What he'd told Bill about heading for the location given via the game, seeing the van then losing it again because of the accident, rang true too. Even his reason for leaving the mobile with Sean.

But he was hiding something. His behaviour in the meeting with Bill and Magnus, that shut-down look, wasn't just because he was awaiting Sutherland's summons.

There was no webpage for the Old Forge Inn, just the owner's name, Megan McKellar, and the hotel number. After a few rings, a pleasant female voice answered.

Rhona explained who she was and that she was calling about Detective Inspector McNab.

The tone immediately changed to worry. 'Is he okay?'

'Pretty knocked about, but okay,' Rhona said.

'I'm glad. Have you found Helena yet?'

'No, and we may need your help with that.'

'Of course.'

'The van that was involved in the accident—'

The woman interrupted her. 'Detective McNab said the

van hit him on purpose. It pushed the car over the bank and into the river. He was trapped inside . . .' Her voice indicated how frightening the incident had been.

Rhona listened to the remainder of Megan's story. When she'd finished, Rhona thanked her, and urged her to call if she remembered anything else that might help find Helena.

When she rang off, Rhona contemplated the disturbing news that Josh Kearney had tried to murder McNab, and that he'd chosen to keep this information secret. But why?

McNab had screwed up as DI. He knew he would be demoted, and was in the shit over his relationship with Iona. Maybe even in the frame for her death, which he probably blamed himself for. At this moment in time, McNab appeared to have nothing left to lose. And that's what worried her.

Rhona fetched her mobile and scrolled down through past calls until she found the number he'd used to contact her. It was a mobile, probably pay-as-you-go. He hadn't gone into the unknown, leaving his phone with Sean, without a back-up.

He answered on the third ring. 'Dr MacLeod?'

'Can we meet?' Rhona said.

He didn't answer immediately and she strained to hear what was in the background. It didn't sound like a pub.

'Better not. We might talk shop and that's against the rules.'

'Why did you lie about the accident?'

A momentary pause. 'I didn't,' he said guardedly.

'I spoke to Megan McKellar.'

Another pause. 'Playing the detective again, Dr MacLeod?'

'She said Kearney pushed your car over the bank into the river.'

'She's mistaken.'

'She sounded pretty certain to me.'

A male voice, which Rhona didn't recognize, called McNab from the background.

'Sorry, I have to go.' Without giving her a chance to reply, he rang off.

Rhona threw down the mobile in frustration. McNab was up to something. What, she had no idea.

She settled down to work. Now at the write-up stage, her reports were in depth, and full of the detailed scientific evidence from the forensic samples collected. In many instances, she wasn't asked to present her evidence in court because her reports were sufficient.

Normally she was juggling a variety of cases. It was less than usual to find herself dealing with multiple murders by the same perpetrator. Serial killings did happen, more often than anyone liked to believe, but they tended to be carried out over a period of years, even over the lifetime of the perpetrator, making it forensically difficult to link them, if the bodies of those missing were ever found.

The *Stonewarrior* case was unique, in that it had been carried out over a period of some nine days, and was linked to an online game, which meant the country, if not the world, was watching the outcome.

Josh Kearney, known as Stonewarrior, had now reached online celebrity status. He was seen to be outwitting and outmanoeuvring the police, both north and south of the border. If the media ever got hold of the McNab angle to the story, things would only get worse.

Which meant it was even more important for McNab to stay out of it.

62

Aware she might attain consciousness soon, he'd driven off the main road onto a farm track. Under cover of trees, he lifted her from the passenger seat and installed her in the bed in the back of the van. He tied her hands and feet and gagged her. Her eyes flickered open momentarily, but the look was glassy, the pupils large. Nevertheless, he prepared another syringe.

Finding an entry point was easy, the blue-black veins obvious in her slim arms. She moaned a little as the needle pierced the skin, then grew quiet again. He studied her, aware that in her present state he could do anything he wanted. The thought excited him and he contemplated rolling her over onto her front, but it would involve untying her again, then removing her jeans. The thought evaporated as swiftly as it had come.

As he exited and locked the door, his glance fell on the black holdall. He unzipped it and took a quick look inside. It had been pure luck that he'd been back checking to see if the body had been found when the bloke discovered the stash, then the body.

It had been Iona's idea to seek him out and get him to help them frame the policeman. How she'd love playing him along. Josh stopped his thoughts there, not wanting to think any more about Iona. He re-zipped the bag. Once the game was over, he would head to London, sell the cocaine. Start afresh.

Checking there was no one about to take note of him, he turned the van and made his way back to the main road. Glancing at his watch, he worked out that at this rate he would be home in a couple of hours, longer if he chose to dispose of her and take photographs to upload later.

He tested his wishes on this, one more time.

He would have to kill her eventually, but found himself unable to contemplate it quite yet. Once she was dead, it was over. The planning, the excitement, the pleasure of outwitting his opponents. But most important of all, while the game had been foremost in his mind, other thoughts and memories had retreated.

Once the game was over, would they come back? He forced himself not to think about that.

As he prepared to draw out of the side road, an incoming message sounded on his mobile. Startled, he released the clutch and the van jerked and stalled. Josh stared, mesmerized, at the mobile. The only people who had that number were *Stonewarrior* players and they were all dead, apart from the female in the back of the van.

He pulled on the handbrake and stared at the name on the mobile screen. *Caylum*.

How had the bitch sent a message when she was tied up? The answer was, she couldn't.

Irritation seized him as he tried to make sense of it. Irritation and a niggling thought that he'd fucked up in some way. He should have checked her pockets for the mobile. He should have killed her at the stone circle, then posted the photograph. He should have played by the rules of the game.

LIN ANDERSON

He tried to calm himself. It was more than likely that her mobile, having finally picked up a signal, had sent him a late text from her.

Josh opened the message.

Steve tried to open his eyes, but they appeared to be glued shut. He didn't want to see who was in the room with him, but just hearing them was worse. There was a great deal of cursing and he was sure he'd heard someone pissing.

Much laughter followed this, together with the suggestion that they shit on the keyboard, or maybe even in the bastard's lap. Footsteps approached. He heard the sound of a zip being pulled down and suddenly an arse was shoved in his face.

Steve struggled desperately to break free of his bonds but only succeeded in rubbing his face further against the backside.

The guy straddling him moaned as though in pleasure.

Steve threw himself backwards and the chair tipped. He landed with a grunt, the air knocked out of his lungs.

'Last chance. Tell us where it is or I take a dump on your face.'

Steve said again that he didn't know.

The guy squatted in preparation.

Steve felt his own bowels begin to move in horror.

'Okay,' he said. 'I'll tell you.'

The guy farted in his face, then stood up.

'The policeman dug it up. I saw him. I thought he'd handed it in, but I found out he hadn't,' he said.

He watched them assess his answer. They looked at one another as though his pronouncement made some sort of sense.

'What does this policeman look like?'

Steve described McNab. The expression on all three faces suggested they knew exactly who he was talking about.

63

McNab waited, his blood pressure mounting. The bastard must have got the message by now. Why didn't he answer?

Ollie threw him an anxious glance. 'He may be out of range.'

'Send it again,' McNab said.

'It's better if we wait.'

McNab was about to issue a sarcastic reply, asking who the fucking detective in the room was, when Helena's mobile pinged.

Both men drew a breath together.

'That's it,' Ollie said.

'It better fucking well be,' McNab said, relief in his voice.

Ollie had attached the mobile to a tracking device. McNab stared at the map on the screen with the small blinking dot.

'Where is he?'

'Near Loch Katrine, an hour north of here.'

Ollie brought up the text message on the big screen.

Entity

DO NOT ATTEMPT TO CONTACT THE STONEWARRIOR CORE.
Ignore communications from anyone seeking information about the Game.
Tune in, turn on, play hard, Live or Die by the Game.

'It's the same fucking nonsense as last time,' McNab said, exasperated.

'He's testing to see who sent the message.'

'*I* fucking sent it.'

'But he thinks you're dead.'

McNab indicated the mobile. 'Then let's show him I'm very much alive.'

'I'm not sure that's a good idea.'

'Do it,' McNab ordered.

Ollie took the picture and McNab added his message. Moments later, the dot on the screen disappeared.

'The mobile's been switched off,' Ollie said. It was obvious by his expression that he thought they'd messed up.

McNab wasn't so sure. His meeting with Kearney had shown him that his death had become a major goal in the game. McNab still being alive would be more than just an irritant. Kearney would see it as defeat, and that's what McNab was counting on.

'We wait,' he said.

'Maybe we should alert DI Wilson that he's somewhere in the Trossachs,' Ollie tried.

McNab shook his head. When they'd sent the photograph, he'd made clear that the fight was now between himself and Kearney. One on one, on the understanding that Helena wasn't harmed.

McNab abandoned Ollie and lay down on the couch. Closing his eyes, he tried to think. Instinct and intuition told him that this was the way to deal with Kearney. He could be wrong and the girl already dead, but nothing had been posted online yet to suggest that. If she was dead, he could still catch Kearney if he got him to play along with *his* game this time.

His own mobile rang, startling him out of his reverie. He glanced at the screen to find Rhona's name. He almost answered. He would have liked to talk to her, to run the whole scenario past her. But then again, he knew what she would say.

McNab switched the phone off in case he was tempted. The truth was, Rhona had been right from the beginning. He wasn't cut out to be a DI. She hadn't said that in so many words, but he'd sensed it, observed it in her reactions.

Well, if he was going down, he would do it his way.

Helena's mobile rang out. In an instant McNab was up and back at the computer.

The dot reappeared on the screen.

'He's back inside the city boundary,' Ollie said, excited.

McNab opened the text from Stonewarrior and read the instructions.

He hated this place even more than he'd hated the house he'd grown up in. He spent most of his time in the van, but he needed to get off the road and this was the place to do it. The first mobile call had unnerved him, then he'd decided it was a fake.

There was no way that detective could be alive. He'd watched the car crash down the bank and enter the water. He'd waited for the water to fill the open windows. Unconscious, the bastard had no chance of getting out before he drowned. So he'd left the scene, content and looking forward to the finale.

Now he realized that killing the detective had made him complacent. He'd lost his edge. Grown soft like his supplicant mother. He'd observed the girl in the back of the van with something resembling pity. He'd been stupid, but he wasn't going to be stupid again.

The backstreet of lock-ups behind the house was deserted. He got out, opened up, and drove the van inside. Dotted around the walls was the boxed debris of Angus's house-breaking days. He'd rummaged through it a few times and found some interesting stuff, which he'd sold. There was nothing of any value left, if you discounted Angus's penchant for stealing women's underwear.

He locked the garage door from the inside and went to check on the girl.

She was moaning softly. He thought of his uncle and what he would choose to do to her at this moment. In the darkness of the garage the thought brought a flashback as powerful as the original. He was in the blackness of the cupboard, only a chink of light allowing him to watch his uncle's sexual antics. For a moment he was his younger self again, fascinated and repulsed, aroused and repelled.

He reached down and checked the pulse in her neck. It beat, but weakly. He couldn't go on dosing her like this forever, but he needed an image that showed her as alive or else the detective wouldn't believe him.

He set the mobile to take a video then untied the gag. Saliva dribbled down her chin and she coughed to clear her throat. He turned the mobile on himself, undid his zip and his prick rose in anticipation. Her eyes flickered open briefly and she gave a small moan.

He stopped recording and re-zipped himself. That should be enough to bring the detective running. He re-tied the gag. He could of course inject her now, but the flashback had brought a desire. One that he would enact.

He would kill the pig, then come back here and reward himself. One thing he could promise. She would die in ecstasy.

64

Her mobile rang out five times, then stopped. The number came up as withheld.

Very few people had her personal number and all of them were identified by their name when they called.

A few minutes later it rang again. This time Rhona answered, but didn't identify herself. A few moments of silence followed. She could distinguish nothing, not even breathing, so not a nuisance call. She decided on a wrong number, until a text pinged in.

It was from McNab. He asked to meet, there were important things he needed to discuss with her. He suggested they meet at his flat as soon as possible.

It was what Rhona had wanted to hear. When she texted back suggesting a time, McNab immediately replied in the affirmative.

Rhona experienced a sense of relief. McNab was going to talk to her and, despite everything, there was a possibility he could come through this. She would tell him about the evidence of Kearney in the flat. That Josh and Iona had obviously set him up. She would urge him to lie low. Let Bill take over. Not interfere.

His possible involvement in Iona's death would be disproved. The statement by Steve Munro was obviously a pack of lies. McNab would survive, maybe even at DI level.

She was aware of the difficulties he faced, but the fact that McNab had got in touch and was planning to meet dispelled some of her worry. If she could persuade him of the right course of action, all might yet be well. She concentrated on finishing her reports with one eye on the clock.

Ollie had gone back to work, leaving McNab alone in his flat. McNab had urged him to do so, to avoid suspicion. Surely he could monitor any progress they had made from the official Starship Enterprise? Ollie had done as ordered with such a worried look on his face that McNab vowed to get the guy drunk when they had a party to celebrate bringing in Kearney.

An hour before the allotted time, McNab took himself into the bathroom. The dressing he'd put on the wound had peeled off, exposing what could only be described as a suppurating mess. He regarded it with one thought in mind: how he might inflict something similar on Kearney. He doused the wound with as scalding water as he could suffer, then searched for something to bind it with. Ollie's bathroom cabinet wasn't much healthier than his own, so he checked out the computer desk and found some masking tape.

He contemplated padding the wound with toilet paper, then decided closing it was more important than a dressing. He patted his skin dry, then cut a long piece of tape, pinched the sides of the gash together, and applied it along the wound. It hurt, but the anticipation of seeing Kearney again served to ease the pain.

Half an hour before the meeting time, he exited the building.

Ollie had proved to have nothing more than a can of high energy drink in the fridge. McNab had taken it and mixed it with a very healthy dollop of whisky from the half-bottle he was carrying.

His head buzzing from a mix of pain and alcohol, he headed for the rendezvous point. Kearney had sent him a video clip to prove Helena's continued existence. It was a short but ugly scene. Ollie had assured McNab that it hadn't appeared online, which he hoped meant she was still alive.

They said you always remembered your first murder scene, often in graphic detail. It hadn't been true for him. He'd forgotten it entirely, until now.

The block of four houses was boarded up, in an already partially demolished street. He parked his car outside, wondering if it would be there when he exited. Or if it was, whether it would still have wheels. Any streets left standing had been empty as he'd wound his way through the housing estate. Across the road, grass was attempting to grow in the rubble left by the bulldozers.

McNab had been raised in a place like this. He remembered well the rules for survival here. He locked the car, aware that anyone with a little know-how could force the lock in seconds, hot-wire the ignition and drive away. And walking out of here might prove more difficult than driving in.

The Kearneys had occupied the flat on the upper level of house number 33. Access to it was gained by a side door that opened on an inner stair. When McNab tried the door he found it open.

The remains of a threadbare carpet covered the narrow staircase, the marks of dirty hands forming a dark and mottled frieze on the right-hand wall. McNab checked behind him, then entered and shut the door.

He stood listening in the silence, sensing no presence other than his own. As he climbed, his feet on the carpet caused dust motes to rise and dance in the jagged light from a smashed window.

He was on the landing now.

In a flash of recognition, he knew that the kitchen lay at the end. A sitting room and bathroom to the right, two bedrooms on the left. Everything about the flat was narrow and cramped. He dipped his head a little as he walked the corridor. Above him, the low roof sagged in places where the rain had found entry.

He checked each room in turn, finding broken furniture and a scattering of syringes and condoms. The kitchen was last.

By now anyone in the flat would know of his presence, despite any attempts at silence. Since all the other rooms were empty, if Kearney was in his former home, he would be in here.

McNab pushed open the door.

The contrast with the rest of the house was dramatic. The kitchen window had been freed of its shutter and sunlight streamed in. The surfaces were clean, a table and two chairs sat in the centre. On the window ledge a posy of seeding grass and wild flowers was arranged in a cracked mug.

The image affected McNab more than he could acknowledge, because just such a bunch of flowers had been on the window ledge the night he'd been summoned here. It was a detail he'd forgotten until now. Then a red poppy had been the centrepiece, its colour matching the pools of blood on the floor and the splashes that streaked the surfaces. Isabel Kearney had been sitting at the table, the knife in front of her, her eyes focussed on the posy on the windowsill, as though by its presence the rest of the scene might cease to exist.

He heard a creak and turned to face the door.

65

Bill regarded the technical assistant with undisguised anger.

'You aided a suspended officer in gaining access to data in a multiple murder enquiry?' he said in disbelief.

The young man before him squirmed. 'Not exactly.'

'Then what *did* you do *exactly*?'

'We engaged with Stonewarrior, as Joe Public.'

Bill gave a harsh laugh. 'Joe Public. I bet that was DI McNab's turn of phrase?'

Ollie gave a slight nod.

'And how exactly did you do that?'

This was obviously the question Ollie didn't want to be asked. He took a few moments to answer. 'Detective Inspector McNab had the missing girl's laptop and mobile.'

Bill couldn't believe what he was hearing.

Seeing Bill's expression, Ollie came back quickly. 'He was going to hand it in after we made contact with Stonewarrior.'

'I bet he was.' Bill waited for the rest.

Ollie rushed on in a breathless voice. 'Inspector McNab sent Kearney a photograph to prove he was still alive. He said he was willing to meet him one to one, provided the girl wasn't harmed.'

Bill fought to control his anger. There was no point shouting at Ollie whatever-his-name-was, when he really

374

wanted to shout at McNab. He decided not to ask for further details on the revelation that Kearney believed McNab to be dead, guessing that the story of the car accident was just that, a story.

'How did DI McNab get hold of the mobile?'

Ollie had no idea.

'Where is the mobile now?'

'He must have taken it when he went to meet Kearney.'

Panic began to rise in Bill's chest. 'He's gone to meet him already?'

Misery filled Ollie's face. 'He told me to go to work. When I checked back at the flat, he wasn't there. Neither was the mobile.'

'When was the last time you saw him?' Bill said sharply.

'Around four hours ago.'

Bill dismissed the Tech guy and sat down to think. Four hours. Jesus, McNab could be in serious trouble or already dead, but trying to find him without a clue where to look was impossible.

He cursed McNab for making the case personal.

Bill had risen from the seat and was pacing. The atmosphere in the room was hot and humid, yet seemed to crackle as he moved through it. From the window he noted the river flowing, grey and sluggish between its banks, as though the heatwave had proved too much for it. Above hung an army of thick black clouds. The storm would break and soon.

Bill brought a halt to his walking, and put in a call to Professor Magnus Pirie.

Magnus's usually healthy complexion, which had weathered the sun, rain and wind of the Orkney Islands, looked unnaturally pale. The dark blue eyes had lost their shine and, more surprisingly, their directness. Bill was faced with the strange experience of having to catch the criminal profiler's eye.

'I don't think I can help. I've been unable to make any more sense of the medium's predictions and I don't believe him anyway.'

'Let's forget Patrick Menzies for a moment.' Bill pushed the file on Isabel Kearney across the desk to Magnus. 'Take a look at this while I fetch us some coffee.' He took note again of Magnus's drawn face. 'And some sandwiches.'

Bill made himself scarce, giving the job of fetching the sandwiches and coffee to someone else before making a beeline for DS Clark. She jumped to attention at her desk on his approach. He waved at her to sit back down.

'Angus Patterson,' he began.

'I've see him, sir. He's suffering from dementia, and,' she hesitated, 'he's an unpleasant character.'

Bill tried to recall Patterson, but could only remember that he'd been associated with endless burglaries. Then something did spring to mind. Angus liked stealing women's underwear. From their homes and their washing lines. He mentioned this to DS Clark, who grimaced.

'That sounds about right, sir. He asked me for a fuck and got quite irate when I ignored him.'

Bill nodded. They never did get Patterson for anything other than burglary, but they'd always wondered what else he'd been up to. Bill dredged his memory. There was something else. The boy had gone to live with Patterson after his mother died. Then Patterson had been caught at his favourite pursuit and banged up again, which meant the boy had had to go into care.

'Has Josh ever visited Angus at the care home?'

'I asked, but the woman there at the time didn't know. She was going to check it out.' DS Clark looked stricken that she hadn't yet followed that up.

'Find out if Josh has ever been there. And find out what happened to Patterson's house when he was admitted to the care home.'

DS Clark looked even more uncomfortable at a further omission.

Bill, sensing this, gave her a few words of encouragement. 'You've had enough on your plate trying to find your commanding officer.'

When he re-entered the office, Magnus was deep in the file. The swiftness with which his eyes travelled the page was pretty impressive and Bill had no doubt that the professor was assimilating the material regardless of the speed he was reading it. The coffee and sandwiches lay undisturbed in front of Magnus. Bill busied himself with his own coffee, cooled now to the temperature he preferred. He took the mug to his favourite seat and waited.

Bill had also found the file interesting reading. Domestic abuse and subsequent murder was ugly to deal with. According to the record, McNab had handled it well. The woman had confessed to stabbing her husband after he'd raped her. But, reading between the lines, questions had arisen in Bill's mind. The son had told McNab that he'd done it, although the mother had denied this. Josh had been only fourteen at the time, below the age at which he could be tried and convicted. McNab had chosen to believe the mother's story and that's the way it had gone. Josh Kearney had stayed briefly with the uncle, Angus Patterson, not a great role model. When Angus went back inside, Josh was sent to a number of foster families, then a home, from which he subsequently absconded. There was no record of him after that.

Magnus was studying the crime-scene photographs intently. The bloody kitchen, the knife, the frenzied stab wounds, some of them obviously stabbed more than once.

Bill recollected Isabel Kearney. Small, slight, bruised and battered. How had she found the strength and frenzied will to inflict those injuries? Although, from his own experience, when women like Isabel finally snapped, often in the face of danger to their children, they were capable of just about anything.

So had Isabel Kearney been covering for her son?

Magnus set aside one photograph in particular. It was a horrific scene. Isabel Kearney was sitting at the kitchen table, the knife in her hand, amidst what could only be described as a bloodbath.

Magnus moved another photograph to sit against it. Now the two men could see what her glassy-eyed stare was focussing on. It was a posy of flowers set in a jam jar on the kitchen window ledge behind the sink. The posy consisted of wilting daisies, a splash of buttercups, tendrils of wild grass and a single red poppy.

'There's no psychiatric report on the boy amidst the case papers,' Magnus said. 'Was an assessment ever done?'

Bill had no idea. 'I'll try and find out.' He waited for Magnus to continue.

'You're contemplating the prospect that DI McNab was wrong and that the boy Josh was the culprit?' Magnus said.

'If that were the case, what would it mean for the boy's state of mind?'

'If he did do it and made that plain, the fact that his

confession was ignored would make him angry, perhaps despairing, and definitely without control. When his mother took her own life, any feelings he had would be exacerbated.'

'How would the boy react to the officer who refused to believe him?'

'Resentment, even fury, if he held the arresting officer responsible for his mother's death.' Magnus paused. 'You're linking Josh Kearney directly to DI McNab in some way?'

'Kearney tried to kill McNab. He even risked capture to do so.'

'That changes everything,' Magnus said.

'I agree.' Bill now came at things from a different angle. 'Assuming Josh Kearney is the puppetmaster of this alternative reality game, what's the psychology behind it?'

Magnus considered the question for a few moments.

'Game playing among adolescent and not so adolescent men allows them to act out their fantasies, ostensibly without directly harming their opponents. To outsmart and outplay your adversaries builds confidence and a strong sense of power and control, when in the real world you may have none of these things.' Magnus went on. '*Stonewarrior* is not a shoot-them-up game, but a game of knowledge which has a mystery behind it. It is filled with pattern. The puppetmaster is like a chess grandmaster, who knows just when and how he will call checkmate. However, when he outwits his opponents, he loses respect for them and in this game they die.'

'And posting the battle online?'

'The interest shown, the followers, even the admiration for the way he outwits his opponents, the police, feeds his confidence and his sense of power still further.'

'And the fact that he failed to outwit and kill McNab?'

'It's the first time his plan has been really challenged. If he thought McNab was dead and rejoiced in it, then finding out he wasn't would seriously enrage him.'

McNab would know that and use it to draw Kearney out. Bill wished again that McNab had confided in him. If he'd still been his DS, he might have, but not now. Not now.

Magnus was regarding him closely. 'What's happening?'

'McNab has set up a meeting with the puppetmaster, and I have no idea where or when it's happening.'

66

When she buzzed, McNab let her in without speaking. Climbing the stairs, Rhona tried to work out what she would say to persuade him into the best course of action. Revealing the fact that Kearney had tried to kill him could be in McNab's favour and would go some way to compensate for his less than wise decisions in the *Stonewarrior* case. But taking advice was not McNab's strong point.

She composed herself before ringing the doorbell. She would remain calm. She would not argue. That never worked. She would reason with him instead. The first ring wasn't answered, so she pressed the bell again. When that too went unanswered, she knocked.

At last she heard approaching footsteps and braced herself. Those first few moments when she and McNab met eye to eye could determine the entire encounter.

The door opened.

It took less than a second for her to realize that it hadn't been opened by McNab. But less than a second was not enough for her to escape.

She was dragged inside and a hand placed over her mouth. The stink of male sweat, cigarettes and alcohol was overwhelming. Mingled with urine, it brought tears to her eyes.

The two hooded figures dragged her through to the

sitting room. Above the hand she spied a third, watching her entrance.

'Who the fuck is she?' He looked peeved.

Rhona tried to mouth words into the hand.

'Let her talk.'

'She might scream.'

The point of a blade poked into her neck.

'No fucking screaming, bitch,' the one in view ordered. He was taller than her captors. Thin as a rake, his cheekbones stood out at sharp angles. The sunken eyes were bright with some substance or other, and righteous indignation.

'Who the fuck are you?'

Rhona shook off their hands and cleared her throat. 'I'm a police officer,' she lied.

The rake regarded her with some consternation. 'You live here?'

Rhona wasn't sure what the right answer should be. If they were looking for McNab, then telling them she lived here wouldn't work. And, as far as she knew, they would have found no female clothes during their more than obvious search.

She took a calculated guess. 'If you're looking for the holdall, it's not here.'

That stopped his muddled thoughts in their tracks. Then a glint appeared in his already bright eyes.

'So you know about the holdall?'

I just made a big mistake, Rhona thought. 'We have it at the station,' she tried.

'No you don't.' He approached her, bringing with him a heinous mix of stale cigarettes, dope, alcohol and body sweat. He shoved his face in hers, adding rotten breath to the mix.

'No you don't. The pig who lives here dug it up and kept it for himself.'

Rhona waited until he withdrew his face a little before opening her mouth to answer.

'It's at the station. I've seen it.'

The slap came from nowhere and met her cheek in a stinging blow, the force of it sending her staggering sideways. As she strove to recover her footing, the knife point prodded her neck again. She had an immediate image of how close it was to a fatal puncture zone. He did too, and smiled to emphasize the fact.

'You're going to call the pig and tell him to get here fast with the holdall or I'm going to practise noughts and crosses on your neck.'

'Okay.' Rhona agreed because the last thing she wanted was for McNab to appear on the premises unprepared. She indicated she planned to get her mobile from her pocket. On the two most recent occasions McNab had called, it had been from different numbers. God knew if he would respond to either of them. She tried the most recent number first. It rang out unanswered.

The guy in charge swore loudly.

'If he's driving, he won't answer,' Rhona said. 'I'll have to text or leave a voice message.'

He grabbed the mobile and listened to the standard 'leave a message' in a female robotic voice.

'We've got your girlfriend. Bring the holdall home now or I slit her throat.' He thrust the mobile in Rhona's face. 'Speak.'

'McNab, it's me.'

He stabbed at her neck and she cried out in pain. He cut off the call and threw the mobile across the room. It skittered out the door. He pushed her onto the couch and told her to keep quiet or he'd mark her face.

Rhona did as bid. Now the initial skirmish was at an end, she took time to survey the room. Every possible hiding place had been raided in their search for the holdall. They'd even found McNab's stash of booze and were in the process of consuming a bottle each of whisky and vodka. The whisky was a single malt, the vodka a premiere Russian brand. McNab would be well pissed off.

Rhona considered her predicament and what she might do about it. Her mobile was out of reach, so no opportunity to make an emergency call unless the trio drank themselves into oblivion. Unlikely, unless they topped up the alcohol with some other substance.

When the thin guy had threatened her neck, his exposed arm had shown needle tracks. She wondered how long before he needed to shoot up again and whether he'd brought the gear with him, or had relied on finding the holdall.

He caught her swift gaze before she looked away.

'Fucking boring waiting here. Maybe we should have a little fun to pass the time.' He came towards her, the grin exposing teeth made in hell.

Rhona swore under her breath. Where the hell was McNab when you needed him?

67

Magnus had departed before DS Clark brought Bill the news.

'Josh Kearney visited his uncle a couple of months back. According to the care home he brought some of Patterson's belongings.' DS Clark's eyes flashed with excitement.

'So Josh has access to his uncle's house?'

'Yes, sir.'

'Where?'

'Castlemilk, not far from Cathkin Braes Park.'

'Let's take a look.'

Until now the only place they'd identified with Kearney was the van that had knocked McNab off the road. If Patterson's old house had been providing a safe haven for him and his computer equipment, they were one step nearer him and his centre of operation. Bill didn't dare hope they would find McNab there too.

Thunder was already rolling over the hills as they approached Castlemilk. Stretching up the lower slopes of Cathkin Braes in an interwoven set of streets, they took a couple of wrong turnings before they finally located the address they'd been given. Bill drew into a parking place. Curtains were already twitching, although with the heat, many of the street's residents were sitting out in the gardens or on doorsteps. The arrival of a police car was of interest, but then again wasn't that unusual, although a few of the younger street residents melted away at the sight of it.

Bill told DS Clark to guard the car, and approached the door of number 25.

'No one there,' he was informed by a man in next-door's garden. Stripped down to his shorts, his exposed belly would have done a pregnant woman proud. 'Old Angus is in a home.' He made a screwing sign next to his head with his forefinger. 'Went doowally.'

'What about his nephew? Name's Josh Kearney. Nineteen years of age. Drives a dark green van,' Bill tried.

A woman emerged from the house. She eyed Bill with suspicion. 'What do they want?' she asked the beefy man.

'Looking for Angus's nephew.'

'Why?'

Bill decided a lie might be in order. 'Angus has asked for him,' he said gravely.

She snorted. 'No way.' She turned to go back in.

'Has Josh been around lately?' Bill tried.

'Never seen him.' The man had taken his cue from the woman.

'What about the van?'

'Didn't know he had one.'

The woman bellowed at the man to get his arse inside and he did. The door was slammed shut, and any remaining audience melted away like snow off a dyke.

Bill knocked on the door, knowing he would get no response. The curtains were shut over dirty windows and the grass in the front garden could have grazed a cow for a week. He walked round to the back of the house. No grass here, just a small stony yard with a high back fence to keep out nosy neighbours, and a padlocked gate.

Bill stood on tiptoe and looked over to find a row of lock-ups, most of them in a dilapidated condition. Multi-coloured graffiti screamed at him from their shuttered doors.

He turned and approached the back door. Without a warrant he had no right to enter the house, but he planned to do it anyway. He removed his jacket and wrapped his hand with it, then punched a hole in the glass. Moments later he was inside.

The kitchen smelt of mould and disuse. Bill flicked the light switch to check for power and a low-wattage bulb came to life. Exposing the shadows confirmed that no cooking had been done in there recently, although there was plenty of evidence of mice, whose droppings littered the table and the area round the sink.

Bill ventured out of the kitchen and into a narrow hall. From there he found the living room, home to a worn three-piece suite and an old-fashioned TV set. He checked the toilet next and found some soap and a razor. He tested the razor on his hand and found it was sharp. The toilet pan confirmed the fact that someone had been in here with the urine on the rim of the bowl still wet.

Bill cautiously climbed the stairs.

There were two doors on the upper landing, both standing open.

One room was Angus's, judging by the contents. A double bed with dirty sheets and a large old-fashioned wardrobe. When opened it proved to contain a few shirts and a couple of heavy coats. The other room resembled a teenager's bedroom stuck in a time warp, the photographs of footballers and rock bands peeling off the walls.

So this was where Josh Kearney had come when his mother was banged up. And was maybe using now. Bill lifted a glass that sat on a bedside cabinet. Tasting the water, he found it still fresh.

He carefully went through the drawers. They were mostly empty. A deep cupboard held a deflated football and a skateboard. He pulled back the curtain a little. This room looked over the yard with the row of lock-ups.

Bill went downstairs. He exited by the back door and headed round to the car where DS Clark waited anxiously.

'Request a team to go over the house. Someone's been there and recently,' Bill said. 'Then drive round the back. There's a row of lock-ups I'd like a look at.'

A group of five youths had gathered across the street. Bill strode directly towards them. He focussed on the one who looked the most defiant on his approach.

'You,' Bill said. 'Come with me.'

'Get to fuck.'

'Swear at me again and I'll book you.'

The guy suddenly became Johnny-no-mates as his pals eased themselves out of the firing line.

'Come with me,' Bill said again in a voice that brooked no refusal.

The guy glanced at the car where DS Clark was busy on the radio and, making a decision, swaggered after Bill.

Bill led him round the corner and into the back court.

'Which of the lock-ups is used by a camper van?'

No answer.

'This is a murder enquiry, which means if you lie or fail to give information, you're an accessory.'

That he didn't like. He shrugged as though it was no

skin off his nose to tell. He motioned to one of the metal doors. 'I seen a van go in there once or twice.'

'Who was driving it?'

He shrugged again. 'A bloke.'

Bill eyeballed him.

'A dark-haired bloke. Maybe twenty. Never speaks. Just ignores you.' He nodded in the general direction of Patterson's house. 'Goes in there too.'

'You can get lost now,' Bill said.

'What the fuck?'

'Beat it, before more of us arrive.'

The guy gave him the finger and hit the road as directed.

It didn't take long to break the chain on the padlock, then he had the shutter up. The first thing he noticed was a strong smell of diesel. An engine had been run in here, and recently. Bill started to rummage in the rotting cardboard boxes that lined the walls, discovering broken ornaments, no doubt pilfered during Angus's numerous burglary sprees. His fetish for women's underwear was represented by a varied collection in sizes and styles of bras and knickers.

He turned to find DS Clark.

'The forensic team's on its way, sir.'

'Good.' Bill tried not to show his disappointment that he'd discovered nothing in the house, or here, that brought them any nearer to finding McNab and the elusive puppet-master.

68

McNab's world consisted of nothing but pleasure. It was better than being drunk, because he felt no need to talk, fight or fuck. A little voice told him that this was what junkies felt like. Why they would do anything to get to this place. At that moment he felt the same. He cared about nothing more than riding the waves that engulfed him.

Just as that thought occurred, his heart, which had been beating like a slow, smooth waltz, kicked into something faster. Every nerve and sinew in his body launched into song. His heart was a massive machine in his chest, pounding out pleasure. He was fast-fucking into ecstasy. He tried to scream, but the sound was sucked into the singing of his nerve ends. He saw a bright light at the end of a kaleidoscopic tunnel and raced towards it. When he emerged he knew he had reached heaven.

He checked for the pulse and found one so faint it felt like a fluttering moth wing. The bastard had survived but only just. He was strong. Many other hearts would have beat their way to death given that level of dose. He would be out cold like this for a while. When he reached the stone circle, he would inject him again before he stuck him with the knife. He opened the van door a little to check the light. At least another couple of hours before it would be dark enough.

The female was moaning softly, her face pressed to the pillow. The pig didn't have a pillow. He lay on the floor alongside the bed. Josh yawned. He would sleep in that bed tonight, well away from here. He would sleep the sleep of the damned and enjoy it. He moved to the equipment that lined the left-hand side of the van. It was time to prepare his audience for the final scene.

Would they be able to work out where it was going to happen?

This particular stone circle wasn't on any map that featured Neolithic sites, yet it was right under their noses. Buried in plain sight. Maybe he would use that phrase when he posted.

He spent some time digitally reworking his pictures, then put them up online. In seconds they were travelling cyberspace, being tagged and retweeted and discussed. He read a few of the comments and guesses, irritated that there were so many stupid people trying to play his game. Sometimes he felt surrounded by idiots.

He listened to the mobile message again and smiled. She too had been easy to fool. Iona had told him that the policeman had the hots for the forensic woman and that she was soft on him, although she pretended not to be. He glanced across at the comatose McNab. He'd planned to let him listen to the message. Watch his face as he realized who had his girlfriend and why. But it had become necessary to quieten him.

He contemplated what he should do about the woman. He checked his watch. The call had come an hour ago. Anything could have happened in that hour.

He made his way round to the driver's seat.

The engine purred into life. He switched on the lights and wound his way down onto the motorway, heading out of the city. Everything was going to plan. The small problem of the female's mobile had been solved. If the pig had revealed that he had it to anyone else, it wasn't apparent. He'd tried to play the big man by reeling him in alone. And he'd failed.

The motorway was a steady stream of light. He headed down the slipway and merged in. A glance at the overhead bridge reminded him that the traffic cops might be looking out for the vehicle. He should maybe have stayed clear of the main road. That small feeling of insecurity was quickly doused by a feeling of control.

He had number four and the cop. They would die together inside the final circle.

McNab had been standing with his back to the kitchen door, listening. He should have turned more quickly. He should have heard the footsteps sooner. He relived the moments, replayed them again and again, but it always played out the same way. One moment he was conscious, alert and ready to meet the bastard face to face. The next moment his legs were crumbling beneath him and he was fingering his neck. Then the whoosh as the drug hit his bloodstream. In the dream he saw a girl lying naked, him climbing on top of her. Her face was Iona's. He tasted metal on his tongue, felt a spike between his fingers as he touched her breast. He entered her only to feel a metal gate shut on him, trapping him there for ever.

He screamed in agony and the scream escaped his brain and woke him. He was in utter darkness and he was moving, although pressed against a floor. He tried to raise his head but it felt like lead. He reached out with his brain to locate his right hand and felt his fingertips touch the floor. Then his left hand. It was twisted at a strange angle and when he tried to straighten it the pain made him gasp.

Making a sound seemed wrong so he smothered it, then tested for his legs and feet. He was in darkness and moving. There was a smell of diesel and sweat and something else? The scent of a woman?

Where the hell was he?

He strove to interrogate his brain but it refused to respond. He had all the intelligence of an amoeba. He could move his body parts a little but think he could not do. He was dumb and dumber.

Then he heard it. A moan.

He reached up with his right hand and felt something soft like a cover. He stretched a little further and found flesh. It was an arm, hanging off a bed. He attempted to rise. His limbs felt numb and he couldn't feel his knees against what he now knew was a metal floor. His world suddenly shook and rattled, then threw him to the right like a fairground ride. He grabbed at the bed and the limp arm swung loosely against him.

He felt for the figure on the bed and knew quickly that it was female. Somewhere in his head he recalled that he was looking for a female and imagined for a moment it was Iona, then Rhona's face appeared before him. The hallucination was so powerful, he gasped. When it passed he tried to focus on the face in the dark. He ran his fingers over the nose, eyes and jawline.

He was looking for a girl.

His voice appeared from nowhere and said the number five. Something about the number five was important. The fairground ride dipped and he slumped back onto the floor, hitting his head a glancing blow, yet feeling no pain. A wave of euphoria hit him and he no longer cared that he was on a ride in the fair with a woman in the dark.

Then the fairground ride stopped.

69

The thin one was growing jittery, his jaw moving like an old man missing his teeth. The other two were less affected. The booze they'd consumed had seemingly dulled their need in the short term, or else they weren't so far down the road as he was.

Rhona rose from the couch.

'Where the fuck do you think you're going?'

'The toilet.'

'Like fuck you are. Sit down.'

'Please,' she tried.

He studied her from behind heavy lids then nodded. 'Leave the door open.' He motioned to one of the other two. 'Watch her.'

Rhona walked swiftly to the toilet, her eye catching sight of her mobile outside the bathroom door. She nudged it inside as she entered, then tried to close the door, but a foot stopped her. Conceding defeat, she allowed it to stay open a fraction, pocketed the mobile, then ran the tap at a rate that sounded like someone urinating, flushed the toilet and made a big show of washing one hand while she rummaged in the cabinet with the other. The first object she fingered turned out to be a razor, its protective cover rendering it useless as a weapon.

It wasn't until the third shelf that she found something

useful. The nail scissors were small but sharp. She'd just grasped them when the door was thrown open.

'Out! Now!'

Rhona exited and headed back into the sitting room where the skinny one was pacing and muttering.

'We could try him again,' Rhona suggested.

'Maybe he likes the gear more than you,' he said sneeringly.

'Or maybe he never had the holdall in the first place.'

He tried to process that idea. 'No way. The fat guy told us he saw him take it.'

'Steve Munro lied because he was threatened by Josh Kearney.'

He tried to compute this and couldn't. All his brain could think about was his next fix. He suddenly made a lunge at her, knocking her back onto the couch. Then he was on her, his sinewy arm tearing at her clothes. Rhona did not fight back but concentrated on positioning the scissors in her hand.

She waited until his fly was down and his penis emerging, before she stabbed at his testicles. The reaction was instantaneous. He literally flew off her, screaming abuse, then started to dance, cradling his balls, as blood spurted between his fingers.

Open-mouthed, the other two stared at him in disbelief. Rhona took advantage of their consternation and made a dash for the toilet. In the background the skinny one was screaming like a banshee. Telling them to get the bitch and slit her throat.

She was back inside before they sprang into action. She'd already spotted that the lock was an old-fashioned turnkey, with a brass handle. It would hold longer than a modern bolt. She hoped it would be long enough.

She shouted her 999 call over the pounding of the door.

70

The photograph was of a woman lying spreadeagled and face down, a man lying on top of her. Both were naked, their faces turned from the camera, but Magnus was in no doubt who they were. The photo looked as though it had been taken in a dark room, but a mock stone circle had been digitally sketched around the bodies.

Below was the caption: *Buried in plain sight.*

Kearney was mocking them. He had no intention of killing them at a Neolithic site. Or, if he did, he had already left the city again, taking his victims with him.

Magnus studied some of the online attempts to guess the next location. Most, to his mind, were nonsense, but others had validity. Some had even worked out the sacred pentagram aspect and were suggesting the police head for the islands of Iona and Lindisfarne on the east–west base-line of the five-sided figure.

One gamester was convinced the puppetmaster was headed for the centre of the pentagram, an island in the middle of Loch Moy, south of Inverness. The island was heavily wooded, with an ancient history. Lying at the centre of the sacred pentagram meant the energy lines met there.

Magnus gave this credence for all of five minutes until he discovered how difficult it would be to transfer two bodies by boat onto an island, miles off the main A9 road.

He stopped looking at other people's solutions and tried to think of one of his own. To his mind the perpetrator would want to finish the game at a stone circle, but he could only do that if he left Glasgow.

Then again, his obsession with McNab seemed to be centred round his mother, her imprisonment and suicide, which he apparently blamed the detective for. According to an update from DI Wilson, they'd checked Kearney's family home and were pretty certain that's where the two men had arranged to meet. That Kearney had chosen the location where it'd all begun, seemed important.

The uncle's house was also being forensically examined, in the assumption that Kearney had hidden the van in the lock-up on his return to Glasgow. What forensics couldn't tell them was where Kearney and McNab were now.

Magnus studied the caption again. 'Buried in plain sight' was a common enough phrase, but what did it mean in the context of Kearney's psychology? If he was right and it had something to do with the death of Kearney's mother, then the word 'buried' had a secondary meaning.

Understanding came in a flashback. He'd been examining the photographs taken in the Kearney kitchen. He'd focussed on the mother staring at the posy of flowers on the window ledge. He'd thought she was trying to blot out the scene of her creation – the body of her husband, her distraught son, desperate in his eagerness to take the blame.

Suddenly Magnus knew what he'd missed, because it had been in plain sight.

The photograph that showed the posy of flowers on the kitchen windowsill, had also shown something else.

*

'I've seen the photos,' Bill said. 'It's definitely McNab and the girl Helena. The Tech department think it was taken inside his van. They were able to make out some computer equipment in the background.'

'I'm talking about the photographs taken in the kitchen . . .' Magnus hesitated, 'on the day of the murder.'

'What about them?'

'I only just remembered. Through the window I saw a hill and on it was what looked like a cemetery.'

'Sighthill cemetery lies behind the house,' Bill said, puzzled. 'It's called that because of the view from the highest point.'

Magnus hesitated. 'It's just, the recent photographs posted online had the caption "Buried in plain sight".'

A moment's silence fell as DI Wilson realized the possible importance of this.

'If Kearney's mother is buried there,' Magnus said, 'that could be a meaningful location to end the game.'

71

This was where the idea had come to him. This was the place where he'd decided to create the game. Focussing on writing the game had kept the demons at bay. Living in a Druid past had made his present bearable.

The Druids believed in sacrifice. That there was no life without death. At first he had been content to make the deaths merely symbolic, a drug-induced unconsciousness from which the player would eventually awake, but it hadn't worked out that way. The first one had died, and it seemed so right, so clean, when that happened, that it was inevitable the others would follow.

Those who live by the game must die by the game.

He chose the stone with the white cross, and sat down, his back against it. It was still warm from the day's sunshine, although clouds now amassed on the horizon. He could taste moisture on his lips. The rain would come soon and wash all evidence of him from this place.

Between the hill and the southern watches of the city, the lights of the motorway linking east to west streamed past in parallel lines. Up here, he was safely encircled by the stones, their energy encompassing him.

He roused himself. The girl was slim and light and, in her current state, easy to drag. The man would be more difficult. Even the power of the drugs wasn't enough to prevent him fighting his way back to consciousness. The man they called McNab was the enemy, yet at times he felt like a version of himself.

Josh stood up and walked the short distance to the parked van.

72

They had given up at the sound of the sirens. When she'd opened the bathroom door they'd gone, although the place still reeked of them. The skinny one had dripped blood everywhere, but he wouldn't die from his injury, although sex might be a problem for a while. Rhona had smiled at the thought.

She'd refused any treatment from the paramedics. There was nothing wrong with her, apart from a slapped cheek which had resulted in bruising and some puffiness. She'd got off lightly, no thanks to McNab. Once again he'd asked her to come and meet him here, then left her in the shit. It was getting to become a habit.

Back in her own car, she tried both numbers he'd used to call her. Neither answered. As she rang off, a call came through from Bill, who'd obviously been told about her incarceration.

'What the hell happened?' he said.

'McNab texted me to meet him at his place. When I turned up he wasn't there but a trio looking for the holdall was. Have you found him yet?'

'We're on our way to Sighthill cemetery.'

Rhona's heart stopped. 'Why?'

'Magnus thinks Kearney's going there and he has McNab and Helena in the van.'

'Alive?' she said.

'We don't know.'

She swore under her breath. It was always like this with McNab. Her fear for him was mixed with fury. Why the hell did he always have to play the hard man and go it alone?

'I'll meet you there,' she said.

As she joined the motorway, a flash of lightning lit up the distant outline of Cathkin Braes. Another downpour, she realized, was inevitable after the heat and humidity they'd endured over the past week. Sure enough, moments later, the first drops of rain met her windscreen. Rhona turned the wipers to fast as, shortly after, the heavens opened. The stream of cars started to slow as the drivers struggled to make out the road in front of them.

Rhona applied the brakes as the tail lights in front flashed.

Minutes later the line of vehicles drew to a grinding halt.

She tapped the wheel impatiently. If she had been in a police car, they could have put on the siren and taken to the hard shoulder. She would give it five minutes and if they hadn't started moving by then she would take to the hard shoulder anyway.

The deluge resounded on the roof in a deafening roar. Peering out the driver's window, the motorway seemed to undulate as surface water quickly accumulated.

She put the car into neutral, turned off the engine and called Bill. There was no answer, so she tried Magnus. When he responded, she could barely hear his voice above the rain.

'We're about ten minutes away, making slow progress,' he said.

Rhona couldn't even claim to be that close.

'Bill's called for back-up from the Air Support Unit, but they're out west. Could be an hour before they can get there.'

Rhona asked the question that had been puzzling her. 'Why do you think he's going to Sighthill cemetery?'

She listened in distress to the news that a photograph of McNab and Helena had been posted online along with the caption, 'Buried in plain sight'.

'He drew a stone circle round the bodies,' Magnus said.

'Then why the cemetery?' she asked.

'His mother's buried there and . . .'

Rhona cut him off, knowing he was wrong. So wrong. 'He's not going to the cemetery, he's headed for the stone circle.'

'What stone circle?'

'Sighthill stone circle. It was built in the late seventies. An academic experiment in constructing a modern stone circle that reflected the astronomical layout of the ancient ones. When the Tories came into power, funding was cut and it was never finished. Most people don't even know it exists.'

She could sense Magnus's bewilderment. 'Buried in plain sight,' he muttered.

'Where are you exactly?' Rhona demanded.

'Almost at the cemetery.'

'You'll have to double back. The circle's just north of the M8 motorway in Sighthill Park. I'm closer than you are.'

She heard him mutter something to Bill, then he came back on.

'Bill's sending the other car to the cemetery. We'll double back and meet you.' His voice fizzled out as the pounding rain took over.

Rhona put the car into gear, indicated, and drew onto the hard shoulder. A chorus of horns sounded their annoyance as she swept past. She didn't think she had missed the exit that would allow her access to Sighthill Park. From there she could wind her way up to the top of the hill where the stones were located. How far she would get by car she wasn't sure.

Peering through the windscreen, her wipers going full pelt, she ignored the angry faces and honking horns and concentrated only on locating the exit. Cars lined the slipway. Rhona swept past them too.

The dark row of trees and bushes that hid the motorway from the park came into view. The rain was easing as she located the entrance. After the lights of the motorway, the single-track road was almost pitch black, dense foliage catching at the car on either side.

Her memory of the hill and the stone circle was sketchy. Her one and only visit had been with an old friend, whose astronomical knowledge had been sought when the place was being planned. She'd been astounded by the level of scientific thought that had gone into the placing of the stones. From what she recalled, there had been fifteen stones to mark various important dates in the astronomical calendar, including the summer and winter solstices, at both sunrise and sunset, and a central stone. Three further stones had been delivered but had never been raised. When Mrs Thatcher came into power the project had been immediately cancelled, because she deemed it ludicrous. There had been moves since to restore it, then she'd heard more recently that it was to be removed altogether to make way for a development.

The road took a sudden turn and she braked, before noting a side track that appeared to climb the hill. Rhona engaged a lower gear and followed it, more slowly this time. The trees melted away as she crested the hill and spotted the jagged outline of the stones set against a purple-red horizon. Thunder still rolled, although the storm had moved further away now, to the north.

Rhona stopped the car and got out.

If Kearney's van was still here, there was no sign of it. She grabbed her high-beamed torch and set off for the stones.

73

The rain had slowed things a little, but he'd welcomed it nonetheless, because pelting rain would discourage any night-time visitors to the place to drink and have sex among the stones. It would also delay any pursuers, if they'd been clever enough to work out where he might head with his captives. Even as he considered this, he knew that McNab had been nearest to his own way of thinking, and McNab was close to death in the back of the van.

He turned off the narrow road and dimmed his lights, then did a three-point turn and reversed. The track led into woodland, mature enough to shield his presence until daylight at least. Raindrops still pattered the roof from the overhead branches, but the clouds hadn't parted to allow the moon to shine through. Perfect.

He shut off the engine and doused the lights.

Excitement beat in the nerve at the corner of his mouth as he opened the back door.

McNab was aware he lay with a woman, but in his dream-like state drifted between pleasure at this, and horror. At its worst moment, the nightmare had him coupling with Iona as a corpse – or was he the corpse and she the living being? At times almost lucid, he fought his way towards the surface and knew that he was in a drugged state. At that moment he knew himself capable of something terrible in his anger. When the drug reclaimed him he was almost grateful.

But its power was lessening and reality returning.

He rolled off the woman, his head sent spinning by the movement. Instinct took his finger to seek for and find a faint pulse in her neck, although her skin was clammy to the touch. The moving darkness told him he was in the back of a vehicle, probably the van that had sent him off the road, and he was seized again by the claustrophobic memory of the sinking car and the weight of the water crushing the air from his lungs.

McNab forced himself to breathe in the stale air, to attempt to slow his heartbeat which seemed to have an erratic life of its own. He began to feel around the surfaces for a weapon of any kind, knowing that his best weapon would be surprise.

The pig still lay on top of the woman. He considered whether the dead weight might have suffocated her and there would be no need to inject her further. As he stood by the door studying them, he knew instinctively that the man was conscious.

'If you move, even a fraction, I will inject her foot with a fatal dose.'

The pig had heard him, because his breathing changed, a little, but enough.

The van dipped as he entered, and her arm dropped free of her body and hung there. He could feel the pig tense, though he strove hard not to show it.

His own movement was swift and practised and the

needle found an entry point behind the right knee. The man tried to wrench the leg back, but too late.

He exited and re-locked the door. Unsure how much he had managed to inject, he would have to wait.

McNab writhed on the floor, his arms and legs knocking against the bed and a chair. Much better to be shot or knived than to be rendered useless by this creeping sensation as the drug overtook him. He began to thrash, not from choice because his body was no longer his own. Then it came again, that sense of freedom and oblivion. A place where he no longer cared, about himself or anyone else.

A man, arms and legs outstretched within a circle. Lines from the head, feet and hands criss-crossed to make a five-pointed star. The image symbolized many things. Man's place in the universe, Jesus's death on the cross. The head, pierced hands and feet, were the points on the circumference of the circle, within the sacred pentagram.

He had kept the single point at the top. There was nothing sacrilegious in his offering. Those who had died sacrificed themselves to the common good.

The man he placed to the north, the woman south of the central stone, their fingers touching. Their moans as he impaled them were only a whisper on the wind that had sprung up after the storm. He stood for a moment before photographing the scene. In that moment the hidden moon chose to show herself, casting her rays over his handiwork.

It seemed to him that his work had been sanctified.

*

She stumbled as she reached the summit, dreading what she would find there. Moonlight encased the stones, the circle reflected by its light so that it appeared to dance with energy. An aurora borealis of stone.

Approaching, Rhona encountered such a powerful force of energy that she was stopped in her tracks. As a scientist she had no evidence to believe in the energy lines that such places signalled or created, but she felt it now, or else her fear fuelled it.

As she stepped inside the circle, the central stone seemed to shimmer. Then she saw them. The image that Magnus had first shown her, only doubled.

Two naked bodies. Male and female. Spreadeagled within the circle, fingertips touching.

It was a scene from heaven. Or a scene from hell.

As she sprang through the stones, she tripped, caught by a wire strung out between them. She fell, hitting the ground hard enough to drive the breath from her body, the torch flying ahead to bounce and extinguish. As she struggled to rise, the weight of a man's body drove her flat against the ground, his hands on her shoulders.

He bent his face to hers. 'You worked it out.' He sounded surprised.

Rhona tried to draw breath. 'The police are on their way.'

He gave a harsh laugh. 'They won't get here in time to save you, or them.'

Rhona let her limbs go lax. There was no point in physically fighting him. She had to engage him, delay him, until Bill and Magnus arrived. It was an old trick but, played well, might yet win the game.

His hands moved to encircle her neck.

'Tell me why your mother killed herself.'

His hands faltered then tightened their grip on her throat.

'That bastard,' he motioned to the pale, lifeless form that was McNab, 'killed her.'

'Your mother tried to save you from your father.'

His laugh came from hell itself. 'I did what he asked. That night. I did what he told me.'

Rhona had no idea what he meant, but kept on, none-theless.

'You did it to save her,' she tried.

'No, to please me.'

His fingers tightened and she choked, trying to drag in air. Even as she strove to remain conscious, she could see, in her mind's eye, the marks of his fingers on Iona's pale throat.

Focussed on her neck, he'd forsaken her hands. Rhona withdrew McNab's scissors from her pocket and thrust them into his side with as much force as she could muster.

She felt the points pierce the cotton of the T-shirt, then his skin.

He grunted, the force and power she'd used impacting. Reaching for his side, he loosened his grip on her neck.

Coughing and spluttering, Rhona attempted to scramble out of reach. He grabbed at her leg to pull her back, and she twisted round and lashed out. The scissor points sliced down his cheek. He screamed an obscenity and threw himself, full bodied, at her.

It was what she'd hoped for.

As he fell, she aimed the point at his neck.

74

His cheek cushioned by grass and earth, his eyes focussed on a moonlit sky, spreadeagled in supplication, he felt no pain, although he was aware that both his outstretched arms were pinned to the ground.

And in that moment, he understood everything about who he truly was. Why he was here. What he had done, and what he would do in the future.

The epiphany lasted seconds, before reality swept back in, swiftly followed by a searing pain that set his hands aflame. His first instinct was to drag them free from the earth, which proved easy to do but made the pain worse.

He uttered every obscenity he could imagine and more, as he pulled out the two nails. On his knees now, he was suddenly aware of the body that lay opposite him in the moonlight on the other side of the central stone.

He crawled towards her.

Pale as a spectre, her lips blue, her skin mottled, he knew she was dead before he felt her neck in search of a pulse. He gently pulled out the nails from the finely boned hands, knowing there was nothing more he could do to help her.

He forced himself to rise as the circle of stones wavered and spun round him like an hallucinogenic fairground ride. Then he heard a voice call his name.

A voice he thought was Rhona's, yet knew it couldn't be.

The voice called again.

He traced it to the southern edge of the circle and made out a large shadow on the grass. McNab forced his legs to move in that direction.

She was pinned to the ground by a body he recognized. Kearney's face nestled in the crook of her neck, like a lover's.

McNab made to pull him off.

'No,' she shouted. 'He's bleeding. If the scissors come out of his neck, we'll lose him. What about Helena?'

'Dead,' he said in a dull voice.

She looked stricken. 'Bill will be here soon. Sit with me.'

McNab did as bid. He reached out and took her free hand. It was cold to the touch. He lifted it to his lips and kissed it.

'Are you okay?' he said, knowing what had to happen before the others appeared.

She nodded and Josh Kearney's head moved a little as though in agreement. An image too terrible for McNab to bear.

He clasped her free hand tightly, then reached for the one that held the scissors in place.

'No,' she shouted, trying to free herself to fight McNab off, without success.

He pulled out the scissors, then rolled Kearney's body off her. The trickle from the artery became a spurt, falling like red rain on the wet grass while McNab watched.

75

One month later

'It's a ridiculous idea,' Rhona said.

Chrissy shrugged. 'I think it's a great idea. People have divorce parties. Why not a demotion party?'

Rhona swore under her breath. 'Where is this party?'

'I thought Sean would have told you. At the jazz club. Everyone's invited. You are going?'

'No way,' Rhona said with gusto.

Chrissy's face fell. 'Look what happened the last time you rejected McNab.'

'You are not going to blame me for that,' Rhona said stoutly.

'Well, it's tonight after work. Bill's going to be there.'

'What?' Rhona continued to voice her annoyed amazement that such a thing as a party to celebrate your demotion should ever happen.

There was a moment's silence as Chrissy interpreted her response.

'McNab fucked up,' she said. 'He didn't kill anybody.'

Rhona looked quickly away, but it wasn't swift enough for Chrissy.

'Did he?'

'Don't be daft,' Rhona said. 'Now let me get on with some work.'

Chrissy flounced out.

Rhona had avoided McNab like the plague since the events at the Sighthill stone circle. He had tried calling her mobile. Had even turned up at her flat one night. She hadn't answered the phone or the door. If they didn't discuss it, she could maybe make herself believe it hadn't happened. McNab had been drugged and half dead. She had been terrified and injured. Everything after she fell into the stone circle was a blur. She had tried to convince herself of that fact, and failed.

She could not, therefore, meet McNab's eyes.

Chrissy made one last attempt to persuade her before she left for the jazz club.

'What the hell's he done?'

Rhona couldn't bring herself to answer. When Chrissy departed, she made herself coffee and tried to drown herself in report writing.

She never heard him enter the lab. Engrossed in her report, she first realized he was present when he said her name.

'How did you get in here?' she said sharply.

'Harry on security thinks you've forgotten there's a party on tonight.' He paused. 'I came to escort you there.'

'I'm working.'

He stood for a moment, nonplussed. It wasn't a demeanour she was used to seeing with McNab.

'I'm back where I belong,' he said.

'In prison, for murder?' she fired back.

'Kearney killed five people, but he was trying for seven, including you and me. And you were keeping him alive.' By his tone he wasn't asking her forgiveness.

'I can't work with you again,' she said.

'I said that once to you, remember?'

'What you did was wrong.'

'Then tell the boss.'

When she hesitated, he said, 'Okay, if you can't bring yourself to, I will, if it makes you happy.'

'You can never make me happy,' she said.

Her remark cut him. She could tell. She wanted to take it back but couldn't.

'Where does all this leave *us* then?' he said.

'Exactly where we were before. Nowhere.'

He nodded and made to leave. At the door he turned back.

'I'll speak to the boss tomorrow, tell him I removed the scissors from Kearney's neck – if you come with me now.'

She fought herself, unsure what to do.

'Go ahead,' she said. 'I'll follow.'

She heard his firm step in the corridor walking away from her. That's it, she thought. That was always it.

Her mobile rang. She glanced at the screen to find Sean's name. She answered.

'Hi, beautiful. Coming to the party?'

'I will if you come for me,' she said.

76

The spiritualist church had greatly increased its membership, judging by the size of the Sunday-morning audience. The warning given by the first victim to his mother had been picked up by the press. Coupled with the online frenzied interest in the search for Stonewarrior, it had sparked a debate about online gaming, stone circles, spiritualism and the afterlife. Which was why Magnus was here.

He still didn't understand how Patrick Menzies had known of Alan's murder before anyone else. Nor how he was able to warn the police that those who played the online game with Alan were also in danger.

He had interviewed Menzies after Josh Kearney's body had been recovered from inside the modern stone circle. Menzies had indicated that he was already aware that the perpetrator was dead. That Amy MacKenzie had had a message from her son to that effect. Since the news had been released almost immediately, that didn't surprise Magnus.

Yet, here he was, still trying to understand what Menzies was all about.

The hymn had drawn to a close. Magnus had stood and mumbled the words under his breath, but had chosen not to sing, although the sound of so many voices resounded in his head, reminding him again of church services in St Magnus Cathedral when he was a schoolboy. Hymn completed, the audience took to their seats in excited anticipation as the medium appeared on stage.

Menzies wore that same apologetic air, as though he couldn't believe he had been chosen to do such work. His expression and the soft sound of his voice grated on Magnus. He fought to free himself from preconceptions. If he wanted to study the psychological power of these events, he had to remain objective.

Menzies scanned the audience and Magnus imagined his eyes lit up at the size of it. He welcomed them and gave his little speech about getting in contact with the deceased, and how he could not summon someone to talk to a bereaved relative.

Then his head twitched left and he nodded. 'God Bless,' he said, and listened.

Magnus was surprised to find himself impatient to hear who would be singled out. By the expressions on those around him, they felt the same.

'Is there a Magnus Pirie in the room?'

A hushed silence followed his question as Magnus suddenly registered that it was his name that had been called.

When he didn't raise his hand, Menzies looked directly at him. 'Mr Pirie?'

All eyes turned on Magnus.

Suddenly he wished himself anywhere but here. He understood for the first time how Amy MacKenzie must have felt when she too had been singled out.

'Yes,' he said, trying to sound nonchalant.

'I have a message for you, from Morvan.'

'I don't know anyone of that name,' Magnus said quickly.

Menzies ignored his response and listened again to his invisible visitor.

'Her message is that you should not feed the gulls.'

Magnus's stomach lurched as he realized why the name Morvan had seemed familiar. It was the avatar of the girl on his jetty. How could Menzies have known about her visit? How could he have known about her dangerous baiting of the gull?

Magnus waited for more, but Menzies' interest had left him. Once again the medium was listening to a silent voice at his left shoulder. A voice not destined for Magnus.

www.panmacmillan.com